⇜YOU'VE GOT MAIL⇝
The PERILS
of
PIGEN
POST

2

⊱You've Got Mail⊰
The PERILS
of
PIGEN
POST

❀2❀

WRITTEN BY
Blackegg

COVER ILLUSTRATION BY
Leila

INTERIOR ILLUSTRATIONS BY
Ninemoon

TRANSLATED BY
alexsh, Tywon Wynne

Seven Seas Entertainment

You've Got Mail: The Perils of Pigeon Post - Fei Ge Jiao You Xu Jin Shen (Novel) Vol. 2

Published originally under the title of 《飛鴿交友須謹慎》
Author© 黑蛋白 (Blackegg)
Illustrations granted under license granted by I Yao Co. Ltd.
Cover Illustrations by Leila
Interior illustrations by Ninemoon
English edition rights under license granted by 愛呦文創有限公司 (I Yao Co. Ltd.)
English edition copyright © 2024 Seven Seas Entertainment, Inc
Arranged through JS Agency Co., Ltd
All rights reserved

Seven Seas press and purchase enquiries can be sent to Marketing Manager Lauren Hill at press@gomanga.com. Information regarding the distribution and purchase of digital editions is available from Digital Manager CK Russell at digital@gomanga.com.

Follow Seven Seas Entertainment online at sevenseasentertainment.com.

TRANSLATION: alexsh, Tywon Wynne
ADAPTATION: Abigail Clark
COVER DESIGN: G. A. Slight
INTERIOR DESIGN: Clay Gardner
INTERIOR LAYOUT: Karis Page
COPY EDITOR: Ami Leh
PROOFREADER: Imogen Vale, Nino Cipri
EDITOR: Hardleigh Hewmann
PREPRESS TECHNICIAN: Salvador Chan Jr., April Malig, Jules Valera
MANAGING EDITOR: Alyssa Scavetta
EDITOR-IN-CHIEF: Julie Davis
PUBLISHER: Lianne Sentar
VICE PRESIDENT: Adam Arnold
PRESIDENT: Jason DeAngelis

ISBN: 979-8-89160-317-2
Printed in Canada
First Printing: November 2024
10 9 8 7 6 5 4 3 2 1

CONTENTS

BACK HOME FOR THE ANCESTORS

"Right, so how did you explain me to your ancestors?"

Wu Xingzi gave a jolt, feeling uneasy. After all, this was what he'd said...

My dear ancestors, your unfilial descendant has brought along the pengornis he is playing with... Please bless me with majestic pengornises every year, and may they always be abundant.

When Wu Xingzi made his prayers, he had been distracted by Guan Shanjin to the point of confusion, so he'd ended up talking nonsense. Now thinking about the content of his prayers, he was a little worried. Would his ancestors punish him after hearing such filth? Ah, what a headache...

IT WAS TWO DAYS before the new year when the travel-worn men reached Qingcheng County. Adviser Wu truly had no horseback riding skills, and Guan Shanjin was afraid of tiring him out. With the adviser's inexperience in mind, they went at a slower pace.

Having been away from home for over a month, Wu Xingzi felt a sort of relieved ease when he pushed his door open. A thin layer of dust covered the tables and chairs. Fortunately, though, the house had been repaired rather meticulously before winter, and despite how much rain fell during the cold season, the roof hadn't leaked.

Wu Xingzi couldn't be concerned with how weak his legs felt after riding a horse for a long period of time. He rolled up his sleeves to start tidying his house.

After he'd fed the horse and tied it up in the stable at the magistrate's office, Guan Shanjin arrived at Wu Xingzi's house to see that the adviser had already collected a basin of water and was wiping down his furniture. Naturally, Guan Shanjin couldn't watch Wu Xingzi sweat and exhaust himself during a cold winter day. What if he caught a chill from the wind? The general walked forward and took over Wu Xingzi's task. Then, as if worried he'd be unable to sit idly on the sidelines, he sent Wu Xingzi out to buy some groceries for cooking.

"I've already asked Su Yang to prepare the New Year goods for us. He'll send them over tomorrow before noon, so there's no need to buy much." After briefing Wu Xingzi, Guan Shanjin pushed him out of the house, not even giving him a chance to refuse.

Blankly, Wu Xingzi looked at the door that had shut behind him. He scratched his nose, secretly delighted.

Human beings were not made of stone. Having traveled together, just the two of them, for the past dozen or so days, Wu Xingzi had seen how meticulously Guan Shanjin cared for him. The general was always worried that the old man would be cold, hungry, or uncomfortable, and he always managed to make sure they arrived at a village just before sunset. Before they left, Mint and Osmanthus had secretly told Wu Xingzi that the general had never allowed anyone else to ride his horse, Zhuxing. Even Mr. Lu never had the good fortune to take a ride on Zhuxing's back—not even once.

"I believe the general must really like you," Mint said, covering her smile with her hand.

"Exactly!" Osmanthus chimed in. "The general is even going back home with you for New Year! He's never returned to the capital for Mr. Lu before."

Wu Xingzi could only give a droll smile. He didn't want to bring the great general of the Southern Garrison back home with him to pray to his ancestors! What was he supposed to tell his ancestors about him?

Father, Mother, my ancestors: this is the...pengornis I've been thinking about. I'll be living with him temporarily. Please bless this cock with the best wishes possible, so that it can reach its utmost potential, be filled with perseverance, garner great achievements, and be forever unyielding.

Wu Xingzi was afraid his parents and ancestors would immediately enter his dreams that night and teach their unfilial son a lesson! He remained conflicted throughout the entire journey home, but he still didn't manage to come up with a decent phrasing that could strike a happy balance.

With his little money pouch in hand, Wu Xingzi strolled over to Auntie Liu's house. By this time, most of the stalls along the street had already packed up, so he had to purchase the produce he needed directly from the farmers. Auntie Liu had two sons, so she had plenty of food at home. She should have no problems selling him a little.

On his way there, he happened to walk past a few villagers. Wu Xingzi greeted them, smiling brightly, and their expressions in response were fascinating. First, they came to an abrupt stop, staring at him; then, they revealed a face full of either malicious amusement or pity. Finally, they gave him a complicated, tight smile. Even the sedate and placid Wu Xingzi registered that something was off after he'd passed a few people.

Finally, he arrived at Auntie Liu's place, mostly avoiding everyone along the way. Knocking on the door, he heard Auntie Liu shout her acknowledgment from within. The wooden door opened, and after seeing that it was Wu Xingzi, Auntie Liu's eyes rounded. She did not speak as she held his hand and started to cry.

"Mother, what's wrong?" Auntie Liu's eldest daughter-in-law, A-Xiu, ran out in a panic. After seeing Wu Xingzi—who sported an awkward expression on his face—she too started wiping her tears.

"Sister, Mother, what's wrong?" Auntie Liu's second daughter-in-law, A-Bao, came over.

For the next fifteen minutes, the entrance of the Liu home filled with sobs. Helplessly, Adviser Wu looked at the three women. His mouth hung open, not knowing what he should say.

In the end, it was Old Liu who came and called for everyone to enter the house. Gently, he patted Wu Xingzi's shoulder. "Good boy. It's nice that you're back."

Huh? Wu Xingzi was baffled. He could guess that this had something to do with the villagers' strange behavior along the way. However, the men of the Liu family were all taciturn by nature. Old Liu's two sons had yet to return, and Old Liu sat to the side and started smoking. Wu Xingzi alone was powerless to persuade the three women to stop crying. With no other choice, he could only pat Auntie Liu's hand. "Don't cry anymore, don't cry," he repeated wanly. "Crying too much is bad for the eyes."

Women were truly made of water! Wu Xingzi had to coax them until his mouth went dry, his throat nearly burning before the three women gradually stopped crying and gave him water and dried fruit in a fluster.

Drinking a large bowl of water in one gulp, Wu Xingzi sighed in satisfaction, but he couldn't bear to touch the dried fruit. Just as he was about to buy some vegetables from Auntie Liu, she spoke. "Xingzi, you pitiful child. Have you lost weight again? That young lord of yours looks like he was born from wealth. Is he so heartless that he didn't even feed you?"

"Hmm?" Wu Xingzi did not understand, looking even more lost. In Auntie Liu's eyes, it seemed as though he was hiding an injured, sorrowful heart—like he was a pitiful victim of some scam.

"Ah, Xingzi! It's all my fault. I should have stopped you from leaving with that heartless son of a bitch!" Auntie Liu exclaimed. Seeing her filled with righteous indignation, and noting how A-Xiu and A-Bao stared at him with pity and heartache in their teary eyes, Wu Xingzi realized what was going on.

He sighed, waving his hands anxiously. "No, no, no, Auntie, you've misunderstood. Haiwang is extremely good to me. He didn't let me go hungry for even a day, and I could even plant cucumbers in the yard where I was staying!"

The mention of crops immediately distracted Auntie. "Planting cucumbers during this season? That's no good, they won't grow well! In this cold weather, you should plant carrots."

"Yes, yes. I didn't think of it at the time. I just felt that the people there had explosive tempers, so I planted cucumbers for them. Cucumbers would help calm their temperaments and remove heat and toxins from their bodies. They'd be nice as gifts." Of course, cucumbers had another use as well, but Wu Xingzi was shy and easily embarrassed, and he would never let Auntie Liu know about that. After all, it was something he had seen in the erotic drawings Manager Rancui had given him. Cucumbers were good for eating, and any "mouth" could swallow them.

A-Xiu could not carry on listening to this conversation. "Mother, planting cucumbers or carrots is not the point." She took a deep breath, then looked at Wu Xingzi. "Xingzi-ge, don't try to hide from us! Everyone has been saying that after that young lord took you away, you were entirely forgotten in a matter of days. There are countless beauties in that young lord's house, and they said that the one in his heart is as beautiful as a fairy. Auntie Li and the rest said that the young lord discarded you, and that he never even liked you."

"Hmph! Wicked women with their wicked tongues." A-Bao was considerably more direct, pursing her lips and scolding the village gossips. "Auntie Li and the others are born with nasty mouths. They just can't stand to see Xingzi-ge living a happy life."

"It's all they've been talking about recently. They even said that Xingzi-ge might get chased home before the new year." A-Xiu closed her mouth, glancing at Wu Xingzi cautiously. "If that young lord is so good to you, why didn't he ask you to stay for New Year?"

"He said..." Wu Xingzi's face flushed a bright red, looking somewhat awkward. Praying to his ancestors together was a big deal, after all!

"What did he say? Don't keep me in the dark!" Auntie Liu could not bear to wait, urging him on hurriedly.

"Um, he said he would come home with me for New Year and make offerings to my ancestors."

Every inch of Wu Xingzi's exposed skin turned red. He was extremely shy about the subject, but a certain sweetness coursed through him like honey.

He knew that there was no future between him and Guan Shanjin. He had always been firm on his direction of life, which was to collect dick pictures. However, he had still been moved by Guan Shanjin's care and concern. There was no need to start thinking about solemn pledges of love, but a taste of sweetness here and there was still rather enjoyable.

"Are you saying that you're really in a relationship with him?!" The corners of Auntie Liu's eyes were still red from crying, but in an instant, she started smiling so widely that her eyes crinkled. "The heavens have blessed you, the heavens have blessed you! You're a good child, and if that young lord has working eyes, he'll cherish you. Hah! Early tomorrow morning, I'm going to the Lis' place to beat up all those old women and take revenge on your behalf!"

Making offerings to one's ancestors was a tremendous matter—outsiders had no right to participate in the tradition. Since it appeared that the two of them were in a serious relationship, they must have already declared their intentions toward each other. Although becoming life partners was not as complicated a process as getting married, and all they needed to do was to go to the magistrate's office to register their household, most couples still invited their families and friends over for a banquet to celebrate.

"Where will you be holding your banquet? When will it be?"

Wu Xingzi was overwhelmed by Auntie Liu's barrage of questions. He waved his hands. "Auntie! Auntie! We did not become life partners! He's only here to accompany me for New Year and to make offerings to my ancestors. He has to return to Horse-Face City before the tenth day of the new year."

"What?! He's already here to make offerings! Becoming life partners is only a matter of time." With a wave of her arm, Auntie Liu turned to enter her kitchen. Soon, she came out with a chunk of preserved meat, a few carrots, a large cabbage, and four eggs, shoving them all into Wu Xingzi's arms. "Here, this is my gift to you. If you ever get bullied in Horse-Face City, just come back and look for me. I'll deal with them for you."

Wu Xingzi stared at the food in his arms. The chunk of preserved meat had streaks of fat running through it, shiny and tempting.

The layers of meat were distinct, without any clumping. Swallowing his saliva, he pushed the meat back into Auntie Liu's hands.

"Auntie, I'm here today to buy some rice and vegetables and things like that. Just enough to make a meal for Haiwang and me. The New Year's goods that he has asked his friend to prepare will be here tomorrow, so keep this meat for yourself. I appreciate that you've always looked out for me."

Auntie Liu was delighted. "That young lord is truly meticulous." She did take the preserved meat back, but she refused to accept any payment for the rest.

Wu Xingzi had no choice but to accept Auntie Liu's generosity. He left with vegetables, eggs, and some rice, and ended up bumping into Guan Shanjin along the way. The general had left in search of the older man, as he had yet to return after cleaning the house. He took the items from Wu Xingzi.

"Is this enough food for you?" Guan Shanjin teased, looking at Wu Xingzi's tummy.

Wu Xingzi blushed faintly, lowering his head. The sight lit a flame within Guan Shanjin. If they hadn't been out in public with a few people around, he would have pulled him into his arms and kissed him to his heart's content.

"There's only some salt left at home. I'm afraid you'd feel unwell after eating that."

Wu Xingzi seemed to be getting used to his situation with Guan Shanjin. When walking next to him, he would unconsciously hold on to his arm. Their body language was fairly intimate, and people who saw them started muttering amongst themselves. After all, Auntie Li had sounded very convincing earlier when she talked about how Adviser Wu would be discarded, how tragic his life would be, and how celestially beautiful the god-like man's real sweetheart was.

Apparently, that sweetheart was even a successful scholar in the imperial examinations! They all said that the divinely beautiful military man had been unable to woo that scholarly sweetheart of his, and so he kept Wu Xingzi by his side as a substitute. However, the general and his sweetheart had recently accepted each other's feelings, so Wu Xingzi was now an eyesore. If not for the kindness of that sweetheart, Wu Xingzi would have long been abandoned in Horse-Face City.

"Hah! If Wu Xingzi has any sense of shame, he'll run back home soon!" This was Auntie Li's conclusion at the time, and many old women chimed in with their agreement. It had been one of the most hotly discussed topics in Qingcheng County over the past two weeks.

But what they saw now was not the disheveled appearance of the much-gossiped-about man walking alone. Instead, with him was that immortal-looking, elegant young lord. The two of them were even intimately exchanging whispers with each other on the street.

"Look at that Wu Xingzi. Doesn't he know how old he is? How shameless!"

"Forget it, Auntie Li must have taken a huge mouthful of sour grapes and spun the rumors out of spite."

"This god-like man must have been enchanted! With Wu Xingzi's ugly mug? You'll despise him even more when you take another look at him. How did that celestial beauty fall for a man like him?"

"Someone clearly thinks he's not attracting enough attention as it is. Someone needs to teach him a lesson!"

Everyone had something to say. But their voices were all very soft, as they didn't dare to let the involved parties hear what they were saying.

However, Guan Shanjin had very strong hearing. Even without paying attention, he ended up hearing all the rumors going around, and a cold unhappiness settled in his eyes.

There was too much overlap between the rumors and the truth. Mr. Lu's existence was practically shining visibly in front of everyone. Someone had to be deliberately working behind the scenes to stir up these rumors.

Who could it be? And what was their objective? If Wu Xingzi was to hear these rumors, would he...have any opinions? The last point made him shudder. Looking down, he glanced over to Wu Xingzi chattering away next to him. His ordinary face was tinted a slight red, and there was not a single trace of Mr. Lu's stunning beauty. However, no matter how he thought about it, Adviser Wu was still pleasing to his eyes.

He could no longer even remember exactly which feature of Wu Xingzi had originally reminded him of Mr. Lu.

If Wu Xingzi were to discover that Guan Shanjin's affection and care all began because he was a substitute for Mr. Lu, would he still be able to smile at him like he did now? Would he still blush upon seeing him? Or would he be completely unbothered, sighing in relief and returning to the Peng Society to continue making friends through the pigeon post?

Guan Shanjin started feeling oddly upset. He held all the food securely with just one hand, then wrapped his other arm tightly around the thin man next to him. He ignored the eyes of the crowd, lowering his head and placing a deep kiss on his sweet, honeyed lips. Curling his tongue, he licked at the pooling saliva in Wu Xingzi's mouth. Only when Wu Xingzi became weak-limbed and panting did Guan Shanjin release him.

The adviser's eyes sparkled, looking at the general foolishly. Only Guan Shanjin existed in those eyes.

"Are you hungry yet?" Guan Shanjin asked gently. His voice was tender, and it seemed to have little claws that clung onto Wu Xingzi, making his heart pound.

Gulping his saliva down, he realized that he could still taste Guan Shanjin in his mouth. Flustered, he answered mindlessly, "I'm hungry now. Can I have you?"

An intoxicating smile bloomed in front of him, and a kiss fell on his ear. "Whatever you want."

When the two men returned home, they didn't even bother to put away their groceries. Instead, they casually tossed them aside and entwined together, kissing passionately.

Wu Xingzi was a little impatient, and the kisses made him weak limbed. Despite trying a few times, he was unable to undo Guan Shanjin's belt. "Take it off!" he complained.

Amused, Guan Shanjin kissed him in consolation. The old man nibbled on the tip of the general's tongue, licking and sucking. It was as though he was enjoying some fine delicacy, unwilling to part from it for even a second.

Allowing Wu Xingzi to clumsily yet feverishly kiss him, Guan Shanjin deftly stripped both of them of all their clothes. Although the hearth was lit, it wasn't warm enough. Worried that Wu Xingzi would get cold, Guan Shanjin wrapped him tightly in his arms.

Wu Xingzi whimpered, grinding against Guan Shanjin. Guan Shanjin's body was fit and sturdy, and he had abundant inner strength. His skin was soft and as hot as a furnace. Plastered against him, Wu Xingzi was so comfortable that he could not stop moaning.

Guan Shanjin's large hands kneaded his buttocks, and his moans rose higher in pitch, sounding sweeter and sweeter. His limbs automatically curled themselves around Guan Shanjin's muscular body as his lips shifted to Guan Shanjin's perfectly formed ear, lapping at it like a puppy.

"Becoming so naughty already?" Guan Shanjin laughed as he grabbed a handful of his ass.

"Ahh..." Wu Xingzi groaned, arching in Guan Shanjin's embrace. His legs tightened around Guan Shanjin's narrow waist, as if he didn't fear falling at all.

Of course Guan Shanjin wouldn't let him fall. He steadily supported his buttocks, pressing Wu Xingzi against the door. His hard cock ground against Wu Xingzi's soft belly as well as his half-erect little prick. When he thrust with a bit more force, the two men panted heavily with delight.

Wu Xingzi had never restrained himself in sexual matters, and he soon became unsatisfied with this sort of clinging friction. Aroused, he urged Guan Shanjin on, "Quick, get inside me. I-It itches..."

He truly was itching for something. Guan Shanjin savagely pinched that plump bottom. He hadn't teased him for long, but his hole was already soaking wet. It was dripping, coating Guan Shanjin's fingers and making everything slick and wet.

This dirty darling was born to destroy him!

Guan Shanjin panted, his finger casually sliding down the drenched cleft and pressing into Wu Xingzi's hole. With only that slight movement, more slick gushed out, flowing down his slender, jade-white finger. The fluids slicked his hand, down to his wrist, and kept on dripping. In a matter of moments, a small puddle had collected on the ground. The old man's entire body flushed pink, his hips twisting about as he cried out in continuous thrill.

"More... Give me more!"

Compared to his thick and bulging cock, Guan Shanjin's finger was a little too slender. Although it was gentler and more agile, Wu Xingzi was used to being fucked wildly and passionately, and he soon grew unsatisfied. He licked Guan Shanjin's neck in an ingratiating plea, his hips never ceasing their movement.

"As you wish." Guan Shanjin bit his shoulder, pushing Wu Xingzi even more firmly against the door. The thick head of his cock brushed along Wu Xingzi's cleft, his balls smacking against his perineum. The little pink cock trapped between their bodies trembled, leaking a great gush of pre-cum.

Guan Shanjin's finger thrust inside, deeper and harder. His fingertip glanced past the slightly protruding sensitive spot within. Without waiting for Wu Xingzi to so much as catch his breath, Guan Shanjin pressed down on that spot, rubbing it mercilessly while intermittently impaling his finger even deeper into his hole. It wasn't long at all before Wu Xingzi's voice trembled, his entire body twitching, as he came on both of their bellies.

"You can't handle the heat, and yet you always like to fan the flames. How slutty." Guan Shanjin's amused words were husky, his breath a little out of control. The words trickled into Wu Xingzi's ears, making his scalp tingle and his body grow weak.

"I'm not slutty..."

"You're not?"

Wu Xingzi's mewling nearly pushed Guan Shanjin to his limit. He yanked his finger out from Wu Xingzi's hole and shoved his cock straight into him.

Despite having been teased until his bottom half was soaked and dripping, Wu Xingzi's hole was still a little too tight for Guan Shanjin's dick. It was soft and slick enough, but penetration was somewhat painful. His buttocks were spread wide open, and the tender wrinkles around his hole disappeared as he was stretched. His sweet moans turned a little shaky, and he gasped pitifully.

"Gently, a little more gently..." It wasn't overly painful, but the old man still bit into Guan Shanjin's firm and muscular shoulder, whimpering unintelligibly.

"Be good." Only a third of Guan Shanjin's cock had entered Wu Xingzi. Guan Shanjin kneaded at his buttocks comfortingly, kissing his cheek. He was sweating with the effort of holding himself back. Still, he did not immediately thrust with abandon. If he ended up injuring Wu Xingzi in the process, it would hurt him too.

Wu Xingzi truly was born for debauchery. Even though he looked extremely pitiful, his lips pale with pain as he acted like he was about to be pierced through, his ass still clenched and flexed around Guan Shanjin's cock, freely fluttering and squeezing down on the large cock head as though it was desperate to take in even more of him.

As expected, it wasn't long before Wu Xingzi yearned for more. Whining, he urged Guan Shanjin to thrust in harder, his limbs wrapping around him even tighter.

"My filthy darling. You asked for it." Guan Shanjin gritted his teeth. He was not going to hold himself back any longer. His sturdy chest pressed Wu Xingzi firmly against the door as his hands tightly gripped his soft buttocks. With a savage thrust, he impaled himself right into Wu Xingzi's core. The old man in his arms kicked and shrieked at the onslaught, yet Guan Shanjin did not stop until he was all the way inside.

In seconds, he was buried deep within. Wu Xingzi's belly protruded outward, revealing the shape of the general's cock.

"You're going to rip me apart! Ahh, gently, a little more gently..." Wu Xingzi cried. Guan Shanjin fucked him until his body shuddered.

Drool hung from his lips and his gaze grew weak. His fingers feebly scratched at Guan Shanjin's well-defined back, leaving only a few light pink tracks.

Guan Shanjin retreated, Wu Xingzi's hole still clinging to his length. The obscene fluids within flowed out with Guan Shanjin's movement, and a salacious scent filled the entire house.

Feeling the thin body in his arms trembling, Guan Shanjin harshly slammed himself in again, forcing a yell from Wu Xingzi. That thick and brutal cock started thrusting away as Wu Xingzi's reddened hole clung to it for dear life. Even without deliberately aiming for the sensitive nub inside, Guan Shanjin's cock was so big that the wild, passionate motions ground against Wu Xingzi's sweet spot with each thrust, making it tingle madly. The spot felt like it was swelling up. Wu Xingzi's ass had long become aroused and dripping; each thrust was accompanied by a slick, wet sound.

Guan Shanjin practically fucked Wu Xingzi's brains out. His eyes became unfocused, and his face was covered with tears and drool. He looked wrecked, only able to moan brokenly.

At first, Wu Xingzi could still thrust his hips along with the rhythm. However, Guan Shanjin's fucking was truly too fierce, and Wu Xingzi could barely even catch his breath. His toes curled tightly before they relaxed again. He shivered nonstop, as if his body was cramping up. Weak spurts of semen were again forced from his delicate little cock, and it seemed like he would soon be unable to come again.

After some time, Guan Shanjin placed Wu Xingzi on the table. Pulling a fair, slender leg onto his shoulder, he gripped one of his hips, pushing himself even further into Wu Xingzi. His balls slapped against the old man's buttocks, turning the flesh red. He covered Wu Xingzi's soft, flaccid little cock with his hand, teasing it with his calloused palm.

Guan Shanjin's hands were very beautiful, his skin fair and delicate. Despite looking as though they were carved from jade, they were hands that had suffered hard work. After all, Guan Shanjin was a military man. He sported many calluses from his training, and the skin on his hands was rough. Brushing against his palms would bring about an itching sensation, and when Guan Shanjin's hand played with Wu Xingzi's sensitive and delicate little prick, the feeling was entirely unusual. With only a few strokes, Wu Xingzi could not help but cry out sharply, and he pushed at Guan Shanjin, wanting to rescue his little dick from the unbearable itch. When Guan Shanjin deliberately rubbed the tender flesh at the tip of his cock with his thumb, Wu Xingzi's high-pitched moan cracked, and he could not make a sound.

Of course, he was unable to push Guan Shanjin away. Gradually, he only ended up even deeper in pleasure, and he was close to orgasm again.

"Don't... Don't do this," Wu Xingzi mewled, shifting and adjusting his body, trying to evade Guan Shanjin's cock deep within him as well as that cruel hand. However, General Guan quickly caught his hips and shoved Wu Xingzi further down on his cock. Again, he reached deep inside him, and Wu Xingzi's pale belly bulged outward.

"Ahh!" Wu Xingzi tilted his head back and howled. Shivering, he reached out and touched his own stomach.

"Do you like it?" Guan Shanjin lowered his head, pressing kisses upon Wu Xingzi's eyelids. Guan Shanjin looked even more entrancing in the haze of pleasure, with a slight crease between his brows and his lustful, gorgeous eyes. Looking at him made Wu Xingzi's heart beat faster and his mouth dry up. Even if he were to die from getting fucked, he would be more than willing to perish.

What a perfect pengornis! It's not just this cock that's like the Prince of Lanling, Guan Shanjin himself is like the Prince of Lanling! Wu Xingzi had never seen him in armor before, nor did he know the imposing, handsome figure he'd strike on the battlefield—but he knew he'd be stunningly beautiful.

"I like it..." Wu Xingzi's small voice faltered. Intoxicated, he stared at Guan Shanjin.

This heated gaze set Guan Shanjin ablaze. He grabbed onto Wu Xingzi's waist, fucking him even more savagely. The egg-sized head of his cock shoved into Wu Xingzi's belly again and again, making Wu Xingzi's senses go blank and his body convulse. Wu Xingzi's ass spasmed and contracted, brutally stretched open once more.

"I can't... No more..." Wu Xingzi's eyes rolled back slightly, drool trickling down from the corner of his mouth. He felt like he was about to go crazy. His orgasm viciously overtook him, carrying him away like the tide. It crashed over him without end, and Wu Xingzi thought he must have been fucked beyond repair. There seemed to be no end to his orgasm; his mouth gaped open, yet no sound came out.

Suddenly, Guan Shanjin kissed him on the lips, his thrusts becoming even more forceful. Wu Xingzi's eyes rolled to the back of his head as he convulsed in pain, his cries stuck in his throat. Guan Shanjin's strong hips rammed into him several more times before Wu Xingzi finally felt spurts of warmth inside. Unable to catch his breath, he passed out cold.

Guan Shanjin came long and hard. After all, during their hurried journey to Qingcheng County, he had not dared to touch Wu Xingzi. Other than the one time before they left, he had held back his sexual desires for an entire month.

Adviser Wu still shuddered slightly after he collapsed on the table. His eyes, cheeks, and nose were red from crying. The sight was surprisingly enticing, causing Guan Shanjin's heart to wrench tightly. With a fondness that he himself was not aware of, Guan Shanjin leaned down and kissed Wu Xingzi's plump lips. Unable to control himself, he hardened again.

Since there was nothing on his agenda, he might as well enjoy himself to the fullest. With this in mind, Guan Shanjin gave up on self-control. With their bodies still joined, he pulled Wu Xingzi up and into his arms. He was still fucking him as he walked into the bedroom.

When Su Yang delivered the New Year supplies, Wu Xingzi was still unable to get out of bed. He had indulged a little too much last night, and on top of that, he was still exhausted from their hasty journey from Horse-Face City. Even significantly sturdier advisers would not have been able to endure such exertion. Wu Xingzi slept like the dead.

This was the first time in Su Yang's life that he saw the strange sight of Guan Shanjin underdressed in a shanku, the plain, simple set of shirt and trousers that villagers commonly wore. Su Yang and some servants he had brought along solemnly unloaded items from the carriage. Even though Guan Shanjin was able to pull off the simple shanku with an elegant flair, it was not enough to abate Su Yang's anger at the sight.

He leaped down from the carriage, shaking with anger as he tugged at the hand of his childhood friend. "Guan Haiwang, how did you end up debasing yourself like this? You're the general of the Southern Garrison! How can you lower yourself to menial labor? Where's that old man?"

"He's still asleep. He's exhausted," Guan Shanjin said. Su Yang's grip was so forceful he managed to stop Guan Shanjin from moving. Guan Shanjin didn't struggle, simply giving the servants some instructions on how to pack away the items before allowing his friend to pull him into the carriage.

"Look at you, all sweaty and smelly, dirtying my golden monkey fur blanket." Su Yang grumbled away, pouring a cup of tea and handing it to Guan Shanjin. "What sort of madness has overtaken you this time?" he asked disdainfully. "Why did you come to such a horrid place for New Year?"

"Because I wanted to." Guan Shanjin's eyes smiled as he drank his tea. He glanced at the little house outside. The man within seemed to be completely undisturbed by all this noise—he must have been sleeping like a rock.

Su Yang snorted. "Have you ever wondered if Mr. Lu is happy about this situation?" He crossed his legs, placing his elbow on his knee and resting his chin on his hand. He looked distinguished, but the image made Guan Shanjin laugh.

"Why would Mr. Lu be unhappy? He knows I'm here. I informed him once I made the decision. He told me to relax and have a good New Year."

When he had mentioned this to Mr. Lu, Guan Shanjin was somewhat testing his reaction. He knew that Mr. Lu would be getting married after the holiday. Although he could understand why Mr. Lu wanted to get married, there was still bitterness in his heart, and he felt like provoking him a little.

"Relax?" Su Yang pursed his lips disapprovingly. "Man Yue has been so busy that he's fatter than ever, right?" When talking about the round, plump man, who came from the same hometown as him and Guan Shanjin, Su Yang's fox-like eyes glimmered with a hint of malice.

"That's not something you should concern yourself with," Guan Shanjin replied with a thin smile. He had never liked Su Yang's antagonism toward Man Yue. After all, there were differences between relatives and friends, and for him, Man Yue was as close as family.

Left speechless, Su Yang was fine with letting the subject drop. After all, he wasn't here to talk about Man Yue.

A silence fell between the two of them before Su Yang finally spoke up again. "Say, what sort of plans do you have regarding Mr. Lu?"

Guan Shanjin did not look at Su Yang, drinking his tea with eyes averted. "I'll be going back before the tenth day of the new year. I need to help him properly manage his wedding affairs."

"You can actually bear to do that?" said Su Yang. "Don't tell me you don't know what Yue Dade's thinking." He really could not endure watching this go on any longer. Su Yang had always appreciated beauty. No matter how much he hated Mr. Lu, he still preferred him to the old man living inside that shabby hut. Guan Shanjin was an idiot, being pecked away by that old quail—it was a complete waste of his beauty.

Faced with Su Yang's interrogation, Guan Shanjin didn't react. He even picked up a pine nut and rose petal pastry and bit into it.

"Don't make me start swearing at the elders!" Su Yang exclaimed, gnashing his teeth.

With perfect composure, Guan Shanjin glanced at his friend and laughed. "If you want to curse at your mother, I can't stop you. At most, I'll just cover up for you—I won't tell Auntie Su about her disrespectful son."

Su Yang spat silently. What was Guan Shanjin even saying? He ground his teeth in anger but was unable to do anything about the general. Who would want to test their own neck against his Chenyuan Sword?

"Actually, there's something I want to ask you," Guan Shanjin said, his tone changing.

Su Yang glanced up at him. "You may ask, but I might not answer."

Guan Shanjin got straight to the point. "Were you the one spreading those rumors in Qingcheng County?"

"So what if I was?" Su Yang didn't deny it, curling his lips into a vulpine smile. "You want to refute the rumors on behalf of the old man? I'll just lay everything out right now. Those rumors are nothing but the truth, and there's not a single bit of exaggeration to them. Is Mr. Lu not the one in your heart?"

As for the exaggerations that occurred *after* the rumors spread among the villagers—that wasn't his responsibility, right?

Having received his answer, Guan Shanjin's brows knitted slightly. His jade-like fingers toyed with the teacup on the table. The cup rolled about, and Su Yang grew frustrated looking at it.

"What?"

"Who asked you to spread such gossip?" Guan Shanjin shot his friend an icy look. Even though Su Yang was acutely aware of the general's disposition, he couldn't suppress a shudder. It took all his might to control the expression on his face, but he still averted his eyes.

"I just don't like that old man. Am I not allowed to? You're not even going to let me be nauseated by him?"

"He's the only thing you feel sick about?" Guan Shanjin laughed.

The teacup Guan Shanjin was playing with shattered, practically turning into powder. Su Yang's brows creased, and he swore under his breath.

"Su Yang, we've known each other for twenty years. Don't I know what sort of person you are? At the same time, you should know very well the sort of person I am." Lightly brushing away the ceramic dust on his hand, Guan Shanjin looked gentle and elegant, even carrying a trace of a spring breeze's warmth. Smiling, he looked at his friend. "I can understand that you don't like Wu Xingzi, but it's out of the ordinary for you to be so preoccupied with an ugly fellow you dislike. According to how you normally conduct your life, Wu Xingzi should be like dust to you—in the amount of time it takes to blow it off your fingers, you'd have forgotten all about it. How would you have the extra time to feel sick about him?"

"What do you *really* want to say? Just come out with it." Su Yang, too, was an intelligent man. The best method for facing Guan Shanjin was to avoid any confusion. When the general decided to be heartless, he could be very inhumane. It was only when it came to Mr. Lu that he could be foolish.

"Was it Man Yue who wanted you to spread the rumors, or was it...Hua Shu?" Guan Shanjin said.

Su Yang laughed when he heard Hua Shu's name. "You already know the answer," he said, slapping his knee and laughing uproariously. "You actually said the name out loud!"

Compared to Su Yang's guffaws, Guan Shanjin was expressionless. He'd naturally had his own suspicions. The rumors he heard yesterday were too close to the truth for comfort—too pointed and specific. He kept worrying that if Adviser Wu heard them, he would discover his selfish motives. He wouldn't be bothered if the truth made the old fellow sad and upset, but he had a feeling that the adviser might instead be delighted. In that case, he'd only use the general for his cock and wait for the day he fell out of favor.

The general had been unable to stop sulking over it, so he questioned Su Yang about the rumors. However, after getting an answer, he didn't feel any better. Instead, he became even more frustrated.

He knew that if the rumors were instigated by Man Yue, they would not have been so crude. Su Yang would also not have been willing to be Man Yue's lackey, no matter how much he wanted to disgust Guan Shanjin. However, if Hua Shu asked, Su Yang might have done it to relieve his boredom.

Still, Hua Shu was only Mr. Lu's servant. Hua Shu often engaged in devious, petty tricks, but this was leaking the private matters of the general's household. If the crime was deemed severe enough, the punishment was death by caning. Did Hua Shu have the guts to commit such an act? Guan Shanjin didn't believe so.

Which would also mean that this entire situation... He kneaded his temples, decisively resolving not to think about it anymore. He knew how noble and unsullied Mr. Lu was as a person.

The year he had returned to the capital from the northwest, he kept feeling like an outsider, completely out of sync with the capital's prosperity and luxury. After all, he had lived in the northwest for eight full years—since he was twelve. The cold and desolate northwest was stained by blood. For him, the line between life and death had been blurred. During the direst times, they even brought the bodies of their enemies back as food.

In his eyes, the world was no longer the pure and beautiful place it had been when he left. He used to be like a treasured bird in a golden cage, arrogant and free from worries. Now, peaceful days left him feeling anxious. Although it could not be seen simply by observing his face, it was as though he had never left the northwest, and his soul had long been trapped in that sickening, smoke-filled wasteland.

Because of his experiences in the northwest, he had lived his days unrestrained for a period of time after his return. Not only did he engross himself in drinking and making merry, he also stirred up trouble in the capital. Many courtiers and imperial court officials complained bitterly about him.

During that year's Spring Lantern Festival, Guan Shanjin brought along a servant with him. They meandered along the riverside to admire the lanterns when unexpectedly, an elegant figure in white captured his attention. Ignoring the alarmed shouts of his guards, he chased after the graceful silhouette. He finally found Mr. Lu under a plum tree, quietly admiring a revolving lantern with his head tilted back.

With one glance, it was as though all the colors in the world faded away. The only thing left was the white color of the snow lotus. Drop by drop, like the clear morning dew, the sight of this man nourished his reckless and frustrated heart.

Having presumably sensed his gaze, Mr. Lu turned around, seeming to recognize him very quickly. The corner of his mouth curved up, and he softly called out, "Haiwang."

At that moment, Guan Shanjin finally felt like he had returned home. He was no longer an outsider, no longer in that place where he had to kill as soon as he opened his eyes. This atmosphere was gentle and warm, with none of the stench of blood and dust. In that moment, he was the son of the protector general, not a sharp blade slicing through flesh.

Guan Shanjin was not dissatisfied with his military life. With his character, he took to the circumstances like a duck to water. Still, no matter how resolute and ruthless he was, he too needed space to breathe.

Mr. Lu had barely changed since the first time they met, when Guan Shanjin was seven. He was still gentle and elegant, kindly and openhearted. It was like a ray of pure moonlight quietly shone upon his heart. Although it was not as bright and scorching as the sun, it still lit a path through the darkness; it was tremendously tranquil and deeply comforting.

Out of all the possible suspects to spread slandering rumors, Guan Shanjin would never suspect Mr. Lu.

Su Yang poured him another cup of tea. Neglecting to bring alcohol along was truly a blunder on his part. Silently finishing the entire cup in one mouthful, Guan Shanjin's expression returned to normal. With a smirk, he looked at Su Yang. "If I ever find out that you tried such underhanded methods toward Wu Xingzi again, expect me to greet you with Chenyuan."

"You're really treating that old man like he's something precious?" The world had to be about to collapse. Was Guan Shanjin's concern toward a mere plaything not going overboard?

"How I treat him is my prerogative. But you know that I hate it when people try to overstep their boundaries and touch things they aren't supposed to. They deserve to get that hand lopped off." Guan Shanjin patted Su Yang's shoulder. Although he did it gently, Su Yang's hair still stood on end. Chills ran through his body, and his face paled.

Indignantly, Su Yang cursed at him. "You must have gone blind!" he exclaimed, but he didn't dare to actually move against him. In the end, even though Su Yang didn't like this ugly little Adviser Wu, why should he concern himself with the advancement of an ant? There were much more important things in life.

It was just that he had never expected Guan Shanjin to actually *like* the old bastard.

"When I started treating you like a good friend, I had already gone blind," Guan Shanjin said. "Be good. Don't be jealous over something small like this." Guan Shanjin patted Su Yang's shoulder again, then jumped off the carriage. He had heard some movement in the house, so he no longer had the heart to chat with his friend any further.

The New Year's goods were now fully unloaded and stored away neatly inside the house. Only the items meant to be kept in the bedroom were still left outside—they had to wait for Wu Xingzi to wake up before they could carry them inside.

Guan Shanjin pushed open the door to the bedroom and happened across a blank and bleary Adviser Wu, still yet to fully awaken. His fair and slender legs were exposed as he sat by the bed, staring at the carriage that just happened to be outside his window.

This soft and sweet image made Guan Shanjin's heart melt, and he walked forward to pull Wu Xingzi into his arms for a kiss.

"Did you sleep well?"

"Huh? Oh..." Wu Xingzi blinked, and his cheeks flushed red. He nodded, embarrassed. It was evident that he was recalling the unbridled things they did the night before.

His body still ached, and his hole felt a little worn out. It felt as if something was still inside him, and he could vaguely feel it dripping. It was somewhat uncomfortable, but he didn't dare to reach down and touch it.

"Su Yang has delivered the New Year's items. There's a new set of bedclothes. Would you like to use them now? Or do you want to change the bed later, right before we sleep?" Pulling Wu Xingzi on his lap, Guan Shanjin wrapped his arms around him and rested his chin on his shoulder with a smile.

Warm breath hit Wu Xingzi's sensitive ear. He inadvertently hunched over, his ears flushing red.

"W-we'll change it later..." Wu Xingzi covered his ears, stammering. "Don't hug me. It's broad daylight, and there are still people outside."

Adviser Wu had always been sensitive. When he was alone with Guan Shanjin, he was bold enough to try many things. However, if there was even a single outsider present, he would be very timid.

"Su Yang will be leaving soon. Don't let him bother you," Guan Shanjin said. He couldn't let the adviser go so easily. He deliberately tightened his hold and began to nibble on Wu Xingzi's glowing red earlobe. As the man in his arms practically hunched into a ball, he couldn't hold back a quiet laugh.

"Come, just ignore Su Yang. Let's talk about New Year festivities. Tomorrow is New Year's Eve—will you be pasting any spring couplets on the windows? How many dumplings should we make? Do you prefer the ones with pork and cabbage filling, or ones with eggs and radish? Bamboo shoots and mutton sounds good, too."

"Dumplings? Why are we eating dumplings?" Wu Xingzi looked confused.

"Don't you eat dumplings during New Year?" Although Guan Shanjin had lived in Horse-Face City for about five years, his close soldiers and guards were all from the north, so they still had dumplings for the New Year.

"You eat dumplings for New Year?" Wu Xingzi blinked. "I eat tangyuan for New Year, and prosperity cake." He greedily licked his lips as he spoke.

"Sure, we'll follow your traditions this year. You can teach me how to prepare the New Year dishes, and we'll make them together."

Guan Shanjin's heart skipped upon seeing Wu Xingzi's pink and delicate little tongue. Unable to stop himself, he lowered his head and captured it with his lips. They kissed for quite some time without pause; the general only stopped when the man in his arms needed to come up for air.

Giving Guan Shanjin an aggrieved glare, Wu Xingzi counted the various New Year dishes on his hand. Time was a little short. Fortunately, he didn't require a long, extensive list. With a large pot of tangyuan, a few prosperity cakes, fried fish, braised chicken, and some stir-fried mustard leaves, there should be enough. It was just that they would be in an even bigger hurry to make offerings for his ancestors, and they would need to visit the cemetery today.

Luckily, Guan Shanjin was a reliable man. He'd already had Su Yang prepare some simple offerings; the candles, incense sticks, and joss paper were all there.

They put their heads together to discuss their schedules and prevent wasting any time. Fifteen minutes later, they'd finally arranged everything. Guan Shanjin patted Wu Xingzi's plump buttocks, laughing. "Aren't you going to go wash up and get dressed? If you end up getting me hard again, we could spend this New Year in bed, too. That'd be nice."

Wu Xingzi gulped upon hearing Guan Shanjin's suggestion, blushing. He got off the general's lap and shot him a resentful look, but he didn't dare say anything.

After getting the offerings, candles, and incense sticks ready, Guan Shanjin wrapped Wu Xingzi up in a big coat. With one hand holding the offerings and the other holding Wu Xingzi's hand, he spoke assuredly: "Let's go."

"Oh." Wu Xingzi kept feeling like something was amiss, but he still led Guan Shanjin toward the mountain.

After walking for about an hour, they reached a valley. In the middle of winter, it was warmer than its exposed surroundings. Silvergrass covered the valley, and small mounds were faintly discernible through the plants. Most of the grave markers were tidied up regularly, so they weren't buried within the silvergrass.

Not far from the Wu family's ancestral grave stood an enormous old tree. There was an empty space to the left of it that was neither too big nor too small. It was rather special: what grew on it was not silvergrass, but a patch of grass that was vividly green. Guan Shanjin glanced at it, then took out a sickle from the basket and started cutting the silvergrass.

"Do you see that patch of ground?" Wu Xingzi asked. His voice was practically exultant, and it made Guan Shanjin curious.

"I see it. Is there something special about it?" Guan Shanjin's actions were skillful and swift. As they conversed, he cleared a large patch of silvergrass, revealing half the grave.

"That's where I'll be laid to rest in the future," Wu Xingzi said in a yearning tone.

Guan Shanjin knew that Wu Xingzi had already purchased his own gravesite. He straightened up, glancing toward the spot. The area was sunny, and it had a good view.

"It's a nice spot." Although his words were polite, he still felt somewhat bitter and upset. He could not explain why the thought came to him, but he realized that this burial spot belonging to Wu Xingzi was perfect for one person—but would be a rather tight fit for two.

"Exactly," Wu Xingzi said delightedly. As he cleared the silvergrass off the grave, he said, "Many people were after that spot!"

"Oh? Then how did you manage to buy it?"

The grave marker in front of the dirt mound was now visible. The words on the wooden tablet had long turned indistinct. Short and covered with moss, it somehow gave off the same bleak feeling that Qingcheng County itself did.

"Uhh..." Wu Xingzi rubbed his nose, laughing a little sheepishly. "So, I'm the county's adviser, right? Qingcheng County is a very small place, and all the documents pertaining to the sale of land go through me. After I found out about this place, I..." Wu Xingzi cleared his throat before continuing, "I took part in a little jobbery."

It wasn't a big deal to talk about it so openly. In a small little place like Qingcheng County, even sales of governmental land were done very innocently.

All anyone had to do was fill in the contract of sale at the magistrate's office. The magistrate didn't waste manpower and time by investigating everything; he just settled things as simply as possible. If too many people wanted the same plot of land, it was up to the magistrate to decide. Wu Xingzi worked earnestly and ceaselessly for many years, gaining the trust of each successive magistrate. Since he wanted to buy this plot of land, the magistrate approved of it immediately.

"It was honestly worth doing a backdoor deal." This was the only time in his life that Adviser Wu actively did something for personal gain. He felt somewhat uneasy about it, but also a little gleeful. Even while mentioning this matter now, his face still reddened.

"I never imagined Adviser Wu was such a devious man," Guan Shanjin teased. Although the old fellow had a very ordinary appearance, no matter how he looked at him, the general found him quite pleasing to the eye. If not for the inappropriate location, Guan Shanjin would have dragged Wu Xingzi into his arms and caressed him all over.

"Hey," Wu Xingzi said as his blush traveled from his ears to his neck. Flustered, he lowered his head and started arranging the candles and offerings.

In the end, Guan Shanjin could not resist leaning over and nuzzling his cheek. On edge, Wu Xingzi hunched over in fright and shyness.

After that, Wu Xingzi avoided Guan Shanjin, always keeping a body's-length distance between them. Only after they had finished burning the joss papers and tidying up the offerings and candles was

Wu Xingzi willing to move a little closer to Guan Shanjin. However, he still refused to let Guan Shanjin hold his hand.

As they walked out of the valley, Wu Xingzi finally shifted closer to Guan Shanjin. "How could you be so indecent in front of my parents and ancestors?" he said, sounding aggrieved.

"How so?" Guan Shanjin stretched out his long arm, pulling Wu Xingzi into his embrace. "If that was indecent, then what was last night?"

Who is shameless enough to answer that question?! Wu Xingzi's face flushed red, and he hurriedly covered Guan Shanjin's mouth. After looking around and confirming no one was nearby, he sighed in relief.

"Shh! Don't mention private matters in public!" Although there was no one around, the ancestors were still behind them! If it was said out loud, wouldn't they hear it? How was he going to keep his dignity intact? Would he be punished by having to kneel on the abacus at night? Just thinking about it made his skin crawl!

Knowing how easily embarrassed Wu Xingzi was, Guan Shanjin didn't tease him any further. With an arm around his shoulders, he started walking back home.

"Right, so how did you explain me to your ancestors?" Guan Shanjin asked. When praying to his forefathers, Wu Xingzi had looked very sincere, and spent a long time muttering at the wooden tablet. If Guan Shanjin had wanted to listen to him, he could have. However, it was already strange for him to participate in the veneration of another man's ancestors. It would really be an egregious act to eavesdrop on Wu Xingzi's prayers.

Although he hadn't listened in, Guan Shanjin was still curious. He had a pressing desire to know exactly what position he held in Wu Xingzi's heart.

Guan Shanjin noticed the man in his arms squirming. Wu Xingzi's unease was evident, and his face had paled. Wu Xingzi looked up, giving the general a placating smile.

Wu Xingzi's palms turned clammy. *There's no way I can tell him about it!*

He normally only took a short while to complete his prayers to his ancestors. After all, what was actually in the grave were clothes and some wooden mannequins meant as substitutes. His parents had vanished, washed away in the massive flood, and the gravesites in Qingcheng County were completely destroyed. When the waters receded, the bones of everyone's family members were all jumbled up together; many of them were left incomplete. Wu Xingzi was still very young at the time. It was only with the Liu family's help that he managed to clean up the grave and get some wooden mannequins and clothes as substitutes for the bodies.

Wu Xingzi wondered, if another big flood occurred after his death—what would happen to him and his ancestors?

"Why aren't you saying anything?" Guan Shanjin asked. Wu Xingzi's face looked awful, as if recalling something sorrowful. Even his lips turned pale. Guan Shanjin's heart ached a little. He reached out and rubbed at Wu Xingzi's lips, consoling him. "It's fine if you don't want to say anything. I have no intention of forcing you."

"Hmm?" Wu Xingzi blinked. After understanding what Guan Shanjin meant, he heaved a breath of relief.

He had told his forefathers:

My dear ancestors, your unfilial descendent has brought along the pengornis he is playing with. Please don't be offended. If there is a superior penis out there, I hope I get the chance to see it. Please bless me with majestic pengornises every year, and may they always be abundant.

When Wu Xingzi made his prayers, he had been distracted by
Guan Shanjin to the point of confusion, so he'd ended up speaking
nonsense. Thinking about the content of his prayers now, he was a
little worried. Would his ancestors punish him after hearing such
filth? *Ah, what a headache.*

Wu Xingzi's ancestors were probably incensed by his prayer. Just
as the two men arrived home, they saw Auntie Li and Auntie Liu
tearing into each other, each with their respective group of friends.

Wu Xingzi could not describe how astonished he was. Standing
there stunned, he watched as Auntie Liu brandished her broom
and Auntie Li blocked her blows with a winnowing basket. A-Niu's
mother held a spatula, and on Auntie Liu's side, another lady wielded
two large carrots as if they were a pair of knives.

What exactly was going on? How did they end up fighting with
the new year's arrival so soon?

Without thinking, Wu Xingzi moved to approach the women,
wanting to persuade them to stop fighting. However, Guan Shanjin
held him back. They instead stood at a distance, watching the show
from under a tree.

"Quick, let me go. The villagers are fighting—what happens if
someone gets injured?" Wu Xingzi said anxiously. He tried forcefully shrugging Guan Shanjin off a few times, but Guan Shanjin held
him tighter still, until he was almost embedded within the general's
embrace.

"If they want to fight, let them fight. You're no longer the adviser
of Qingcheng County, and you'll be returning to Horse-Face City
after New Year. There's no need for you to get yourself involved in
such unseemly affairs." Guan Shanjin clearly heard what the dispute
was about. He sneered at Auntie Li's group.

The gossiping of these ignorant women utterly disgusted him.

However, as the dignified general of the Southern Garrison, Guan Shanjin did not argue with women. He knew who the source of the rumors was, and he would resolve the matter after going back to Horse-Face City. As for these vulgar villagers, he knew Auntie Liu would seek justice on behalf of Wu Xingzi. He could not let this old quail with a stubborn mind go and spoil it.

"I'm no longer the adviser of Qingcheng County?" Wu Xingzi's breath caught. Only then did he realize he'd been absent from work for nearly two months without any official excuse. Knowing that he had probably caused quite a lot of trouble for the magistrate's office, his heart jolted. He became nervous, feeling like he was falling.

"Since you're staying with me in Horse-Face City, you naturally are unable to fulfill the obligations of an adviser. Li Jian has already found a replacement, so you don't need to worry about it."

How could he *not* worry? Wu Xingzi's anxiety increased the more he dwelled on it. He had always assumed he would remain a frog in the well, happy to stay in the same place forever—who would have guessed that he'd be scooped out of his puddle in the blink of an eye? The well had even turned dry in the time he'd been gone, and he was unable to return to it even if he wanted to.

"But...how could I stay in Horse-Face City forever? My gravesite is here..." When his fling with Guan Shanjin reached its end, what would he do after returning to Qingcheng County? He still wanted to continue collecting cocks!

It seemed like he would need to start planting crops. Although it would be tiring, he still had a stash of slightly over nine taels. He might not be able to afford a fir coffin in the future, but he could still buy a cedar coffin for four or five taels...

After making his calculations, Wu Xingzi's mood improved again. As long as he had pengornises, he would be satisfied with life.

After all, life was unpredictable, and a cock might be right around the corner!

Wu Xingzi pondered his pengornises while Auntie Liu and Auntie Li continued to brawl. They tossed away the broom and basket in their hands and rolled up their sleeves to fight with their fists.

Guan Shanjin was very entertained. Auntie Liu proved to be a superior fighter compared to Auntie Li. Although she was thin and small, her strength was tremendous. With one slap from Auntie Liu, Auntie Li's left cheek swelled up, and she fell onto the ground in a sorry state.

"Hah! Just continue to spread your nonsense!" Auntie Liu's anger had yet to be completely unleashed. Lunging onto Auntie Li, she gave her another three loud slaps. Auntie Li's face looked like a bright red bun, swollen and burning.

A-Niu's mother saw that her friend was now at a disadvantage. "You bitch!" she shrieked, lunging over.

Great. It was New Year's Eve tomorrow, and the atmosphere was supposed to be bustling with joy. Now, everything was a mess. Over half a dozen women tussled with their sleeves rolled up. The two carrots were swung several times in Auntie Fang's face until they finally broke into two. Disoriented from the beating, she fell to the ground with a shrill cry.

"Auntie Liu is truly impressive," Guan Shanjin said, nibbling on some melon seeds. He took out some dried fruit from the basket of offerings and shared it with Wu Xingzi.

Auntie Liu and Auntie Li seemed to have each brought three people with them. On Auntie Li's side, other than A-Niu's mother, who still resisted stubbornly, the other two women had turned into bright red buns as well. Just as it seemed like the chaos would end with Auntie Liu's complete victory, Auntie Li suddenly screamed, "Wu Xingzi!"

Wu Xingzi was biting into the dried fruit at that very moment. "Ack!" he choked, coughing fiercely.

Suddenly reinvigorated, Auntie Li scrambled toward Wu Xingzi, and even Auntie Liu was unable to stop her. Grabbing at his lapels, she screeched, "Say it! Say it! What sort of demonic charms did you use to enchant that god-like man? How can a bald chicken think of himself as a phoenix? How the hell did you manage that?! How?!"

The fruit was now stuck in Wu Xingzi's windpipe. He gave a racking cough, unable to speak, his face turning red.

"Remove your hands." How could Guan Shanjin allow Wu Xingzi to be bullied right before his very eyes? He reached out and directly twisted both of Auntie Li's wrists. With a scream of pain, she stumbled backward and fell onto her behind. Tears and snot covered her face, and she glared at Guan Shanjin both pleadingly and fearfully.

"You divine man!" she howled, "you have to wake up! Wu Xingzi has blinded you with a demonic enchantment! What I'm telling you is the truth!"

"Pah!" Auntie Liu had caught up. She swung her broom about, striking and scolding her at the same time. "You're just jealous! Who here doesn't know you've always resented Wu Xingzi?! Hah! The bald chicken you mentioned is that son of yours, right?! He can barely read, and yet he wants to replace Xingzi as the adviser? Who gave you the gall, huh?! Who gave you the audacity?!"

Auntie Liu beat Auntie Li to the point where she could not escape. Together with the pain from her twisted wrists, she screamed like a pig in a slaughterhouse. Auntie Fang and A-Niu's mother had both already stopped fighting. They knew when to back down—

putting aside the matter of Wu Xingzi employing demonic charms, there was no way they could win against Guan Shanjin!

Guan Shanjin took no notice of what the women were chirping about. He only cared whether Wu Xingzi was in pain from choking, gently patting his back. Removing the bamboo container from his waist, Guan Shanjin poured water into Wu Xingzi's mouth, sip by sip. Finally, he managed to remove the dried fruit from his windpipe. Wu Xingzi's eyes, nose and face were all flushed red, and Guan Shanjin's heart ached looking at him. Guan Shanjin hugged him and spoke a few words of comfort.

However, Wu Xingzi was only concerned about the aunties. "Auntie Liu, Auntie Liu! Don't fight anymore." With eyes still wet from choking, he hurriedly waved his arms at Auntie Liu, attempting to stop her.

"Xingzi, don't be scared! I know when to stop. The Li family's skin is thick and coarse—they won't be injured easily. If I don't teach them all a proper lesson, Auntie Li will never control her mouth!" Auntie Liu was just like a female general. Despite her harried breathing, the energy spreading within her was enough to make her glow. It was impressive compared to how disheveled Auntie Li looked.

"Auntie..." Wu Xingzi wrung his hands and rubbed his nose, not knowing how to persuade her to stop. He was fully aware that today's chaos was caused by the rumors that they'd heard yesterday, and Auntie Liu was only acting in his defense. He was quite touched by her actions, but he was also afraid that Auntie Liu would end up embroiled in legal trouble. Wu Xingzi was no longer the adviser, and he had no way of protecting her. What could he do?

When Wu Xingzi was about to persuade her to stop again, Guan Shanjin covered his mouth. "Let Auntie Liu vent her anger. I'll handle Li Jian."

Uhh... Wu Xingzi smiled brightly as Guan Shanjin essentially proclaimed that the back door of the magistrate's office was as wide open as the city gates.

After another bout of turmoil, Auntie Li finally stopped crying. Only then did Auntie Liu stop wielding the broom in her hand, heroically wiping the sweat from her forehead. Holding the broom like a spear, she declared, "If you ever talk nonsense about Xingzi again, I'll kick your ass!"

Auntie Li glared resentfully at Auntie Liu. She then glanced over at Wu Xingzi and Guan Shanjin snuggling together, her eyes almost bloodshot from anger. However, she no longer had the guts to squabble. Snorting, Auntie Li stood up with the help of Auntie Fang, grudgingly leaving the scene with her friends.

Confirming that her nemesis had retreated, Auntie Liu triumphantly patted the dust off her skirts, looking cavalier as she addressed Guan Shanjin. "See? Although I'm but a humble woman, I'm still someone Xingzi can count on. You two should spend your days happily together...but if you hurt Xingzi, I won't let you off the hook, either!"

Guan Shanjin admired such heroic words, and he nodded in agreement.

Satisfied, Auntie Liu and her friends gave Wu Xingzi some consoling words, then gleefully returned to their individual homes, their chests puffed up with pride.

There was still evidence of the fight in front of his house. Wu Xingzi stared at the scuff marks for a moment, and then burst out laughing.

"Why are you so happy?" Guan Shanjin asked, tightening his arms around Wu Xingzi. Looking at his reddened, fleshy nose, his teeth itched to bite. He lowered his head to nip at it.

"Hey, no biting." Wu Xingzi shyly ducked away, pulling at Guan Shanjin as they headed home. "I just feel that this New Year doesn't seem so bad."

The little interlude of the fight amongst the aunties did not cause much commotion in the county. The public displays of affection between Wu Xingzi and Guan Shanjin had been witnessed by many people, and news of their closeness spread rapidly throughout the village. Only Auntie Li and her gang still insisted that Wu Xingzi had cast demonic enchantments.

Rumors never bothered Wu Xingzi. Since Auntie Liu had acted on his behalf, he glossed over the matter. What was most important now was making tangyuan.

Previously, he'd lived alone. As it was rather troublesome, and he was afraid of not finishing them all, Wu Xingzi often only prepared tangyuan with savory fillings. Since Guan Shanjin was around this year, Wu Xingzi was seized by a sudden whim to prepare sweet tangyuan filled with pine nuts and sesame.

The meat for the savory filling was top-quality pork belly, well-marbled with fat. The texture was smooth and tender, and it was first marinated with alcohol and ginger slices to get rid of any smell. After that, it was minced finely and seasoned, then mixed with chopped celery and fried red onions to complete the filling.

One by one, Guan Shanjin skillfully formed round and plump dumplings with deft fingers. Just one look was enough to make Wu Xingzi's mouth pool with saliva.

Wu Xingzi prepared the sweet filling. He placed red dots on the sweet tangyuan to differentiate them from the savory ones, making them look even more festive.

With four hands working, the two men were soon done. They made nearly sixty dumplings in total.

Wu Xingzi was a little worried. The dumplings he'd made were not small, and he did not know if they could finish all of them.

However, he didn't have too much time to ponder this dilemma, as there were still many things to do: pasting the paper cutouts, writing the spring couplets, changing the bedclothes, and other tasks. Wu Xingzi didn't know why there were so many tasks. Previously, when it was just him, he spent New Year very simply. Even if he waited until New Year's Eve to do all these things, there was more than enough time!

Occupied with their New Year's preparations, time flew by. Guan Shanjin took charge of nearly all the kitchen tasks. The only thing Wu Xingzi did on New Year's Eve was cook the savory tangyuan— Guan Shanjin didn't know how to season the soup, so he had no choice but to let him enter the kitchen.

CHAPTER 2

MURDERING THE TOP TEN PRIZED PENGORNISES

"So, who am I?" Guan Shanjin laughed at him. In his drunken state, Wu Xingzi was even more bewildered than usual.

Staring at Guan Shanjin's dewy lips, an enchanted Wu Xingzi wriggled into the general's arms, answering proudly: "You're the pengornis spirit," he said between hiccups, "come to life!"

The what spirit?!

Guan Shanjin didn't know if he should be angry or amused. Pinching Wu Xingzi's cheeks, he said calmly, "You're drunk. I'll settle this with you tomorrow!"

ONCE THE DISHES for the New Year's Eve dinner were all placed on the table, the two men cleaned themselves up, changed into fresh clothes, and sat down together to share the meal.

It had to be said that Guan Shanjin possessed fantastic culinary skills. He had even prepared a dish of chrysanthemum fish. It was crispy on the outside and tender on the inside, and the sauce was sweet and sour with a hint of spice. The fried fish looked like a flower blooming in water, and it tasted so delicious that Wu Xingzi was tempted to swallow his own tongue along with it.

"Would you like to have a small drink with me?" Guan Shanjin knew that Wu Xingzi was a lightweight. However, since this holiday only came once a year, he figured a small drink wouldn't be a big deal, so he'd had Su Yang prepare a light and sweet plum wine. It was a weak wine that had only fermented for two years; not even a child could get drunk on it.

"Yes, yes." The bottle had only been partially unsealed, but Wu Xingzi could already smell the delicate fragrance of the wine. He couldn't really hold his liquor, but he liked the atmosphere that drinking cultivated, so he promptly nodded his head.

As expected, the wine was excellent. The flavor of the plum was slightly tart, yet it tasted dry and sweet on the tongue. Holding onto the cup, Wu Xingzi took one sip after another. They spoke few words, but the ambience was warm and intimate.

Guan Shanjin didn't eat much. He preferred drinking his wine with the accompanying sight of Wu Xingzi enthusiastically eating. Wu Xingzi finally managed to devour all the dishes on the table and empty his cup too.

"Another cup?" Guan Shanjin asked casually. He thought that Wu Xingzi would refuse him. After all, the old man was grinning foolishly, his face already flushed and his eyes shining brightly.

He didn't expect that Wu Xingzi would happily hold up his cup to Guan Shanjin, eagerly awaiting his next cup. "Sure."

He looked docile and innocent. Caught off-guard, Guan Shanjin ended up pouring him a second drink. Wu Xingzi downed this cup even faster than the first, emptying it in a few mouthfuls. He burped, and his drunken smile turned even more dopey.

"Wu Xingzi?" Guan Shanjin reached out to shake his arm, realizing that things had gone awry.

This only aggravated the situation. Guan Shanjin's jostling made Wu Xingzi fall backward. Alarmed, Guan Shanjin quickly pulled him into his arms. The old fellow wobbled wildly and squinted at the general. There was a solemnness in his gaze that Guan Shanjin had never seen before.

"What are you looking at?" Guan Shanjin asked. With a sigh, he tried to remove the cup from Wu Xingzi's hand. However, Wu Xingzi refused to let it go, even licking the lip of the cup with the tip of his tongue, as if savoring the taste of the wine.

"I... I recognize you," Wu Xingzi said.

As soon as the adviser spoke, Guan Shanjin knew that Wu Xingzi was drunk, and he resigned himself to the inevitable. He still remembered how chatty an inebriated Wu Xingzi had been at the Restaurant of Songs.

"What a coincidence—I recognize you too." Reasoning with a drunkard was a waste of time. Wu Xingzi wouldn't remember anything after he sobered up, so Guan Shanjin decided to just humor him.

"Oh?" Wu Xingzi leaned his face closer to Guan Shanjin's, staring at him for quite some time. "Ah, you're really handsome," he praised the general, blushing.

Guan Shanjin chuckled. "I feel the same way." When they drank in the Restaurant of Songs, Wu Xingzi had repeatedly mentioned how good looking he was. The old man had ordinary features, but he sure liked looking at beauties.

"Mm... Who are you?" Wu Xingzi asked.

Though drunk and unsteady, Wu Xingzi was more daring than usual. He reached out, cupping Guan Shanjin's face in his hands, almost pressing his nose right against the general's handsome profile. Guan Shanjin let him do it, supporting him slightly to prevent him from falling.

"Can you see clearly, now that you're up close?"

"Can... I can..." Wu Xingzi hiccupped drunkenly, twitching his nose to take in Guan Shanjin's scent. A look of realization suddenly swept over his face. "I know who you are!"

"Oh? So, who am I?" Guan Shanjin laughed at him. In his drunken state, Wu Xingzi looked even more bewildered than usual as he stared at Guan Shanjin's dewy lips. They were stained crimson, but they didn't look effeminate; he was tempted to lean in for a taste.

Enchanted, Wu Xingzi wriggled into the general's arms. "You're the pengornis spirit," he said proudly, between hiccups, "come to life!"

The *what* spirit?!

Guan Shanjin didn't know if he should be angry or amused. Pinching Wu Xingzi's cheeks, he said calmly, "You're drunk. I'll settle this with you tomorrow!"

He knew he shouldn't have let Wu Xingzi touch the wine. All he wanted was to share a small drink to brighten the festive mood, but he didn't anticipate Wu Xingzi getting drunk off a mere two cups. What the hell was he saying? A pengornis spirit?!

If he were a spirit, the first thing he would do would be to swallow this dizzy old quail down, bones and all! Then he wouldn't be able to anger him anymore.

Wu Xingzi was preposterously drunk. Twisting about in Guan Shanjin's arms, he nibbled on Guan Shanjin's lips and neck and exclaimed about how delectable he was. It seemed like Wu Xingzi planned on fondling the general's head and gnawing on it all night.

With him fussing about like this, would they even be able to sleep tonight?

Wu Xingzi suddenly calmed down, obediently nestling in Guan Shanjin's embrace and staring at him with bright eyes.

"What are you looking at now?" Guan Shanjin asked patiently.

"I want to show you my darlings." With his cup in his mouth, Wu Xingzi smiled blearily. His expression turned gleeful and mysterious. "You can't tell anyone about it, especially that...that...Prince of Lanling."

Prince of Lanling? Who? Guan Shanjin felt dour, but he still nodded in agreement.

Of course, the inebriated Wu Xingzi did not care if Guan Shanjin sincerely wanted to see his darlings. Hazily, he knew that the person in front of him was someone very close to him—they had venerated his ancestors together. He couldn't resist the desire to show off his prized possessions to this man.

"Follow me." Wu Xingzi tried getting up a few times. He started to stand, but his limbs were weak. He was like a turtle flopping around on its back: no matter how much he tried, he was unable to flip himself over.

Guan Shanjin sighed and lifted him up in a bridal carry. "Come. Show me the way and I'll take you there."

"Sure, sure, sure. Hey, for a pengornis spirit, you're really nice. Can I keep you?" Wu Xingzi asked in an almost yearning tone. He compliantly leaned his head on Guan Shanjin's chest, not looking at him.

Instead of answering, Guan Shanjin nudged the man in his arms, reminding him not to forget what he was supposed to be doing. Under Wu Xingzi's direction, Guan Shanjin entered the bedroom and opened the cabinet. He took out the meticulously maintained rattan case, placing it on the bed alongside Wu Xingzi.

It was obvious Wu Xingzi treasured this rattan case. He even carefully wiped his hands before opening it. The faint scent of insect-repelling herbs wafted out of the box. To no surprise, the first thing taken out was an herb sachet. Sitting near the bed, Guan Shanjin saw that there were some drawings inside the case.

An ominous feeling welled up within Guan Shanjin. He opened his mouth, wanting to ask Wu Xingzi to stop. However, Wu Xingzi's actions were faster. He carefully took out the drawings with pride, waving Guan Shanjin over to show them off. "Come, come, take a look. These are your brothers."

Brothers? Guan Shanjin was an only child—how could he have brothers?

When the general finally saw what his "brothers" were, he was so outraged that he could only laugh.

Damn you, you old scoundrel! I've always said that you repress your sexual desires—but you're actually this shamelessly horny?!

"These are your darlings?" Each and every picture was a rendering of a penis. Guan Shanjin had used the pigeon post before, so of course he knew how these drawings had come into the adviser's possession!

Exactly who was it that started this tradition? Guan Shanjin gnashed his teeth. He had done everything he could to prevent Wu Xingzi from mailing drawings of his own penis to others, but he had completely forgotten that such illustrations were sent *and* received. Wu Xingzi didn't mail any out, but that didn't mean other people wouldn't mail any to him! There were at least forty or fifty dick pictures in that pile!

Guan Shanjin must have had too much to drink. His blood surged within him, and a pressure rose in his throat. He felt like he might cough up blood.

Wu Xingzi didn't register that anything was wrong with Guan Shanjin. He flipped through each phallic illustration with great tenderness. "I've collected fifty-plus pengornis pictures! Look, these ten drawings are my favorites. Do you think they'll come to life as well?"

"They won't." How could they? Guan Shanjin gritted his teeth, his enthralling eyes almost turning bloodshot. He looked like a huge leopard about to violently pounce.

If any drawing dares to come to life, don't blame me when I pull out Chenyuan!

"They won't...? What a pity." Wu Xingzi gazed at Guan Shanjin's pretty face before letting out a small sigh. However, his eyes still shone brightly. "Can I kiss you? You're beautiful, and you smell so good..."

"You can't." Guan Shanjin rejected him with a sneer. Surrounded by penis pictures, Guan Shanjin was unwilling to let Wu Xingzi get his way.

"Ah. Can I lick you, then?" Wu Xingzi had no choice but to ask for the next best option. He licked his lips as he stared at the elegant, perfectly chiseled hands of the pengornis spirit. He had just filled his stomach, but now he was hungry again.

"You can't." *Your mind is absolutely filled with filth, you old quail! The audacity!* Guan Shanjin pointed at his "brothers" with a grimace. "Weren't you going to introduce my brothers to me? Tell me about them!" Sooner or later, he would ferret out all of them and destroy each one!

Once the dick drawings were mentioned, Wu Xingzi's eyes sparkled. The sight of him treating the drawings with such care made Guan Shanjin so angry his insides hurt. However, he had to suppress his temper if he wanted to understand the origins of these "darlings." With more information, he would be able to track these men down.

"Look, look. These ten drawings are my favorites. When you were inside the wax paper, did you talk to them?" Wu Xingzi held up the carefully wrapped drawings.

How would he be able to talk to them? It was only today that he learned they existed—that it wasn't *The Pengornisseur* that Wu Xingzi liked, but the pengornis drawings mailed to him!

"It's stuffy inside the paper, so it's not conducive to conversation."

"It's stuffy?" Wu Xingzi exclaimed in alarm and hurriedly undid the paper packaging. He quickly apologized, "Ah, I've made you all feel cramped. My mistake!"

"Mm." Staring at the revealed drawings, Guan Shanjin's vision suddenly seemed awash with blood. Great! Now he knew why Wu Xingzi was so open about sex.

This old fellow seemed to have always been partial toward thick and sturdy cocks. Observing his ten favorite pengornis drawings, every single one of them was long and girthy—almost filling up the entire paper. All of them looked hot and hefty, as if their heat emanated from the paper.

"This drawing is the first one I saw with bumps on the tip. Say, why is it that some faces grow marks like that, and cocks have them, too? Would it feel ticklish if I rubbed them?" This was the second drawing. The phallus it showed was not especially large or thick, just extremely savage looking. The veins stood out, bulging in certain areas. Wu Xingzi lightly caressed the bulging parts, his face blushing red.

"It's ugly." Guan Shanjin absolutely abhorred it. He preferred the ones that were pale and delicate looking—for instance, Wu Xingzi's was very nice.

"This thing is useless. Only men who can't stay hard grow such bumps." Pursing his lips, Guan Shanjin pinched Wu Xingzi's cheek. "Continue."

"Really? Wow, I didn't even know that could happen. I'll have to ask you, a pengornis spirit, to teach me more." Wu Xingzi put the dimpled dick down with clear dejection. Pointing at the next draw-ing, he said, "Then look at this one—see how it tilts to the right? I keep wondering, a cock this thick with its head at an angle...how wonderful will it feel when it enters?"

"It is thick enough, but this angle wouldn't hit the right spot. As they say, a boat leaves no traces moving through the water. It's probably referring to that sort of sensation." Guan Shanjin slan-dered all the other cocks with great vigor, criticizing each one that he saw. Wu Xingzi sneaked a few peeks at him, and the general was unsure if Wu Xingzi felt offended, or if he simply liked looking at his face.

Eventually, they reached the ninth illustration. This time, Guan Shanjin shut his mouth, not saying a word. Wu Xingzi's attitude toward this pengornis picture was different from the previous ones. He even held up the drawing, comparing it with Guan Shanjin's face, thinking that he wouldn't notice! The adviser clearly wondered if this was the cock that had come to life. *Damn. Wu Xingzi really deserves a good fucking!*

"So, do we look alike?" Guan Shanjin asked in a low voice. His fingers twitched, restraining himself from pushing Wu Xingzi down and having his way with him. After all, there was still one pengornis left at the top of the ranking!

It was unfortunate that due to his temper, he did not notice that the final phallus was very similar to his own.

"Hmm..." Wu Xingzi squinted, earnestly comparing the drawing to the general several times. Finally, he shook his head. "You don't. I remember that he's a scholar, very refined and elegant. I really liked his face, so my first letter was to him. Ah, it really is a lovely pengornis! How hot do you think it'd feel? What would it taste like? Would it be able to reach my belly?"

"He wouldn't dare." Guan Shanjin pinched the corner of the drawing with two fingers, gradually pulling it toward himself. The previous few pictures made his chest feel tight, but this drawing felt like a threat to him. It was evident that Wu Xingzi liked this cock very much, even remembering the appearance of its owner.

This old pervert! How can he be so debauched?! Every single drawing smelled like incense and insect-repelling herbs, but there was an additional vague scent with which Guan Shanjin was very familiar—the scent of Wu Xingzi's cum.

Guan Shanjin was almost about to explode. Not only did Wu Xingzi look at erotic illustrations of other men's penises, he even used them when masturbating!

He had to destroy all of them!

"Hey, don't kidnap my cock!" Wu Xingzi held on to the drawing tightly, but of course Guan Shanjin refused to let go either. Seeing that the paper was about to be torn into two, Wu Xingzi released the drawing, unwilling to hurt it. He could only watch as his prized penis picture fell into the hands of the pengornis spirit and was torn into tiny pieces right in front of him. Tears started to well up in Wu Xingzi's eyes. He was devastated.

"That... That cost a coin..."

Glancing at him, Guan Shanjin took a coin out from a pouch hanging on his waist and tossed it at Wu Xingzi. "Here's your money back."

Wu Xingzi clumsily caught the coin. Blinking, he stuttered his thanks.

"What about the last drawing?" Guan Shanjin asked. He gritted his teeth so hard that they creaked. He decided that once Wu Xingzi held up the next drawing, he would grab it and tear it up as well, to prevent it from becoming an eyesore.

"The last drawing..." Wu Xingzi suddenly swallowed his saliva. His face was red from the alcohol, and he still looked rather intoxicated. "Ah, this one is really attractive."

This drawing was clearly larger than the rest, and the sketched image was so thick and long that it almost burst from the page. Its slightly open tip glistened a little. It looked like a real object with heat and heft. Guan Shanjin was fairly certain that Wu Xingzi was thinking about sucking it.

Just as he was about to snatch it up, Guan Shanjin realized that the shape of the cock looked somewhat familiar. He took a closer look and was suddenly enlightened. Wasn't this top-ranking cock... his very own?

"At least you have taste." Guan Shanjin's chest still felt tense, but he also felt somewhat proud. He gathered up the other penis illustrations and shoved them back into the rattan case, immediately undoing his pants. Pulling out his cock that had yet to fully harden, he shook it at Wu Xingzi. "Look. See what sort of pengornis spirit I am."

After one glance, Wu Xingzi's eyes were completely glued to the cock before him. He gulped his saliva down, and his entire body felt hotter. He blushed even more intensely, and he could not resist licking his lips.

"Yes... So you're the one that came to life..." Carefully packing the drawings back into the rattan case, Wu Xingzi placed the sachet inside before closing the lid. After placing it under his bed, his slightly trembling fingers reached out toward that Lanling Prince of penises, but he dared not touch it so readily. "Ah, now I know. If there is a Lanling Prince of pengornises, it would definitely look just like yours."

So the Prince of Lanling was referring to *him*. Guan Shanjin laughed out loud. This old fellow always aimed right for the soft spot in his heart.

"Come here," Guan Shanjin commanded gently. His voice sent shivers up Wu Xingzi's body, traveling from his ears to his brain. With a jolt, Wu Xingzi started panting heavily.

He shifted and shuffled, moving closer and closer to the pengornis spirit. The scent of white sandalwood and orange blossom filled his nose, and it was more intoxicating than the dry and sweet plum wine.

"Don't cry and faint tonight, all right?"

That affectionate tone stole all strength from Wu Xingzi's body. Boneless, he fell into the arms of the pengornis spirit, his thigh pressing right into that huge, hard cock. It gave off enough heat to make his entire body tingle in excitement.

"Yes..."

Stripping a drunk man naked was an easy task, especially when the drunkard was handsy. Guan Shanjin effortlessly took off all of Wu Xingzi's clothes, then got off the bed to remove his own.

Wu Xingzi stared at Guan Shanjin as he disrobed, utterly captivated. The candles in the bedroom flickered, casting shadows upon his body. His pale, fair skin was illuminated with a gentle glow, accentuating firm and sharply defined muscles, full of hidden power. This was a body that had been thoroughly strengthened, and it could not look more perfect.

Wu Xingzi's breathing sped up just from looking at him. He licked his lips, his throat going dry.

"You always like doing this, don't you?" Guan Shanjin laughed, returning to the bed naked after removing his trousers. His massive member was rising to the occasion, its head glistening wetly.

Wu Xingzi swallowed his saliva with a gulp. Enchanted, he threw himself into Guan Shanjin's arms, trembling as he touched the pengornis spirit. As expected, it was hot and hard to the touch, just like a searing bar of iron. The thrilling heat pierced right into his nerves and leached into his brain, weakening his entire body.

"Do you want to taste it?"

"Yes..." Wu Xingzi stroked it continuously, his face full of yearning. "Can I?"

"Go ahead." Guan Shanjin caressed Wu Xingzi's chin with his cock, making Wu Xingzi moan.

"You have to last a little longer tonight," Guan Shanjin said. He dragged his fingers along Wu Xingzi's cheek, then brushed past his eyebrow. Finally pressing against the back of Wu Xingzi's head, Guan Shanjin pushed him down toward his dick.

Wu Xingzi's lips bumped against the heated head of Guan Shanjin's cock, and the slightly salty and bitter-tasting pre-cum seeped into his mouth. The tip of Wu Xingzi's tongue swirled around, enjoying the taste. He opened his mouth wide and took in the head of the huge, hard cock. As he sucked on it, his tongue swiped along the slit on the tip, back and forth.

His actions were still a little curious, but there was no sign of hesitation. Wu Xingzi's soft, tender tongue slid down the shaft, licking around it. Next, he stretched his mouth even wider, entirely unafraid. Inch by inch, he slowly swallowed the remarkably long, thick cock.

"Mm..." Guan Shanjin moaned. Wu Xingzi only felt more enchanted at the charming sound of it. Obsequiously—although it was a little selfish of him, too—he took the cock all the way to his throat and didn't stop until he started to choke and cough.

"Why are you in such a hurry?" Guan Shanjin asked as he kneaded Wu Xingzi's bulging cheeks. The general's alluring eyes looked starry in the candlelight.

Ah, he's really handsome! A pengornis spirit was a kind of demon, but this demon was truly pleasing to the eye.

The atmosphere was effortlessly erotic. Wu Xingzi himself had been hard from the start, and he unconsciously ground his buttocks against the bed—the obscenely slutty sight lit a fire in Guan Shanjin's heart. His cock grew even harder in Wu Xingzi's mouth, trapping his tongue. The corner of Wu Xingzi's lips whitened under the strain, looking as though they were about to split, but Wu Xingzi was undeterred. He kept swallowing the cock down, all the way until a prominent bump could be seen in his throat. Tears smeared across his face, and he couldn't stop gagging.

Guan Shanjin was impossibly thick. Wu Xingzi could scarcely breathe. He faltered, holding onto Guan Shanjin's thighs as he shifted backward and pulled his mouth back slightly. The general's cock shone with saliva, making it look even more fierce.

When just the head remained in his mouth, Wu Xingzi lowered his head again, taking the shaft back inside. After he repeated this several times, Guan Shanjin's movements turned savage. He grasped Wu Xingzi's hair and forced him harshly down onto his cock, greedily fucking his mouth.

After only a few thrusts, Wu Xingzi's eyes were just about rolling to the back of his head. It was as though his throat's only purpose was to be fucked by Guan Shanjin. The shape of Guan Shanjin's cock could be seen in Wu Xingzi's throat as he pumped himself inside. Wu Xingzi's tongue couldn't even move, and he had no choice but to allow the egg-sized head of Guan Shanjin's cock to have its way with him.

Wu Xingzi started crying, but he tightened his grip on Guan Shanjin's strong thighs even further, obligingly moving his head with the general's thrusts. Suddenly, his entire body convulsed—it was clear that Wu Xingzi had just climaxed.

Guan Shanjin hurriedly removed his cock from Wu Xingzi's mouth. Feebly, Wu Xingzi collapsed against his legs, retching pitifully. His face was flushed red, and his saliva, along with Guan Shanjin's fluids, flowed out of his mouth in a thin stream. A delicate thread of saliva stretched between Guan Shanjin's cock and Wu Xingzi's mouth.

"You have to increase your endurance." Guan Shanjin's gaze darkened. He patted Wu Xingzi's blushing cheeks with his cock, speaking seductively. "Do you want to try something different?"

Wu Xingzi was adventurous in bed, and he had never refused anything Guan Shanjin wanted to do with him. Wu Xingzi blinked innocently and sold himself out with a hoarsely spoken agreement.

"Good boy," Guan Shanjin said. As he leaned over and kissed Wu Xingzi on the ear, the general undid his own hair ribbon. His silky, soft hair flowed downward, making him look less aloof and greatly increasing the gentle seductiveness of his charm. Wu Xingzi gazed at him, so enraptured that his mouth fell open and he forgot to breathe.

Guan Shanjin held the ribbon in front of Wu Xingzi and tugged on it, apparently pleased with its durability. He then wound the ribbon round Wu Xingzi's soft, spent cock, wrapping it around over and over again. Finally, he tied a knot at the base.

"What are you doing?" The fatigue from the alcohol and his orgasm made Wu Xingzi a little slow to react. He had a sinking feeling that something was amiss, but he had lost his chance to refuse.

"Something fun." The general's laughter came out half muffled in his long hair. Wu Xingzi instantly had no other questions.

Guan Shanjin picked the old quail up, placing him on his lap as his fingers prodded Wu Xingzi's hole. Wu Xingzi's hole was well acclimated to sex, and relaxed from his recent orgasm, he took in two fingers with no difficulty at all. When Guan Shanjin pressed against that special spot within, Wu Xingzi released a long and sweet moan. His hips tensed up and his backside swayed in delight. His ass greedily mouthed at the two fingers, desperate to have them even deeper.

"How naughty." While nibbling at Wu Xingzi's fleshy nose, Guan Shanjin skillfully maneuvered his fingers. He shoved them in and out of Wu Xingzi's hole, then scraped against that sensitive spot with his fingernails, alternating between soft and hard pressure. Teased relentlessly, Wu Xingzi spilled lewd fluids everywhere. His little cock twitched continuously as it started to harden; he felt close to climax, but the hair ribbon bound tightly around his prick prevented him from reaching relief.

"T-take... Take it off..." Aching, Wu Xingzi reached down and tried to remove the ribbon. However, Guan Shanjin swiftly blocked his hand; he trapped both of Wu Xingzi's wrists with his free hand and yanked them behind his waist.

"It hurts..."

"Bear with it for now. Didn't you want to try something different?" Guan Shanjin heartlessly thrust his fingers directly against Wu Xingzi's sensitive spot.

"Ah—!" Wu Xingzi cried out, his body jerking in Guan Shanjin's arms. He raised his buttocks up high, but he was still unable to come. Desire that could not be satisfied thrummed through his body. Sniffing pathetically, Wu Xingzi pleaded, "Take it off... Please, please..."

Guan Shanjin didn't say anything in reply. He simply removed his fingers and positioned his cock against Wu Xingzi's soft, relaxed hole. He impaled himself, pushing his entire length inside; he nearly shoved his way into Wu Xingzi's stomach in one thrust.

"Ahh!" Wu Xingzi raised his slender neck, his throat bobbing delicately. He looked as though he wanted to plead for mercy, but he was unable to utter a single word. He was at a perfect angle for Guan Shanjin to lower his head and nip his Adam's apple. The impassioned general opened his mouth and took a bite, leaving a bruise on that little bump.

Then Guan Shanjin began to fuck Wu Xingzi, wildly and passionately. Wu Xingzi's hands were trapped behind his waist, so it was impossible to keep his balance; as the general pounded into him, he became very unsteady. Each savage thrust made his buttocks tilt up high, and when Guan Shanjin's cock retreated, lewd juices escaped his little hole. The huge, thick cock pierced right through him, grazing past his sensitive spot each time. Wu Xingzi's hole quickly became swollen.

This did not give Guan Shanjin pause. Instead, he thrust rapidly into that shamelessly slutty hole, making Wu Xingzi cry and shout. His bound little cock hardened desperately again and again, only to soften without climax each time. Not only was he unable to relieve the overwhelming pressure rising within him, but it built up even further. His pleasure surged until tingles spread throughout his body, leaving aching trails of want. Wu Xingzi couldn't think of anything other than coming.

"Please... I beg you..." Wu Xingzi was crying so hard that he started hiccupping. Confused, he murmured nonstop about things that even he himself did not understand. Another shrill howl came as his stomach began to protrude with the shape of Guan Shanjin's cock.

Wu Xingzi's mouth gaped open, his tongue hanging out halfway. Saliva flowed from the corner of his lips as his body spasmed uncontrollably. He did not know exactly what he was feeling, only knowing that if he was unable to come soon, he might die.

Guan Shanjin still refused to show mercy. After releasing his hold on Wu Xingzi's hands, Guan Shanjin gripped Wu Xingzi's backside, fucking him even more violently. The harsh thrusts made fluids seep out of Wu Xingzi's hole, leaving a huge wet patch on the new bedsheets.

"Ah... Ahhh!" Wu Xingzi yanked on his own hair as he shouted in madness. His blank eyes stared into nothingness, and he began to shudder again.

Wu Xingzi truly thought he would die on that bed. However, even that desperate thought was soon too much for him to keep his head. All he could perceive was white. As soon as he reached the mountaintop, he once again was forced to climb another. Taller and taller mountains stood before him, and he had no choice but to continue climbing.

Wu Xingzi was crying, shouting, and pleading; his eyes began to roll into the back of his head. In the end, he reached his orgasm without ejaculating. He had been fucked open completely, to the point where his mind went blank. The actions of the man fucking him turned even more vicious, each thrust going straight into his belly. Finally, when Guan Shanjin shot his hot cum inside of Wu Xingzi, he yanked the ribbon away.

"Ahh!" A wild pleasure swept through Wu Xingzi, and it was too much for him to bear. His eyes rolled back, twitching, and his little cock wetted itself, the liquid spattering onto the bed. Even then, he did not ejaculate.

Holding Wu Xingzi and panting for a moment, Guan Shanjin flipped him over on the bed and spooned him from the back. His cock, having just come, was still very hard. As it twisted around in Wu Xingzi's ass, it made him cry, and he pissed himself again. Wrapping his hands around Wu Xingzi's slender waist—which was marked with bruises from his own fingers—Guan Shanjin slowly pushed himself further into Wu Xingzi. He grabbed hold of Wu Xingzi's hands, placing them on his stomach and making him feel his gradually bulging belly.

"Since it's such a rare opportunity for a pengornis spirit to come to life, let's not waste it," Guan Shanjin laughed.

Wu Xingzi was incapable of understanding him. He could only shake his head and cry.

After a few strokes, that little cock hardened again. He was once again dragged into another stint of passionate sex. Fucked into multiple orgasms, Wu Xingzi's balls became pitifully shriveled. He had nothing left, unable to even piss himself, but Guan Shanjin still did not show him mercy.

After all, on New Year's Eve, it was tradition to stay up all night.

Wu Xingzi was unable to get out of bed for the first five days of the new year.

Forget visiting friends or walking around the village—he couldn't so much as say hello to Auntie Liu, Ansheng, and a few close neighbors who had dropped by. Guan Shanjin had stopped them all at the door, dismissing them curtly.

As for Wu Xingzi, he slept in the nearby bedroom, unaware of whether it was night or day. When he finally woke up, he was once again pressed against the bed and fucked savagely.

According to Guan Shanjin, this was to help improve his memory. However, Wu Xingzi only felt fucked stupid. It was even worse for his poor hips; they could barely straighten.

He was now truly afraid of the great Southern Garrison general's stamina. Wu Xingzi convulsed as Guan Shanjin fucked him, apologizing tearfully, "I was wrong! I was wrong... Please have mercy on me! Please let me go!"

"Tell me, what were you wrong about?" Guan Shanjin remained calm and composed, playing with Wu Xingzi's little prick. Having ejaculated too many times, the tip now looked pitifully shrunken. A layer of skin threatened to flake off from the friction.

Sniffling, Wu Xingzi truly did not know what exactly he had done wrong. He only remembered that he'd had too much to drink on New Year's Eve. After the second cup of wine, he remembered nothing.

By the time he had woken up, his hips ached, his legs were weak, and his entire body hurt—even his bones. Just like usual, Guan Shanjin had cleaned him up and made him comfortable. He sat by the bed, reading as he waited for Wu Xingzi to wake.

Guan Shanjin noticed Wu Xingzi was up. "Not too long ago, Auntie Liu and her family came over to visit for the New Year," the general said gently. "I sent them back."

"Eh? Why didn't you wake me up?" Wu Xingzi asked, surprised. He wanted to get up from the bed but found that he could not move even a single finger. "Huh? Wh-what's going on?" Did he become paralyzed?

"Hmm? It's nothing much. We just went a little overboard last night." Putting down his book, Guan Shanjin gently cupped Wu Xingzi's face. "Are you hungry? I've made some porridge. Would you like a little?"

"Yes, yes, yes."

As expected, Wu Xingzi's stomach felt unbearably empty. Only then did he realize that the sky outside was growing dark, and he had basically slept half the first day of the new year away.

Drinking really is bad for you! Wu Xingzi took a furtive glance at Guan Shanjin. He was dressed in a crimson robe, and since he was in the bedroom, his hair wasn't tied up in a bun. Instead, he wore his thick, silky hair simply gathered up behind his head in a ponytail, and the lines of his incredibly attractive face were now less harsh. The original ferocity faded away significantly, lending a touch of gentleness to his expression.

This was the first time Wu Xingzi had seen Guan Shanjin so relaxed. He blushed as he stared, and while he was distracted, Guan Shanjin fed him an entire bowl of porridge.

Wu Xingzi could not recall the taste of the porridge. After Guan Shanjin fed him three large bowls, he then removed his robe and got into bed beside him. His seductive eyes narrowed as he smiled at Wu Xingzi. "Are you full now? Still feeling weak?"

"Uhh..." A chilling wave rose from Wu Xingzi's feet to his head. He did not dare speak, giving a placating smile back.

"Seems like you're all right now." Guan Shanjin caressed Wu Xingzi, nibbling on his lips. "Since you like pengornises so much, I'll fulfill your wishes," he said huskily.

Huh? Ahh! Before Wu Xingzi could understand the meaning of the general's words, Guan Shanjin lifted his hips and impaled him once again. The sky turned dark, and Wu Xingzi cried out until his throat was weak. He was completely filled with Guan Shanjin's cum—he practically looked pregnant. Guan Shanjin even deliberately rubbed his belly, making Wu Xingzi spasm on the bed like a fish out of water. It was as if his soul had departed from his body. And this was only the first day of the new year!

The next few days carried on in a similar fashion. Kept warm and sexually satiated, Wu Xingzi didn't have a chance to so much as think about anything else.

Soon, it was the sixth day of the new year. Wu Xingzi was freshly fucked, drowsily sprawled across the bed. As for Guan Shanjin, he felt completely revitalized. Having prepared a basin of water, he wiped Wu Xingzi clean.

After cleaning up the old quail nesting in the bed, Guan Shanjin slapped Wu Xingzi's plump buttocks in satisfaction, noting that they seemed to have grown a little larger in size from all the squeezing and rubbing. All the gloom within the general finally dissipated. No matter how lively his "brothers" in that rattan case might be, they would never be able to compete with the pengornis spirit who had come to life.

Wu Xingzi groaned from the slaps, but he could barely keep his eyes open. "I was wrong... Please let me go," he begged for mercy pitifully.

"I will. We'll talk once you're awake." Kissing his cheek, Guan Shanjin cleaned himself up as well and got into bed, holding Wu Xingzi until he fell asleep.

It took Wu Xingzi another two days to become fully conscious. When he woke up in the morning, the man next to him had disappeared. In his bed were two hot water bottles to keep him from getting cold. Guan Shanjin had always been good at taking care of others. He was meticulous and considerate, but never made anyone feel that he was too clingy.

The room smelled like the two of them, and slightly like fish soup. As Wu Xingzi sniffed the air, he rubbed his belly. Slowly pulling his clothes on as he got off the bed, he inexplicably felt as though he was separated from the world the moment his feet landed on solid ground.

Probably because he had been lying in bed for too long, Wu Xingzi was unable to hold himself up; his legs kept feeling weak.

After trying a few more times, Wu Xingzi finally stood up and tottered about. The first thing he did was not to wash his face and change his clothes, but to make his way to the cabinet where he hid his pengornis drawings with faltering steps. Opening the cabinet, he took out the rattan case. He wanted to take the opportunity to examine the sachet within. *Maybe I can still change it?*

"Hmm? Something seems wrong," Wu Xingzi said to himself. After opening the lid of the rattan case, he gave a rare frown, his expression turning solemn. Carefully, he took out the sachet. Its positioning was not quite right—it lay directly on top of the pictures. The color of the sachet might stain the illustrations, so he had always placed the sachet to the side.

Could it be that Guan Shanjin had moved it when tidying up the house? As Wu Xingzi pondered the subject, he held up his treasured pengornis drawings and felt sorry for them. Examining them one by one, he checked to see if they were dirtied. Fortunately, the phallic fellows were all undamaged.

Just as he heaved a sigh of relief, Wu Xingzi gasped in shock. With his eyes opened wide, he stared at the wax paper within, his face paling.

Inside that wax paper sat his ten most beloved penis pictures, including Guan Shanjin's. He was extremely particular about the way the wax paper was folded.

First, the paper had to be smoothed out with not a single bump, to prevent it from choking the cocks within. Next, the lines of the folds had to be as straight as a ruler, so that the penises would not be distressed. Finally, the portion of paper used as the seal had to face up and slide inward. It could not be folded under the dick pictures. If it was placed like this for too long, the drawings would become crumpled, and the pengornises would no longer be able to stand upright.

The wax paper in front of him was very neat, but the seal was facing down. Before he could think carefully about how the paper packaging had flipped, Wu Xingzi, with a pained heart, hurriedly took it out of the case. Only after he had meticulously repacked the drawings did he sigh in relief, and then he decided to examine whether there were other mishaps regarding his top ten cocks.

"My word, you're only just able to get out of bed, and you're running straight for your darlings?" Guan Shanjin's voice was gentle and full of amusement, but Wu Xingzi was so scared that all the hair on his body stood up.

"Uhh... These... These are books left behind by my father." Wu Xingzi hurriedly put the wax paper bundle down, pushing the rattan case into the cabinet. Turning his head around, he smiled placatingly at the beautiful Guan Shanjin. "I-I've always...had the habit of reading the books my father left me while I stay up late on New Year's Eve. This year, I got drunk, so I didn't read any—and I missed them."

"Hmm?" Guan Shanjin folded his arms, smiling at him with narrowed eyes. "Continue spinning your tale, I'm listening."

How can I keep lying to him?! Wu Xingzi withered.

"How... How did you find out?" Wu Xingzi had never been good at telling lies. Now that he had been caught, he could only admit to it immediately with an ashen face. In his heart, he knew today did not bode well for his box of darling dongs; his heart truly ached!

"It's a long story. Do you want to calm yourself down with a bowl of fish soup first?"

The thick, aromatic scent entered the room through the open door. As usual, Wu Xingzi's stomach betrayed him, immediately gurgling away. He was starving, unable to stop swallowing his saliva.

Naturally, Guan Shanjin noticed all of this.

"Sure, sure." Nodding his head incessantly, Wu Xingzi closed the doors of the cabinet and walked over to Guan Shanjin. "Let's finish the entire pot of soup!" *Any moment of delay is still a delay!*

Amusedly staring at Wu Xingzi's incredibly expressive face, Guan Shanjin leaned down and kissed him. "Eat as much as you want. The past few days have been exhausting for you. You need to nourish yourself."

Upon mentioning the past few days, Wu Xingzi instantly reddened. "Ah, my back still hurts. Today, you...probably shouldn't..."

"Don't worry, we have to return to Horse-Face City in a couple of days. I'll let your back rest for now." With a swing of his arm, Guan Shanjin directed Wu Xingzi to the dining table. Besides the fish soup, there were a few light side dishes, as well as some plump white buns.

Wu Xingzi gulped down his saliva. Without any consideration for Guan Shanjin, he buried his head in the food and started eating. He had eaten nothing but porridge over the past few days. Although there were variations, and they all tasted good, they still couldn't compare to a proper meal.

The fish soup was a milky-white shade. With a garnish of sliced scallions, it looked remarkably mouthwatering.

The first mouthful was fresh, thick, and sweet; it felt as though he was drinking the fish itself. At the bottom of the bowl, there were tender slices of fish, and they melted with the slightest pressure of his tongue. As the soup went down his throat, Wu Xingzi's entire body warmed up.

The meal made Wu Xingzi look positively radiant, and he mostly forgot about the disaster of Guan Shanjin discovering his cache of cock drawings.

Seeing that Wu Xingzi had finished his meal, Guan Shanjin tidied up the table. He cleaned and wiped the table before he spoke to Wu Xingzi. "Come, let's talk about your box of darlings. Take them all out."

"Uhh..." Wu Xingzi rubbed his nose. He sat up straight as a board. "It's actually nothing much. Th-they're just... the replies from the pigeon post."

"I know." Guan Shanjin sat across him, his long fingers tapping lightly on the table. "Wu Xingzi, if you're not going to take them out, I'll take them out. Think about it—once those pictures are in my hands, what do you think will happen to them?" This was a blatant threat!

Wu Xingzi's face paled, swiftly glancing at Guan Shanjin in despair. With drooping shoulders, he spoke dejectedly. "I-I'll go take them out right now. D-don't, you can't..."

You can't hurt my darlings!

"Go." Watching Wu Xingzi's desolate expression, Guan Shanjin repressed his laughter. "Don't try to hide anything. You've already let me see every drawing inside. For every missing drawing, I'll tear one up to accompany it, understood?"

Wu Xingzi's thin figure shuddered violently. He was clearly terrified by the general's bloodthirsty words—or maybe he was embarrassed that his thoughts had been perceived. In any case, the old quail hunched further down, walking unsteadily into his bedroom and fiddling about for a while before emerging. Hugging his rattan case, Wu Xingzi tried to put on a brave face.

When he placed the case down on the table, Wu Xingzi's eyes glistened with tears.

"Th-they're all here." He had contemplated the issue for a very long time and ended up hiding the drawing of Guan Shanjin's pengornis.

He wasn't shameless enough to admire the cock drawing right in front of its owner!

This also meant that there would be an innocent pengornis that would have to suffer in the cruel hands of the great general of the Southern Garrison... Wu Xingzi's heart hurt terribly, and he tried to console himself. *How many penises are there in the world? Falling to the Great Southern Garrison General... It's a blessing passed down from his previous life!*

How could Guan Shanjin not be able to read the expressions on Wu Xingzi's face? He could tell that Wu Xingzi had hidden his pengornis drawing.

"They're all here?" Guan Shanjin deliberately repeated the question, only to see Wu Xingzi tremble violently. Even his lips were pale. The sight made Guan Shanjin's heart ache, and his wicked intentions lessened. Reaching out and pulling Wu Xingzi into his arms, he soothed him a little, before patting the old fellow's hips and flipping through the drawings one by one.

The Peng Society's artist did have excellent technique. Every drawing was lifelike. Compared to the hazy, dim glow of the candles that illuminated these drawings before, the late morning sun threw every detail of the dick pictures into light.

They truly had their own individual qualities; each cock was attractive in its own way.

"Do you like these men?" After going through nearly fifty drawings, Guan Shanjin gestured toward the wax paper package that was missing two pictures.

"Uhh..."

Wu Xingzi's chest tightened. All he could do was watch as Guan Shanjin's exquisite hand unfolded the wax paper. His mind was completely vacant.

"Hmm?" Guan Shanjin kneaded his waist. "Do you like them? Or not?"

"I... I guess so?"

Wu Xingzi answered with a question, and it made Guan Shanjin burst out laughing. Like flowers blooming in spring, Wu Xingzi was unable to drag his eyes away from the sight.

"You yourself don't know if you like these men or not?" Guan Shanjin asked. Wu Xingzi was too adorable. The general pressed a kiss to the corner of his lips. "Then, these few drawings that have been specially wrapped up with wax paper... You must *really* like them, right?"

"Yes, yes..." Just like that, the truth was teased out of Wu Xingzi. He quickly covered his mouth, but it was too late. Not knowing that he had already sold himself out on New Year's Eve, he now blinked frantically in fear, staring straight at Guan Shanjin's hand as it flipped through the phalluses.

Guan Shanjin snorted. He wanted to frighten Wu Xingzi. If he did not properly deal with the old fellow right now, it was likely he wouldn't give up this bad habit of his. He picked up the penis covered with pockmarks, waving it in front of Wu Xingzi. "So you like this sort of ugly thing?"

"Umm... Yes, yes... I'm simply curious," Wu Xingzi replied cautiously, lowering his eyes. How could he possibly say that these ten cocks were the ones he had fantasized about over and over again through countless nights? At least he did manage to use the Lanling Prince of penises.

"Curious?" Guan Shanjin sneered. He still remembered what Wu Xingzi said that night! How was Wu Xingzi only curious? If the actual prick appeared before him, he would definitely lunge over to have his way! What a naughty, slutty man.

Guan Shanjin was annoyed. No matter how he looked at this pockmarked pengornis, he hated it. He gave up pretending, and right in front of Wu Xingzi, he tore the drawing to shreds.

"Ahhh..." Wu Xingzi gasped and shivered. Before he could recover from the shock of having the pengornis torn to pieces, the general shoved a coin into his hand.

"Huh?" He looked blankly at Guan Shanjin, his mind still muddled.

"Isn't each drawing worth a coin?" Guan Shanjin asked. Seeing Wu Xingzi nod stupidly, he smiled. "May I continue?"

Continue what? What is there to continue? Wu Xingzi's eyes widened as he pressed his palm against his chest. Amidst the chaos, he watched Guan Shanjin take out another phallic illustration, tearing it into bits as well.

"Ahhhh..." He received another coin. Wu Xingzi stared at the coin, dazed. On the verge of tears, he shuddered. "D-don't tear any more of them!"

"What about two coins?" Another drawing was torn.

"No, no, no..." Wu Xingzi shook his head repeatedly.

"Five coins?" One more was destroyed.

"Please...stop!" Wu Xingzi's heart ached, his eyes red.

"Ten coins?"

Seeing that Guan Shanjin was about to tear another one, Wu Xingzi rushed over, the coins in his hand scattering on the ground.

His heart ached so much that his entire body trembled. Ignoring his fear, Wu Xingzi tightly held onto Guan Shanjin's hand, pleading: "These are only drawings, why are you taking them so seriously? There's no need! Please let them go!"

"They're only drawings—why are *you* taking them so seriously? So what if they're torn?" Guan Shanjin retorted using Wu Xingzi's own words, making him choke in silence. Finally, tears rolled down Wu Xingzi's face.

"Why are you crying?"

"I... I..." *I don't know why, either.* Wu Xingzi cried in great sorrow. Sprawled in Guan Shanjin's arms, tears, snot, and saliva smeared all over his face. Choked sobs tumbled from his throat, and his voice became hoarse.

He too knew that these were only drawings, and the point of making friends through the pigeon post was not obtaining these illustrations. However, for Wu Xingzi, they were incomparably important. When there had been no one by his side, it was the pengornis drawings that had stayed with him. Once Guan Shanjin left, only these drawings would keep him company. Days and years and thereafter, as long as he kept these drawings, he wouldn't be alone.

Wu Xingzi had originally decided to depart this world at the age of forty. These illustrations saved him from his despair. He never desired nor demanded anything—it was his nature—but that did not mean he was able to tolerate the loneliness of the past twenty years... He was truly, sincerely, strikingly lonely.

"I won't tear any more of them... I've gone too far." Sighing, Guan Shanjin put the dick pictures back into the rattan case and focused on consoling the man in his arms. Each low, thin cry felt like a needle stabbing into his heart. He had only heard such cries on the battlefield from despairing soldiers when they missed their homes, their families—they too would cry quietly, just like this.

"I was wrong. Don't cry," Guan Shanjin said in a rare moment of regret, pressing Wu Xingzi's face into his embrace.

Wu Xingzi continued to cry. He did not wail loudly, nor did he resent the general or feel embittered. He only cried quietly, his acrid, stinging tears soaking Guan Shanjin's chest.

Wu Xingzi cried in anguish, and Guan Shanjin didn't know how to comfort him. He had never comforted anyone before. Mr. Lu was an introverted man, and he never revealed much emotion in front of Guan Shanjin. Guan Shanjin was good at tending to others with careful cosseting, and his past lovers for the most part only cried when he was leaving them. And no matter how upset they were, those tears were unable to inspire even a flutter in the general's heart.

However, Wu Xingzi was different. The tear-stained spot on Guan Shanjin's chest burned as if it were on fire. The heat left him feeling guilty, depressed, and full of heartache. He was angry that a few cold pieces of paper ranked higher in Wu Xingzi's heart than him—a living, breathing being—but he regretted his rash actions.

He thought that the old man had a gentle temperament, not desirous or needy. He thought that Wu Xingzi would probably feel unhappy for a period of time after losing a few of his pengornis drawings, but he would not be *too* upset. He couldn't have been more wrong.

"Don't cry anymore... It's my fault, I went too far..." Guan Shanjin repeated himself, apologizing and consoling Wu Xingzi. However, Wu Xingzi ignored him. Although the sounds of crying had stopped, tears still flowed down his face.

A hoarse, tearful voice came muffled from his arms: "Let me go." Guan Shanjin froze, not wanting to comply with the adviser's request. However, due to his moment of hesitation, he ended up releasing Wu Xingzi from his arms.

Having gained his freedom, Wu Xingzi immediately put distance between them, standing far away. He turned his head around, wiping away the tears on his face with his sleeve. Other than the redness of his nose and eyes, his face held a deathlike pallor.

"On the tenth day of the new year... I won't be returning with you to Horse-Face City."

"Hmm?" Guan Shanjin's face darkened, and his hand, hidden in his sleeve, clenched tightly. Worried that he would scare the old man, he tried his best to control his expression—but it still looked as cold and sharp as ice.

"I won't be going to Horse-Face City with you." Wu Xingzi exhaled, his voice still a little hoarse from crying. "I want to stay home. I've seen the world outside, and that's enough for me."

Out of nowhere, Guan Shanjin asked, "What about your cucumbers?"

Momentarily stunned, Wu Xingzi foolishly glanced toward him. While sniffling, a large snot bubble came out of his nose. Instantly, he blushed red with shame. The courage that he had mustered up with great effort vanished in a flash. Flustered, Wu Xingzi lifted his sleeve to hide his face.

Guan Shanjin stood up and brought a basin of water, wringing out a wet cotton cloth and handing it to Wu Xingzi to wipe his face.

"Thank you, thank you..." Wu Xingzi accepted the cotton cloth, reproaching himself internally for not being able to stand his ground. However, he was secretly a little delighted, and it made him feel all too useless.

Wu Xingzi! Think about the innocent cocks that lost their lives!

His eyes fell to the torn remnants of the drawings on the table, and Wu Xingzi immediately pulled himself together. Sparing no effort to put on a stern expression, he carefully wiped his face clean. Once he was sure that he would not produce another snot bubble, he stared at the wet patch on Guan Shanjin's chest left by his tears. "I've said it before, all I want is to be a frog in a well. Mint and Osmanthus will watch over the cucumbers. Once they are harvested, you can eat some. They'll be very sweet."

"You don't want me to send some over to you?" Guan Shanjin asked, his voice surprisingly soft.

Wu Xingzi blinked, nearly losing control of his expression. He had to take a few deep breaths to keep a firm grasp on his emotions.

"Mm, you can send a couple cucumbers over." Wu Xingzi did worry over those cucumbers. *Did any of them get eaten by worms? Were they growing well? They were about to flower, right?*

"Just two?"

"Five is fine, too. I won't be able to eat many of them." He could even gift two cucumbers to Auntie Liu for her to try.

Seeing that Wu Xingzi was now distracted by the thought of his cucumber crop, Guan Shanjin took the opportunity to stride forward and pull him tightly into his arms. Grazing his chin against the top of Wu Xingzi's head, Guan Shanjin spoke gently. "I want to return to Horse-Face City with you. I've been insolent—don't be angry with me anymore, all right?"

Oh... Wu Xingzi's tender-hearted nature made him soften.

Guan Shanjin backed down, so Wu Xingzi's anger wilted. Rubbing his nose, he did not know how he should respond.

"Are you still mad at me?" Not getting a response, Guan Shanjin became anxious. He reached out and gently lifted Wu Xingzi's head by the chin, frowning slightly. "Are those drawings truly so important to you?" His guilt turned into bitterness. It felt like a huge boulder pressed into his chest, and he didn't understand why he felt so gloomy.

"Are... Are you going to keep tearing them up?" Wu Xingzi did not answer readily. If he were to agree, would his entire case of drawings be brutally murdered?

He cares too damn much about them! Guan Shanjin's eyes darkened, releasing the man in his arms. Clenching his fists tightly, he had to huff out a few breaths before his temper settled. There was an iron taste in the back of his throat, which he could only forcefully swallow back into his stomach.

Was this old fellow sent by the heavens to test him? He was *the* great general of the Southern Garrison, famed demon of the battlefield. His Chenyuan Sword left rivers of blood and bodies in its wake. Seeing his figure from afar, his enemies trembled in their boots, throwing down their weapons and fleeing in a panic. Even in the Imperial Court, there was no one who dared to steal his glory—even the emperor spoke warmly to him.

But this man had made him angry enough to cough up blood. Where was his dignity?

With bloodshot eyes, Guan Shanjin stared at those cock drawings on the table. He gritted his teeth, and amidst Wu Xingzi's alarmed cries, he shoved them all back into the rattan case—including the torn shreds.

"We're going to Goose City." He lowered his head halfway to hide the ferocious look on his face. "Dress warmly. I'll bring the horse over." Without turning his head to look at Wu Xingzi, Guan Shanjin sped away.

Wu Xingzi was left confused. He paused for a long moment before moving to tidy up his treasures. When he put the torn shreds of paper in another pouch, his tears nearly fell again. He was now left with less than half of his ten favorite drawings. Were the owners of those pengornises still making friends through the pigeon post? If he were to send them another letter, they might not reply with another picture.

Wu Xingzi had no idea why Guan Shanjin wanted to bring him to Goose City. Was he going to stir up trouble with Rancui?

The prospect made Wu Xingzi even more nervous. Pushing his anxiety aside, he pulled on his clothes and stepped outside his house to see Guan Shanjin's upright figure upon his horse, Zhuxing.

Compared to Wu Xingzi who was wrapped up like a bulky dumpling, Guan Shanjin was lightly dressed. His fitted clothes made him look even taller, and his expression was distant, like a god banished to the mortal realm. When he saw Wu Xingzi, his lips curved up slightly, his faint smile somewhat melancholy. Wu Xingzi immediately forgot what he was going to say.

"Come on," Guan Shanjin held his hand out toward him, and once Wu Xingzi grasped it, the general pulled him onto the horse. Guan Shanjin's actions were very careful, making sure Wu Xingzi felt no discomfort.

Leaning into the general's warm, solid embrace, Wu Xingzi finally collected himself a little and hurriedly asked, "Wh-why do you want to go to Goose City all of a sudden?"

"I'm bringing you to the Peng Society to look for someone. Now, stop talking." Guan Shanjin used his cloak to cover Wu Xingzi's face. Spurring his horse on, they sped away, leaving a trail of dust behind.

They arrived at Goose City two hours later. Leading the horse with them, they headed straight for the antique shop that housed the Peng Society. Since it was so close to New Year, the shop was quiet, but it was decorated very cheerfully. The antiques meant for admiring in the main hall had been replaced, and the salesman Wu Xingzi knew was still there. When he saw them arrive, he came forward to welcome them with no change in his expression.

"Welcome. May I ask if there's anything you're looking for?"

"Is Rancui around?" Guan Shanjin got straight to the point. He headed inside with his arm wrapped around Wu Xingzi.

"The manager hasn't awakened yet. Please wait, Guan-gongzi!" The salesman hurried after him, but he didn't know how to stop Guan Shanjin from entering the courtyard. The patio had only just been repaired before New Year, but if he tried to physically block the general, he'd probably just be kicked away.

"Call him up. Tell him there is business knocking at his door." Guan Shanjin knew where he was going; he headed toward the pavilion where Rancui had always received Wu Xingzi. Despite the general's calm tone, the salesman was still scared enough to hunch over. Wringing his hands, he paced around Guan Shanjin.

"Y-you better not do anything to Manager Rancui!" Wu Xingzi said, overly anxious. However, he was trapped in Guan Shanjin's arms, forced to move along with him. He could only attempt to persuade him verbally. "Manager Rancui has nothing to do with my pengornis drawings. I-if you're still upset, I'll throw them all away when we go home, all right? I'll prepare the cucumbers for you when we return to Horse-Face City—they'll be very sweet!"

"Will the cucumbers be fully grown when we return?" Guan Shanjin snorted. His chest felt so stifled that it hurt. He was unwilling to explain himself to Wu Xingzi, practically carrying him forward.

"Uh... It's hard to say. Perhaps another two months? It's difficult to grow cucumbers in winter, but once spring sets in, they'll grow faster."

Guan Shanjin huffed. The mention of spring annoyed him further. Mr. Lu would be getting married then, yet this old fellow didn't care at all.

They soon reached the pavilion. The curtains around it were drawn closed, and there was a small hearth burning within. Rancui sat inside. However, it was evident that he was not deliberately waiting for them, only coincidentally drinking tea there.

When the curtain lifted, Rancui looked up in surprise. After registering who his visitor was, he stood up, giving a superficial smile as he cupped his hands together. "It's the general," he said coldly. "Do you have a request for our little shop?"

"I'd like to take a look at the latest *Pengornisseur*." Guan Shanjin spoke stiffly, but his actions were very mellow as he cleaned a chair for Wu Xingzi to sit on. "If it's not inconvenient, I'd like to borrow a brush and paper from you as well."

He wants to see The Pengornisseur? Rancui frowned. He glanced over at the restless Wu Xingzi and rubbed his stomach absentmindedly, thinking about the dowry cakes he'd eaten a couple of months ago.

Guan Shanjin had never been interested in *The Pengornisseur*. Rancui was intimately familiar with the temperament of such men—they never allowed the person they liked to look at anyone else. Anything could happen when their tempers exploded. Why was the general taking the initiative to read *The Pengornisseur*? Who was he planning to torture?

Rancui speculated on all sorts of possibilities, but he still ended up motioning for his employee to collect the *Pengornisseur*, as well as the requested writing instruments. Replacing his cold stare with a warm, smiling expression, he exchanged some New Year's greetings with Wu Xingzi.

"Adviser Wu, you haven't dropped by in a long time. How have you been?" Rancui secretly studied his customer. The usually gentle and detached adviser looked somewhat panic stricken. His eyes were slightly bloodshot, and it seemed like he had cried recently.

Furious, Rancui considered how he should rescue his customer from the general's demonic claws. When he had a chance, he needed to force his boss to ban Guan Shanjin from harassing any of the Peng Society's members!

"He's been a troublemaker," Guan Shanjin said. He could see what Rancui was thinking, and he snorted as he slapped a corner of the stone table. The square edges were smooth, as though they'd been carved by a knife, but the table was originally round.

"Would the general feel uncomfortable if he didn't destroy a few of my little shop's items every visit?" Rancui glared at that corner of the table, unafraid. What storms had he not endured? Since the general liked to tear things down, let him tear down the entire shop! New year, new beginnings! Rancui would just take the opportunity to renovate the place.

"You sure are relentless." Guan Shanjin's fingers twitched, and a subtle snap of air shot toward Rancui's shoulder. Rancui had no time to dodge—it hit him, and numbness shot through his arm and half of his body. He could barely maintain his expression, his face twisting.

"Being too willful can sometimes hurt you."

"Manager Rancui? What's wrong?" Wu Xingzi couldn't see what Guan Shanjin had done. He stood up, wanting to help and support Rancui, who was bent over, hunched in his seat, unable to move.

"What... What did you do?" Wu Xingzi was not a fool. He could tell at once that Rancui's grimace had something to do with Guan Shanjin. Now he truly was angry, feeling sorry for Rancui. Snorting coldly, Wu Xingzi turned his head away, not wanting to look at Guan Shanjin any longer.

Even a saint had his limits, and Wu Xingzi was only human! No matter how placid his disposition, his temper could occasionally flare. He had no idea why Guan Shanjin was behaving like this. Forget about tearing up his pengornis drawings and making him cry—Manager Rancui was such a good person, and he ended up being involved in Wu Xingzi's problems. Manager Rancui should have been celebrating New Year, but now he had to face the general's ire, suffering such pain for no reason.

"I didn't do anything. You saw, didn't you? I didn't go near Rancui at all." Guan Shanjin would not allow Wu Xingzi to ignore him. He backed away from Rancui, wrapping his arms around Wu Xingzi. "I brought you to the Peng Society because I wanted to make it up to you," he said, his voice consoling. "Why would I make you angry again? Hmm? Won't you look at me?"

"Really?" Wu Xingzi turned his head toward Guan Shanjin doubtfully. "Then why is Manager Rancui in so much pain? And you're not even letting me help him!"

"He may have eaten too much oily food this New Year, so his stomach's feeling uncomfortable. If you go up and help him, you'll make his employees feel awkward." The lies came smoothly, and Rancui nearly exploded with indignant laughter.

It was clear that Wu Xingzi didn't believe him. But he couldn't find any fault with the general's words, so he turned to look at Rancui.

"Thank you for your concern, Adviser Wu. I'm fine." Half his body still felt numb, and he was so incensed that his chest hurt, but what could he do? The odds were not in his favor. So what if Guan Shanjin was a scumbag? His fist was harder than anyone else's—and he also had his Chenyuan Sword!

"It's good that you're all right..." Wu Xingzi was still doubtful, and he looked as though he wanted to continue asking if Rancui was unharmed. In the end, he shut his mouth and turned away, refusing to look at Guan Shanjin's enchanting face.

Fortunately, the salesman came back quickly. He placed *The Pengornisseur* in front of them. To evoke festive New Year's feelings, the cover was a cheerful red. The words "The Pengornisseur" were even dusted with gold. Such colors could easily be tacky, but they complemented the book very well. It was very celebratory, yet still exquisite.

"Here, see if the owners of those pengornis drawings are still listed." Guan Shanjin shoved *The Pengornisseur* into Wu Xingzi's hands, then started grinding ink on an inkstone.

Wu Xingzi still did not understand what was happening. In a daze, he held onto *The Pengornisseur*.

"Hmm? Why aren't you looking through it?" Guan Shanjin asked. Wu Xingzi's foolishly blank stare was adorable; Guan Shanjin leaned over and kissed him.

"Wh-why are you asking me to look for them? Do you want to..." Wu Xingzi bit his lip, alarm and fear flooding his face. "Haiwang, they're just penis pictures. Don't hurt the owners as well! I'll burn that entire case of drawings when we go back, all right?"

Rancui happened to be drinking tea at that very moment, and when he heard Wu Xingzi's words, he spat out his drink. Did he eavesdrop on a secret that he shouldn't have heard? From what he knew, Wu Xingzi did mail out a great deal of letters, but the Peng Society would never stop a member from making more friends. Did Adviser Wu keep all the drawings of penises that had been sent in response?

Guan Shanjin glared at Rancui with loathing. The tea he'd spat out had gotten all over the inkstone, and Guan Shanjin called the salesman over to exchange it for another one. "It seems like your surroundings this New Year are rather damp," he snorted. "Is your chest so congested that you're not able to even drink your tea?"

"I'm afraid it hasn't been as stuffy as yours. Choking on tea is nothing. It's not like I'm spitting out blood," Rancui said, showcasing his sharp tongue. If Wu Xingzi had really kept all the penis illustrations, he reasoned, Guan Shanjin must have discovered them. This had clearly caused considerable turmoil. Although he was on the verge of coughing up blood, Guan Shanjin would still help Wu Xingzi collect those pengornis pictures once again.

Rancui's verbal stab landed harshly and accurately. Guan Shanjin's brows creased further, and he nearly unsheathed Chenyuan.

However, he held himself back, lowering his head and placating Wu Xingzi. "What nonsense are you talking? Why would I kill these men over such a small matter? I only thought that since I tore up your pengornis drawings, I should get you a new set. If we use my name to send them letters, we'll be able to receive the drawings, won't we? Come, take a look. Let's see if they're still in here."

This time, Wu Xingzi was extremely moved. With tears in his eyes, he held *The Pengornisseur* with one hand and Guan Shanjin's sleeve with the other. His mouth was shut tightly, and it took him a long while before he softly said, "Thank you."

"Don't thank me. I was wrong. However..." Guan Shanjin held Wu Xingzi's hand, his beautiful eyes narrowing into a stern expression. "You have to return to Horse-Face City with me. Also, you can't add any additional drawings to your collection. Understood?"

Wu Xingzi nodded his head repeatedly, blushing and smiling. "Definitely, definitely."

Seeing the two reconcile with just a few sentences, Rancui sat by the side, drinking tea with a sour face.

Ugh. It was New Year, but his eyes were sore.

Finally, Wu Xingzi did manage to find the owners of all his collected pengornises, except for his second favorite. Adviser Wu had been too drunk to remember its brutal murder at the hands of the general, so it was naturally passed over.

With a dark expression, Guan Shanjin shot Rancui a sneer. "They say that even through a distance of a thousand miles, *The Pengornisseur* can help a man seek his beloved. Seems like the rumors are false."

Rancui sighed loudly and deliberately. "We aren't responsible for men who do not seek their beloved, but instead sleep with embroidered pillows." He looked toward a lightly blushing Wu Xingzi—who seemed to be in a better mood—and laced his words with meaning: "In my opinion, Adviser Wu is not the type who likes embroidered pillows. After all, good pillows should be simple and sturdy."

"Yes, yes." Adviser Wu made all his own pillows by hand. Every autumn, he would replace the old rice husks inside with new ones. The pillows were perfectly firm, there was no need to worry about dirtying them, and they even smelled pleasant.

Seeing how easily Wu Xingzi fell into the trap, Guan Shanjin was displeased but resigned to the situation. He hurriedly finished writing the letters, and after instructing Rancui to deliver the replies to the Peng Society branch in Horse-Face City, he stood up and hauled Wu Xingzi away.

His actions were so rushed that Rancui didn't even have time to say his goodbyes. Pressing his palm against his chest, Rancui grabbed the still-wet brush and threw it into the hearth.

This brush was a gift from his boss. It was crafted by a renowned expert using elder tree wood and weasel hair. The brush head was smooth, and the longer it was used, the better its strokes became. Rancui had been using it for seven years, and its tip was so smooth and shiny that it could almost be used as a mirror. It felt weighty and comfortable to carry around; it was one of his most beloved items.

However, since Guan Shanjin had used it, Rancui was loath to ever touch it again.

"What a waste of a good brush..." Rancui stared at the hearth, rubbing his chest. He was unable to distinguish if he felt angry or heartbroken. When the entire brush had been consumed by the licking flames, Rancui tightened his fists firmly and summoned his employee. "Immediately return to the capital and relay this to the boss."

"Yes," the salesman said, though he was a little confused. If something needed to be reported, wouldn't sending a letter be more prudent? The one thing the Peng Society had in droves was homing pigeons.

"Tell him that this is what Manager Rancui has to say: 'Fuck you! If you want me to stay in the Peng Society, you'll get rid of Guan Shanjin. And if you don't kick him out, I'll leave! You're an ass, and all you give me is lip service. I now have two members who have fallen victim to Guan Shanjin! There is no room in the Peng Society for this kind of heartless, unfeeling man. Run the damn thing yourself, you miserable motherfucker! I'm going to go to Horse-Face City now—there's no need to send me off.'"

Rancui's voice was bright and clear. He was usually mild and tactful, weighing his words before he spoke. He spoke gently and politely, even toward his subordinates. This salesman had worked for Rancui for over seven years now, and he had never heard a single unpleasant word from Rancui before, let alone such vulgarities. Manager Rancui had a clever tongue; when he wanted to scold a person, he never needed to use any curse words.

But now they spewed from Rancui as if he was reciting poetry. The salesman stood there, frozen for quite some time, before stiffly picking at his ear and asking with a shaky voice, "M-manager, I didn't quite hear your message to the boss clearly... Did you really say something about a mother...?"

"I did. You heard me perfectly. Remember, you can't change a single word when passing the message to the boss—you have to relay it exactly. Understood?" Rancui knew that sending a message via pigeon would be much faster, but that would not allow him to properly express his anger! He could already imagine his boss reading a letter full of vulgarities. He would laugh loudly, entirely unbothered, and tell his lover, "Look, little Rancui is all grown up. He even knows how to swear now." Just thinking about it made Rancui so enraged that he felt physical pain. If not for his concern for Wu Xingzi, he would have returned to the capital to scold him himself.

"Bring the other employees here. Send a letter to the Horse-Face City branch. Tell them that I'll leave tomorrow, and they should get ready."

Did this mean that he was going to abandon the Goose City branch for the Horse-Face City branch? A-Heng, the sales assistant, mopped his sweat. He was not stupid enough to ask the manager why he was doing this. It was clearly to cause trouble for General Guan, as well as to find a suitable opportunity to rescue Adviser Wu!

Only Manager Rancui put in such great effort to look out for the Peng Society's members. It was truly thanks to him that the Peng Society had grown to the organization it was today.

"Manager, Horse-Face City is a dangerous place. Aren't you afraid that General Guan will use underhanded means to stop you?" A-Heng was very worried. Guan Shanjin was the local despot of Horse-Face City; he could secretly do away with Manager Rancui with just a crook of his finger. Even if their boss had the ability to save him, General Guan was beyond his reach!

Fed up, Rancui grumbled, "Let him come at me with his devious ways!"

Rancui was a thorn in the arrogant general's side. If Rancui really followed Guan Shanjin and Adviser Wu to Horse-Face City, no matter what his intentions were, the general would certainly give him a beating. All General Guan could think about was Mr. Lu, who was soon to be married—Rancui's sole worry was that the general would end up kicking Wu Xingzi to the side. In that case, Rancui would be compelled to rescue the adviser.

In the end, Rancui's boss was to blame for giving him so much trouble.

"Did you remember everything that I've said?" Rancui asked, drinking some tea to calm himself down. Looking at A-Heng, he emphasized his instructions: "Remember, you must repeat every single word to the boss, verbatim. He won't punish you."

The boss would not, but the boss's lover might! A-Heng looked troubled, but he could only nod and agree. Rancui shoved a jade pendant into his hand. A-Heng stared straight at Rancui, only to see the manager waving him off. "That's a present the boss gave me. When you relay the message, just hold the jade pendant up. No one will dare touch you. After you've finished, look for me in Horse-Face City. Don't waste a single second."

A-Heng finally relaxed, hurriedly storing the jade pendant on his person. "I understand," he said. Then, following the manager's orders, he left to begin his preparations.

Once Rancui finished settling matters in Goose City, he headed straight for Horse-Face City.

As for Guan Shanjin, he did not return straight to Qingcheng County after he'd dragged Wu Xingzi away from the Peng Society. Instead, he brought the old quail to the Restaurant of Songs for a meal.

Due to their vigorous bedroom activities the past week, and having only eaten one meal before all this trouble, Wu Xingzi was hungry and exhausted. Since the issue was finally settled, Guan Shanjin was in no hurry to head back, so he thought he might as well give Adviser Wu a good, proper meal—it certainly was *not* to compete for favor with those lifeless pengornis drawings.

Now that his collection of dick pictures had been exposed, Wu Xingzi was a lot less self-conscious. He ate an extra two bowls of rice with a bright smile, even ordering two more dishes and a bowl of soup. When his stomach was full and bulging, he put his chopsticks down in satisfaction and thanked Guan Shanjin sincerely.

Although he was unwilling to speculate about the real meaning behind Guan Shanjin's actions, the fact that the general would protect his pengornis pictures and even bring them along with him to Horse-Face City was enough for him.

CHAPTER 3

AN INNOCENT IN INNER-CIRCLE INFIGHTING

*"Wu Xingzi," Guan Shanjin called out. When that name rolled off his
tongue, it somehow tasted sweet.*

 *His own mind felt foreign to him—somehow, entirely
without his say-so, Wu Xingzi had found an inexplicable place in
his heart. For the first time in his life, Guan Shanjin was panicking.*

AFTER THEIR MEAL, Wu Xingzi and Guan Shanjin strolled about
the marketplace. Goose City was a prosperous place, and its citizens were already preparing for the Spring Lantern Festival. The
lantern market bustled with activity. There was a great variety of food
and drink available, as well as some delightful-looking toys.

Wu Xingzi had never explored the lantern market before. In his
childhood, his father had been strict, preferring peace and quiet to a
busy crowd; at the very most, they would light a single lantern for the
occasion. And as an adult, Wu Xingzi lived entirely on his own. He
found this sort of festival, where families gathered to walk through the
marketplace, rather awkward. Since he happened to be both shy and
poor, he had felt less and less inclined to visit the market as he grew
older.

As such, it was his first time at the festival's market, and Wu Xingzi
found everything entertaining. Guan Shanjin accompanied him
from the first stall to the last. To protect him from being pushed

around by the crowd, Guan Shanjin shielded him between his arms with his intimidating stature, completely ignoring the probing eyes of passersby.

As they walked down the street, lanterns were lit one by one.

The lanterns in Goose City were not as lavish or exquisite as the ones in the capital, but they were delicate and charming. All sorts of lanterns lined the broad market street. There were palace lanterns and revolving lanterns, with numerous different designs. There were lanterns with birds and flowers and lanterns with rivers and mountains. Some featured the Eight Immortals, while others displayed words of luck. There were too many varieties to count!

"Ah, look! It's a revolving lantern with the Eight Immortals," Wu Xingzi exclaimed, his eyes filled with delight.

The revolving lantern was exquisitely crafted. In a sea of lanterns that looked simple by comparison, it stood out prominently, hanging high up in a tree. The two men stood at a slight distance from the crowd—it was a peaceful pocket amongst all the commotion. The few people walking by them were all couples, intimately entwined with each other. Guan Shanjin looked at the lantern, as well as the man standing under it, and his expression contorted slightly.

Wu Xingzi happened to be dressed in white today, and his winter clothes gave him some bulk. Because of his thin figure, he looked a little plumper and handsomer wearing thicker clothes. His smiling face looked plain and commonplace, with a fleshy nose and plump lips. His philtrum was too short, and his forehead was too narrow, but his sparse eyebrows and small, round eyes looked adorable when his eyes curved in delight. When he froze in thought, he looked just like a foolish little quail. Nothing in his face resembled Mr. Lu's luminous, flower-like features.

However, seeing Wu Xingzi dressed in white, standing under a tree and gazing up at a revolving lantern, Guan Shanjin felt as though he was looking at Mr. Lu from the Spring Lantern Festival years ago.

Wu Xingzi looked graceful, tranquil, and content. If Mr. Lu was the soft and luminous moonlight, Wu Xingzi was the brook below reflecting it. Guan Shanjin was unable to reach the moon in the sky, but he could touch its reflection in the water. He tightened his arms, snugly embracing Wu Xingzi.

"Haiwang?" Feeling the arms around him suddenly tighten, Wu Xingzi flushed red, unconsciously lifting his arms to try pushing him away. However, he was sorely lacking in strength, and Guan Shanjin had a knack for trapping him. Wu Xingzi struggled and panted but was unable to gain even an inch. He could only lower his head and hide his face to prevent others from seeing him and laughing.

"What's wrong? Are you feeling shy again?" Guan Shanjin asked. Looking down at Wu Xingzi, the general smiled. He lovingly stroked the tip of Wu Xingzi's nose, but it wasn't enough to satisfy him, so he gave him a kiss. The old fellow burned red with embarrassment and his eyes filled with tears.

"No one will notice us—they're all admiring the lanterns," Guan Shanjin said.

"Oh?" Wu Xingzi quietly raised his head to glance through the crowd. As expected, the couples drifting about were either looking up at the lanterns, or they were just like him and Guan Shanjin: tucked into a dark corner, closely wrapped in each other's arms.

Although Wu Xingzi still felt shy, he finally relaxed. He allowed Guan Shanjin to continue hugging and caressing him while they finished viewing the rest of the lanterns. Eventually, they reluctantly left the lantern market.

It was already past seven when they returned to Qingcheng County. Wu Xingzi had originally wanted to visit Auntie Liu and her family to wish them well during the new year, and to present them with some gifts that he bought at the lantern market. However, by now, it was probably too late. Farmers woke up early—they must be getting ready for bed around this time.

Wu Xingzi contemplated for a moment and decided to go to Ansheng's place instead. For the duration of the New Year festival, no one in Qingcheng County opened their businesses. The largest teahouse would reopen on the tenth day. As for the rest of the stalls in the market, they only reopened after all fifteen days of the festival had passed, so Ansheng didn't have much to do at the moment. The magistrate's office had yet to officially reopen, as well. If Wu Xingzi were to visit, he would not be disturbing Constable Zhang's rest.

Having made the decision, Wu Xingzi told Guan Shanjin of his plans, implying that he should go home first. He didn't want Ansheng and Constable Zhang to feel awkward around someone they didn't know well.

Naturally, Guan Shanjin refused. He held tightly onto Wu Xingzi's hand, and after leaving his horse in the stable at the magistrate's office, he insisted that Wu Xingzi lead the way.

With no other choice, Wu Xingzi bashfully brought Guan Shanjin along for the visit. Both Ansheng and Constable Zhang were even more sure of their relationship now than they were previously.

Ansheng tried talking to Wu Xingzi in private several times, but he was continuously blocked from doing so by Guan Shanjin. Constable Zhang saw this happen more than once and was not very happy about it. He glared darkly at Guan Shanjin, and if not for Wu Xingzi's sake, he might have even thrown a punch or two.

Because of this, Wu Xingzi was unable to stay for a longer visit. Before Guan Shanjin dragged him away, he hurriedly delivered his gifts and promised to get some tofu jelly the next time he returned to the stall.

On the way home, Wu Xingzi got a little angry. "When we visit Auntie Liu tomorrow, you can't act like that," he warned the general. He kept feeling that something had been off with Guan Shanjin these past few days. The general seemed to be deliberately preventing others from coming close to him.

"Mm," Guan Shanjin casually acknowledged him. Ignoring everything else, he kissed the man in his arms. When Wu Xingzi became teary-eyed and short of breath, the general peeled himself away, licking his lips in satisfaction.

"After we visit Auntie Liu tomorrow, let's go back to Horse-Face City," Guan Shanjin said, gently caressing Wu Xingzi's kiss-swollen lips.

"We're heading back so soon?" Wu Xingzi was a little hesitant. If he was going to be away for quite some time, he would need to bring his pengornis collection, as well as his father's books. Although there would not be too much luggage to pack, he was reluctant to leave so soon after coming back in such a hurry.

Over half his life had been spent in this little house. He had always been alone here, but nonetheless, it was where he lived in peace.

However, he didn't know how he could get Guan Shanjin to stay for a few more days. Mr. Lu would be getting married after the New Year festivities, and there were only so many days left. It was understandable that Guan Shanjin wanted to return to Horse-Face City to help with wedding arrangements.

"Is there still something you need to do?"

"No, not really…"

They arrived home as they talked. Wu Xingzi looked at his little house with the feeling that he was unlikely to return to it for quite some time. He shook his head, laughing at himself inwardly for overthinking things.

"Haiwang, why are you willing to let Mr. Lu get married and start a family?"

The question caught Guan Shanjin off guard. He stood in silence for quite a while.

The man who asked the question, however, kept chattering away without thinking too much of it. "I can see that Mr. Lu really likes you too," Wu Xingzi said. "It's really quite funny that I didn't realize the nature of your relationship before. It was Auntie Li's words that allowed me to understand."

"Understand what?" Guan Shanjin's voice was hoarse. He had wanted to light a candle, but now his fingers were stiff, and he had forgotten the candle entirely.

"Hmm? That you and Mr. Lu aren't simply teacher and student! He's your beloved, isn't he?" Wu Xingzi blinked. It was terribly dark inside the house, and the moon outside was dim. He could not see clearly; he could only hear Guan Shanjin's abruptly hoarse voice and harsh breathing.

Feeling a little flustered, Wu Xingzi groped about, searching for a candle to light—but Guan Shanjin tightly gripped his wrist, with such terrifyingly powerful force that his arm nearly broke. It was painful enough to make Wu Xingzi cry out, but the pressure did not abate.

"H-Haiwang, you're hurting me. Please, let go…"

"You *know*?" Guan Shanjin gritted his teeth so forcefully that a grinding sound could be heard. The pressure he exerted in his grip increased, causing the bones of Wu Xingzi's wrist to creak. Wu Xingzi howled in pain.

"Answer me! Do you know *everything*?"

"Wh-what do I know?" The agony made tears stream down Wu Xingzi's face. His complexion paled, and it felt like his wrist could shatter at any moment. Trembling, he begged, "P-please let go of me... It really hurts!"

"Do you know..." *That I've only been treating you as Mr. Lu's substitute? You know that I have feelings for him...* "Have you always been pretending?" Guan Shanjin pressed on. Not only did Guan Shanjin not release Wu Xingzi, he dragged him closer, inch by tortuous inch.

"Huh?" Wu Xingzi could not comprehend what he was saying. His perplexed face would have made Guan Shanjin soften in the past, but now, it only enraged him further.

So he'd been using this sort of befuddled expression to lie to him? Did he know everything all along? Why did he stay by his side—did he have other intentions? All sorts of thoughts flashed through Guan Shanjin's head, but for some reason, his mind landed on a pengornis drawing. Guan Shanjin froze. Then, as though burned by flames, he quickly let go of Wu Xingzi.

Wu Xingzi cried out softly in pain, his body unsteady. He started to fall, but Guan Shanjin pulled him into his embrace just before he hit the floor.

Wu Xingzi gasped, quaking with lingering fear. The pain in his wrist radiated through his whole body, and he didn't know if it was truly broken. He didn't even dare to move it.

"What exactly should I do about you?" Guan Shanjin asked. He was unsure if he was asking Wu Xingzi or himself. Just now, he had been possessed by madness, and ended up hurting Wu Xingzi. His heart pounded in shock.

He knew Wu Xingzi was not a fool. Since he had heard Auntie Li's rumors and witnessed the interactions between him and Mr. Lu in Horse-Face City, he definitely would have been able to guess the situation. So what exactly made him erupt in rage?

Guan Shanjin fell into a rare state of confusion.

"I'll help you massage it. Don't be afraid of me." Guan Shanjin relaxed his posture, his tone lightly pleading.

Wu Xingzi wiped his tears away. Nodding his head, he extended his hand toward him.

Wu Xingzi was a thin man, so his wrist was slender as well. The bones in his wrist protruded prominently under the skin. His skin was very fair, showing the greenish blood vessels trailing down his arm.

Now, his entire wrist was bruised, red, and swollen. It had grown nearly twice its original size, and it was obvious how much strength the man who left this mark had used.

Guan Shanjin found the medicine that he had stored in their bags. There were topical treatments as well as oral medications. After bringing Wu Xingzi to his bedroom and onto his bed to lie down, he carefully applied the ointment, massaging his wrist at the same time to help promote blood flow.

Fortunately, Wu Xingzi's bone was not broken, and it didn't hurt as much once the treatment was applied. Wu Xingzi closed his eyes as if he was dozing off, and Guan Shanjin's movements became even lighter and more cautious.

The soft breathing steadied Guan Shanjin's emotions a little, and he gradually stopped moving as he fell into his thoughts. Guan Shanjin dared not say how good a lover he was. He had treated everyone in the past as Mr. Lu's substitutes, and even in the midst of heightened emotions, he still knew how to take care of someone.

In other words, as he pampered these substitutes, he convinced himself that he was taking care of Mr. Lu. The two of them were so close yet so far; they were always so courteous and proper when interacting with each other. Since all his previous lovers were shadows of Mr. Lu, he would not treat them harshly. He could never frighten Mr. Lu.

This was truly the first time... How could he bear to leave such a brutal mark on Wu Xingzi's arm? Why had he acted so crazed?

Guan Shanjin wasn't stupid either. In fact, he was too clever. This loss of control was completely out of the ordinary for him. There had never been a single time when he had lost his wits like this, not even as he struck down enemies in the battlefield. He shuddered unconsciously as he thought about that iciness he felt when he heard Wu Xingzi mention the relationship between him and Mr. Lu.

Why exactly was he so on edge?

Something seemed ready to emerge from a cocoon in his mind. It was not a sentiment that he could currently control, so he clenched his teeth and harshly shoved it back down, unwilling to think further about it.

Wu Xingzi had a gentle temperament. Even after being treated roughly, he didn't complain, nor did he rebuke Guan Shanjin. The general was caught between feeling assured and discouraged. More than anything else right now, he felt guilt—he could not speak of it aloud, but he felt he needed to do something about it. How could he make it up to this old fellow?

Wu Xingzi's sleeping face appeared content in the candlelight. It was as if his injury had never occurred, and his bone had not nearly been broken. It was the instigator who felt more afraid.

Sighing, Guan Shanjin confirmed that the bruise had been thoroughly massaged before he applied a new layer of ointment across it and wrapped it in clean linen. He got into bed, still dressed, and held his lover until he fell asleep.

The next morning, Wu Xingzi woke up, had his breakfast, and packed his bags. He did not mention what happened the previous night at all. There were a few times when Guan Shanjin wanted to ask about it, but he found that when he opened his mouth, he didn't know what to say. He resented Wu Xingzi's inattentiveness to the matter.

Wu Xingzi packed away the pengornis drawings and his father's books securely under his clothes. He left the room with his bags and saw Guan Shanjin looking annoyed, sitting at the table and drinking tea.

"What's wrong?" Wu Xingzi asked.

Only after he heard the adviser speak was Guan Shanjin willing to look at him. "It's nothing," he said as he poured some tea for Wu Xingzi. He frowned slightly. "Does your wrist still hurt? Why are you in such a hurry to pack?"

He felt he shouldn't offer to help Wu Xingzi pack his things. Noticing how Wu Xingzi fiddled about, he knew that the old man was bringing along his treasures with him. Not only was the case of penis pictures included, but there were other things that were even more important, things that he could not know about. Guan Shanjin felt even more melancholic as he thought about it. Compounded with the guilt about what happened last night, his chest felt achingly stifled.

"Huh? Oh..." Wu Xingzi smiled and shook his head as he looked at his own wrist. "It doesn't hurt much anymore. Thank you for applying the ointment last night, it was very effective."

This fool! He's been injured. Doesn't he know how to get angry?

Guan Shanjin would rather Wu Xingzi scold him. It would be better than how he was acting now—like he was about to forget it entirely.

"It's what I should do. After all, I was in the wrong." Guan Shanjin's tone was stiff. He stared at the old fellow happily drinking tea and eating snacks, looking no different from his usual self.

The general's mood was indescribable. He wasn't just angry with himself for his peculiar attitude, he was angry with Wu Xingzi for not knowing how to stand up for himself. But what could he do about it? To Wu Xingzi, the matter was already over and done with. Even if Guan Shanjin became enraged to the point of spewing blood, the old thing would only look at him in blank confusion.

Rubbing his chest, Guan Shanjin had no choice but to force himself to temporarily leave this matter behind. With a hard voice, he said, "Since you're already packed, let's give all the things that we haven't finished eating or using to Auntie Liu. We'll depart for Horse-Face City in the afternoon."

"Yes, yes."

The New Year goods that Su Yang had prepared were a little too elaborate. There were more than enough provisions here to last Wu Xingzi and Guan Shanjin if they stayed here for another ten days. All the ingredients were of excellent quality, too, but they would not be able to take them along, so it was fortunate that they could give them to Auntie Liu.

Having made their decision, the two of them soon finished packing. They took as many snacks with them as they could. The rest of the food, as well as other kitchen ingredients and daily necessities, were all given to Auntie Liu.

Knowing that they were leaving, Auntie Liu didn't refuse any of it. She kept on at Wu Xingzi to take care of himself, telling him that city folk were calculating and secretly scheming and that Wu Xingzi had to be more aware of it.

"We shouldn't set out to harm others, but we also cannot let others take advantage of us, understand? People like that woman from the Li family—you must be more wary of them. They bully the good and fear the evil. You should deal with them when and if it's needed, all right?"

"I understand," Wu Xingzi said. He patted Auntie Liu's hand in consolation, only to reveal the linen bandage around his wrist. Auntie Liu's eyes sharpened, and just as she was about to open her mouth, Wu Xingzi waved his hand. "Auntie, it's not a big deal. Don't worry about it."

Since Wu Xingzi said it was all right, Auntie Liu suppressed her anger, even if she was unhappy about it. She glared savagely at Guan Shanjin and deliberately raised her voice. "If anyone ever does you wrong, just tell Auntie about it! I have always protected you in the past, and I will still protect you in the future."

It was unclear if Guan Shanjin heard her. He silently remained sitting at the head of the table with his eyes half-lowered, as if distracted.

The anger in Auntie Liu's heart flared up. She almost rolled up her sleeves to teach that fellow a lesson, but once again, Wu Xingzi stopped her. Before they even had lunch, Wu Xingzi said his farewells and dragged Guan Shanjin away.

He didn't know how long he would be staying in Horse-Face City this time. Before leaving the world of Qingcheng County, Wu Xingzi reluctantly turned to look back at the familiar grounds: the bleak and desolate scenery, the hard, dry earth, and the weeds that refused to flourish.

"We're going." Seated on Zhuxing, Guan Shanjin trotted the horse around Wu Xingzi once. He hesitated for a moment before placing an arm on Wu Xingzi's shoulders. "I'll come back with you next year to make the offerings to your ancestors again, all right?"

Wu Xingzi blinked. "I'll have to be back for Qingming,"[1] he said matter-of-factly.

Guan Shanjin laughed lightly, brushing Wu Xingzi's nose with his finger. "Exactly. We'll need to come back for Qingming. It's settled."

They would be returning together for Qingming? Wu Xingzi's face turned grim. How was he going to explain it to his ancestors this time? This tryst was becoming a full-blown affair!

Wu Xingzi's riding ability had improved greatly, so the journey back to Horse-Face City was much shorter. Guan Shanjin only just made it into each city before sunset, but the journey back to Horse-Face City took them two fewer days than the journey from it.

Just like before, Guan Shanjin sent Wu Xingzi to Shuanghe Manor and took his leave.

The New Year festivities were over, and various military decrees came one after another. Man Yue was pale with exhaustion and looked like a deflated balloon. His body was as round and plump as always, but he gave off the distinct impression he was on the verge of collapsing.

Mint and Osmanthus were truly delighted when they saw Wu Xingzi. They surrounded him and chattered away, asking about all sorts of things. They even showed off the maturing cucumbers to him as though they were revealing treasures, and both of their delicate faces were full of pride.

---

1   Qingming takes place during the spring. Traditionally families visit the graves of their ancestors on this holiday to clean them and make offerings.

"Mr. Wu, look! My sister and I gave it our best, and there's not a single bug on your cucumbers. When they're fully grown, they'll definitely be crisp and sweet." Mint lifted up the little growing cucumber. The flower had yet to wilt; the fresh and bright blossom was adorable.

"Yes, yes." Wu Xingzi carefully lifted one of the small cucumbers as well, caressing it admiringly.

It was quite warm in Horse-Face City, and the cucumbers were growing a lot faster than he had anticipated. Covered with soft, downy fuzz, they were actually quite cute.

"However, there seem to be too many of them." Osmanthus crouched down by the side, checking for insects. "If we don't pluck some now, I'm afraid they won't taste as good when they're fully grown."

"Why don't we harvest half of them and pickle them?" Mint suggested.

"That's not a bad idea," Wu Xingzi said. He discussed with the two young ladies how they should pickle the cucumbers. Should they make them more sour or more salty? Perhaps they should be a little spicy?

In the days that followed, Wu Xingzi returned to the leisurely life he'd led before the new year. The cucumbers grew quickly, reaching the size of his palm within a couple of weeks. The small, pickled cucumbers were also nearly ready to be eaten. Wu Xingzi's heart skipped with joy, and he inexplicably thought of Guan Shanjin, whom he had yet to see in the last few weeks.

The two girls told him many things regarding Guan Shanjin. They said that the general was very busy these days, and he didn't even visit Mr. Lu that much.

Is he eating properly? But Wu Xingzi understood that his concern was rather pointless. Guan Shanjin was the general, so there must be people taking good care of him. It wasn't his duty to worry over such small matters like eating and sleeping; Mr. Lu would definitely remember.

Mint and Osmanthus had preserved the cucumbers in soybean paste and added some spices. However, the two young ladies were afraid that they would over-season the pickles, so they left the final touches to Wu Xingzi.

He still remembered the promise he made to Guan Shanjin—he told the general he would make him cucumbers to eat!

What a coincidence. Wu Xingzi hesitated, wondering if he should send some over.

Mint was able to quickly guess what Wu Xingzi was feeling conflicted about. "Let's send some over," she said. "I heard from the kitchen auntie that the general's appetite hasn't been very good lately."

Mint hastily prepared a plate of pickles with her sister, and they urged their master to go. The day they had been waiting for had finally arrived! Wu Xingzi was about to secure the general's favor! They had read a few new picture books over the holiday, and there was finally an outlet for them to release their romantic zeal.

However, before they could leave Shuanghe Manor, Osmanthus murmured to her sister that an unwelcome guest had appeared.

The intruder was Hua Shu. The haughty, arrogant air he'd exuded the last time they saw him was gone. He acted friendly and servile, and he had a slight smile on his face as he greeted Wu Xingzi. "Mr. Wu, it's been a long time since we last spoke. How have you been?"

"I've been doing well. How are you, Hua-gongzi?" Wu Xingzi hurriedly cupped his hands together. He had only met Hua Shu twice, but this exquisite-looking man was indelibly engraved in his memory. Previously, his attitude had been pompous; this time, Wu Xingzi felt a little overwhelmed by his warmth.

The two girls hid behind Wu Xingzi, looking down to hide the roll of their eyes. Hua Shu was such a nuisance. He was merely an attendant, but he was able to rely on Mr. Lu's favorable position within the general's estate to act rudely without consequence. He was overbearing toward the younger servants, and unabashedly put on airs.

"Thank you for asking, Mr. Wu." With eyes lowered, Hua Shu spoke respectfully, but he still could not hide a hint of conceit in his tone. "I would like to invite you to join me for lunch, Mr. Wu. Please follow me."

Mint couldn't bring herself to wait for her own master to speak. She knew how soft-hearted Wu Xingzi was; he would not refuse the invitation, and he would simply follow Hua Shu. *Hmph!* Could her master be ordered to heel as if he were a dog?

"Hold on!" she exclaimed.

"Hmm?" Hua Shu glanced at the little girl blocking Wu Xingzi, a sneer on his lips. "Where did this servant come from, and why is she so rude? Who taught you your manners?"

"My mother did." Mint was a local girl from Horse-Face City, and her female relatives were able to support the entire extended family by themselves. She had no patience for Hua Shu's peculiarities. "May I know who taught *you* your manners, Hua-gongzi? Are you inviting someone to lunch, or are you calling a dog?"

Hua Shu frowned, his cheeks burning. "Why, you—!"

"What? Your master wants to invite Mr. Wu for a meal, so he *has* to go? Was this how Mr. Lu taught you to invite people?" Mint put her hand on her hip, pursing her lips. "Mr. Wu isn't available right now. He's going to see the general."

"The general?" Hua Shu's face paled, but he soon recovered, and his brows knitted together. "The general has been busy with the military recently. Did he really say that he was going to see Mr. Wu?"

"Uhh..." Wu Xingzi was about to respond, but Osmanthus stepped out, smoothly taking over the conversation.

"Does this have anything to do with you, Hua-gongzi?" she said. "At the end of the day, the general still has no intention of seeing you." Osmanthus had a sort of childlike naïveté that her sister lacked, but she did not want to seem less sharp-tongued.

Every word stabbed right into Hua Shu's heart. His complexion turned uglier; even his lips were pale.

"It's true that the general does not want to see me, but the general left early in the morning, and he has yet to return," Hua Shu said, trying to smile at the two girls. "Who are you planning to see?"

"He left?" Wu Xingzi sighed, feeling rather regretful as he looked toward the earthen jar of pickled cucumbers.

Seeing how they failed to scare Hua Shu, Mint and Osmanthus both pursed their lips. After exchanging a glance, Mint remained calm. "Even if the general is not seeing Mr. Wu right now," she said, "I doubt Mr. Lu asked you to call a dog over! Shuanghe Manor has no dogs, so you can leave now."

"This young lady has a very sharp tongue," Hua Shu scoffed.

"How could it be sharper than yours, Hua-gongzi? Your tongue doesn't even know how to invite a person over. Has it been whetted by a stone?" Mint waved her hand, smiling innocently. "Hua-gongzi, please return to your master. Shuanghe Manor is too small, so we won't invite you for tea."

"Is this Mr. Wu's intention as well?" Hua Shu glanced over at Wu Xingzi, who was being blocked by the two girls.

"No, no." Wu Xingzi waved, tugging at the two girls. "Since Mr. Lu has invited me, I won't refuse him."

"Mr. Wu!" Mint shouted unhappily.

"Hey, we still have to eat," Wu Xingzi said. Hua Shu's haughty tone didn't bother Wu Xingzi. He had been an adviser for half his life, and he'd met every kind of person under the sun. Some people only felt secure if they treated others with contempt. He was content to just let it be.

"Please follow me, then, Mr. Wu." Hua Shu lowered his eyes, hiding a flash of disdain. To him, Wu Xingzi's submission proved his inferiority, a failure carved directly into his bones and flowing freely in his blood. How could the general have feelings for someone like this?

"Many thanks to Hua-gongzi for guiding the way," Wu Xingzi said. He patted the two girls in consolation and hurried after Hua Shu.

Mr. Lu stayed at Wang Shu Residence. It was a tranquil location in a forest of plum trees. The buildings were constructed tastefully, crafted from green bamboo. The location exuded a remarkable feeling of serenity amongst the tumult.

The plum trees were flowering; brilliant red petals bloomed everywhere. It felt like even the breeze blowing by was tinted with rich colors. The view was elegant and vivid, and Wu Xingzi was entranced.

This place suited a man like Mr. Lu. Wu Xingzi recalled the slim figure dressed in white, beautiful and fair-skinned. The man was scholarly and refined, like a clear spring or a ray of moonlight that glimmered in one's eyes and captured people's hearts. He was completely unforgettable. Mr. Lu was not a young man anymore—

after all, he was Guan Shanjin's teacher. Still, he looked very youthful, like a young man of twenty.

Hua Shu realized that Wu Xingzi had stopped and was staring into the forest. He could not disguise the annoyance in his eyes, so he bowed his head a little as he urged the adviser on. "Excuse me, Mr. Wu. Mr. Lu's mealtime cannot be delayed, so please follow me closely."

"Ah, sorry, sorry." Wu Xingzi jerked back to awareness. He reddened, hurriedly cupping his hands in apology and following behind Hua Shu properly. They walked into the bamboo house on the left.

"Mr. Lu, Mr. Wu is here," Hua Shu called.

"Mm." In the bamboo house stood a dainty, round table with a few platters of food upon it. Two sets of bowls and chopsticks were set across each other. The house's decor was simple, but laden with subtle elegance. The bamboo screen-covered window was halfway open, showing the plum tree forest outside. A light breeze filled the entire place with the scent of plum blossoms.

Mr. Lu reclined on the daybed under the window to the right. He held a book between his nearly translucent fingers, seeming to be halfway through reading it. After hearing their footsteps, he lifted his eyelids slightly and looked over. Wu Xingzi quickly cupped his hands together.

"It's been a while, Mr. Wu. How have you been?" Mr. Lu put the book down, standing up in a rather awkward manner to welcome him. His leg looked as though it had recovered greatly, but he still needed to rest it.

"Many thanks. I'm doing well. How is your injury, Mr. Lu?"

"There's no need for you to be concerned, Mr. Wu. My leg is better now. The only thing is that I'm still rather ungainly with it—please excuse my clumsiness."

Hua Shu helped Mr. Lu take a seat by the table, then retreated a few steps and stood subserviently in a corner of the house.

"Mr. Wu, please quickly take a seat. I apologize for having only vegetable dishes; I've been a vegetarian for many years. Please forgive my discourtesy."

Wu Xingzi took a seat when Mr. Lu finished speaking. He swiftly glanced at the dishes on the table.

It was true that the dishes were all vegetarian—not a trace of meat could be seen. However, the colors of the dishes complemented each other very well. The dainty serving plates were simple, with a green color that deepened toward the center. They looked just like lotus leaves, tender and delicate. The rice bowls were jade-colored, making the light brown hue of the bamboo chopsticks stand out prettily.

Wu Xingzi felt rather lost. First, the portions of these dishes were all fairly small. Even if he ate them all, he would not likely feel full. They could only be considered an appetizer at most. Furthermore, the placement of the bowls and chopsticks looked like a work of art. They gave off the feeling that they should not be touched, and Wu Xingzi was unable to bring himself to move them. He absent-mindedly wrung his sleeves.

"Are these not to Mr. Wu's liking?" Mr. Lu's brows knitted, looking very self-reproachful. "It seems that I have been impolite. Mr. Wu is here all the way from Qingcheng County as a guest. I should have prepared a more sumptuous meal."

"No, no, no, you're too courteous. It's just that I'm an unrefined man, and I'm afraid of offending Mr. Lu..." Wu Xingzi rubbed his nose, looking at Mr. Lu before lowering his head. He really wanted to eat, but seeing that Mr. Lu had no intention of picking up his chopsticks, he could not display his greedy hunger. The pair of chopsticks in front of him looked very slippery and difficult to maneuver, too...

"It is I who has been thoughtless. I ended up slighting you, Mr. Wu." Mr. Lu wrinkled his forehead and sighed softly. He summoned Hua Shu. "Please ask the kitchen to prepare a bowl of steamed eggs for Mr. Wu."

"But..." Hua Shu glared at Wu Xingzi resentfully, only to discover that the man was currently drooling at the sweet and sour cabbage. With how eager he looked, it was highly likely that he would not pay attention to what they were saying. Hua Shu gnashed his teeth. "Mr. Lu, you've remained a vegetarian for a dozen years just to accumulate good luck for the general. Why..."

"Hush, just go." Mr. Lu cast a sidelong glance at Hua Shu, a faint smile curling his lips. There seemed to be a mocking glint in his eyes. Hua Shu quickly bowed his head to hide his own expression and hurriedly retreated.

"Hmm?" Wu Xingzi's attention was finally pulled away from the fragrant sweet and sour cabbage that stirred his appetite. He saw Hua Shu leaving rather hastily. The adviser looked at Mr. Lu in confusion, blushing slightly as he secretly reminded himself not to reveal his timidity.

"I've embarrassed myself in front of you, Mr. Wu. Hua Shu is not a cruel young man, he's just overly protective of me." Mr. Lu sighed lightly. Seeing Wu Xingzi nodding along perfunctorily made him angry. Hua Shu's words had been unexpected, but they were not very surprising. However, they clearly had not been heard by the man who was supposed to hear them, and it was a completely moot point.

"I understand. The two girls at my place are the same as well, and they're quite adorable." Wu Xingzi thought about Mint and Osmanthus. They were clearly young enough to be his daughters, yet they protected him as though he was their child. It warmed his heart.

"Oh?" Mr. Lu laughed shallowly. "It'll be a pity if the food turns cold. Mr. Wu, have some first. Hua Shu will come back later with the steamed egg."

"There's no need for all the trouble. You're too polite." Wu Xingzi waved his hands. He was already hungry, and to continue declining would make him seem small-minded. Although he was a little hesitant, he still picked up his bowl and started eating.

The dishes were all delicious, showcasing the excellent skills of the kitchen in the general's estate. Wu Xingzi ate with great relish, but worried about how Mr. Lu barely picked up his chopsticks. He had no choice but to put down his own pair after finishing a bowl of rice. He sipped his tea to curb his hunger.

At this time, Hua Shu returned with the steamed eggs. The fragrance of egg and chicken broth filled the air. Wu Xingzi had eaten a bowl of rice and half the dishes already, yet his stomach still gurgled, growling out without any consideration for the situation.

His face turned as red as a beet. Bowing his head, he apologized as he rubbed his stomach firmly.

"Mr. Wu, don't stand on ceremony," Mr. Lu said. "This steamed egg has been prepared for you. Please eat it while it's still hot."

Mr. Lu's face was a little pale, and his head angled slightly as if he was avoiding something. Hua Shu quickly handed over a handkerchief. Frowning, he held back his words as he glared at Wu Xingzi.

"Uh... Mr. Lu, if you're not feeling well, then I won't bother you anymore..." Wu Xingzi had no idea what was going on. Could it be that Mr. Lu hated eggs?

"Mr. Lu has not eaten anything from an animal over the past several years. The smell of this steamed egg and chicken broth is strong—of course he feels uncomfortable!" Hua Shu spoke rudely, apparently pushed to his limits. "Mr. Wu, just sit there and eat your food. Why do you insist on making things difficult for Mr. Lu?"

He clearly did not remember that it was not Wu Xingzi who had requested the steamed egg, or that it was Mr. Lu who had insisted on having this meal.

"Ah... Oh... I've been improper! Oh no, I'm sorry, I'm really sorry!" Distressed, Wu Xingzi apologized as he quickly pulled the steamed egg toward himself. Scooping a large spoonful, he raised it to his mouth. The steamed egg was still piping hot—he would end up scalding his throat badly if he swallowed it.

Seeing this, Mr. Lu took a breath and quickly reached out to stop him. In the confusion, the steamed egg somehow ended up spilling out of the spoon. By chance, it spilled onto Mr. Lu's flawless hand. He cried out softly, his face paling. A red mark appeared on his hand, and it began to blister. The bowl containing the steamed egg rolled to the edge of the table. Still boiling hot, it fell and shattered on the ground.

The house was momentarily silent. At a loss for what to do, Wu Xingzi looked at Mr. Lu as he endured the painful burn. Hua Shu gasped in alarm, then glared at Wu Xingzi hatefully. He hurriedly carried over a basin of cold water for Mr. Lu to submerge his blistered hand before calling out loudly for the other servants.

Hua Shu was not the only one taking care of Mr. Lu in his residence. With a few shouts, two serving boys appeared out of nowhere.

"Quick, call the physician over! Mr. Lu has burned his hand!" Hua Shu commanded in a rage. The two serving boys seemed to be alarmed by the situation as well, and they flew off to carry out their orders.

The physician came very quickly. Before Wu Xingzi could even figure out what was going on, the two serving boys pushed him away, and he could only watch from afar as the physician applied ointment to Mr. Lu's hand. After Mr. Lu quietly gave Hua Shu some instructions, Hua Shu glared at Wu Xingzi indignantly, looking as though he wanted to lunge at him and bite him. Still confused, Wu Xingzi's shoulders came up to his ears in fear.

"The general is here!" someone shouted suddenly. The scene turned chaotic, and the only people standing firmly were the two serving boys holding onto Wu Xingzi.

In no time, Guan Shanjin strode over, followed by Hei-er and Man Yue.

"What's going on?" Upon stepping inside, Guan Shanjin immediately saw Wu Xingzi trapped in the hold of the two tall, sturdy serving boys. His already grim face turned even colder.

"General, Mr. Lu…" Seeing that something was not quite right, Hua Shu hurriedly spoke up, only to be stopped with a raised hand from Guan Shanjin.

"Go take a look," he instructed Man Yue, while he himself walked over to Wu Xingzi and pulled him into his arms. "Why are you here?"

"Uhh… I came… for a meal…" Wu Xingzi's stomach grumbled again. Guan Shanjin's lips curved up, as though he was about to burst out laughing. He suppressed his laughter only because he did not want to embarrass Wu Xingzi too much.

"You're not full yet?" Guan Shanjin rubbed Wu Xingzi's stomach affectionately and was very dissatisfied by the emptiness within. "You haven't eaten?"

"I had a bowl of rice." Wu Xingzi's face burned, feeling so embarrassed that he dearly wished that a hole would open up and bury him alive.

This was too embarrassing! Why was his stomach so useless in front of everyone? And Guan Shanjin even heard it!

"Only one bowl?" Guan Shanjin again rubbed the adviser's stomach, his brows knitting together tightly as he looked up and glanced at Man Yue.

Man Yue stood next to Mr. Lu and asked the physician about the situation. On the other side, Hua Shu's eyes glared with resentment and anger. Guan Shanjin did not pay attention to him at all. However, Wu Xingzi was unable to ignore it, and he tugged at Guan Shanjin's sleeve lightly.

"You're not going over to take a look at Mr. Lu?"

"I'm not a physician." Guan Shanjin eyed him, amused. However, with the feelings that he had cultivated for his teacher over the years, he was still rather worried about Mr. Lu's injuries. "If you're hungry, just go back and eat. There should be some food left in the kitchen. I'll have Hei-er get something for you."

"Uhh..." Wu Xingzi was a little tempted. After that bowl of rice and vegetables, his appetite had completely awakened; he was fiercely hungry. Still, he bore some responsibility for the injury on Mr. Lu's hand, and to just depart like that would be very rude of him.

Seeing the two men huddling together intimately, Hua Shu finally opened his mouth. "General! You, you have to stand up for Mr. Lu!"

"Oh?" Guan Shanjin raised a brow. He had been very busy ever since he returned, and he did not yet have the time to deal with Hua Shu's attitude. Since he clearly wanted to throw himself into the fire, Guan Shanjin was more than happy to play along.

"Teacher, are you all right?" Guan Shanjin asked.

Man Yue silently mouthed at him, telling him that Mr. Lu had a blister from scalding his hand. Guan Shanjin's heart ached a little, but he did not feel the usual desire to wrap Mr. Lu up and take good care of him. He was more worried about Wu Xingzi's stomach.

This old fellow needed to eat a lot, and he could never endure his hunger. It was already long past mealtime—what would happen if he became sick from hunger?

"It's nothing, only a blister," Mr. Lu replied gently. After a pause, he continued, his voice carrying traces of worry, "It's actually Mr. Wu who has been wronged. I've been an inconsiderate host."

"Mr. Lu! Isn't this injury all because of Mr. Wu? Why are you still defending him?" Hua Shu asked, displeased. Without waiting for Mr. Lu, he bowed toward Guan Shanjin. "General, you're more aware than anyone of Mr. Lu's character. Today, Mr. Lu invited Mr. Wu over for a meal, and he was very meticulous and attentive to every aspect of it. Mr. Lu has remained a vegetarian for many years to seek blessings for you, so you know that he never touches animal products. He still specially arranged for the kitchen to prepare steamed eggs for Mr. Wu. However, Mr Wu..."

"Steamed eggs?" Guan Shanjin frowned. He knew that Mr. Lu did not eat anything that came from an animal. Even things like garlic and onion never appeared on his table.[2] "You've been very thoughtful, Teacher. So, where is the steamed egg now?" It would be perfect to pad Wu Xingzi's stomach.

Guan Shanjin did not realize how partial he was to Wu Xingzi. With the adviser in his arms, he took a few steps forward and glanced at the table. He only saw a few plates of vegetables, including sweet and sour cabbage. This dish would normally not appear on Mr. Lu's table. After all, it was full of scallions, ginger, and garlic. It seemed like Mr. Lu truly put in great consideration for his guest.

Since Mr. Lu could not eat this dish, Guan Shanjin had Wu Xingzi take a seat. Scooping a bowl of rice for him, he poured the entire

---

2 In Buddhism, garlic and onions are among the "five pungent spices" (五辛), which may be traditionally abstained from along with alcohol and animal products.

plate of cabbage into the bowl. The rice turned golden yellow from the sauce, and the tart aroma wafting from it was extremely tempting.

"Go ahead and eat. Don't starve yourself," Guan Shanjin said. As long as he was around, he would never let the old fellow go hungry.

Since Guan Shanjin gave him permission, Wu Xingzi forgot the formalities and picked up the bowl to eat.

A peculiar atmosphere permeated the house—even Man Yue stared straight at Guan Shanjin and Wu Xingzi, unable to look away. *Ah, look how clingy they are!* He wanted to retch.

"General, Mr. Lu is still injured. You…" Hua Shu looked utterly insulted as he tried to gain Guan Shanjin's attention.

"How was Mr. Lu injured?" Guan Shanjin asked. Since Hua Shu insisted on him handling this matter, Guan Shanjin hoped that he would be able to take whatever he dealt.

"It's only a small injury," Mr. Lu said, before Hua Shu could reply. He smiled faintly at Guan Shanjin. "Have you eaten yet, Haiwang? You've been so busy these days. You even have to split your attention between overseeing the military and helping me arrange my wedding. I'm really sorry."

"Don't say that, Teacher. I'm just doing my duty as your student." He looked at Mr. Lu's serene and elegant face. It moved his heart, but the feeling was not as strong as before. The man who was once as luminous as moonlight now seemed to have dimmed.

Mr. Lu sighed, reaching out as though he wanted to touch Guan Shanjin, only to pull his hand back and press it against his chest. "I know that Mr. Wu is your beloved, and you must treat him well. In the future, I will remain a vegetarian and pray for you—so don't force Mr. Wu."

"Force?" Guan Shanjin asked. That word, no matter how it was said, sounded very uncomfortable. Guan Shanjin was willing to play clueless for Mr. Lu's sake, but that didn't mean he truly was an idiot. No matter how unwilling he was to admit it, he could still perceive the vague malice in that word.

Mr. Lu turned his head away, refusing to elaborate. His sad expression was overwhelming, and in the end, Guan Shanjin softened. At the end of the day, he did not want to think negatively of Mr. Lu.

"Teacher, don't worry too much about it. After your marriage, you'll still be my teacher. I know that you're always worried about me." Guan Shanjin lightly lifted Mr. Lu's hand. Mr. Lu struggled a little, but he didn't manage to break free. Guan Shanjin discreetly used a bit of strength to hold on tightly, examining the injury.

The physician had clearly made a timely appearance. Other than the redness of the skin, the injury was not serious. After expelling the fluid from within the blister, applying ointment, and taking care of it, it would likely recover completely in a few days.

"Teacher, you should have someone smarter attend to you. It will prevent people from stirring up trouble when you're married."

"What does that mean?" Mr. Lu asked, trying to pull his hand away once again. This time, Guan Shanjin let him go. The general's eyes curved as though he was smiling, but the emotion was not there. Mr. Lu had never seen such a cold look before. Guan Shanjin had always been gentle and considerate in front of him, afraid that he would accidentally alarm him.

"Hei-er, drag Hua Shu outside." This command was neither cold nor angry; it was as gentle as the wind in early spring. However, it sent a chill down the spine of every person present.

"Haiwang, you're..."

"Teacher, I'm doing all of this for you." Guan Shanjin gently tucked Mr. Lu's hair behind his ear.

On the other side, Hua Shu's face turned white with fear. He fell to his knees, crying, "General, please make your decision wisely!"

Guan Shanjin ignored him, gesturing at Hei-er. Hei-er covered Hua Shu's mouth and dragged him away like a butcher carrying a chicken. There was no telling what would happen to him.

Wu Xingzi looked on as the drama unfolded. Holding onto his empty bowl, he was completely confused. Everything had happened so quickly, even quicker than that steamed egg catastrophe—he still had no idea how he had spilled it. There was something wrong with Guan Shanjin!

"You..." Wu Xingzi opened his mouth but realized he could not say a word.

"Hmm?"

This Guan Shanjin was too similar to the one he had seen when they first met. Arrogant and indifferent, there was a ruthlessness about him that could not be concealed. He was poised like a wild beast, ready to bite at any moment. Wu Xingzi had almost forgotten that this side of the general existed.

Swallowing, Wu Xingzi put down his empty bowl. After a pause, he stiffly sat up on his seat and timidly asked, "D-do you eat pickled cucumbers? They're very delicious."

Guan Shanjin did not understand how he ended up following Wu Xingzi back to Shuanghe Manor to eat pickled cucumbers.

The little cucumbers, which had yet to fully mature, were somewhat stiff. They still retained their crunchiness after being pickled. Chewing on them aroused one's appetite, and even without any other side dishes, they finished two big bowls of rice.

The two young girls tidied up the table, serving desserts and tea before vanishing completely. How thoughtful of them!

The evening's winter breeze was no longer that cold, and even carried a little of spring's vigor. Guan Shanjin mulled it over for a moment, then decided to just pull Wu Xingzi along. They sat on stools by the cucumber trellis, drinking tea.

Only when they were about to finish their tea did Guan Shanjin finally break the silence: "What happened between you and Mr. Lu?"

"Hmm?" Wu Xingzi blinked. He swallowed a pine nut candy and drank a mouthful of tea to wash it down, and then replied guiltily, "I wanted to quickly finish the steamed egg to prevent him from feeling sick from the smell. Mr. Lu only wanted to stop me because he was afraid that I would burn myself in my rush... I didn't think that I would end up causing him to be burned instead."

"It was he who asked the cook to prepare the steamed egg for you?"

"Ah, yes. Mr. Lu is so very kind, yet he hurt himself because of me," Wu Xingzi said. Mr. Lu's hands were so pretty. For them to suffer an injury for no good reason made Wu Xingzi's heart ache.

"Mm... Teacher has always been meticulously considerate." Guan Shanjin turned his head to look at Wu Xingzi, letting out a sudden laugh. "He's not like you. You don't even care about me at all. Your pengornis pictures are much more precious to you than me. If I were to lose an arm or a leg, it still wouldn't compare to you losing a corner of one of your darlings."

"Hey, don't talk such nonsense," Wu Xingzi answered seriously, furrowing his brow. "After all, as a living being, blood runs through your veins. If you were to lose an arm or a leg, my heart would hurt even more. Don't say such silly things. If you repeat them often enough, they'll come true."

The cautious, worried look on Wu Xingzi's face thoroughly warmed Guan Shanjin's heart. He couldn't resist gathering Wu Xingzi into his arms and nuzzling him. They cuddled together like this for a while. In a low voice, Guan Shanjin tenderly asked what other dishes could be made with the cucumbers. Wu Xingzi was familiar with various preparations, and he recited them one by one. His gentle voice sounded even more enchanting than the delicacies he described.

Guan Shanjin carefully listened to each and every recipe with his eyes closed. Wu Xingzi's voice was neither too high nor too low, and it wasn't agitated or scratchy. He occasionally drawled his words together with a very strong southern accent. When he spoke in his native dialect, it sounded like he was singing, the words sticking together like candy.

It was said that the words of the Wu clan were graceful and light. Wu Xingzi's tone was so gentle and warm that it seemed impossible to imagine him losing his temper.

Guan Shanjin liked his accent.

This sort of accent often melded together some of the heavier-stressed, throaty consonants, sounding rather honeyed and sweet. To a northerner like Guan Shanjin, it sounded a little effeminate coming from a man. The words joined together in a lackadaisical way.

It had been some time now, though, and he had grown used to it. He loved listening to Wu Xingzi babble away. He would always talk about irrelevant, trivial matters—they were clearly very minor issues, yet Wu Xingzi would end up laughing while talking about them. Smiling with a pair of squinting, narrow eyes, he looked like sunlight reflected in water—soft around the edges, only leaving warmth behind.

For the last couple of weeks, he had truly missed Wu Xingzi. If he hadn't been so swamped with work, he would've visited this old fellow every day. He wanted to listen to his chatter, watch him eat everything he made with great enthusiasm, and hold him as he lay timidly and softly in his embrace.

"Wu Xingzi," Guan Shanjin called out to him. When this name rolled off his tongue, it somehow tasted sweet, and Guan Shanjin inadvertently licked his lips.

"Yes?" Wu Xingzi pillowed his head on Guan Shanjin's shoulder. His stomach was well satisfied, and the winter sun was warm. In Guan Shanjin's sweet-smelling embrace, Wu Xingzi was about to nod off.

"The injury I gave you... Has it recovered completely?" The moment the words were out of his mouth, the man leaning lazily on him tensed up slightly. Guan Shanjin patted Wu Xingzi, speaking hesitantly, "I was wrong to do that. I've been thinking about that night ever since. Wu Xingzi, do you think that I hurt you because of Mr. Lu?"

Upon returning to Horse-Face City, Guan Shanjin had sought Man Yue immediately.

He was unable to comprehend his own mind. He had always kept Mr. Lu in his heart, treasuring him. Ever since their first meeting, he'd been attracted to him. Guan Shanjin was quite aware that he himself was not a good man. It was only when he was next to Mr. Lu that he wished to be better—to be gentle, considerate, kind, and restrained. That place in his heart was an extremely special one, a place that no one else could enter.

But somehow, entirely without his say-so, Wu Xingzi had found a place in his heart, too. It was inexplicable. For the first time in his life, Guan Shanjin was panicking.

"Oh, is that so?" was Man Yue's reply. He sighed. "Haiwang-gege, if you can't figure it out, who else can?"

"You haven't addressed me like that in a long time," Guan Shanjin laughed, cocking a brow as he pinched Man Yue's full and fleshy chin.

"I get upset hearing it myself," Man Yue said, jerking away. "However, Great General, you should go look for Adviser Wu and have a chat. If you can't stop worrying about him, there'll only be trouble later."

What Man Yue said was the truth. The man they were going to deal with next was rather troublesome. Guan Shanjin would need to make a decision before placing Wu Xingzi in any sort of place in his heart.

Who would have thought that the place they would finally meet would be in Mr. Lu's abode? An incident that was neither big nor small had shaken his feelings for Mr. Lu.

"Hurting me because of Mr. Lu?" Wu Xingzi blinked. He lowered his head, staying silent.

Guan Shanjin was in no hurry. There were things that he wanted to say, so he would take his time to do so!

"The first time I met Mr. Lu, I was only ten years old." Guan Shanjin picked up Wu Xingzi's hand, caressing it. The old fellow's hand was smaller than most. Apart from a few calluses, it was shapely and smooth—the hand of a scholar.

"You were ten years old? He was your childhood teacher?" Wu Xingzi's palm itched from the strokes. Absentmindedly, he tightened his grip, capturing Guan Shanjin's long, slender fingers within his hand.

"No, I wouldn't say that. Before him, I had already gone through a few teachers. I was a clever child—exceedingly precocious. The previous teachers either left because they were angered by me, or they left of their own accord. None of them stayed for long." Guan Shanjin chuckled. "At the time, Mr. Lu himself was only seventeen, and he had just achieved a juren rank in the imperial examinations.[3] He was from the same province as my maternal grandfather. He had some literary fame among the neighbors, and he was known for his

---

3   A juren rank was awarded to imperial examination candidates who passed the provincial examination. It was the second highest rank a scholar could achieve, and entitled its holder to a variety
of social and legal privileges.

open-mindedness, and so he was recommended to my mother to become my teacher."

Guan Shanjin exhaled, and Wu Xingzi discreetly raised his head to observe him. That breathtakingly beautiful face gazed into the distance with a longing expression that Wu Xingzi didn't understand.

"The first time I saw Mr. Lu, he was dressed in a white robe. He always liked dressing in white, saying that it was a reminder to practice self-respect and avoid making mistakes. When a drop of ink falls on a piece of white paper, would you look at the paper or the ink?" Guan Shanjin suddenly bent his neck to glance at Wu Xingzi. Their eyes met, and Wu Xingzi hunched his shoulders, feeling somewhat embarrassed about being caught watching him. Guan Shanjin let out a low laugh. "Hmm?"

"I'd probably look at the ink stain on the white paper." It would be so conspicuous. Even if he wanted to tear his eyes away, it would be difficult!

"That's right. Teacher said that, too. So he dressed in white to always remind himself that he should keep himself clean. He said that this was also a way to always be prepared, so misfortune could be prevented." Guan Shanjin chuckled again, shaking his head. "Mr. Lu's life has always been planned meticulously. He takes each step cautiously, and he never takes any unnecessary risks."

"Exactly! One should seek peace, not fortune. It's good to just live a down-to-earth life." Wu Xingzi deeply believed in this way of life. He spent his days peacefully, and he could not help but empathize with Mr. Lu. "Mr. Lu is truly a good teacher. It's no wonder that you like him."

"You don't seem to be bothered at all that I like him." Guan Shanjin felt somber. Wu Xingzi was in his arms right now—how could he remain so easygoing? He should at least feel jealous that the general's cock had other interests! Guan Shanjin snorted sourly. "Haven't you ever thought about it before?" he asked. "If my pengornis no longer pursues you, but turns toward Mr. Lu instead—wouldn't you be upset?"

"But...your pengornis isn't pursuing me, either!" Wu Xingzi exclaimed.

The hand around Wu Xingzi's waist tightened and held him down, and something hard and bulging ground between his buttocks. Startled, Wu Xingzi cried out in alarm. "Y-y-you..."

"Isn't it pursuing you right now?" Guan Shanjin grinned wickedly at him, his eyes dancing with delight.

Wu Xingzi's cheeks reddened. He shifted his buttocks, wanting to run, but Guan Shanjin held him tighter.

"Stop squirming. If you can't stay still, my cock might plunge into a certain little hole."

What is he saying?! Wu Xingzi stared at him, stupefied. The general was so handsome; how could something so obscene come out of his mouth?

Having lived a long time in the military, Guan Shanjin had picked up some of the bad habits of foul-mouthed soldiers. His appearance could be quite deceiving. He had little care for outsiders and didn't speak with them more than what was strictly required. He was aloof and dignified, and his presence was like a harsh, bone-chilling wind. When filth sprung from his lips, it sounded anything from enigmatic and profound to lovingly flirtatious.

These dirty words would inevitably end up sounding especially amorous to his lovers. Now that Wu Xingzi thought about it, he had heard such vulgarities from him many times before, each one more shameless than the last. How did he only realize it now?

Wu Xingzi's behavior lit a fire within Guan Shanjin. He couldn't resist leaning over and capturing his plump, pouty lips. The tip of his tongue dove straight in, sweeping past Wu Xingzi's sensitive gums, licking across every delicate surface within. He twirled around that soft little tongue, suckling and nibbling.

This kiss left Wu Xingzi breathless and giddy. His trembling body fell limp, allowing Guan Shanjin to have his way with him.

Guan Shanjin wanted to fulfill his desires right then and there, but he remembered there were still matters he had to attend to. He hadn't touched Wu Xingzi in half a month, and this kiss ignited his hunger. His cock was painfully hard as he ground it against Wu Xingzi's round, soft ass.

Wu Xingzi's lips were finally released. "You... You..." he panted. He tried to protect his trousers from prying hands, but his limbs were weak and his body still shivered. Guan Shanjin's scent wafted through the air, a mixture of white sandalwood, orange blossom, and the slight tang of iron. Wu Xingzi had almost forgotten that Guan Shanjin carried the smell of blood on him. He had been immersed in the battlefield for many years, and it etched itself into his bones long ago.

Perhaps their days in Qingcheng County had been too comfortable; the smell of blood had faded quite a bit. Now that he'd returned to his life in Horse-Face City as the feared general of the Southern Garrison, that sharp, bloody scent hung around him once more. He was like a mighty leopard licking the blood off his paws; he appeared idle on the surface, but his eyes were always alert. He could leap toward his prey at any moment.

Guan Shanjin easily divested Wu Xingzi of his trousers. With his outer robe still on, his pale legs peeked out from the fabric. Guan Shanjin undid his own trousers as well, freeing his thick, dripping member. It slapped against Wu Xingzi's plump buttocks, making the adviser cry out in shock.

Guan Shanjin nibbled on Wu Xingzi's sensitive earlobe. "Be good," he murmured. "I won't go inside."

Wu Xingzi was rather thin, but the fleshy parts of him still had some heft. As Guan Shanjin caressed his slender legs, they felt smooth and sleek. His thighs were especially soft to touch and knead.

His perky, plump buttocks were even more sumptuous. They seemed to have grown bigger from all the squeezing and kneading Guan Shanjin had done in their arduous lovemaking. Guan Shanjin's colossal cock became trapped between those buttocks, growing harder with every movement. The more he slid between Wu Xingzi's buttocks, the slicker the passage became. He tightened his embrace, his actions gradually growing rougher.

The fat head of his cock was already wet, smearing across Wu Xingzi's ass. Occasionally, it would press against his hole, the pressure making Wu Xingzi hyperventilate. His hips squirmed uncontrollably, and it was unclear if he was trying to evade the general's cock or seek out its touch.

"Stay still," Guan Shanjin said. After repeatedly glancing past the hidden entrance without entering, Guan Shanjin's forehead was covered in sweat from the effort of holding himself back. The veins in his temples visibly throbbed with the beat of his pulse.

Wu Xingzi panted heavily, moaning and mewling. Each cry lingered, every sound spilling slowly from his lips. His narrow waist twisted and thrashed; he couldn't have looked more wanton if he tried.

Unable to stop himself, Guan Shanjin gave those slicked buttocks two sound slaps. Wu Xingzi's ass cheeks, already pink from friction, looked absolutely obscene as Guan Shanjin's handprints appeared.

Guan Shanjin was at his wits' end, trying to resist thrusting his cock into Wu Xingzi's hole. The fluids glistening on his cock hadn't come entirely from him—a large amount dripped from the old fellow's slutty little hole, soaking Guan Shanjin's trousers.

"Come on... Harder," Wu Xingzi urged. Despite his shy personality, Wu Xingzi always let loose in bed. He sounded tearful, whining as he spurred Guan Shanjin on. The teasing friction heated his body, warming him through.

Wu Xingzi felt an incredible emptiness within him. Impatiently, he tried to grind himself against the thick, burning cock beneath, but the general gripped his waist so tightly that he could not move. Guan Shanjin took his sweet time, thrusting unhurriedly against his thighs and buttocks. He brushed along Wu Xingzi's sensitive perineum a few times, fanning the flames of his desire; Wu Xingzi's body fell limp at the sensation, unable to think straight.

"My dirty boy..." Guan Shanjin sucked on Wu Xingzi's earlobe and smacked his ass again, the pale flesh rippling upon impact. "Clamp your thighs together and let me fuck them."

Lust burned within him, his cock painfully hard—he desperately wanted to hold the man down and fuck him senseless. However, General Guan promised he would not fuck his hole, and he was true to his word. He had official duties to attend to, so he did not have the time to slow down and play with this naughty quail. He could only choose the next best thing, which was to fuck Wu Xingzi's thighs to relieve his aching desire.

Wu Xingzi obediently clamped his thighs shut. The tender skin on his inner thighs was extremely sensitive. His legs trembled slightly with the fear of being burned by that huge, hot cock.

And it really was huge. Just the part of it sticking out from between Wu Xingzi's thigh seemed nearly as long as Wu Xingzi's own little dick. Guan Shanjin's shaft jabbed away, jostling Wu Xingzi's half-hard cock and making him lose his balance. Swaying with the general's thrusts, Wu Xingzi whimpered. With tearful eyes, he looked down at his little pink prick turning red from the friction. It twitched and jerked as pre-cum drooled from its tip.

"Ahh... Gentler, be gentler..." Wu Xingzi begged, unable to bear the sensation. His inner thighs burned with pain and his little cock tingled with pleasure. Gripping Wu Xingzi's waist, Guan Shanjin held him firmly on top of his lap. Every bristly strand of the general's pubic hair rasped against Wu Xingzi's sensitive taint, and the pleasure was almost as good as the feeling of his hole getting fucked.

"Hmm? Weren't you the one who wanted me to move?" Guan Shanjin teased. He was in ecstasy between Wu Xingzi's slick thighs. It couldn't match properly fucking into him, but it was still delightful.

Guan Shanjin's gentle and sentimental tone swept past Wu Xingzi's ear along with his warm breath. "Ahh..." Wu Xingzi exclaimed, his shoulders lifting a little. "I was wrong... It hurts... N-not so hard," he begged.

Guan Shanjin's hard cock suddenly prodded Wu Xingzi's balls. Wu Xingzi cried out, shuddering violently as he suddenly orgasmed. Shots of white cum landed on his belly, followed by small droplets that dribbled out from the tip of his cock. The man behind him gasped before reaching out to caress the tender head of Wu Xingzi's prick, stroking it with his calloused fingers.

Pleasure lanced into Wu Xingzi's heart and mind. His mouth gaped open as he raised his chin. No sound left his lips as his perineum was harshly jabbed. With a twitch of his hips, he came again, thin streams of cum spurting from his cock to landing in Guan Shanjin's palm. The general spread the fluid over Wu Xingzi's softened dick, and gripped it along with his own hard member, rubbing them together. Wu Xingzi cried for mercy, with nowhere to run.

"Hold on a little longer. I'm not there yet." Guan Shanjin bent his neck, kissing Wu Xingzi's sweaty cheek. He was breathing hard, filthy words falling from his mouth like rain. He could no longer keep a casual pace. Letting go of their cocks, he grasped Wu Xingzi's waist and fucked into his thighs with abandon.

Wu Xingzi panted and cried out. It felt like the skin of his inner thighs was about to be rubbed raw. Although it was slick from their combined fluids, there was still not enough lubrication. His little cock and his taint were sore from the friction, and he couldn't get hard anymore. As the general's shaft ground against him wantonly, Wu Xingzi could no longer tell if he felt pleasure or pain.

"J-Just put it inside me... Ahh!" Wu Xingzi begged, sniffing pitifully. Guan Shanjin slapped his ass again. What was the point of Guan Shanjin grinding against him? He would much rather be fucked!

Having never felt this kind of painful sensation when having sex with Guan Shanjin, Wu Xingzi tried to twist his hips away from the general, only to be trapped, unable to free himself. Whenever his thighs fell apart slightly, Guan Shanjin would thrust between his buttocks instead. Wu Xingzi could only cry and plead for mercy as he felt both pleasure and agony.

While Wu Xingzi was trapped between dueling sensations, Guan Shanjin enjoyed himself greatly. The smooth thighs brought him great pleasure, forming a perfect sheath for his cock. The sight of Wu Xingzi's soft little prick was adorable as it flopped about.

Eyes red from pleasure, Guan Shanjin lifted Wu Xingzi up and turned him around, hooking his legs around his waist. His heated cock dragged between Wu Xingzi's swollen, fleshy buttocks.

"Does it hurt?" Guan Shanjin asked, gently caressing Wu Xingzi's inner thigh. He slid his hand toward the reddened patch of skin. It felt scorching hot, and Wu Xingzi let out a low cry when he touched him there, his hips shifting to avoid his touch.

But Guan Shanjin didn't allow him to escape. He caught hold of Wu Xingzi with one hand as he used the other to stroke his heated thigh with more force.

"Ahh!" Wu Xingzi cried, twitching. "I-It h-hurts," he stuttered.

"Be good." Guan Shanjin's eyes curved as he smiled at Wu Xingzi, consoling him with a peck to the tip of his nose. He then moved down to press kisses on his lips before tugging Wu Xingzi into his arms. "Look, pengornises aren't that special. They don't dote on you like I do."

Huh? Wu Xingzi blinked. Two single tears rolled down his cheeks, only for them to be licked away by Guan Shanjin. Guan Shanjin then slid his tongue between Wu Xingzi's lips, swirling about in his mouth. Wu Xingzi's body fell limp from the kiss. He was unable to catch his breath, his mind melting into a puddle.

Guan Shanjin seemed to have let go of some of his anger. His smile bloomed like a flower as he caressed the man in his arms.

His cock, still hard, pressed against Wu Xingzi's buttocks, grinding slowly. It nudged its way slightly into Wu Xingzi's hole but did not fully enter. After repeating this several times, Wu Xingzi's thighs no longer hurt like before, and his desire began to build again.

Wet sounds echoed in the room as their tongues twined together. Guan Shanjin could no longer hold himself back. Grabbing onto the old man's narrow waist, he decided to drive straight in. If anything came up, Man Yue could handle it. It was all right for him to indulge himself occasionally.

But just as Guan Shanjin was about to thrust all the way in, Hei-er's voice came from outside Shuanghe Manor.

"General! The third daughter of the Yue family is asking to see you!"

Guan Shanjin paused. The flames of desire within him abated abruptly. Although his cock could not fully soften so suddenly, he had lost his interest in continuing; it was rather awkward.

"Hmm?" Wu Xingzi was still in a daze. He absentmindedly nudged his buttocks back toward Guan Shanjin, who patted them in consolation.

"There's something I need to attend to. I have to go. You..." Guan Shanjin helped pull Wu Xingzi's trousers up, returning him to his stool. He then straightened himself out, becoming the Great Southern Garrison General in the blink of an eye. If not for that erotic red gleam in his eyes, he would have seemed as cold as ice.

"You..." Wu Xingzi had yet to regain his wits. Blankly, he stared at Guan Shanjin. The man in front of him could neither be described as a stranger nor a close friend, but Wu Xingzi could vaguely see annoyance and loathing in those charming eyes of his. The fire within Wu Xingzi slowly died down as well, and he sat awkwardly on his seat, not knowing where to put his limbs.

"Hmm?" Bending down and placing a gentle kiss on Wu Xingzi's mouth, Guan Shanjin stroked his earlobe. "Let's have dinner together tonight."

"Sure, I'll have the girls prepare a few dishes." Wu Xingzi nodded, gently pushing him away. "Don't let that young lady wait."

Wu Xingzi remembered who the third daughter of the Yue family was. Wasn't she Mr. Lu's fiancée? No wonder Guan Shanjin had lost all interest. Wu Xingzi began to feel somewhat sad without being able to explain why. He rubbed his chest as he watched

Guan Shanjin leave. He was sure he'd felt this way before, but he couldn't remember what the feeling was, exactly...

"Mr. Wu?" Mint quietly approached him, softly calling out. "Shall I prepare some hot water for you to clean up?"

"Ah, sure." Wu Xingzi smiled and nodded at her. He could see the worry in the girl's eyes, but he didn't know how to reassure her.

After all, he didn't know what he was feeling, either.

CHAPTER 4

THE TASTE OF A HEART STIRRING

Rancui's impression of Wu Xingzi was that he was gentle and soft, but he would never easily give up his heart. When someone who guarded his heart so carefully gave it away, there was nothing that could make him take it back; he would fall deeply and quickly.

When Wu Xingzi realized that he had truly fallen for Guan Shanjin, would that fickle general still continue to dote on him?

Ah, Rancui's stomach really hurt...

T HE THIRD DAUGHTER of the Yue family was named Yue Mingzhu. Enchanting and adorable, she was as pretty as a peony in full bloom. She had bright eyes and white teeth, her skin was creamy and smooth, and her eyebrows were thick and arched. She exuded a strength of spirit that was common among the girls of Horse-Face City.

Yue Mingzhu was eighteen this year, and by usual standards, she should already be a mother to a few children by now. However, she had always been the apple of her father's eye and the youngest child at home. Having one more mouth to feed was no burden on her family, so her father was delighted to keep her at home to dote on her. Her father felt no need to discuss marriage until an appropriate man appeared in her life—one with a background that matched the family's, who knew how to spoil Yue Mingzhu, and for whom she held great affection. As a matter of course, Mr. Lu was a good candidate.

Although he was a little old for her, his clean, fair, and heavenly appearance made him a great match. His disposition, too, was refined and cultured; toward Yue Mingzhu, he was both loving and respectful. The two of them looked good together. Old Master Yue was very satisfied with the prospect.

And of course, what was most important was that Yue Mingzhu liked Mr. Lu a great deal. When she first saw him in the Mingjing Temple, she immediately fell in love.

There were two large temples in Horse-Face City, each situated atop a hill. One was in the south of the city, the other in the north. Perhaps due to the many years of war at the border, many residents in Horse-Face City were in the habit of praying to Buddha. People would flock to the temples to pray, especially during New Year and other festivals.

It was during the Spring Lantern Festival a year ago that Yue Mingzhu caught sight of Mr. Lu as she said her prayers.

Buddhist temples were sacred and tranquil places; however, due to the celebratory occasion, a few lanterns with scriptures inscribed on them were hung up in the temple. Plain, simple brushstrokes vividly displayed each character within the verse. Mr. Lu happened to be standing beneath one of the lanterns, gazing up at it.

Yue Mingzhu's first thought was that this man was too frail. He was dressed in white, accentuating his slight figure. Despite that, his posture was very straight, and Yue Mingzhu thought he looked as beautiful as a jade statue. After observing him closely, she could no longer drag her eyes away. Until now she hadn't believed someone like this could exist: a man who truly transcended the material world, glowing like moonlight in the sky.

Mr. Lu was half-turned away from her, so she could only see his profile. The outline of his face was so gentle, it looked as if it was carved by water. His facial features were perfectly placed—if anything about him changed, he would look imbalanced. His crystal-black eyes were especially striking; they were so serene, one could almost drown in them.

Yue Mingzhu's wits flew out of the window. Unable to bring herself to care how she was embarrassing herself, she stood there foolishly in the corridor, staring impolitely at this man. At last her burning gaze startled Mr. Lu, and he looked around in uncertainty before darting a cautious glance back at her.

Most girls would feel sheepish if caught staring like this, but Yue Mingzhu didn't. She walked straight ahead, and her two maidservants were helpless to stop her. They could only tag along, trailing behind her until she stopped in front of the man.

"I am the third daughter of the Yue family, and my name is Mingzhu," she said.

One of Yue Mingzhu's maidservants, Changyi, widened her eyes. Her face paled and she nearly keeled over in shock. Her mistress was still but a girl! Although interactions between men and women were not forbidden in Horse-Face City, a maiden simply didn't go around telling strange men her name!

Mr. Lu looked rather awkward. He cupped his hands together in greeting, quietly taking a half step back. "Miss Yue..."

Who would have expected that the young lady would take a half step closer? She stared at him with beautiful eyes sparkling like the night sky, and said, "May I ask for your name?"

"Ah..." Mr. Lu retreated half a step more, but Miss Yue kept approaching. He had no choice but to turn his head away to avoid arousing any suspicion. "My family name is Lu," he replied gently. "Miss Yue is much too polite."

"Lu-gongzi," Miss Yue said with a nod, her smile blooming like a flower. "Do you have a wife?"

Mr. Lu glanced swiftly at Miss Yue. He was momentarily stunned into silence. "Um…"

"You have the bearing of an immortal, Lu-gongzi. It would not be strange if you were already married," Miss Yue said. She misunderstood his astonishment as him having difficulty in responding. "I am eighteen this year. Although I'm a little old, I fell in love with you at first sight, Lu-gongzi. I wish only to be able to stay by your side. I want to be close to you, even if I am merely your concubine."

"Miss!" Changyi couldn't keep her exclamation contained; she almost wanted to keel over right there. What exactly had she just heard? Did her mistress *really* want to get married so badly?

"Uh… Since you are not betrothed, young lady, these words directed at a strange man may harm your reputation. I wish for you to conduct yourself with dignity, Miss Yue." Mr. Lu finally came back to his senses; he realized that the pretty girl in front of him was declaring affection for him. A blush of embarrassment suffused his pale cheeks, and his exquisite brows knitted together sternly. Cupping his hands together in farewell, he was about to leave with a flourish of his sleeves.

However, Miss Yue was willful and proud. Girls in Horse-Face City were very candid and unreserved to the point of being unbridled. Now that she'd finally found a man who'd moved her heart, how could she let this person go so easily? Without even thinking about it, she reached out and grabbed Mr. Lu's sleeve. However, in her haste, she exerted a little too much strength, tearing the sleeve of Mr. Lu's outer robe.

Now both of them were frozen in embarrassment. Miss Yue finally realized that she had been too rash, and a blush flooded her pretty face. Mortified, she hung her head down low and stammered an apology. "L-Lu-gongzi, I've been rude. Please, Lu-gongzi, don't take offense. Why don't you come to my residence so I may express my sincere apologies?"

Mr. Lu blushed a discomfited red. He looked at his torn sleeve, which was still trapped in the young girl's hand.

After a long moment, he replied in a low voice, "I suppose I will have to trouble you."

Yue Mingzhu smiled brightly. Attentively, she welcomed Mr. Lu to her home, even diligently mending his sleeve for him. Through her father, she learned that Mr. Lu was teacher to the Great General of the Southern Garrison. She also learned that, according to the private consensus of many people, he was the general's beloved.

But Miss Yue didn't care about the general. If Mr. Lu had any feelings toward him, how could he still be single after all this time? She was convinced that the general was holding Mr. Lu captive, and this was the reason he'd remained unsullied by romantic entanglements all these years.

She would be the girl who rescued Mr. Lu from his prison.

Her decision made, the third daughter of the Yue family began to pursue Mr. Lu in earnest.

Over the next six months, with the support of her father and brothers—as well as Mr. Lu acquiescing, despite putting on a show of reluctance—the relationship between Miss Yue and Mr. Lu progressed rapidly. Not too long after autumn began, they promised themselves to each other forever.

However, once the general found out about this, Yue Mingzhu suddenly discovered it was now very difficult to meet with Mr. Lu.

She was unable to catch even a glimpse of her betrothed, especially after Mr. Lu was hurt in a fall from his horse. She and Mr. Lu were to marry once spring arrived, but she was unable to nurse her intended through his injuries and was barred from entering the general's estate! How could Yue Mingzhu take this lying down?

However, her father asked her to be patient. Although the Yue family was the most aristocratic in Horse-Face City, their influence was minuscule compared to that of the lauded Great General of the Southern Garrison.

Yue Mingzhu was filled with fury, her entire body in pain: chest, stomach, and everywhere else. Lacking in both sleep and appetite, her entire being became frail. Seeing her like this made Old Master Yue incredibly anxious. Disregarding his dignity, he went to the general's estate to plead for a meeting with him, hoping General Guan would permit his daughter to see Mr. Lu and alleviate her heartsickness.

Three times he went to the door of the general's estate, and three times he was spitefully rejected under a veneer of politeness. Old Master Yue seemed to age several years in just a short time. However, when it was close to the new year, it appeared the general finally took pity on Old Master Yue and his daughter. They were allowed to see Mr. Lu, and Miss Yue could even bring him back to their residence to recuperate.

Unfortunately, those good days didn't last. Not too long after New Year festivities had ended, Vice General Man sent his men over to bring Mr. Lu back home. The reason given was hard to refute—custom dictated that it was bad luck for a betrothed couple to see each other before their wedding. Would it not be worse to be seeing each other every day, living in the same residence? The general did not want Mr. Lu and Miss Yue's future to be blighted in such a manner, so it would be best if they stopped seeing each other before the wedding. It was better to heed such superstitions than to accidentally bring about misfortune, wasn't it?

It made sense. Old Master Yue cared for his daughter. Naturally, he wasn't willing to break such a taboo. He allowed Man Yue's people to bring Mr. Lu home.

However, this made Miss Yue quite unhappy. In her eyes, the general was deliberately keeping her apart from Mr. Lu. The general was up to no good! She was convinced that Guan Shanjin had feelings for Mr. Lu, but that he just didn't want to tear down the veil of pretense between the two of them. As Mr. Lu's betrothed, she could not leave her fiancé in such a dangerous place!

Thus, Yue Mingzhu kicked up a huge fuss every day, from the moment she opened her eyes each morning to the moment she fell asleep at night. It troubled Old Master Yue, so he made his eldest son take Yue Mingzhu to the general's estate. Whether or not Mr. Lu moved into the Yue residence was Guan Shanjin's decision. However, if the general could say just a few words to appease Miss Yue, that would be enough.

If someone asked Vice General Man to describe this situation, he'd say Yue Mingzhu was knocking on Guan Shanjin's door to collect her man.

These days, the vice general couldn't be more annoyed. Besides his official duties, he still had to help Guan Shanjin make arrangements for Mr. Lu's wedding, and every little detail had to be approved by him first. When Guan Shanjin still had feelings for Mr. Lu, these trifling things would be handled by the general himself. Now that Advisor Wu occupied the general's heart, most of the decisions now fell to Man Yue. Man Yue wanted nothing more than to curse and swear his heart out!

What did Mr. Lu have to do with him? They were two completely unrelated individuals! This marriage should have been left to the Yue family to deal with, and the general could simply provide some assistance as needed. However, Guan Shanjin's feelings for Mr. Lu were still rather profound, and he'd chosen to take over many of the decisions...

Damn it! If the general wants to be involved so badly, he should be the one making the plans!

Man Yue silently rebuked Guan Shanjin over and over again, but not a trace of it could be detected on his face. He welcomed the eldest young master and the third young miss of the Yue family with a warm smile, inviting them to take a seat.

Yue Mingzhu snorted. "In no way am I distinguished enough to drink the general's tea! I just want to ask Vice General Man where my husband is!" she exclaimed angrily. With a proud, unbending neck, she cast a sideways glance at Man Yue. Not only did she refuse the vice general's invitation to sit down, her expression was unpleasant as well. If not for her brother calming her down, she might have started spouting a litany of curses.

"He's currently in the Wang Shu Residence," Man Yue answered swiftly.

Yue Mingzhu froze, momentarily unable to respond.

"If you'd like to see Mr. Lu, I'll have someone bring him here. Miss Yue doesn't have to be so aggressive," Man Yue said, not bothering to feign courtesy. This third daughter of the Yue family had come to the general's estate to pitch a fit one too many times, and he no longer had the patience to deal with her tantrums.

"What are you saying?!" Yue Mingzhu's entire face was flushed red, enraged. With her hands on her hips, she started to unleash her wrath, only to be held back by her brother and pushed down into a chair. He then shoved a cup of tea into her hands.

"Brother!" Miss Yue protested loudly.

"That's enough," Young Master Yue chastised her, his brows deeply creased. "Vice General Man is only sparing the time to see us thanks to Mr. Lu. You ought to mind your tongue!" His spoiled little sister was giving him a massive headache.

"Exactly, Miss Yue's face itself isn't enough to draw me here." Man Yue still smiled pleasantly, but his tongue dripped with acid. Young Master Yue found himself laughing awkwardly at the vice general's remark.

Yue Mingzhu clearly did not have her brother's patience. She leaped up in anger, pointing at Man Yue. "Who the hell do you think you are?!" she shouted. "In Horse-Face City, the Yue family is the highest above all. Without the support of the Yue family, would your Great General of the Southern Garrison be able to maintain such a steady foothold in this city? Hounds are killed for food once they've caught all the hares—no wonder you're the size you are!"

Man Yue skimmed the thin layer of scum off the top of his tea. Hearing Miss Yue's words, he burst out laughing, looking straight at her, interest piqued. "I never knew that the General of the Southern Garrison needed the Yue family's support! Six years ago, you were already around thirteen years old, yes? Do you still remember the Battle of Fuyang?"

Once the Battle of Fuyang was mentioned, Miss Yue's expression changed. Her stiff neck and arrogant demeanor were the same as ever, but she was no longer as belligerent as before; she shrank back a little in her seat.

"It seems you do." Man Yue took a sip of his tea, clicking his tongue. "Miss Yue, there are things that shouldn't be said, so you need to know when to shut your mouth. The general's estate is not the Yue family home. We don't cater to your whims here, understand?"

Man Yue's words were light and casual, but embarrassment crept its way across Young Master Yue's face. He glared reproachfully at his sister before standing up and cupping his hands toward Man Yue in apology.

Even now, the memory of the Battle of Fuyang was fresh in the minds of Horse-Face City's citizens. It was the most heroic battle the Great General of the Southern Garrison had led against Nanman. Nanman had the custom of massacring all remaining citizens within a conquered city, and if General Guan had not managed to hold Nanman back then, Horse-Face City would have met an ugly fate.

Horse-Face City had not always been the last city before the border; there was once a Centipede City. About thirty years ago, Centipede City had fallen to Nanman, and barely anyone was left alive. The entire city was set ablaze, the flames soaring into the skies— the fires took seven days and seven nights to subside. If not for Guan Shanjin's army fiercely fighting against Nanman, Horse-Face City would have followed in Centipede City's ill-fated footsteps.

Miss Yue's words today made the Yue family seem like ungrateful wretches.

"You don't have to stand on ceremony, Young Master Yue. I'm not going to argue with a little girl." Man Yue waved him off before continuing with a smile. "I've already sent someone to invite Mr. Lu over. He should be arriving soon; just wait a little longer. Have some tea and snacks. Let it not be said that I don't know how to treat my guests."

"Vice General Man is much too polite," Young Master Yue said, shooting his sister a glare warning her not to further aggravate the situation. Only after he saw Yue Mingzhu give a reluctant nod in assent did he exhale in relief and sip his tea. The truth was, he shouldn't have let his guard down so early.

Man Yue was not just going through the motions. He really did send someone to fetch Mr. Lu. After a few moments of waiting, Mr. Lu entered, his steps slow.

He was dressed in his usual white attire, but looked a little haggard. As he cupped his hands together, it was obvious that he was hiding his right hand; it was impossible to turn a blind eye to it.

Yue Mingzhu was the first to act. Flying straight to Mr. Lu, she pulled his right hand out from his sleeve. Her displeasure toward Guan Shanjin—and her conviction that he would do something awful to Mr. Lu before the wedding—were the reasons she was so insistent on taking Mr. Lu away with her.

Mr. Lu's hand was wrapped in clean white bandages all the way up to his wrist. It seemed like he'd been injured, and his complexion was paler than normal. He hurriedly pulled his sleeve back down to hide his injury, and Yue Mingzhu's heart fiercely ached. With great distress, she asked, "What's the matter? Are you badly injured? How did this happen?"

"It's nothing, don't worry." Mr. Lu smiled somewhat sadly as he comforted her in a gentle voice. "I was careless and ended up burning myself. It has nothing to do with Haiwang, so don't let your imagination run away with you."

Hmm? Man Yue's eyebrow quirked up as he sneered internally. Mr. Lu's words sounded quite sincere, and they were technically true. However, saying them in such a way, in this exact moment, would certainly cause one to...speculate.

Just as the vice general expected, Yue Mingzhu exploded at Mr. Lu's words. Tears of anger welled up in her eyes. Ignoring the pleas of her brother and her fiancé, she pointed at Man Yue. "Bring me Guan Shanjin!" she roared.

If the third young miss of the Yue family wanted to see the general, Man Yue had no reason to stop her. He turned his head, instructing Hei-er to go to Shuanghe Manor and invite the general over. He made a point to tell Hei-er that at all costs, he mustn't enter that residence—it would be enough to call the general from outside.

Although Hei-er did not understand why, he had always listened to Man Yue. He did not take a single step inside.

As Guan Shanjin exited the residence, his expression was dark, as though a storm was brewing beneath. "Miss Yue wants to see me?" he asked.

"Yes," Hei-er said, bowing his head. As one of the general's personal bodyguards, he knew how to read the expression on his master's face. Silently, he thanked his lucky stars. Interrupting Guan Shanjin's "personal matters" was not a problem, but if Hei-er were to accidentally catch even a glimpse of Adviser Wu's naked body, he would be in for a serious beating. When he thought about how Guan Shanjin had disciplined him before, Hei-er couldn't suppress a shudder.

"Where's Mr. Lu?" Guan Shanjin asked, dusting off his clothes. It seemed he had no intention of meeting that self-important little girl.

"He's in the front hall."

Guan Shanjin snorted. The Yue child must have seen the injury on Mr. Lu's hand and wanted an explanation from him. Guan Shanjin was fed up. He turned back and glanced at Shuanghe Manor; only upon seeing the indistinct shadow moving around inside the house did his expression brighten.

The Yue family still had some use to them, and he had no plans to replace them with a new family. If not for that and the impending marriage between Mr. Lu and Miss Yue, Guan Shanjin would have acted already… However, since there was still someone eagerly rushing toward their death, he might as well fulfill that wish.

"Stay here and watch over Wu Xingzi," the general said. Although he didn't like Hei-er and Wu Xingzi being too friendly, he was unwilling to leave Wu Xingzi unprotected.

The Yue family had been getting increasingly involved with forces in the capital. General Guan and Vice General Man had already laid a trap for them. The family could not be given any opportunity to stir up trouble, lest they spoil his plans.

"Yes." Hei-er accepted the general's command and hid himself in a flash.

Annoyance shot through Guan Shanjin, and all the gloom inside of him shifted toward Miss Yue. His distaste toward this impudent and arrogant young lady increased even further.

Entering the hall to see Miss Yue twined affectionately around Mr. Lu, Guan Shanjin sneered. He headed straight for the main seat in the hall. One of his servants handed him a teacup; he accepted it and took a sip.

Guan Shanjin's attitude made Miss Yue's chest burn with fury. She leaped out of her seat, pointed at the general, and immediately started cursing. "Guan Shanjin! Lu-gongzi is your teacher, so you should be treating me with the all the respect that your teacher's wife is due. Did everything you studied in the old scrolls get eaten by dogs?"

My teacher's wife? What a wife! Guan Shanjin thought with a snort, crushing the teacup in his hand to powder in an instant. Scalding hot tea splashed on the ground and his hand, leaving reddened patches on his fair, jade-like skin.

Mr. Lu let out a gasp, anxiously rushing forward to hold Guan Shanjin's hand. Before he could call out for a servant, Guan Shanjin stopped him with an unconcerned wave.

"Teacher, you don't need to worry. This is only a small injury," Guan Shanjin said. After all, he was not a pampered young master. In the blink of an eye, the red marks on his hand faded away without a trace.

Mr. Lu still looked worried. Pulling out his handkerchief, he carefully wiped away any droplets of tea that remained.

Standing to the side, Miss Yue's expression was quite entertaining. She glared harshly at Guan Shanjin, as if she wanted to pounce and bite him to death. She knew she was powerless, though, and she could only stand there, the rims of her eyes turning red in anger.

Man Yue watched this little show in delight. His control slipping for a moment, he laughed out loud.

Guan Shanjin cast his vice general a chiding glance. "Do you have a lot of free time right now?"

Unlike in the past, the general was in no hurry to placate Mr. Lu. Instead, he sat there haughtily. His demeanor was elegant and awe-inspiring, making Mr. Lu's attentiveness seem overly familiar. Mr. Lu's face paled as he realized his behavior was rather inappropriate for the situation. With knitted brows, he tucked the handkerchief into Guan Shanjin's hand, straightening up and preparing to retreat.

"Teacher," Guan Shanjin said.

"Hmm?"

Mr. Lu refused to look at him, instead looking down. The sun's rays shone through the window upon his gentle face, and he looked as exquisite as jade. His long eyelashes trembled lightly with every breath, hiding the shame and anger in his eyes.

Guan Shanjin sighed silently. He had never seen Mr. Lu show his distress so outwardly before. His approach—and his heart—softened a little. "Thank you, Teacher, for your concern."

"It's only what I ought to do," Mr. Lu said, glancing at him swiftly out of the corner of his eye. Although it was quick, Guan Shanjin was a skilled martial arts expert, and his vision was exceptional. He easily caught the cloud of dejection in Mr. Lu's eyes. He could not help but reach out and hold his hand, grasping it firmly within his palm.

Miss Yue saw that things were not quite right. How could she endure it? Striding forward, she intended to yank Guan Shanjin's hand away. Man Yue, receiving a look from Guan Shanjin, ordered two tall, strong maidservants to block her path. They all but physically subdued her.

"Guan Shanjin! What is the meaning of this?!" Yue Mingzhu cried, stamping her foot. The two maidservants seemed well trained in martial arts; they completely obstructed her from reaching Mr. Lu. No matter how she tried to force herself through, she was unable to move a single step forward.

"Yue Chonghua, I've already made myself very clear: it's inappropriate for the couple to see each other before the wedding," Guan Shanjin said. He completely disregarded Miss Yue, who was dancing about like a clown trying to get past those servants. With his alluring eyes, he watched the young master of the Yue family shift about uncomfortably in his seat.

"Yes, yes," said Young Master Yue. "We understand the general's intentions! It's all because of my father and me—I'm afraid we've spoiled my sister. General, for Mr. Lu's sake, please don't take her offensive behavior to heart." He earnestly cupped his hands together, his handsome face blushing red. However, beside him, his sister was still making a scene. His forehead dripped with cold sweat.

"Miss Yue is still young and ignorant; I can understand her lack of manners. However, no matter how immature she is, she shouldn't treat Mr. Lu's fortune like a game," General Guan explained. "Such a reckless teacher's wife is not one I can afford."

"Haiwang," Mr. Lu chided, his brows furrowing a little. He seemed to only just realize that he was acting too intimately with Guan Shanjin. He tried to free his hand of Guan Shanjin's grasp, only for it to be gripped even tighter. "Miss Yue is simply the straightforward type," Mr. Lu said. "As the Great General of the Southern Garrison, why let her anger you?"

"Straightforward?" Guan Shanjin barked out a doubtful laugh. He studied Mr. Lu calmly for a while before abruptly letting him go. "All right, I'll listen to you, Teacher. I won't be angry with your wife." Guan Shanjin waved at the two maidservants and they quickly withdrew, only for Miss Yue to shoot forward.

"Zhu-er!" Young Master Yue yelled in alarm, losing his composure. He could not believe his eyes. His sister had actually raised her hand, swinging it toward Guan Shanjin. Did she *want* to die?!

"Hmph!" Moving just his head, Guan Shanjin avoided Miss Yue's slap.

The force of her swing made her stumble and nearly fall. Fortunately, Mr. Lu reached out to support her, so she was saved from making a greater fool of herself.

Yue Mingzhu's face turned blood red; even her eyes turned crimson. Breaking all formalities and politeness, she roared, "Guan Shanjin, don't think that no one knows about your filthy intentions! Lu-gongzi has told me that he had no choice but to stay by your side

because he didn't want to hurt you! A teacher for a day, a father for
life. He cares so deeply for you, but you..."

"*No choice* but to stay by my side?" Guan Shanjin interrupted Yue
Mingzhu's complaints and looked at Mr. Lu, his expression cold and
unreadable. "Hmm?"

Mr. Lu took two unsteady steps back, his face ashen. His back,
however, was as straight as a pine tree. This strong yet fragile image
had once held the dearest place within Guan Shanjin's heart.

When Mr. Lu arrived at the protector general's residence years
ago, Guan Shanjin was only ten. He was so unruly that no one could
subdue him; he'd recently caused a famous scholar to quit in a fit of
rage. This elegant and shy Mr. Lu was not even enough for Guan
Shanjin to toy with.

Unexpectedly, in stark contrast with his appearance, Mr. Lu had
the naivety of a scholar. Every time he was humiliated and teased
by Guan Shanjin, he'd always end up looking utterly haggard, and
there were a few times he was truly angered. Unlike Guan Shanjin's
previous teachers, he neither fled for his life, nor strode away in fury.
He was extremely patient; the only thing he thought of was how to
get closer to Guan Shanjin.

Once, during a poetry competition, Guan Shanjin had caused
Mr. Lu to be outrageously embarrassed. Guan Shanjin no longer
recalled the specific details of that matter, only remembering that
Mr. Lu's placid face had paled, and he'd glared at him. In those eyes
was embarrassment, hurt, misery, and a faint hopelessness.

However, Guan Shanjin didn't care. Ever since he was a child, his
feelings had always been fickle, and he was loyal to no one. The pain
and sorrow of others did not move him; it was as if nothing in this
world was his problem.

The concept of blood relatives did not come naturally to him. No child had to learn how to love their parents, but Guan Shanjin did. He'd known that that man was his father, and that woman was his mother, but it was only the kind of superficial knowledge that one could glean from words.

As a boy, he was already aware that he was different from other people. However, he was a clever and precocious child; before others could notice that something was wrong with him, he'd discovered how to hide his nature and act like a normal child.

With a bright smile, he watched as Mr. Lu awkwardly stood there at the poet's society. He was both surprised and excited by Mr. Lu's tenacity. He could not wait to test the limits of Mr. Lu's patience, to figure out what he had to do in order to rip the mask of fortitude from his teacher's face.

Guan Shanjin had stared at the man clad in white. Under the warm spring sun, his gauzy robes had looked woven from light, and his breathing seemed extraordinarily loud in the silence. His slender back was rigid, as if nothing could bend him. His resilience and strong will were surprising.

After the poetry session, Mr. Lu was quieter than usual. However, he still stayed by the boy's side, calmly discussing the ongoings of the session. Guan Shanjin listened, his ear starting to itch.

He suddenly spoke. "Sir, did you have fun during the session today?"

Mr. Lu fell abruptly silent. He shifted uneasily in his seat, facing the boy properly for a few moments before responding. "The spring weather was wonderful," he said. "There was excellent writing to be heard, and friends were plentiful."

Guan Shanjin burst into laughter. "Sir, you're the most shameless person I've ever met."

Mr. Lu's face lost all color. With knitted brows, he stared at the smiling Guan Shanjin. "A teacher for a day is a father for life," he said, his voice quavering slightly. "Since I've become your teacher, I'll stay by your side. If I'm shameless, then so be it."

Guan Shanjin understood that this was Mr. Lu mustering all of his courage and casting aside his dignity. He was miserable, yet very sincere. Guan Shanjin himself was heartless, but he noticed the feelings of others very well. He could tell whether or not a person was sincere, or if they intended to use him. No emotion could hide from his eyes.

No matter the reason for Mr. Lu gritting his teeth and tolerating Guan Shanjin's cruel words and actions, it still moved him. Would this sort of sincerity last forever? Would such a strong will ever snap? From then on, he no longer deliberately humiliated Mr. Lu; his image was carved indelibly in Guan Shanjin's heart.

Mr. Lu couldn't teach him much, as his talent wasn't particularly exceptional. Before two years had even passed, there was nothing more he could teach Guan Shanjin. From then on, Guan Shanjin was thrown into military training by his father.

Before he left, Mr. Lu came specially to see him. He gave him a sturdy, heavy bag with a few newly published collections of works and some snacks. It made Guan Shanjin laugh; all of these were useless on the battlefield. This was undeniably Mr. Lu: old-fashioned to the point of silliness. His attitude toward him had never changed.

Slowly, somehow, Guan Shanjin had come to treasure this person in his heart. It was a position that no one—other than his family and a few childhood friends—could occupy.

He treated Mr. Lu like he was something sacred, and he loved him deeply. He dared not defile him in the slightest. Despite loving him, Guan Shanjin never thought of keeping him exclusively for himself.

Whatever Mr. Lu wanted, he would give to him, only wishing that he could see this beautiful man smile. Guan Shanjin was willing to endure anything if it meant Mr. Lu could obtain his heart's desires— even if it was costly for him.

"Teacher," Guan Shanjin said. Seeing that Mr. Lu did not respond, the general could not be bothered to wait any further to hear Mr. Lu's reasons. "Since you think that way, Teacher, I won't hold you back any longer."

Guan Shanjin then gestured to Man Yue. "See our guests out."

"Understood." With a broad smile, Man Yue stood up and cere-moniously cupped his hands toward Young Master Yue. "Yue-gongzi, you heard it for yourself. It's not that I don't want you here, but the Yue family has made enough of a fuss in the general's estate today. Since Miss Yue wants Mr. Lu, then she may simply take Mr. Lu and leave! I'll get people to bring Mr. Lu's things over to your household. I hope that Mr. Lu and Miss Yue can live together to a ripe old age, hand in hand!"

"Haiwang..." Mr. Lu called out, his voice quiet yet hoarse.

It seemed Mr. Lu had not expected this treatment. In a blink of an eye, Man Yue was able to kick Mr. Lu out of the general's estate—right in front of the general himself. Guan Shanjin didn't even look at him.

"Hmm?"

"I don't..." Mr. Lu looked sorrowful. He seemed to want to ex-plain something, but Miss Yue grabbed his hand.

She huffed. "Since you said you'd let him go, General Guan, you'd better keep your promise! If Mr. Lu's heart softens toward you, don't come to the Yue family's estate to ask for him!"

Guan Shanjin waved his hand lazily, as though he was shooing away some kind of vermin. "Scram."

"Hmph!" Yue Mingzhu was so angry that her teeth hurt, but she did not dare cause any more trouble. Pulling Mr. Lu along, she sauntered off of the general's estate.

Young Master Yue was more restrained than his sister. He hadn't intended to take Mr. Lu with them today, and the swift progression of the matter caught him off guard. There were times when he wanted to intercede, but he did not know what he could say to avoid kicking the hornet's nest. In the end, he could only watch bitterly. After cupping his hands together in a farewell gesture, he left.

The room was finally quiet. Man Yue drank his tea with half-closed eyes. "Haiwang-gege," he jeered, "how could you bear to push Mr. Lu away? Don't tell me you believe what that Yue child said."

In truth, Man Yue did not believe that Mr. Lu had no choice but to stay. When Guan Shanjin was faced with Mr. Lu, it was like he was blinded by him; his brain became utterly useless. Whatever Mr. Lu wanted, he would give, spoiling him without a second thought. There were no words that could describe just how much Guan Shanjin doted on Mr. Lu. And although he did not like how Mr. Lu led Guan Shanjin along, Man Yue still believed that Mr. Lu had feelings for Guan Shanjin.

Guan Shanjin laughed lowly, pinching Man Yue's plump chin. "I don't believe the Yue child. Even if Mr. Lu did say such a thing to her, it was only to charm her. Mr. Lu has always been softhearted. I know this very well."

"Then why did you—"

"I've indulged Mr. Lu too much." Guan Shanjin lowered his lashes, elegantly skimming the film off the surface of his tea before sipping it. "He is my teacher, and he should understand what that means. Why did he invite Wu Xingzi for lunch this afternoon? How was his hand injured?"

"Huh?" Man Yue asked, then laughed out loud. Guan Shanjin really couldn't be any more biased.

"If the Great General of the Southern Garrison is no longer behind Mr. Lu, do you think Yue Dade will be able to tolerate that?" Guan Shanjin sneered.

In the past, Guan Shanjin was willing to cross any line for Mr. Lu. He loved him, and thus indulged him. But in the end, Mr. Lu was still only a commoner! After so many years, that foolish and honest youth from the past had finally changed. Guan Shanjin felt a little bitter.

Mr. Lu was not a man who was good at plotting and calculating. Guan Shanjin, on the other hand, was able to see to the heart of many things, as long as he thought about them carefully. He knew very well that it was not that Mr. Lu had no feelings for him; it was just that his feelings were like a beautiful treasure covered in dust— a sad, decaying sight.

"Do you still want to tie Mr. Lu to your side?" Man Yue pursed his lips, displeased.

"He's the one I treasure most dearly," Guan Shanjin said with a chuckle, his eyes crinkling. "In the future, I'll need him by my side." His tone was soft, but within it was a bone-chilling cold.

Man Yue frowned and shuddered, understanding what Guan Shanjin had in mind. Now, he actually pitied Mr. Lu a little.

Guan Shanjin truly was a fickle man with no sense of loyalty.

Things rapidly changed in the general's estate, and it caught everyone off guard.

The day after the general's beloved Mr. Lu was taken away by Miss Yue, Vice General Man directed servants to move all of Mr. Lu's belongings in the Wang Shu Residence to the Yue family's manor.

Next, the Wang Shu Residence was sealed. Of the ten people working there, about eight or nine of them were shuffled off to other estates. Everyone knew very well that the servants who were taken away had all broken the rules of the general's estate.

Under the management of Guan Shanjin and Man Yue, the rules of the general's estate were very strict. No information or news from the estate could be leaked to the outside; this was even more vigorously enforced when it came to the privacy of the various residences within.

However, for the past two years, there had been plenty of rumors outside the estate. No one knew who the source of these rumors was, but somehow, half the citizens of Horse-Face City knew that the general had feelings for Mr. Lu. Mr. Lu was not getting any younger, yet he was still unmarried. Most citizens believed that it was the general hindering him, trapping him in his estate for his own private use.

Despite all of the gossip, many people did not take the rumors seriously. After all, who was this Mr. Lu? Wasn't he betrothed to the third daughter of the Yue family? If the general had really locked him up, how could Miss Yue be involved?

Still, as the rumors spread, people would embellish the stories with all sorts of details from their own imaginations. Considering the general's estate hadn't done anything to stop the rumors for the past two years, they spread even more wildly and grew even more vivid.

The servants in the general's estate were aware of the rumors. It wasn't that the general did not care; he ignored the rumors for Mr. Lu's sake. If the servants had to name a culprit, everyone knew who the most likely candidate was. Mr. Lu was elegant and refined, and he was the recipient of the general's respect and concern. Naturally, there was no need for Mr. Lu himself to spread such rumors.

However, this was not the case for the people around Mr. Lu. If Mr. Lu was noble and kind, the servants of his residence were arrogant and proud. It was a mystery how Mr. Lu managed these people, especially Hua Shu. Hua Shu's nose always pointed up at the sky—he even refused to interact with other servants on the estate that he deemed to be below him. But toward the servants with a little more status, he would be respectful and deferential. Outside the estate, he had a wide circle of connections.

Apparently, on the same day Mr. Lu left, Hua Shu was fed a medicine that made him mute, and he was sold to a brothel. Everyone knew that the rumors had most likely been his doing.

Previously, Mr. Lu had been around to protect him. Now that Mr. Lu had somehow lost the general's favor, he was unable to shield Hua Shu from harm.

No matter how fiercely all the citizens of Horse-Face City secretly discussed the matter of Mr. Lu leaving, the servants living and working inside the general's estate could not. Despite having their own speculations, all the servants saw the example made in front of them. They were smart enough to keep their mouths shut.

Because of this silence from the servants, Wu Xingzi knew nothing about these matters. Mint and Osmanthus knew, but they did not dare tell their master. Besides, Wu Xingzi seemed to be troubled these days. The cucumbers had just been harvested, and he was already busying himself with planting tomatoes, chives, and bitter gourds. In one breath, half the courtyard of Shuanghe Manor had turned into a vegetable farm. They'd even begun to raise a few chickens on the other half. They'd surrounded part of the courtyard with a bamboo fence and placed three hens and a rooster within, allowing them to move around freely.

When he was not planting vegetables or raising chickens, Wu Xingzi would sit in the yard in a daze. Mint and Osmanthus tried cheering him up a few times, and Wu Xingzi did smile for them.

In the next moment, though, a crease would appear between his brows, and he would once again fall into a stupor.

The two girls were awfully worried, but they were unable to guess what was running through Wu Xingzi's head. It wasn't about missing the general... It had been couple of weeks since Mr. Lu left the estate, and the general practically lived in Shuanghe Manor now.

The sisters personally witnessed the general embracing Wu Xingzi several times as they conversed in the courtyard. Guan Shanjin smiled as he listened to Wu Xingzi talk about his bitter gourds, his tomatoes, and how the hens each laid an egg every day. One of the eggs was always double-yolked.

The two girls were quite young, but they could see how the general looked at Wu Xingzi. His gaze was gentle and soft, and his charming eyes were like glimmers of light, filled to the brim with joy.

The general always spent the night in Shuanghe Manor, accompanying Wu Xingzi at every meal. He would even occasionally step into the kitchen himself to prepare a few dishes. In the eyes of Mint and Osmanthus, the general had never been this caring toward another person, even when he'd doted on Mr. Lu the most.

All Guan Shanjin wanted to do was carry Wu Xingzi in the palm of his hand and cherish him. He was also very cautious, afraid that he would fall. Anyone observing this could not help but be moved.

Things in the general's estate had truly changed. All the servants knew that the general's beloved had long since changed from Mr. Lu to Wu Xingzi, the adviser of Qingcheng County.

One morning, Wu Xingzi groggily awoke, his lower back still aching from the night before. Guan Shanjin had fucked him relentlessly through half the night. Treating him like a pliable ball of dough, he'd folded him in half, coaxing him to lick at his own prick. *Is this even something a person can do?* Wu Xingzi had thought, abashed. However, in his folded position, he was completely unable to escape. He could only reluctantly lick the cock that stood erect in front of him.

The sight had set off a storm within Guan Shanjin. His eyes turned bloodshot as he thrust into Wu Xingzi harshly and continuously. Wu Xingzi was forced to take the leaking head of his own cock into his mouth as Guan Shanjin practically pierced right through him.

Wu Xingzi cried, begging for mercy. Guan Shanjin paid him no heed, fucking him until he reached orgasm. Wu Xingzi came into his own mouth, swallowing it all down without spilling a single drop. Guan Shanjin finally turned him over and pressed him down onto the bed, fucking him so hard that the bed nearly broke.

Wu Xingzi was barely in his right mind. Drool and tears smeared across his face, and his pink tongue hung limply from his mouth. Leaking fluids from both the front and behind, he reached the point where nothing else could come out of him. Only then did Guan Shanjin fill him up with his come; completely spent, Wu Xingzi fainted clean away.

Watching Wu Xingzi whimper and mewl on the bed, adoration swelled within Guan Shanjin. He pulled him into his arms and kissed him, then pressed his lips to his ear. "I'll be out of the estate for the next few days," he whispered. "If you're bored, you can go and explore the city. Those pengornis drawings of yours have already arrived—why don't you go collect them?"

In truth, the drawings had arrived nearly half a month ago. The Peng Society had sent someone to the general's estate to inform him. However, those illustrations were Guan Shanjin's mortal enemies—how could he allow Wu Xingzi to obtain them so easily? So of course he kept delaying and delaying. Since the general had to be away for the next few days and would not have to see those eyesores, it was a perfect time for Wu Xingzi to get his precious drawings back.

Wu Xingzi's eyes brightened. "Oh! They've arrived?" Instantly, his body was refreshed and alert; his back no longer ached, and his legs were no longer weak.

Guan Shanjin grew sullen seeing how delighted Wu Xingzi was. He bent down and nipped Wu Xingzi's cheek harshly, leaving a mark behind. It was painful enough for Wu Xingzi to let out a quiet yelp. Clasping a hand to his cheek, he turned to give Guan Shanjin a pitiful look.

"Aren't you going to ask where I'm going?" Guan Shanjin said. He pulled Wu Xingzi's hand away from his face, admiring the bite mark he'd left with great satisfaction. Although there was no blood, it was fairly deep; it would probably linger for most of the day.

"Where are you going?" Wu Xingzi figured Guan Shanjin might not reply even if he asked! Besides, Guan Shanjin was a fully grown man, and the Great General of the Southern Garrison. It wasn't possible for a man like him to get lost, right? Nanman had also been very docile as of late, and Horse-Face City barely looked like a city on the border of its enemy in war.

Wu Xingzi's expression openly revealed his thoughts. Guan Shanjin chuckled and patted Wu Xingzi's buttocks. "If you really want to know, it's not that I can't tell you—it's just that you'll need to pay a little price," he teased.

"I..." *...didn't want to know in the first place!* Fortunately, Wu Xingzi was still able to understand what Guan Shanjin wanted. Biting his lip, he decided to ask, even if he was unsure about it. "What price would I have to pay?"

Guan Shanjin laughed heartily, planting a firm kiss on Wu Xingzi's lips. "You don't have to do anything," he said. "I'll leave Hei-er behind for you. Bring him along when you leave the estate, all right?"

Huffing out a breath of relief, Wu Xingzi hurriedly nodded in agreement.

"Just sleep a little longer. I'll get Mint to make some porridge for you later," Guan Shanjin said. "As for the Horse-Face City branch of the Peng Society, you only need to ask Hei-er where it is. When you've collected the drawings, don't stay too long...and don't take this opportunity to bring home a new copy of *The Pengornisseur*." Guan Shanjin brought Wu Xingzi into a strong embrace before reluctantly putting him back into bed and tucking him in. Once all these things were done, the general turned and left the room.

Wu Xingzi watched until his view of Guan Shanjin's back was blocked by the door. He then curled up under his blanket, lightly rubbing his chest.

Over the past few days, his chest had felt suffocated. Wu Xingzi had secretly asked Mint to fetch the physician to come examine him, but no illness was found. Finally, the doctor said that it was mere melancholy. He wrote a prescription for a medicine that would settle his mind, asking him to drink it for two days.

Spring had come. Occasionally, Wu Xingzi would smell the scent of peach blossoms in the air. However, Mint and Osmanthus had told him that there were no peach trees in the general's estate, nor any in all of Horse-Face City. Their entire lives, Mint and Osmanthus had yet to see what a peach blossom even looked like!

Wu Xingzi could vaguely guess what was happening to him. *If this is not madness, then that means...* He sighed. He tossed and turned about on the bed, tired but unable to fall asleep. He felt lethargic, but he did not want to lie in bed.

He got out of bed and pulled on a coarse robe before walking out of the room.

He busied himself in his garden again, pulling weeds, tilling the soil, spreading fertilizer, and eradicating any pests. There were many insects in the south; Horse-Face City was home to all varieties of pesky bugs. Spring had only just arrived, and they'd all marched out in a parade of pests. Wu Xingzi and the two servant girls needed to spend quite a lot of time swatting bugs each day.

When Mint discovered him, Wu Xingzi had already cleared more than half the garden. He was currently taking a break to drink some tea.

"Master, why didn't you call me when you woke up?" Mint asked. In her hand was a steaming bowl of porridge. Wu Xingzi could smell the captivating fragrance even from a distance. He rubbed his belly, realizing that he was famished.

"There wasn't anything important, so I didn't want to disturb you or Osmanthus." Wu Xingzi was still not used to being waited on. His interactions with the two girls were more familial, even if the two girls he saw as nieces always called him Master or Mr. Wu.

"But my sister and I are meant to serve you! What's there to disturb? You must be hungry! Quick, hurry up and eat some porridge. Fill up your stomach." Mint strode forward and handed the bowl of porridge to Wu Xingzi, then picked up the rest of the gardening work.

Not long after, Osmanthus hurried over. When she saw Wu Xingzi, she heaved out a huge breath of relief, patting her chest.

"Master, why didn't you call me when you woke up?"

"Ah, next time, next time," Wu Xingzi said with a wry smile. He blew across the bowl of porridge to cool it down before digging in.

The porridge looked plain, but it had been cooked slowly with bone broth. The rice had turned so soft it had a thick, almost paste-like texture, melting at the slightest pressure of his tongue, but in the bowl, he could still see each individual grain. Fried garlic chives decorated the top. Salty and aromatic, the flavor was refreshing and nourishing for his body and cut through the slight greasiness that came from the bone broth. The taste was rich and perfect. Wu Xingzi finished the porridge in just a few gulps.

Osmanthus took the bowl from him. "I'll bring another bowl. The general specially prepared this porridge for you before he left. He instructed us to watch over the fire. Master, do you like it?"

No wonder it tasted so familiar. "It's great. My thanks to all of you," Wu Xingzi said. His heart was absolutely delighted. Guan Shanjin was skilled in the kitchen, and he never liked to cook anything too ostentatious. The dishes he made were simple but exquisite, and they always left Wu Xingzi wanting more.

Osmanthus ran nimbly back to the kitchen. Mint bent over to diligently swat pests and pull weeds. As Wu Xingzi observed the scene in front of him, he once again fell into a daze. Watching the cotton-like clouds in the sky, he only returned to consciousness when Osmanthus came back with a second bowl of porridge.

After finishing three bowls of porridge, Wu Xingzi realized that he shouldn't trouble the girls to run back and forth. He could have gone to the kitchen himself to get his porridge.

When his stomach was almost full, Hei-er appeared next to him out of nowhere. Hei-er followed him around quietly, even helping him sweep up the chicken coop.

Hei-er only spoke when all the garden chores were done. "Would you like to visit the Peng Society today, Mr. Wu?"

"Ah... Of course, of course." Thinking about the pengornis pictures that awaited him, Wu Xingzi's eyes curved as he smiled. He became more alert as well, shoving the melancholy emotions stirring within his heart deep down.

Mint and Osmanthus wanted to come with them to the city. At thirteen years old, they were in the most playful period of their lives, so Wu Xingzi didn't want to hinder them. However, he was worried the Peng Society wasn't exactly suitable for young girls to visit. Hei-er did say that the branch in Horse-Face City was disguised as a treasury, though, and that there were many interesting trinkets that could broaden the girls' horizons.

Having settled the matter, the four of them marched onward to the Peng Society.

When they stepped inside, a familiar voice drifted over. "Is that Adviser Wu?"

"Huh?" Wu Xingzi turned toward the voice. He was shocked to see a familiar salesman welcoming him with a bright smile.

"The manager has been awaiting Adviser Wu's arrival for many days! Please follow me." The salesman shot Hei-er a sideways look, his smile fading slightly. "I see Commander Hei is here as well. I hope that you will not be destroying our little shop again."

"The general hasn't made to do so, therefore I wouldn't dare." With hands lowered, Hei-er's tone was respectful. The salesman stifled a cough.

Mint and Osmanthus were already entranced by all the baubles and knickknacks displayed on the shelves. Tilting their little heads together, they whispered to each other as they examined some bright glass beads, their faces red with excitement.

Having confirmed that the two girls were enjoying themselves, Wu Xingzi followed the salesman to the courtyard.

Compared to the Peng Society's location in Goose City, the Horse-Face City branch was considerably larger, but less ornate. The pavilions all exuded an aura of simplicity, and the paths did not wind as much. Soon, the salesman led them to a bamboo pavilion.

A beautiful lady dressed in a set of light yellow palace robes sat within. She had a brush in her hand, but Wu Xingzi couldn't see what she was writing. Her long, slender fingers were breathtakingly beautiful, and the brush between them was a prominent, inky black. The contrast between the paleness of her fingers and the black of the brush was striking.

Seeing that it was a lady, Wu Xingzi's face immediately blushed a deep red. Standing outside the pavilion, he hesitated, not daring to step inside. Hei-er was much more direct, cupping his hands toward the person sitting inside the pavilion.

"Manager Rancui, we meet again."

Manager Rancui? Wu Xingzi was stunned. He hurriedly focused his eyes, and he recognized the familiar face of Manager Rancui. The only difference was that he seemed to be wearing cosmetics, making him look even more gorgeous and alluring. Hearing Hei-er speak, he looked up, his brows furrowing slightly, but when he noticed Wu Xingzi, he revealed a warm smile.

"Adviser Wu, it's been a while." Rancui straightened his back and bowed to him. His smile turned even brighter. "You came at a perfect time. Would you like to take a look at the latest copy of *The Pengornisseur*?"

"Ah, certainly!" Wu Xingzi responded, delighted. In an unguarded moment, he had absolutely forgotten Guan Shanjin's instructions.

Rancui waved his hand, signaling his employee to retrieve the book as well as the adviser's beloved phallic illustrations. He then invited Wu Xingzi to sit down and have some refreshments.

Only when half the plate was empty did Wu Xingzi remember something he wanted to ask. He looked at Rancui with a questioning gaze for a moment before asking, "Manager, why are you in Horse-Face City?"

"It's nothing. I just had the urge for a change of scenery." Rancui covered his smile with his hand, then nodded toward Hei-er, who stood outside the pavilion. "Adviser, aren't you annoyed by Commander Hei constantly following you?"

Wu Xingzi anxiously waved his hands. "What are you saying, Manager? I'm the one who is troubling Hei-er." He really didn't understand why Guan Shanjin had insisted that Hei-er follow him. Hei-er was a commander in the military; he surely had many duties to attend to, yet he still had to follow Wu Xingzi around. It must be irritating for him!

"Commander Hei, don't stand there like a statue. There's already so little sunshine, and you're blocking it," Rancui said. The more he looked at Hei-er, the more annoyed he felt. Despite how honest the olive-skinned commander looked, Rancui still remembered that when Guan Shanjin destroyed the Peng Society, Hei-er had rolled up his sleeves without a word of protest and gone to work trashing the place. Guan Shanjin was more verbal than physical, but Hei-er did not say a thing, speaking only with his actions.

Rancui's distaste for Guan Shanjin was based on his concern for the society's members. However, when it came to Hei-er, he simply did not like him. The bastard looked like a dog—it was only when he grinned that the wolf hidden within was revealed.

"My apologies for my discourtesy," Hei-er said with his head bowed. He meekly moved out of the way, acting very submissive. Rancui seethed internally, but he could not openly express his distaste. He could only give a bitter snort.

The salesman returned with the drawings then, so Rancui simply ignored Hei-er.

"Adviser Wu, take a look. All seven replies are here. Would you like to examine them here?"

"Ah, um..." Wu Xingzi blushed crimson. He stroked the seven letters, his action revealing a little of his yearning. However, he pulled his hand back as though he had been burned. "I-I'll look at them when I get back. I have full trust in how you deal with things, Manager," he said, shaking his head continuously.

Wu Xingzi really did want to look at them. After all, these were seven of his top ten favorite phalluses. Still, under bright daylight, with the ethereally beautiful Rancui in front of him, Wu Xingzi was too shy to pull out the illustrations.

"You flatter me, Adviser Wu." Rancui chuckled outwardly but sighed internally. He had tried so hard to protect Wu Xingzi, but he had failed to save him from the dastardly Guan Shanjin. How could he have the audacity to think that he had dealt with things well?

"Here is the newest edition of *The Pengornisseur*, Adviser. Please enjoy." Rancui nudged the new edition of *The Pengornisseur* forward; it had been printed just yesterday. It was monstrously thick, and Wu Xingzi's eyes bulged out at the sight of it.

"This is..." The previous issues he owned were only about a hundred pages each—this copy probably had three or four times as many pages! The book felt solid and weighty in his hands, and in one corner was a small inscription: *Great Xia*.

"Oh, this *Pengornisseur* is a special edition. We've selected the most handsome, talented members of the Peng Society throughout the entirety of Great Xia. The editions you owned previously only consisted of gentlemen from the south." Rancui flipped open the exquisite-looking book, introducing the people within. "The first fifty pages are citizens from the capital. Such a remarkable place produces remarkable men. There are many talents there, and people like General Guan are as numerous as cobblestones on the ground."

This was a bald-faced lie, but Rancui did not care.

Looking through the book, Wu Xingzi couldn't tear his eyes away.

After spending much time with Wu Xingzi, Rancui had come to understand the shy adviser's preferences. Wu Xingzi loved the beauties above all else, especially the elegant, refined men who looked cultured and scholarly. So, for this particular issue of *The Pengornisseur*, Rancui had selected the members who fit Wu Xingzi's tastes.

As expected, Wu Xingzi's face flushed as he carefully studied the pages. Everyone within this book was the best of the best, with both artistic and moral integrity. The most striking thing was that no one came from the aristocracy—at the most, they came from wealthy families, but they were not the ruling class.

"Oh, this gongzi is so young, yet he has already passed the provincial-level imperial examinations?" Wu Xingzi exclaimed.

"Ah, this gongzi's appearance is like an immortal, and he is very adept at the zither. If I have the opportunity, I would love to listen to him play," he continued.

"Wow, this gongzi is a physician! Recently, my chest has been feeling a little stifled. I wonder if he'd be able to tell me what's wrong." Wu Xingzi's eyes sparkled, looking like they held a galaxy of stars.

Rancui detected that something was not quite right. He eyed Hei-er, frustrated to see the bastard standing there like a statue, his head bowed and motionless, acting as though he was paying no attention to their conversation. However, Rancui knew very well that this scoundrel had sharp ears, and he was very loyal to the general. Rancui was certain that whatever they said would be conveyed to Guan Shanjin word for word.

Forget it, let him tell the general whatever he wants. As the manager of the Peng Society, why would Rancui be afraid of the Great General of the Southern Garrison? Rancui had the support of his boss *and* his boss's lover behind him!

With this in mind, Rancui poured another cup of tea for Wu Xingzi. "Adviser, have some more refreshments," he said, his voice carefully casual.

"Ah, thank you, thank you." As expected, Wu Xingzi was pulled away from *The Pengornisseur*. He rubbed his hands on his thighs before picking up a walnut pastry and placing it into his mouth.

"Adviser, I heard you say just now that your chest has felt stifled recently. Have you seen a physician?" Rancui asked as he sipped his tea.

"Uhh... Ahh... Yes, a physician did come..." Wu Xingzi could not help but sigh. Picking up another walnut pastry, he nibbled at it, wondering whether or not he should talk to Rancui about this.

"Adviser, there's no need to discuss it if you're not comfortable. Why don't you pick a gentleman who interests you and send him a letter to make friends?" Rancui signaled the salesman to bring out some writing materials.

Wu Xingzi shook his head in refusal. "No, there's no need. Don't trouble yourself. I've already promised Haiwang not to make friends through the pigeon post again. If he discovered I'd started writing to other men, he'd burn all my pengornis drawings." Even though it was something that had happened a while ago now, just thinking about how Guan Shanjin's hands had torn his pengornis pictures to shreds made Wu Xingzi's heart tremble in fright.

"Oh?" Rancui pursed his lips.

"However, it's hard to say when he'll end this tryst of ours. When that time comes, I'll once again be able to make friends through the pigeon post."

Rancui noticed that this sentence elicited a reaction from Hei-er—he seemed to have quickly glanced up at Wu Xingzi. However, the action was too fast to catch, and before Rancui could confirm anything, Hei-er had returned to his motionless state.

Rancui clicked his tongue. Although he was glad that Wu Xingzi had not fallen for Guan Shanjin's cosseting, he felt that something was off about this entire situation. Curious, he asked, "Have you considered that the general might want to spend the rest of his life with you?"

"The rest of his life with me?" Wu Xingzi blinked, then laughed aloud. "Manager, you're thinking too highly of me. I'm very aware that Haiwang prefers noble and unsullied men like Mr. Lu. I'm ugly and old, I don't have any skills, and I eat too much. When it comes to scholarly matters, I barely passed my examinations—what would Haiwang even like about me?"

For some reason, Wu Xingzi recalled a perfume sachet. He'd nearly forgotten about it. He'd once kept it right next to his skin and taken care of it meticulously. One day, he'd finally snapped out of it, taking the sachet out and hanging it on his belt. After using it for three or four more years, it wore out, so he simply tossed it and replaced it with a new one. He had no particular sense of nostalgia toward it.

What scent had that perfume sachet held? Wu Xingzi could no longer remember. However, that sachet made him think of luxuriant peach blossoms.

He shook his head, smiling sadly at Rancui. "Manager, there's nothing special about me—other than that I know myself very well."

Adviser Wu's words sounded bitter, and Rancui didn't know how to respond. He could only chuckle along and drink his tea.

Wu Xingzi had long since learned to be content with his situation. In no time at all, he recovered from his melancholy. There was no point in dwelling on these things, so why trouble himself? His days were rather pleasant right now, and perhaps he'd feel better after drinking some of the medicine he'd been prescribed. There was no need to seek out more trouble for himself.

And so he resumed cheerily and diligently reading through *The Pengornisseur*, periodically giving compliments and tittering over the details within. He was quite content.

There was no way for the adviser to finish looking through this edition in just one sitting. Wu Xingzi recalled Guan Shanjin's instructions, and he dared not bring the book back to the residence. He could only tell Rancui to hold it for him in the Peng Society, informing him that he would be coming to visit often over the next few days.

Of course Rancui agreed. Seeing that it was about time for lunch, he wanted to invite Wu Xingzi for a meal. However, Wu Xingzi remembered the two girls who were waiting for him, so he decided to bid Rancui farewell.

After sending Wu Xingzi and the other three away, Rancui's face fell. Wu Xingzi's current situation was not looking good. The adviser himself may not have realized anything, but Rancui was an expert when it came to romance; he was extremely sensitive toward matters of love. No matter how much Wu Xingzi tried to convince himself that it was merely a fleeting affair between himself and Guan Shanjin, his heart was soon to be swept away by love. That stifling feeling in his chest was most likely due to suppressed feelings that he dared not express!

Previously, Rancui had thought Wu Xingzi was gentle and yielding—in simple terms, that he was very easy to fool. With the way Guan Shanjin doted over his lovers, sooner or later, Wu Xingzi would fall for him deeply, and fall for him hard.

However, Wu Xingzi was full of surprises. Despite the way his eyes would fixate on beautiful men, and how *The Pengornisseur* was always on his mind, he had no intention of devoting a crumb of his feelings to another. He'd built an iron wall around his heart, and he dared not give it to anyone so easily.

Using his boss's connections, Rancui had spent over a month investigating before he finally found out about Yan Wenxin. As for what specifically had happened between Yan Wenxin and Wu Xingzi, he was unable to find out any further details, but Rancui speculated that it had something to do with an unfaithful man and a devoted one. Why else would there still be this barrier around Wu Xingzi's heart?

He must have been badly hurt to want to be a frog in a well!

Rancui's stomach began to ache again. When someone who guarded his heart so carefully gave it away, there was nothing that could make him take it back; he would fall deeply and quickly.

It seemed Wu Xingzi would be unable to protect his heart for much longer. When he realized his feelings and truly fell for Guan Shanjin, would that fickle general still continue to dote on him?

Ah, Rancui's stomach really hurt...

CHAPTER 5

A SONG OF HEARTFELT EMOTIONS

"Miss Yue said that you see me as a substitute for Mr. Lu. Is it true?"

"And if I say yes?"

"Do you have some kind of illness or internal injury?"

"Oh? Why?"

"Well, there's absolutely no trace of similarity between Mr. Lu and me, so how were you able to see me as his substitute? Unless..."

Unless you have a problem with your eyes?

As wu xingzi led Mint and Osmanthus away from the Peng Society, they started discussing where they should have lunch. Unlike Goose City and Qingcheng County, Horse-Face City was divided into two sectors. There was a curfew at night; the gates to the city square were closed at seven in the evening and opened again the next morning at five. The city was separated into the east and west sides, and stalls selling food were located mainly in the west. Mint and Osmanthus knew the city well, and they showed their master a place where all sorts of restaurants were located. They pointed to one of them in particular.

"Master, do you like mutton? Our aunt owns this shop, and the stir-fried mutton here is the best in the city. Since you can't eat food that's too spicy, we can ask our aunt to adjust the taste."

"Then I must give it a try," Wu Xingzi said, licking his lips. He wasn't picky about food—he'd eat anything. The two girls were good cooks, so he was sure their aunt must be even more skilled.

Their eyes dancing, Mint and Osmanthus chattered away, telling Wu Xingzi about which of their aunt's dishes were the most delicious. Saliva pooled in the adviser's mouth as he rubbed his belly. However, just as they were about to step into the restaurant, someone called out behind them:

"Mr. Wu!"

Wu Xingzi hurriedly turned his head toward the voice. It was a young lady with an impeccable appearance; her starry almond eyes stared straight into him. He reddened in response, not knowing how to react.

Hei-er stood right next to him, so he naturally saw the lady as well. He was typically a stoic man, but his tanned face twitched minutely at the sight of her. With a single stride, he stood directly in front of Wu Xingzi, blocking him from the young lady's bold stare.

It was Yue Mingzhu.

Her expression darkened as Hei-er blocked her view. She opened her mouth to scold him, but managed to hold herself back. Instead, she said sullenly, "Commander Hei, it's good to see you."

"Miss Yue, you're very courteous." Hei-er cupped his hands together in greeting. He did not move an inch, clearly signaling that he wanted the woman to back down.

However, Yue Mingzhu was infamous for being a spoiled brat and as reckless as a wild horse. As an unruly young aristocrat, how could she back down? Furthermore, she had finally bumped into the much-talked-about Mr. Wu. No matter what, she had to at least speak to him.

Even though Hei-er was blocking her line of sight, Wu Xingzi should still be able to hear her. "May I ask if you're Mr. Wu?"

"Ah, yes, I am. May I ask who…" Wu Xingzi poked his head out from behind Hei-er. He could not be impolite toward a young lady.

Mint lowered her voice, privately introducing her to Wu Xingzi. "Master, this is Mr. Lu's betrothed, the third young miss of the Yue family. Be careful. Miss Yue is arrogant and domineering—don't let her take advantage of you."

"Yes, yes," Osmanthus chimed in. "Master, you're too softhearted. It's best if you let Commander Hei deal with her." Both she and her sister had heard about Yue Mingzhu, as she was well-known in Horse-Face City. Even in a place where women were known to be strong, bold, and unrestrained, Yue Mingzhu still stood out among the crowd. Other than her father and brothers, no man could hold her back—of course, the people in the general's estate did not count.

Truth be told, Mint and Osmanthus secretly admired Yue Mingzhu's recklessness. However, they could not allow her to bully their master.

"I'm Yue Mingzhu. Nice to meet you, Mr. Wu." Yue Mingzhu could not hear what the girls were whispering about, but judging from how sneaky they were acting, it was probably nothing positive. Her beautiful eyes narrowed sharply, frightening the girls enough to make them hang their heads.

"I've heard much about you, Miss Yue. It's nice to meet you…" It was only after speaking that Wu Xingzi realized his words weren't quite right, and he smiled in embarrassment.

"Mr. Wu, are you about to have lunch?" Yue Mingzhu asked. She didn't have the patience for any more frivolous talk. She was not the sort to chat aimlessly, and she didn't know if Hei-er might interrupt them. It was extremely frustrating.

"Yes, yes. Have you eaten yet, Miss Yue?" asked Wu Xingzi, only for Mint and Osmanthus to tug on his sleeves. Blankly, he turned to look at the girls.

For Yue Mingzhu, this was the perfect opportunity. She put on a bright smile. "No, not yet. What a coincidence! Mr. Wu, why don't you let me treat you to the local specialties of Horse-Face City?"

Mint couldn't allow her master to answer. "There's no need! Our master doesn't eat spicy food, but many thanks for the invitation, Miss Yue," she said, immediately rejecting Yue Mingzhu's offer.

"Impudent girl, you talk too much. Mr. Wu is my guest, so of course I will respect his preferences. Is there any need for trash like you to run your mouth?" Yue Mingzhu sneered at Mint before turning toward Wu Xingzi. "Mr. Wu, what do you think? Everyone needs to eat, and I'm not some naïve, clueless little girl. You don't have to worry."

There was no reason for Wu Xingzi to refuse her. It was time for lunch, and he was truly hungry, but...why did he feel a sense of déjà vu? For some reason, he found himself on edge. He looked at the worried faces of the two girls, and couldn't help but laugh.

"Thank you for your invitation, Miss Yue, but I've already promised the two girls that I'd be eating at this restaurant. I hear their fried mutton is the best in Horse-Face City. My apologies."

"Exactly! Our aunt is extremely skilled in the kitchen, and her cooking is just as good as the general's! Not only is her fried mutton amazing, but her braised mutton, offal, and sheep's head are also delicious!" Mint delightedly listed some of her aunt's dishes. Wu Xingzi kept swallowing his saliva, hunger written across his face.

"Oh? It's simple, then. I'll just treat Mr. Wu to a meal in this restaurant. We'll kill two birds with one stone." Yue Mingzhu walked straight into the restaurant with her maidservant trailing behind.

Mint and Osmanthus stamped their feet in anger, but they were powerless to stop Miss Yue.

Wu Xingzi, however, was unbothered. No matter who he dined with, food was still food, wasn't it?

Just as he was about to follow her inside, Hei-er caught hold of Wu Xingzi. Wu Xingzi paused, looking at the usually silent man.

"Adviser Wu, don't let Miss Yue's words get to you. People like her only say things to their own benefit."

"Ah, yes, yes..."

Hei-er's sudden words of warning baffled Wu Xingzi. Why did Miss Yue want to invite him to lunch? The two of them had nothing to do with each other, so he didn't think anything of consequence could come of this meal.

As Wu Xingzi pondered over it, he entered the restaurant.

Mint and Changyi, Yue Mingzhu's maidservant, went to see the restaurant owner, while Osmanthus greeted the server she knew, asking him to prepare a quiet table for them. As for Miss Yue, she stood rigidly upright with a supercilious air about her; the people around kept sneaking looks at her and whispering to each other.

Hei-er followed Wu Xingzi, as silent and taciturn as ever. He moved to stand directly in front of Wu Xingzi, blocking him from the restaurant-goers' probing eyes.

Wu Xingzi heard some vague whispers.

"Could this be Mr. Wu?"

"Seems like it. Ah, so that's what he looks like."

Wu Xingzi was a little confused. Since coming to Horse-Face City, this was the first time he'd actually walked around the city streets. Why were people talking about him? Ill at ease, he lowered his head, hiding behind Hei-er. Was there some kind of trouble brewing?

They were fortunate to have brought Osmanthus along. Because she knew the server, they were led straight to the back patio. The staff set up a table and a few chairs next to a stand of wisteria.

It was not yet time for the wisteria flowers to bloom; all that could be seen were luxuriant green leaves. Osmanthus told Wu Xingzi that the wisteria plant was over a hundred years old—but from the size of the base of the plant, he would have been able to guess as much without her explanation.

"If you'd like, Master, we can come and enjoy the flowers once the wisteria blooms. We can even pluck a few to make pastries."

Mint returned, having ordered their food. She dragged Wu Xingzi along, deliberately ignoring Yue Mingzhu—who was sitting at the head of the table.

Hei-er was a ranking military officer; of everyone in their group, he had the highest status. According to custom, the seat at the head of the table should be his. However, Hei-er was currently attending to Wu Xingzi, so everyone knew who should *really* be sitting in that seat.

Yue Mingzhu must have been aware of it, but it was evident that her obstinance was meant to embarrass Wu Xingzi and, by extension, disrespect Guan Shanjin. Mint and Osmanthus could not say a word about it, but their hearts were filled with indignation.

Changyi wanted to persuade her mistress to change her seat. After all, the intent behind this meal was to ask for a favor. It only made sense for her to lower her status a little. Her mistress was usually not *this* pigheaded!

"Ah, how nice. I've never seen wisteria in bloom before," said Wu Xingzi, his eyes glued to the plant. "I've heard that the sight is quite spectacular—I really should come take a look."

Among the letters his father had left behind, one mentioned wisteria flowers. A few lines were enough to make Wu Xingzi yearn for them, but there wasn't a single wisteria in Qingcheng County. Although they could be found in Goose City, the plants were all located in private gardens, and Wu Xingzi did not have the means to view them. Time passed, and his mental impression of the wisteria faded away, but the unexpected opportunity to see a century-old wisteria plant today had reignited his desire to see the blossoms.

"When do they usually bloom?" he asked. Taking a closer look, he saw tiny, tender buds among the leaves. It shouldn't be too long before the plant blossomed.

"The flowers should come in about one or two months from now," Osmanthus replied, counting with her fingers. Seeing how brightly Wu Xingzi smiled, Mint and Osmanthus were even more determined to let Wu Xingzi see the splendid sight of blooming wisteria.

Yue Mingzhu's face grew darker as she watched Mr. Wu and the two young maids ignore her. They laughed and gestured at the wisteria plant as they conversed, enjoying themselves. Unfortunately, Miss Yue was unable to let out any of her anger in front of Hei-er. Her cup made dangerous noises as her fingers tightened harshly around it, nearly shattering it. She had not come to meet this old fellow of her own accord; she was forced to do so by her father and brother.

Wu Xingzi's mousy old face repulsed Yue Mingzhu. Such a vulgar and crude person—in what way could he dare to compare to the otherworldly Mr. Lu? Was Guan Shanjin not nauseated by taking in this old thing as Mr. Lu's substitute?

The dishes arrived quickly. Although only three people were seated around the table for the meal, Hei-er and Wu Xingzi both had big appetites. With this in mind, Mint had ordered enough food for ten people, mainly stir-fried dishes. Plates of sheep's heart, liver, stomach, lungs, and kidneys—nothing was missing from their table. There was also mutton leg, shoulder, neck, and trotters. The dishes ranged from tender and rich to fatty and chewy. As expected of a restaurant specializing in mutton, the meal was accompanied by a bowl of mutton soup. Even though there were a dozen or so dishes, not a single one tasted similar to another. The taste lingered in Wu Xingzi's mouth, making him wish for more.

Of course, it was only Wu Xingzi who was so impressed. When the dishes arrived, he was like a country bumpkin in a big city. Entranced by the food, he could barely restrain himself. Wriggling his nose and inhaling deeply, he filled his nostrils with the delicious aromas. He picked up his bowl and buried himself in the food.

Though eager, Wu Xingzi had surprisingly refined table manners. His behavior in general had always been rather reserved. He held his bowl and chopsticks in the proper manner, and did not eat too quickly. However, food disappeared from the table at a noticeable pace. He left Yue Mingzhu no time to speak. She gritted her teeth and started eating.

Originally, this had been a feast offered with ill intentions—at least in the eyes of Yue Mingzhu. She needed to take control of the situation. Step by step, she would force Wu Xingzi's hand to achieve her objective.

Unfortunately, her plan had gone off-track. Wu Xingzi had truly only come for a meal, and he was absolutely engrossed in his food. Yue Mingzhu couldn't get a word in edgewise; with her anger yet to dissipate, she finished two bowls of rice.

Adviser Wu smiled, his stomach finally satisfied. Out of the entire table filled with dishes, nothing was left other than bones. The onions, ginger, and garlic were all gone; even the gravy from other dishes had been mixed into rice and eaten. Covering his mouth, Wu Xingzi burped quietly, then apologized to Miss Yue, embarrassed.

"It's fine. Mr. Wu certainly has a voracious appetite." Yue Mingzhu looked this skinny old thing up and down, shocked. Where had he put all that food?

"Many thanks to Miss Yue today for the invitation. I'm overwhelmed by your generosity. Next time, please let me return the favor by treating you to a meal."

Mint had secretly informed Wu Xingzi of the cost of the food. As this was a restaurant located in the market streets, the price was very reasonable, which came as a huge relief for Wu Xingzi—otherwise, he would have been too ashamed to accept Miss Yue's generosity. When he thought about it, he'd eaten far more than she had.

Yue Mingzhu exhaled in relief. She could finally bring up what she had come here to discuss. "Mr. Wu, you're too courteous. My objective today wasn't just to treat you to a meal." She shifted in her seat, her expression turning grave. "I'm sure you heard many people talking about you around the stalls outside."

She got straight to the point. Wu Xingzi froze in place.

"This sort of gossip that people bandy about when they have nothing better to do—the Yue family has nothing to do with it," she continued. "Lu-gongzi would never stoop so low. I have always lived out in the light, and I've never done anything to be ashamed about. I hope Mr. Wu is aware of this." Yue Mingzhu didn't need Wu Xingzi to respond. Her aim today was to clear her name and Mr. Lu's—she was only intent on presenting her own opinion.

"Uhh... I haven't..." Wu Xingzi blinked. The meaning lying underneath Miss Yue's words implied that he was biased against her and Mr. Lu, and that he'd only listened to one side of the story. He wanted to explain his position.

"You don't have to say more," Yue Mingzhu said, before Wu Xingzi could try to explain anything. "I understand that you must be displeased to hear such filthy talk, Mr. Wu, and to complain about it to the general is very understandable. I have no intentions of reproaching you for your unhappiness. However, I don't appreciate that you are sowing dissent." She had no patience for whatever Wu Xingzi might have to say. She summoned Changyi over.

Changyi hurriedly held out the little parcel she'd been carrying around. Yue Mingzhu unwrapped it. Inside was an exquisitely constructed red-hued lacquer box. She pushed it toward Wu Xingzi.

"This is a little gift from me. Consider it an offer of friendship, Mr. Wu." She raised her chin slightly, the center of her brows furrowing with disdain and impatience. "Mr. Wu, since you've gained the affections of the general, you should remain his pet without a care in the world, even if, in the beginning, the general only took you as Lu-gongzi's substitute..." She laughed abruptly. Even a young child could recognize the contempt and malice in it.

Wu Xingzi's face flushed red, then paled dramatically. He forced a smile toward Miss Yue, wanting to speak in his own defense, only to have Yue Mingzhu raise her hand to stop him.

"Perhaps the general's eyes have failed him, or his heart itself is blind—but it is certainly true that he saw you as a substitute for Lu-gongzi. You can ask the general yourself how much of his feelings for you are due to Mr. Lu," Miss Yue said. "I'll leave you with this reminder: the general may cherish and dote on you now, but it's all because of Mr. Lu."

"Um, I..."

Yue Mingzhu frowned, glaring at Wu Xingzi in disgust. "Mr. Wu, I don't have the time to listen to your excuses. I know the sort of person you are—I've seen it time and time again. There are only so many methods of gaining favor, and there's no point in mentioning them to me. You were upset, so you tattled to the general in bed, planting the seed of discord in the teacher-student relationship between Mr. Lu and the general. Such methods are truly repulsive— pardon my rudeness."

"I didn't..."

There was no way Wu Xingzi could explain himself, as Yue Mingzhu had no intention of allowing him to speak. She cut him off again. "Go back and convey this to the general: a teacher for a day is a father for life. At the end of the day, Lu-gongzi is his teacher. If he has feelings for him, he should gracefully accept his rejection. This is how a man should behave. All these underhanded tricks... Although I cannot compete with the general's immense political power, I can easily cause a fuss that will harm both sides. The general cannot afford to offend the ladies of Horse-Face City. The same goes for you. You need to know your place. Since you've already benefited from your association with Lu-gongzi, stop making a fool of yourself. You think by smearing Lu-gongzi's name, you'll be able to gain greater favor? Hmph! A lousy adviser from some poor county! How primitive."

Yue Mingzhu was very satisfied with her words. She tapped on the lacquered box.

"That is all. Accept this gift, Mr. Wu. In the future, I hope you'll think before you act."

Not caring whether Wu Xingzi really wanted the gift or not, Yue Mingzhu stood up and hurried out of the restaurant with her maidservant.

Wu Xingzi sat there, at a total loss for what to do. He didn't understand what any of this was about. At last, he looked toward Hei-er, baffled.

"I have been commanded by the general not to discuss such matters," Hei-er said, cupping his hands apologetically. "However, if you were to chat casually with the girls...I won't hear a thing."

Mint and Osmanthus were quick to jump in, knowing that Commander Hei was offering to turn a blind eye. They were worried for Wu Xingzi, so they started making their complaints known quietly.

"That Miss Yue is so unreasonable. How could you ever speak ill of others, Mr. Wu?" Mint said as she deliberated over how to downplay the severity of the situation.

"Master, don't listen to Miss Yue's nonsense," Osmanthus said. She was much more direct. "Things between the general and Mr. Lu are not like she said. It's just that Mr. Lu is about to get married, so the general can't spoil him like he has in the past. Shouldn't Miss Yue be delighted about it?" Osmanthus didn't try to hold back. She even spat at the end.

Wu Xingzi was perplexed. He'd known for some time that there must be a reason behind Guan Shanjin's affections toward him, but he'd never once considered that he could be a substitute for Mr. Lu—their appearances and personalities were completely different. Who could ever think there were any similarities between the two of them? Did Guan Shanjin have a problem with his eyesight? Perhaps he should get a physician to take a look at him. Could it be an unknown injury from the battlefield? Instead of Miss Yue's accusations, Wu Xingzi began to worry over Guan Shanjin's health.

"Ah, exactly! In the past, I felt that Mr. Lu was an angelic being. But now I know his perfect demeanor is a lie," Mint said, pursing her lips. Naturally, she was on Wu Xingzi's side.

"Yes, the general treats Mr. Lu like an outsider now," Osmanthus added. "The Yue family were originally hoping that through Mr. Lu, they could rely on the general's support. Instead, our general is wise and decisive, and he cut off such thoughts directly. No wonder the Yue family is anxious. Without our general's support, Mr. Lu is useless to them." She snorted. Despite her young age, she was very knowledgeable, and well aware of the situation. Of course, the Yue family would know this even better than she did.

The Yue family was the richest merchant family in Horse-Face City. However, under Guan Shanjin's orders, there were many goods that could not be sent in great quantities to Nanman. Goods imported from Nanman also had to go through the general's estate, and the estate would then distribute them to various merchants. Each year, the merchants would have to pay for a permit to sell products from Nanman, and the amount each merchant family could receive was explicitly stated on the permits. The most a seller could hope to get was 40 percent of the total goods.

Although Nanman was barbaric, they had many items of great quality that Great Xia lacked. Great Xia merchants wanted to buy low and sell high, as well as have an easy way to import and export goods. However, as the guard of this border city, Guan Shanjin's greatest priority was to destroy the city's enemies before they could rise. He could not allow the people of Nanman to live too comfortably, but he still granted them a certain amount of stability and spirit. Since he could not obliterate Nanman outright, he would simply employ the boiling frog method: adapt them to the situation as slowly as possible, crippling his enemies by providing them with just enough of what they needed.

Mint and Osmanthus did not understand such matters, but they knew that the general must have had his reasons for the trade sanctions.

Many citizens of Horse-Face City were unhappy with the rules laid out by the general's estate. However, Horse-Face City being so peaceful came with its own advantages as well, which was enough to make everyone deeply grateful. No one would quarrel with the general's estate. After all, a mere six years ago, the war-torn Horse-Face City was mired in violence—no one knew if they would live to see the next day!

"But Mr. Lu is still the general's teacher, after all..." Thinking of that kind and open-minded man dressed in white, Wu Xingzi was sympathetic.

Seeing that things were about to veer down the wrong path, Mint quickly advised Wu Xingzi, "Master, you cannot feel sorry for him. So what if Mr. Lu is the general's teacher? It has nothing to do with us. The general is keeping his distance from Mr. Lu because the Yue family wants to gain the general's favor through his teacher. The general has no choice but to cut him off."

Wu Xingzi contemplated for a moment before agreeing with Mint. "That makes sense," Wu Xingzi said, bowing his head. Using Mr. Lu's closeness to the general to coerce him would make things difficult for Guan Shanjin. Of course, Wu Xingzi's heart sided with Guan Shanjin, so his bit of sympathy for Mr. Lu faded quite a bit.

"I wonder what Miss Yue has prepared for you," Mint said, looking at the lacquered box on the table with open curiosity.

"Shall we open it and take a look?" Wu Xingzi always indulged the two girls. He picked up the box to open it, and froze at what he saw inside.

The interior was lined with fine, shimmery silk of a light golden-yellow hue. In the center were five gold ingots. It was absolutely shocking.

Mint broke the silence. "Is she bribing you?"

"Th-this...this is too much," Wu Xingzi said. He pressed his palm against his chest, exhaling slowly. But it was the perfect gift for him. No matter whether Miss Yue wanted to humiliate him or flaunt her wealth, to Wu Xingzi, money was more useful than anything else. With five gold ingots, he would be able to start a small business and earn a living when he returned to Qingcheng County. He could afford a coffin from Liuzhou, one of the finest[4]—he could even hire people to sweep his grave after his death!

Ah... Miss Yue really has a bright and clever heart!

Wu Xingzi deliberated over the gift for quite some time. In the end, his old-fashioned honesty took the lead. A little reluctantly, he closed the lid of the box and handed it to Hei-er. "Sorry to trouble you, but please help me return this to Miss Yue. I cannot accept such a valuable gift."

"I understand," Hei-er said. He took the box and tucked it into his clothes. He knew very well that Wu Xingzi was sincere, so he didn't try to persuade him to keep it; it would only make the adviser feel awkward. "Do you still plan on taking a look through the market streets, Adviser Wu?"

Wu Xingzi had wanted to, but when he remembered all the gossip about him on the streets, he had to dismiss the idea. "There's no need for that. Let's go back."

"But who spread the rumor this time?" murmured Osmanthus as they left, her brows knitted.

Hei-er glanced at her, then at Wu Xingzi. In the end, he lowered his head and did not say a word.

This time, Guan Shanjin was away for quite a while. Wu Xingzi could not really put it into words, but he kept feeling an emptiness in his heart. Not even gardening and taking care of his chickens improved his mood.

---

4   Liuzhou is a city with such a prominent historical reputation for its high-quality coffins that in modern Liuzhou miniature coffins are sold as souvenirs.

By the seven-day mark, Wu Xingzi couldn't even summon up the enthusiasm to visit the Peng Society. Drearily, he finished his breakfast, then, just like always, he tidied up his garden plots and cleaned up his chicken coop. He stared at one round, plump hen in a daze. His fixed gaze made the hen cluck in alarm and look for a place to hide.

"Master," came Mint's sweet and crisp voice. The girl lifted the hem of her skirt to sprint toward him from outside, her eyes shining with delight.

Wu Xingzi couldn't help but smile too. His days would be truly boring without these girls around. "What's the matter?" he asked, patting Mint's head. She was still catching her breath as she held her hand out toward him as if presenting a treasure. Clutched in her tiny, pale hand was a branch full of peach blossoms.

Wu Xingzi's smile stiffened, and he looked at Mint in astonishment. "These are…peach blossoms! But I thought there weren't any peach trees in Horse-Face City?"

"There didn't used to be, but I asked my aunt and found out that the Zhu family planted a few peach trees in their courtyard. They bloomed this year!"

Mint explained that the Zhu family was among the upper class of Horse-Face City. Unlike the Yue family, who were merchants, they were one of the rare scholarly families that lived here. In their last few generations, the Zhus had produced officials who held positions in the capital. The current head of the family had originally held a position there as well, but later retired to his hometown. This was the reason why the family had such an interest in planting peach trees.

These peach trees had been sent from nearby counties, and it was really impressive that the Zhu family had managed to cultivate them.

There'd been no buds to be seen the past two years, but now the branches were filled with blossoms.

"Master, didn't you say you could smell the scent of peach blossoms for the past few days? It must have come from the Zhu family. Zhu Manor is only one house away from the general's estate." Mint cautiously handed the branch over to Wu Xingzi, speaking earnestly. "Master, I know you're homesick, so I asked them for a branch on your behalf. Let's plant it here!"

How could Mint and her sister not notice that something was wrong with their master lately? Before, Wu Xingzi had been so tranquil and carefree. It didn't matter to him whether the general came to see him or not, and he relished each new day. However, ever since that meal with the young lady of the Yue family, their master had changed. A sadness could vaguely be seen between his brows, and he would periodically rub at his chest. He always seemed to be in a daze, staring off into the distance.

This made the two girls curse Miss Yue out in their heads over and over again. They were so worried!

After that, with some prompting from Hei-er, they found out that the Zhu family had planted peach trees. Osmanthus recalled that Wu Xingzi had asked a few times if there were any peach trees in the general's estate, so she guessed that their master probably liked these flowers. Perhaps seeing them would make him feel a little better.

And so the two sisters mustered up the courage to ask the Zhu family for a branch of peach blossoms. Fortunately, the Zhus were respected scholars, and they were kind and gentle to the girls. Without asking any questions or causing a fuss, they broke a branch off for them.

Wu Xingzi was lost for a moment. A thousand thoughts tangled in his head, and he stared at the peach blossoms for a long time without uttering a word. Only after noticing Mint's flushed face from the corner of his eye did he manage to steady his emotions. He smiled at the girl. "Thank you very much. These peach blossoms have grown nicely."

Mint joyfully watched Wu Xingzi's smiling face, feeling a huge sense of relief. "Yes! It's actually the first time my sister and I have ever seen peach blossoms. They look a little similar to plum blossoms because they're both pink, but if you look closely, they're different."

"Where's Osmanthus?" Wu Xingzi asked, holding the branch. The scent of the peach blossoms made his chest feel worse, but he was unwilling to let the girl notice any difference in his demeanor. He could only change the subject.

"She's gone to the main kitchen to ask for some flour and sugar. The eldest daughter of the Zhu family told us about a dessert made with peach blossoms, and we'd like to make it for you to try."

"Oh? You girls really have so many tricks up your sleeves." Wu Xingzi smiled and ruffled Mint's hair. "I'm a little tired, and I'd like to return to my room to rest for a bit. There's no need to wake me up for lunch; we'll figure it out when I'm awake. You and Osmanthus should go ahead and eat, all right?"

"Ah, yes, I understand." Mint nodded her head continuously. She wanted to help Wu Xingzi back to his room, but she was sent away to help her sister prepare the peach blossom pastries. Thinking that Wu Xingzi must be itching to try one, Mint obediently listened and left.

When she was some distance away, the smile on Wu Xingzi's face vanished, and his complexion turned ashen.

He looked down at the peach blossoms. It was as if he held a burning flame in his hand; he didn't know what to do with himself.

It was then that Hei-er appeared out of nowhere to solve his problem, affably taking the branch from his hands.

Wu Xingzi was unable to spare any words of gratitude for Hei-er. He turned away and practically fled back into his room, where he closed the door and windows and then collapsed onto his bed. There was still a trace of Guan Shanjin's scent on the blanket, but it was fainter than ever. In a few more days, it might dissipate completely.

He took in a harsh deep breath, feeling a lot more composed. However, he was unable to stop himself from remembering that name...

"Zaizong-xiong..."

Wu Xingzi once thought that he had forgotten about that time in his life, but as soon as the man's name left his lips again, he felt heartrending pain; the throbbing ache blurred his vision.

He remembered that tall figure standing in the peach grove, his clothes fluttering in the wind; he looked like a peach blossom deity. At that time, Wu Xingzi had been only eighteen, and the image dazzled him.

From that moment on, Yan Wenxin, Yan Zaizong... He was deeply engraved in Wu Xingzi's heart.

Wu Xingzi had always liked elegant and refined-looking men, but Yan Wenxin did not exactly fit those criteria. Yan Wenxin had been around twenty back then, and had a face that was a little too feminine. He'd been mocked for looking like a fickle and disloyal man: his lips were too thin, and his eyes were slanted and narrow. When he did not smile, he looked very unkind. When he smiled, though, it was like flowers blooming in spring.

Wu Xingzi fell for his smile. The world grew warmer every time he saw it.

His parents had only been dead for two years back then, and Wu Xingzi was still not used to living alone. However, because of his old-fashioned and shy demeanor, he had been unable to find a partner with whom he could spend the rest of his life. Yan Wenxin had added color back into his world: in the biting cold winter, a warm spring breeze finally blew.

Although Great Xia did not ban homosexual relationships, it was still rare for two men to fall in love. Yan Wenxin was passionate about becoming an official, and he naturally had to pay great attention to his personal virtues. Wu Xingzi had originally only wanted to keep his affections secret. Even if they could not be romantic partners, as long as he could be near Yan Wenxin, reading alongside him and talking with him...it would be enough.

The first one to break the thin barrier between them was Yan Wenxin.

Wu Xingzi thought that he had long forgotten the past, but now he knew there were some things that could never be forgotten. He'd simply locked away the memories within his heart; out of sight, out of mind.

It had been raining that day. By the time he'd reached Goose City, it was already afternoon, and when he finished his errands, it was getting late. There was an empty room in the magistrate's office of Goose City where he could stay temporarily. He couldn't get back to Qingcheng County in time, so Wu Xingzi decided to stay. However, though his accommodations had been settled, his stomach was empty! He contemplated for a moment, his cheeks blushing a light pink, and hurried off to look for Yan Wenxin with his little money pouch in tow.

To prepare for the imperial examinations, Yan Wenxin lived a rather destitute life. Despite his poverty, he had great mental fortitude.

He would rather starve and drink rice water for his meals than borrow a single coin. During the day, he would sell some of his writings on the street, earning a pittance and saving most of it in preparation to travel to the capital for his examinations.

Wu Xingzi's heart ached for him. However, he was reluctant to hurt his pride, so he found all sorts of excuses to bring food and other necessities to him.

That day, Wu Xingzi bought a roast goose, a few pieces of flatbread, two big bowls of noodles, and two large bowls of porridge from the market before hurrying to Yan Wenxin's residence.

The sun had set completely. When Wu Xingzi looked in through the window, the room was dark and gloomy. Inside was a flame so meager it looked like a thin thread, twisting about in an alluring pattern.

After knocking on the door, Wu Xingzi immediately pushed his way in, calling out, "Zaizong-xiong, are you here?"

"Xingzi? Why are you here?" Yan Wenxin's voice was not far away. With a bit of fiddling, the candle grew a lot brighter, and Yan Wenxin's sharp chin was now clearly lit.

"I want you to keep me company while I eat my dinner." Wu Xingzi smiled and lifted up the food in his hands. The roast goose looked marvelous.

Yan Wenxin chuckled quietly. "Come over here. You keep finding all sorts of ways to feed me. You're a good friend... I have no way of repaying your kindness."

"Ah, what are you saying that for?" Wu Xingzi blushed in embarrassment, feeling a little awkward at being found out. However, an inexplicable sweetness sprang up within him.

The two men set the table and ate heartily as they sat across from each other.

Yan Wenxin did not own many things. His bowls and chopsticks had actually been left there by Wu Xingzi in the past.

With Wu Xingzi's usual appetite, he would've eaten the entire roast goose down to the bones by himself. However, in front of Yan Wenxin, he only ate a small part of it and left the rest for him. Whether it was the noodles or the porridge, he was determined that it would keep Yan Wenxin full until lunch tomorrow.

"Ah, Xingzi, your appetite isn't that big—why do you always bring so much with you every time?" Zaizong looked at the smiling Wu Xingzi, who had already placed his chopsticks down as if he had eaten his fill.

Wu Xingzi lowered his head, scratching at his cheek. He was too embarrassed to say that he'd purchased the food according to his usual appetite, and he'd have no problem finishing every single bite. He had purposefully left a large portion for Yan Wenxin to have for himself.

Yan Wenxin carefully packed away the leftovers, smiling and saying he had enough to last him until dinnertime tomorrow.

Since they were both fed, Wu Xingzi planned on making his farewells. Unexpectedly, Yan Wenxin suddenly caught hold of his hand.

As a scholar, Yan Wenxin's hands were soft and smooth. They were much more supple than Wu Xingzi's hands, with only a few calluses. Still, his hands were broad and firm, and well proportioned. His fingers were long and beautiful, and his palm felt burning hot. The warmth seeped into Wu Xingzi's skin and spread through his veins.

Wu Xingzi trembled slightly. He quickly glanced at Yan Wenxin before turning his reddening face away. "Is there something you need, Zaizong-xiong?"

"Yes," Yan Wenxin replied with a smile. He took hold of Wu Xingzi's other hand as well, slowly closing the distance between them. "It sounds like it's raining outside. Are you in a hurry to leave?"

When Wu Xingzi listened carefully, he could hear the patter of raindrops. But it was not a heavy rain. In the time it would take him to reach the magistrate's office, he might not even get that wet.

"Zaizong-xiong means...?" Wu Xingzi felt a swell of anticipation, but he quickly pushed away the thought. They had been interacting for months now, and they had always treated each other like good friends. Yan Wenxin had even told him once that he wanted to succeed in both civil and military matters, marry a beautiful bride, and bring honor to his family name.

"Xingzi." Yan Wenxin tightened his grip on Wu Xingzi's hands, his grip on Wu Xingzi's heartstrings tightening with it.

They stood in silence as the rain outside began to fall more heavily. The raindrops drummed upon the flagstone path outside, and the air in the room grew damp. However, the two of them remained motionless and silent. All they could hear was each other's breathing.

Wu Xingzi didn't know how much time passed. Yan Wenxin gave a sudden small sigh, which made Wu Xingzi's heart leap violently into his throat.

"Xingzi," Yan Wenxin called out.

"Yes," replied Wu Xingzi, his mouth dry.

"I love you."

The Wu Xingzi of the past gasped along with the Wu Xingzi of the present, lost in his memories. However, the past version of himself had gasped in joy, while his current self was gasping in pain.

As Yan Wenxin's words reverberated in his ears, it felt like an awl jabbing into him exactly where it hurt the most, piercing and prodding until his vision turned blurry with tears. He could only grit his teeth and suffer.

Wu Xingzi knew that he was clumsy; he knew he was ugly, and he knew he was not that clever. But he was sincere and earnest. He had only ever loved one person in his life. For Yan Wenxin, he felt joy; for Yan Wenxin, he felt sorrow. For Yan Wenxin's future, he could give everything he had.

"Why didn't you say goodbye?" After many years, this was the first time Wu Xingzi gave voice to the question he had for Yan Wenxin.

He understood that a person's heart could change, and he never expected Yan Wenxin to repay everything that Wu Xingzi had given to him. All he wanted was a word of farewell—that would have been enough.

Wu Xingzi skipped both lunch and dinner. Worried, Mint and Osmanthus kept glancing toward his room the entire day, but the general had instructed that unless he or Wu Xingzi called for them, no one was allowed to enter the bedroom of their own accord.

Even when the moon rose and the stars stippled the skies, not a single candle was lit in Wu Xingzi's room. Eventually, even Hei-er came to the door, a solemn expression on his face as he contemplated forcing his way inside. It was nearly seven in the evening, but no sound or movement could be detected in the bedroom.

Carrying a bowl of food and some peach blossom pastries, Mint and Osmanthus called out to Wu Xingzi a few times, so anxious that they wanted to knock the door down.

As the three people buzzed with worry, a pleasant voice came from behind them.

"What's going on?"

Upon turning her head around, Mint almost leapt for joy. "General!"

Guan Shanjin was standing there, travel-weary. He frowned and patted away the dust on his clothes.

Mint rushed over with the food. "Mr. Wu has been hiding in his room all day, and he didn't have lunch or dinner. We've all called him several times, but he hasn't responded."

Guan Shanjin's complexion grew uglier. "He hasn't eaten at all?"

On the general's back was a long item wrapped in cloth. Judging from its size, it looked quite heavy. Guan Shanjin had not put it down at all, so it must be something precious.

Glancing at the cold food in Mint's hands, he waved her off. "Take that away. Go to the main kitchen and ask for some eggs, meat, and vegetables, and bring them here. I'll prepare food for him later. You can all leave now."

Osmanthus raised the box of pastries in her hand. "How about we let Mr. Wu have some peach blossom pastries to settle his stomach first?"

"Peach blossom?" Guan Shanjin's brows creased, and he glared at Hei-er.

"General, the Zhu residence has planted three peach trees in their backyard, and they flowered this year. Mr. Wu caught the scent of the peach blossoms over the past few days and asked about it several times. That's why the girls went to ask for a branch," answered Hei-er with a bowed head. Nothing amiss could be detected from his tone or his attitude.

Guan Shanjin simply looked at him and snorted coldly. "You actually know how to give a perfunctory report now? All right, then." Guan Shanjin walked past Hei-er, tapping on the door with his finger. "Wu Xingzi."

No reaction came from within, so Guan Shanjin went ahead and pushed the door open. He immediately closed the door behind him, not allowing the others to see inside the room.

It was completely dark inside. No candles were lit, and Guan Shanjin did not bother lighting any himself. Moonlight filtered through the window, covering everything in the room like a thin piece of silk gauze and shattering into pieces with each of Wu Xingzi's slow, sedate breaths. Guan Shanjin walked toward the familiar sound of his breathing.

The bed curtains were down, and a vague ball shape could be seen within. Guan Shanjin smiled to himself; he was in no hurry to wake Wu Xingzi. Covered in days of dust and travel stains, he had to clean himself up first before he could caress the man who was delightfully wrapped up in blankets. Judging by his breathing, Wu Xingzi sounded deeply asleep, and he was not ill. Guan Shanjin relaxed.

After untying the bag on his back and placing it on the table, Guan Shanjin went outside to call for Mint and Osmanthus to bring him warm water for washing up. Once he was clean, he changed into a set of comfortable clothes. By now, it was nearly nine in the evening. He lifted the curtains and sat down on the edge of the bed, patting the sleepy old quail through the blanket.

"Wu Xingzi," Guan Shanjin gently called out to him. After he'd called his name nearly a dozen times, an indistinct response came from within the bundle of blankets. "Are you hungry?" Guan Shanjin asked.

"Mmph..." Wu Xingzi mumbled sleepily. Only after a bout of stretching did he pop his red, flushed face out from the blanket. It looked like he had been crying before he fell asleep; he could not fully open his eyes. Tilting his head, he looked at Guan Shanjin with eyes that had swelled to the size of walnuts. Guan Shanjin's heart ached at the sight.

"What happened?" he asked.

Wu Xingzi wasn't fully awake. He had slept for a very long time and was still somewhat groggy. Without thinking, he scrunched up the blanket and repeated Guan Shanjin's question: "What happened?"

"Your eyes are swollen. You've been crying," Guan Shanjin sighed. Frowning, he carefully picked Wu Xingzi up from within the blanket and pulled him into a tight embrace. "Who made you so unhappy, hmm?"

Of course, Guan Shanjin had an idea. Although he hadn't been around the past few days, he still paid meticulous attention to anything and everything that had to do with Wu Xingzi. The peach blossoms were the only thing that had managed to escape his notice; who knew what Man Yue had instructed Hei-er to do behind his back?

Wu Xingzi blearily nuzzled his face into Guan Shanjin's chest and took a deep breath. After holding it in for some time, he slowly and reluctantly exhaled.

Such affection made Guan Shanjin melt. Wu Xingzi would never act this way in front of Guan Shanjin when he was fully awake. He always kept a cautious distance from the general—perhaps worried that if he waded in too deep, he would fall into a bottomless abyss.

After spending so much time with him, Guan Shanjin understood Wu Xingzi's mind; there was nothing he could do about the old fellow's nature. He was a gentle soul, but he was as stubborn as a mule. In the end, Guan Shanjin was often the one who ended up frustrated.

"Shall I make you some rice porridge?" Guan Shanjin suggested. "Then massage your eyes?"

"Mm, I'd like rabbit porridge," Wu Xingzi mumbled. Rice porridge with rabbit meat was the first dish Guan Shanjin had made for him, and it was marvelous. Wu Xingzi had never tasted a porridge so delicious. Although Guan Shanjin had prepared ten different types of porridge for him since, each one more exquisite than the last, they could never compare to that first bowl.

"We don't have any rabbit meat right now, but I'll make some for you next time. I'll go hunting in the next few days for you, all right?" Sympathetically, Guan Shanjin kissed both of Wu Xingzi's swollen eyelids, and lightly rocked him in his arms to make sure that he was truly awake before letting him go. "I have a gift for you. Play with it while I'm cooking?"

"Ahh..." Only now did Wu Xingzi realize he was cradled in Guan Shanjin's arms like a fool. Blushing a bright red, he pulled away, lowering his head as he responded quietly, "I-it's good that you're back. Why did you bother bringing me a gift?"

Had he just been cuddling in Guan Shanjin's embrace and breathing in his scent? *Ah, Wu Xingzi, you useless thing!*

But Guan Shanjin smelled wonderful! How befitting of the man who wielded the Lanling Prince of all pengornises. Even after it sprang to life from the page, his cock was not lacking. It had been a number of days since Wu Xingzi last greeted it, and he did rather miss the spectacular specimen.

"Where are you letting your imagination run off to this time?" Guan Shanjin asked, gazing at Wu Xingzi's face. He never could hide his expressions; right now, his clear eyes wandered to the general's crotch. Guan Shanjin didn't know how to feel about it. No matter the reason why Wu Xingzi had cried before he fell asleep, his sadness had melted like snow under the sun—all because of Guan Shanjin's cock.

"No, no, no, I'm just...hungry." Wu Xingzi still could not keep his eyes from drifting down toward the Lanling prick. If not for the earth-shattering grumbling of his stomach, he'd have drummed up the courage to request a meeting with that perfect pengornis.

"There'll be plenty of time to play later. Why are you in such a hurry?" Guan Shanjin pinched Wu Xingzi's fleshy nose and gently pushed him back down to the bed. Pointing at the cloth-wrapped package on the table, he told him, "Here, amuse yourself with this. I'll go make you some food first. I don't want you to get a stomachache from hunger."

"Thank you, thank you." Wu Xingzi carefully unwrapped the package. When he saw what was inside, his eyes widened in astonishment. "Th-this...this is a qin?"

The musical instrument in the package looked rather roughly constructed at first glance; however, on closer examination, the exquisite air it exuded was clear.

Wu Xingzi was momentarily at a loss for what to do next. He placed his hands behind his back, his fingers fidgeting a little. He wanted to touch the qin, but he dared not put his hands on it so readily. He couldn't tell if this qin was good or not, but he couldn't imagine Guan Shanjin would gift him something of poor quality.

Guan Shanjin helped him properly set up the qin. He moved Wu Xingzi to sit down behind the instrument and placed the adviser's hands on the strings, so that his fingers would stroke it lightly. Although the strumming was out of tune, it still sounded pleasant and sweet. It must have been crafted by a renowned artisan.

But Wu Xingzi wanted to pull his hands away. This time, Guan Shanjin did not stop him; he pinched his palm affectionately before turning to go to the kitchen. Left alone in the room, Wu Xingzi stared at the qin, his face burning red.

"We gather the duckweed, both short and long,
From left and right, both sides of the pond,

The quiet young lady, both modest and pure,
With qins big and small, let us welcome her..."⁵

Finally registering what he was reciting, Wu Xingzi nearly fell off the chair. Was he still such a fool at forty years old? He was neither modest nor quiet, nor was he a pure young lady. What was going through his head? How could he be so shameless?!

Wu Xingzi admonished himself silently, but he couldn't suppress the sense of shy delight welling up inside him. He'd never received anything this lovely in his life. The only other gift he'd ever received was that perfume sachet from Yan Wenxin, and even if he were to ignore who the gift was from, there was still no way it could compare to this qin.

Did it represent something, this gift of a qin...?

"No, no, no, Wu Xingzi, you fool! Guan Shanjin is young and accomplished, and his beloved is clearly Mr. Lu," he said to himself, finally managing to calm down. He nodded and patted his chest. *Exactly!*

Miss Yue had said it already: the only reason why Guan Shanjin was so good to him was because of Mr. Lu. Guan Shanjin loved Mr. Lu too deeply, so he did not dare to ask him to reciprocate his affections. That was why he had chosen Wu Xingzi to be Mr. Lu's substitute.

"Ah, in any case, I don't really know how to play the qin..." Thinking that he had resolved the questions in his head, Wu Xingzi felt the blush on his cheeks gradually recede. He was still happy, but he no longer felt that shy sort of pleasure from before. At the very least, the gift was a sign that Guan Shanjin treated him well.

Now that he'd quashed any unrealistic fantasies, Wu Xingzi calmed down considerably. However, as he looked at the qin,

5   A verse from Guan ju, the first poem in the Classic of Poetry. It is one of the most well-known poems in Chinese literature.

the yearning within him did not subside. Although he had no musical talent, he really did enjoy the sound of the qin. His father had been very adept at playing the qin—Wu Xingzi had heard that no one in the neighboring cities could compare to his father's skill. When he was a child, his father wanted to teach him how to play, but after a month of challenging lessons, his father had no choice but to give up.

Wu Xingzi could not be considered tone-deaf, but he had a tendency to play every note behind the beat. If he was asked to play faster, he would end up a beat ahead. He was always too fast or too slow, and the melody would completely fall apart. Worse still was that Wu Xingzi himself could not hear the problem. He delighted in playing, causing his father to suffer ringing ears that lasted for more than half a month. As a result, his father was forced to give up.

In the end, his father's qin drifted away during the flood and was lost forever. Wu Xingzi never had the chance to touch a qin again until now.

Oh, the sound of the qin was so lovely!

Wu Xingzi wiped his hands a few times on his trousers before strumming the strings again. He only knew one song. He straightened his posture, tuning the instrument, then closed his eyes, recalling what his father had taught him:

"It's said that many years ago, when Fuxi crafted the qin, he suppressed evil and stood away from lust.[6] Cultivating a moral and sensible disposition, he was unpretentious and sincere. As a result, the qin can communicate with all things in the world, and nurture one's integrity.

---

6   Fuxi is a mythological figure said to have created humanity and civilization, along with numerous other inventions.

"Your character is too soft and indifferent—you always back away from disputes and never fight for anything. In the long run, you can live your life calmly; but in the present, you can easily be bullied and taken advantage of. You have to be cautious."

His father told him all of this on his first day of qin lessons, on a lovely day in early spring. His mother was shelling peas nearby, observing father and son with a smile.

"I understand." Wu Xingzi was not yet ten years old. He listened obediently with his head bowed, but didn't really understand what his father meant.

Noticing his confusion, his father sighed. "I hope that the sounds of the qin can cultivate your character," he said sincerely. "You cannot always retreat or give in. You need to know how to assess a situation."

"I understand." Naturally, Wu Xingzi still did not understand.

His father ruffled the hair on his little head and started lecturing about the nine virtues of the qin, going into depth about "the remarkable, the ancient, the diaphanous, the quiet, the smooth, the whole, the clear, the even, and the fragrant."

Wu Xingzi's father expounded greatly on the qin: everything from the crafting of the instrument to its sound when played. Wu Xingzi was practically dozing off at his father's words. When his mother noticed, she secretly tossed a pea at her son to wake him up, so that her little darling wouldn't be reprimanded by his father.

Only when he was finally satisfied with imparting his knowledge did Wu Xingzi's father then lift his son to his knees, teaching him how to play the qin.

Those days were still vivid in his mind. A smile curled Wu Xingzi's lips as he lightly plucked the strings, playing *Melody of the Transcendent and Venerable One*.

Playing on and on, Wu Xingzi repeated the song a number of times, his fingers becoming more nimble. Satisfied, he heaved a big sigh and caressed the body of the precious qin. He was so fascinated by the instrument, absorbed in meticulously studying all of its components, that he entirely forgot about his hunger. However, once Guan Shanjin returned with a bowl of porridge, its thick, delicious aroma caught Wu Xingzi's attention. He rubbed his empty belly, drooling over the food.

"Fill your stomach first," Guan Shanjin said, handing over the porridge. It was an enormous bowl of rice porridge with lean cuts of meat and egg yolk. The golden-yellow grains formed a thick, fluffy layer, and the minced meat was mixed throughout. The blend of gold and brown looked like a constellation of stars, and diced green onions daintily adorned the top. It looked so perfect, Wu Xingzi almost didn't want to eat it.

Wu Xingzi hurriedly stood up and accepted the bowl. Ignoring all etiquette, he scooped a spoonful and delivered it straight into his mouth. Although he burned his tongue on the hot porridge, he couldn't stop eating.

After he'd brought Wu Xingzi to sit at the table in the outside room, Guan Shanjin headed back into the kitchen and ladled a bowl for himself as well. He used a large bowl—the same size he gave Wu Xingzi—but he would most likely be unable to finish it. It was evident that some of it was for Wu Xingzi.

When he returned to the room, Wu Xingzi's bowl was already more than half empty. Guan Shanjin exchanged their bowls, saving them the trouble of ladling porridge from one bowl to another.

Wu Xingzi was truly starving. With his huge appetite, he normally wouldn't be able to stand such hunger. If he hadn't been crying over his memories of Yan Wenxin, how could he have ever skipped two meals? Those days with Yan Wenxin were many years ago. Even if he could not understand why Yan Wenxin never bothered to bid him farewell—even deceiving him with a cheap perfume sachet bought off a street peddler—there was no chance that they would meet again in this life, and therefore Wu Xingzi saw no point in dwelling on it any further.

A bowl and a half of porridge was clearly not enough to satisfy Wu Xingzi. Guan Shanjin never really made a habit of eating supper, and he was only eating with him for fear he might feel awkward otherwise. He only took a couple of bites before readily giving Wu Xingzi the rest of his porridge; then he went back into the kitchen and brought out some egg pancakes that he'd prepared earlier.

Like an autumn breeze scattering the leaves away, the egg pancakes quickly vanished. Guan Shanjin was silently satisfied at the sight. He took out some pastries from his bag for Wu Xingzi to change things up.

He wished he knew how to plump up this old fellow. Wu Xingzi ate with gusto, yet his body was still so thin. Guan Shanjin dearly wanted to fatten him up a little.

When Wu Xingzi was finally full, it was already past eleven. Contented and well fed, Wu Xingzi let Guan Shanjin massage him to help with his digestion. The atmosphere in the room was warm and cozy.

"Why did you get me a qin?" Wu Xingzi finally couldn't resist asking.

Guan Shanjin cocked an eyebrow and smiled. "Don't you like it?"

"I do." Wu Xingzi hurriedly straightened his back to thank Guan Shanjin properly. "Thank you so very much—you're too good to me. But how did you know that I like the qin?"

Guan Shanjin snorted in amusement. "You've been to the Peng Society. Have you collected all your drawings yet?" he asked out of nowhere.

"Ah, yes, yes. I'm very grateful. I've packed them away already." Wu Xingzi's eyes brightened when he spoke of his beloved pengornis pictures. He earnestly cupped his hands in thanks. "I'll never be able to repay your kindness."

Wu Xingzi had evidently forgotten that Guan Shanjin was making amends. After all, it was the Lanling Prince of Pengornises who'd been jealous enough to commit fratricide against his phallic brethren.

Guan Shanjin obviously was not about to remind him of that incident. He nodded slightly with his beautiful face, accepting the thanks without protest.

"So, what else did Rancui show you?"

This follow-up question made Wu Xingzi hunch over abruptly. He looked nervous, a servile smile appearing on his face.

"What else could there be? I-I only picked up the drawings." No matter how foolish Wu Xingzi was, he knew that he could not mention that exquisitely crafted issue of *The Pengornisseur*! Never mind Guan Shanjin throwing a fit at him; he was more worried about implicating Rancui.

"Oh?" Guan Shanjin tapped on the table. His long fingers were symmetrical and slender, yet very powerful. Although the tapping seemed very light, the table was in danger of collapse.

Wu Xingzi gulped, faltering for a moment before bracing himself and answering, "I-I also peeked at the new *Pengornisseur*. However, I didn't have any intentions toward it other than curiosity!" He nodded frantically in emphasis. He was deeply afraid that Guan Shanjin did not believe him.

Of course Guan Shanjin didn't believe him. If he had, he wouldn't be trying to preoccupy him with the qin.

Guan Shanjin sneered. His fingers tapping on the table pierced right through the solid boxwood surface.

Wu Xingzi trembled. "Ah, the table, what a pity..."

This remark made Guan Shanjin laugh; he could no longer keep up his threatening aura. He brushed away the sawdust on his hands and looked at the old quail with tender affection.

"Didn't you want to listen to the gentleman from *The Pengornisseur* play the qin? You have a good eye. That's Bai-gongzi from Qingzhu Lane, and his father is the best qin player of Great Xia—second to none. He is so popular that even the emperor is not always able to summon him to play. His son, Bai-gongzi, is skilled enough to have a chance at surpassing him."

Wu Xingzi blinked. "Ah..." His mouth was open, and he could not put his thoughts into words. He *did* see a young man in *The Pengornisseur* who was skilled in the art of the qin, and he did mention to Rancui his wish to listen to the man play—but how did Guan Shanjin know about this? He no longer even remembered the gentleman's name. "So his family name is Bai?"

Guan Shanjin huffed. "You don't even remember his family name, but you didn't forget that he's skilled in the art of qin. How attentive," he said, his tone sour. "Just now, I heard you play *Melody of the Transcendent and Venerable One* a few times. Do you know any other songs?"

"No, I don't know any other songs. My father only taught me this song in his introductory lessons, but my grasp of music and melody was very poor. In the end, we left it at that." Blushing, Wu Xingzi rubbed his nose. He was too embarrassed to say that for the next week or two, his father had tinnitus, and his playing of the qin was off-key for two months afterward—all thanks to Wu Xingzi's terrible playing.

"What song would you like to listen to Bai Shaochang play?" Guan Shanjin pulled Wu Xingzi back to the qin.

"Uhh... How about *Wild Geese Descend on a Sandbank?*" Wu Xingzi wasn't sure if that was the proper title, but he remembered it had something to do with big birds.

Guan Shanjin eyed him, his handsome lips curling into a faint smile. Sitting down at the qin, he strummed a few notes. "Since you like to listen to the qin, I'll play for you."

He began to pluck the strings, and the sound of the qin flowed from Guan Shanjin's fingers. The melody undulated in the air under the clear, calm moonlight.

Although Wu Xingzi couldn't play on tempo himself, he did know how to appreciate fine music. After all, he had listened to his father's qin for years, and an amateur level of qin-playing skill could not satisfy his ear.

Guan Shanjin was quite adept at the qin—he was almost as skilled as Wu Xingzi's father. Wu Xingzi thought that perhaps the best qin player in Great Xia couldn't be much better than Guan Shanjin. However, his playing was stained with the feeling of bloodshed. In principle, *Wild Geese Descend on a Sandbank* was meant to evoke the autumn sky and crisp air, with light breezes blowing across the flat sand. One was meant to sense the clouds stretching out endlessly, with birds in flight calling out across the horizon. The soaring ambition of wild swans was drawn upon to convey the heart of a reclusive scholar. From the fingers of the general, though, it sounded more like a soldier who could finally catch his breath in a vast desert.

The song had yet to end, but Guan Shanjin's fingers stopped.

Wu Xingzi looked at him in confusion, only to see him laugh at himself before waving Wu Xingzi over.

"What's wrong?" Wu Xingzi asked as he drew closer. With light pressure, he fell into the general's warm and solid embrace, and he started to feel a bit bashful.

"It's nothing... I'm not good at *Wild Geese Descend on a Sandbank*, so I don't want to defile your ears." Guan Shanjin kissed the man in his arms, then caught Wu Xingzi's hands and placed them on the strings of the qin.

"Let me teach you how to play," he said.

"Ah, we'd better not. Even my father could not teach me." Wu Xingzi wanted to pull his hands back, but they were firmly caught in Guan Shanjin's. The general's hands were very warm, like little braziers. The nights of early spring were still rather cold, and it was comfortable to have his hands held like this. Although Wu Xingzi was somewhat shy about it, he stopped struggling and obediently let Guan Shanjin knead his palms.

"I'm not your father, and I'm happy to teach you," Guan Shanjin said. How could he not be aware of how lacking Wu Xingzi's qin playing was? The few repetitions of *Melody of the Transcendent and Venerable One* he had just heard were...unique. The rhythm was severely lacking—sometimes the beat was too fast, sometimes too slow—and because of the lack of strength in Wu Xingzi's fingers, the melody sounded weak.

Wu Xingzi's technique was naturally very poor, but it had a sort of calmness and peace to it that belonged solely to him.

Guan Shanjin had always been attracted to things that were pure and uncorrupted. Perhaps it was due to the complexity of his innermost thoughts; perhaps it was how easily he could see people's foulness and treachery. To him, there was nothing unsullied in this world. He always wanted to keep untarnished things close to him, observing them, pampering them, loving them. Whether it was a cat, a dog, or a human being, in the end, they would all be spoiled by his cossetting—and they all forgot their pure beginnings.

Mr. Lu was the most pampered of them all, the one he'd kept at his side for the longest time, and in the end, Mr. Lu had still changed. Compared to anything or anyone that Guan Shanjin had kept by his side, Mr. Lu's change had been more thorough than any of them. Recently, Guan Shanjin kept questioning why he had failed to see the layer of dust gathering over Mr. Lu's luster.

The sound of Wu Xingzi's qin playing was very clean and bright. The sound of the instrument mirrored a person's character; the type of person they were was reflected in the tone of their playing. Because of this, Guan Shanjin did not like the sound of his own playing. It was too ferocious, too violent. Like an army stampeding past, it was terrifying enough to make children cry.

Once, Bai Shaochang had listened to him play, and he'd been so frightened that he left his seat with his face covered. From then on, he did not dare associate with Guan Shanjin, and this became a laughing matter among the capital's elites. They said that Guan Shanjin's formidable aura and unsurpassed military achievements truly made him seem like the reincarnation of a demigod. Just a short verse of his qin playing was enough to scare the wits out of Bai Shaochang, causing him to run a high fever for several days.

Hmph! How foolish.

"But it's already so late at night, we shouldn't..." Wu Xingzi declined Guan Shanjin's offer. "What if Mr. Lu misunderstood?" The words spilled unbidden from Wu Xingzi's lips.

A tense silence fell between them. The air grew dense and icy cold.

Wu Xingzi shuddered, bowing his head in helplessness, silently scolding himself for being stupid. Of course he didn't mind that Guan Shanjin and Mr. Lu shared an intimate connection, but why were his words so sour? Why did he sound so jealous?

"Mr. Lu? Misunderstood?" Guan Shanjin cocked a brow and chuckled lowly. "Mr. Lu is about to be married. What would he be misunderstanding, exactly?"

After hesitating for a moment, Wu Xingzi realized that he really had taken Miss Yue's words to heart. He sighed and straightened his posture before speaking cautiously. "Ah, I... I'd like to ask you..."

What *would* he like to ask? What was there even to ask about? The words were already at the tip of his tongue, but Wu Xingzi swallowed them back. From the start, he'd never thought that this relationship between them could be more than a fleeting tryst, as ephemeral as the morning dew. Even a flood would recede one day—he would be a fool to let himself drown in it.

He had made a mistake in the past, in giving his heart to Yan Wenxin. Why would he foolishly repeat such a mistake? He pressed a hand to his chest. He had yet to realize that his heart was already bound to Guan Shanjin's.

Not hearing Wu Xingzi continue, Guan Shanjin gently nudged the man in his arms, urging him on. "Hmm? What did you want to ask?"

"It's...nothing, actually..." Wu Xingzi's head sagged. Absentmindedly, he caught Guan Shanjin's hand and started fidgeting with his slender fingers. Surely, he thought, this matter had long been decided, so why would he seek to trouble his mind? Guan Shanjin would obviously not tell him the truth!

A little moody, Wu Xingzi floundered in Guan Shanjin's arms, wanting to stand up. However, Guan Shanjin's arms only tightened around him further. His broad palms patted Wu Xingzi's back in comfort, gradually brushing away the unusual feelings welling within Wu Xingzi.

"Ah," Wu Xingzi sighed, lounging back into Guan Shanjin's embrace, all his internal defenses lowered. "Miss Yue treated me to a delicious meal. Do you like mutton?"

"I do. Why, do you want to invite me to a mutton feast?" Guan Shanjin teased. He was in no hurry to ask what was wrong.

"Yes, I'd like that. The restaurant is owned by Mint and Osmanthus's aunt. She's an expert cook, and her selection of dishes is exquisite. You've been busy outside for so many days—you should eat a good meal." Wu Xingzi mentally counted the amount of spare coins he had in his money pouch. In the last few weeks living in the general's estate, he had gained some income. He received a fixed allowance every month, and Wu Xingzi accepted it with much reticence. As luck would have it, he would now be able to use that money to treat Guan Shanjin to a meal!

"She's even more skilled than me?" Guan Shanjin harrumphed. He did not like Wu Xingzi admiring anyone else more than he admired him.

"That's different," Wu Xingzi said truthfully. "You're the best cook."

Smiling in satisfaction, Guan Shanjin asked another question. "Then why don't I buy some mutton and prepare a feast for you instead?"

"No, no, no, I've already said that I'll treat you." Wu Xingzi hurriedly shook his head, but he could not help swallowing his saliva at the thought of Guan Shanjin's cooking. With the general's culinary skills, that mutton feast would be delicious.

"All right, as long as you're happy." Guan Shanjin caught his hand, kissing at it a couple of times. "When that Yue child treated you to a meal, did she say anything?"

Not having expected Guan Shanjin to be so direct, Wu Xingzi cowered a little. He gave Guan Shanjin an appeasing smile. "I-it's nothing, just... Ah, Haiwang, should you ask the physician to look at your eyes?"

Wu Xingzi sounded serious. Guan Shanjin frowned, not understanding. "What's wrong with my eyes?"

"Miss Yue said that y-you..." Wu Xingzi faltered for a moment before exhaling deeply and speaking with determination. "Is it true that you see me as a substitute for Mr. Lu?"

"What will you think if I say yes?" Guan Shanjin had no intention of concealing this matter. Hei-er had already reported everything Miss Yue had said to Wu Xingzi word for word. The general had only been waiting for Wu Xingzi to mention it.

Wu Xingzi's heart ached for a moment, but he did not pay any attention to it. Instead, he turned around, cupping Guan Shanjin's face and studying it solemnly. "Do you have any illness or internal injury?"

"Oh? Why?" Guan Shanjin knew that Wu Xingzi was a silly old fellow and went about things somewhat unusually. However, the general felt a little dejected and anxious. Even if Wu Xingzi wasn't disheartened at being Mr. Lu's substitute, he should at least throw a tantrum! However, Wu Xingzi refused to participate in such behavior. What exactly was going through this man's head?!

"Please don't get angry. This could be a big problem, so you really should let the physician take a look at you. You're still so young— you don't want any consequences from an untreated illness."

"An illness?"

"Ah, yes. I mean, there's absolutely no trace of similarity between Mr. Lu and me, so how were you able to take me as his substitute? Unless..." *Unless you have a problem with your eyes?*

Although Wu Xingzi did not finish his sentence, how could Guan Shanjin not understand him?

Guan Shanjin was angered to the point of laughter. A sudden pain jolted in his chest, and he nearly spat up blood. If he didn't have any internal injuries already, Wu Xingzi would certainly cause some!

"This is what you wanted to ask me?" Guan Shanjin asked, gritting his teeth.

"Ah, this is no small matter," Wu Xingzi mumbled.

Wu Xingzi was promptly picked up by Guan Shanjin. Amidst his shrieks of protest, the general tossed him onto the bed.

CHAPTER 6

A Way to Attain His Desires

"Did you miss me at all these last few days?" Guan Shanjin murmured to himself. "I've been thinking of you constantly."

Wu Xingzi couldn't help but be moved; a bittersweet sensation welled up within him. He never asked for much, but if there was one thing he yearned for. He honestly wished to be in someone's heartfelt thoughts. His mind spun, twisting and turning over and over. He reached out and hugged Guan Shanjin, nuzzling his cheek against the man's chest as he softly replied.

"Ah, I did miss you quite a bit..."

ALTHOUGH GUAN SHANJIN was careful about tossing him onto the bed, Wu Xingzi still felt a little dizzy from the impact. He collapsed onto the soft blanket and gasped a few times before pushing himself up. He looked at the beautiful man savagely grinning at him next to the bed, confused, before shrinking into himself timidly.

"Y-you're...angry?"

"Oh? You can tell?" Guan Shanjin took his sweet time untying his sash, letting his outer robe slide down his body. Holding onto his waist sash and wearing only his inner robes, he moved onto the bed and cornered Wu Xingzi.

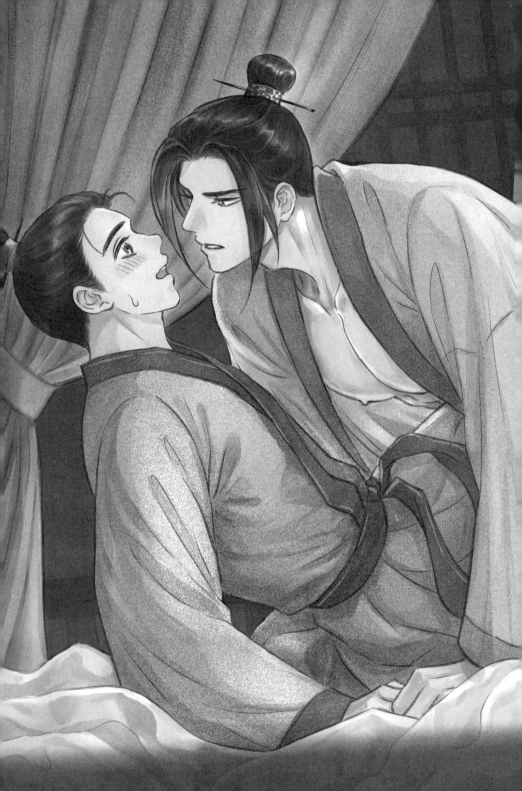

"Why are you angry?" Wu Xingzi asked with a gulp, blinking at Guan Shanjin in panic. He thought back on what he'd said, but he couldn't think of anything that would've angered the general.

But he had to admit, an angry handsome man was handsome nonetheless. Guan Shanjin had extremely emotive and seductive eyes, and within them glimmered a hint of insolence. They shone bright with his riled temper; Wu Xingzi could almost see his own reflection in them, and he was entranced. It would be a great pity if this pair of eyes turned blind, he decided. The physician needed to come and examine Guan Shanjin.

Noticing that the old fellow was once again drifting away with his thoughts, Guan Shanjin could neither stay angry nor laugh. His chest felt tight to the point of pain. He leaned down to bite Wu Xingzi.

"Ahh..." Wu Xingzi recoiled in pain as Guan Shanjin's sharp, shiny teeth dug into his cheek. Stupefied, he clasped a hand over the bite mark. Why did Guan Shanjin keep biting him? This old face of his wasn't tasty at all.

"Wu Xingzi."

With a flick of Guan Shanjin's hands, his waist sash snapped like a whip. Wu Xingzi trembled along with the sound, huddling further into the corner.

"Just now, you insinuated I was blind."

"Huh?" Wu Xingzi blinked, then shook his head violently. "No, I know that you're not blind," he said with great sincerity. "I'm only worried that you might have some unknown illness... Haiwang, you've fought through years of war. It's not shameful to have an undetected disease or injury. There is such a massive difference between Mr. Lu and me, yet you still... Ah, I'm really worried for you."

Such earnest and genuine concern soothed Guan Shanjin, yet also frustrated him. It was as though after drinking cool spring water, a searing iron was pressed into his body. Caught between the heat and the chill, he couldn't put what he was feeling into words.

"Aren't you going to ask why I took you as a substitute?" Guan Shanjin asked, reaching out to wrap an arm around Wu Xingzi's thin back. It had been days since he was last able to hold Wu Xingzi close, and Guan Shanjin had missed him deeply. Not even Mr. Lu had been able to occupy his thoughts so totally.

In the crook of his arm, Wu Xingzi's body was slender and soft. He fit perfectly into Guan Shanjin's embrace, so much so that it would be difficult to separate the two of them. Guan Shanjin held him more tightly, his warm, broad palm resting against Wu Xingzi's back. He felt the man in his arms shudder, then melt into his embrace.

"Hah…" Wu Xingzi wasn't *that* foolish—he wouldn't answer that question. Having spent so much time together, he was able to use some discretion now when dealing with Guan Shanjin. After all, he was certain he knew the answer.

He and Mr. Lu were an ocean apart. One man was up in the clouds, the other down in the dirt. If they were to ask a hundred people, every single one of them would agree that the two men were not alike in any way. What other reason could there be other than Guan Shanjin's eyesight being impaired?

Wu Xingzi was not one to seek trouble for himself. He was aware of his lowly position, and he acknowledged it.

Guan Shanjin huffed. How could Wu Xingzi not realize how half-hearted his response was? He pinched Wu Xingzi's slim waist, making Wu Xingzi's breath catch. Somewhat satisfied, Guan Shanjin bent his neck to kiss the bite mark he had left on Wu Xingzi's cheek.

For a moment, the two of them quietly settled in the tangle of each other's arms. Breathing in Wu Xingzi's faint scent, Guan Shanjin felt immense comfort spread through his body.

"Wu Xingzi."

"Yes."

"Ah, Wu Xingzi."

"Yes?"

"Did you miss me at all over these last few days?"

Did he miss him? Wu Xingzi shifted uneasily, only to be held tighter. He could already feel the heat of the general's groin between his thighs. He blushed, conflicted. Should he remain motionless, or seek what he desired? He dared not ponder too deeply over whether or not he'd missed Guan Shanjin—but he definitely did miss Guan Shanjin's dick.

Guan Shanjin did not wait for his reply. "I've been thinking of you constantly."

The general's words traveled gently to Wu Xingzi's ear with an air of undeniable affection. Even Wu Xingzi couldn't help but be moved; a bittersweet sensation welled up within him.

It had been a long time since anyone openly expressed they were thinking of him. Of course, Auntie Liu and her family were always concerned about him and took care of him. However, they were not blood relatives, so there was still some distance between them.

Wu Xingzi had never asked for much. But he honestly wished to be in someone's heartfelt thoughts. After all, everyone had someone they loved in this world, but Wu Xingzi was always left behind.

He knew that Guan Shanjin's heart was set on Mr. Lu, that he was only doted upon as a substitute, that a day would come when he would return to Qingcheng County alone—when that day came, would he still have the desire to kill himself like before?

His mind spun, twisting and turning over and over. Wu Xingzi reached out and hugged Guan Shanjin, nuzzling his cheek against the man's chest as he softly replied.

"Ah, I did miss you quite a bit..."

Guan Shanjin's muscular figure tensed up slightly in his arms, as though he had not expected to hear such an answer. He pressed a burning kiss against Wu Xingzi's lips—forceful, direct, even a little brutal. Guan Shanjin bit Wu Xingzi's lips, then twined their tongues together. He swept against every sensitive spot in Wu Xingzi's mouth as if he wanted to swallow Wu Xingzi whole.

"Mm..." Wu Xingzi couldn't breathe from the passionate kiss, his entire body collapsing into the general's firm chest. However, Guan Shanjin was still unsatisfied. With loud, wet sounds, he slid his tongue as deeply as he could into Wu Xingzi's mouth. He tightened his arms further around the older man's body, dissatisfied with the distance between them.

It was a wet, sloppy kiss. Wu Xingzi's vision flashed white as he breathed in the scent of Guan Shanjin. With great difficulty, he took in a gasp of air, but it was immediately stolen with another kiss.

Wu Xingzi's mind was left completely muddled by what was happening. He couldn't say when his clothes had disappeared, but he found himself nude; upon contact with Guan Shanjin's heated skin, a blush suffused his slightly chilled body, and goosebumps dimpled his flesh.

Guan Shanjin panted heavily. He managed to pull his lips away from Wu Xingzi's, mouthing down his neck.

"H-Haiwang..." Wu Xingzi fell back onto the bed with the force of Guan Shanjin's kisses. Somehow, he felt a little shy, and he reached out in a futile effort to push at the man on top of him. But even if he'd been strong enough to shove Guan Shanjin off, Wu Xingzi did not actually want him to stop.

"You don't like it?" Guan Shanjin pulled away, a smile accompanying his question.

"I...I do..."

Wu Xingzi had always been straightforward in his desires. He bashfully turned his head away, the tips of his ears flaring a bright red as he exposed his delicate neck to Guan Shanjin. The soft, slender line of his neck was very pleasing to Guan Shanjin's eye; all the marks and bruises scattered across it were the result of his handiwork just now.

Guan Shanjin's heart melted completely, and the fire blazing within him could no longer be contained. Accompanied by Wu Xingzi's shrieks of alarm, Guan Shanjin flipped him over. He raised the older man's buttocks up high, making his thin, fair waist arch enchantingly.

Wu Xingzi wanted to turn around and look at the general, but his current position was too embarrassing. Suddenly, his vision went dark. Something that felt like cloth covered his eyes; Guan Shanjin wrapped the fabric around his head twice before knotting it firmly behind his head. Wu Xingzi was unable to remove it.

In the dark, Guan Shanjin's breath felt extremely hot beside his ear. "Don't be afraid. We're just playing, hmm?"

Guan Shanjin sure knew how to play!

Wu Xingzi whimpered and tried to struggle. He couldn't see anything, and his skin seemed to become even more sensitive because of it. His skin tingled when Guan Shanjin's loose hair brushed gently against his back; it felt like insects crawling across him. Wu Xingzi's limbs turned to jelly.

Seeing that Wu Xingzi wouldn't cooperate, Guan Shanjin went straight to smacking his buttocks. Wu Xingzi twisted and turned, so aroused that he could feel fluid dripping out of him. Between his cheeks, his hole winked shyly; its wetness was evident.

"My dirty boy," Guan Shanjin said. He loved how shameless Wu Xingzi was in bed; it stood in delightful contrast to his otherwise reserved personality. However, he was still quite resentful of Wu Xingzi's penchant for other penises! How could he let anyone else see Wu Xingzi this lustful, this lascivious? There was no way in hell! He would bind Wu Xingzi to himself, even if he had to resort to tying the old man up.

Guan Shanjin inflicted two more harsh slaps on Wu Xingzi's round, perky buttocks. The impact made them jiggle, and the general was absolutely entranced by the sight. His cock rose up to the sky, its tip dripping with pre-come.

Wu Xingzi couldn't be more embarrassed. He couldn't see anything, and his extremely attuned senses felt Guan Shanjin's attention roaming his body, gradually drawing closer to his hole. Warm, heated breaths swirled across his entrance, sending a thrill through him. Curling up, he wanted to escape, only to be caught.

"I haven't tasted you here yet," Guan Shanjin said.

Where? Wu Xingzi's head exploded. He stuttered, "Y-you, you w-want to taste..."

He couldn't mean *there*, right?! That was far too dirty!

"You smell so very lovely here. I wonder if you'd taste just as sweet." Guan Shanjin tasted Wu Xingzi's juices before, but only a little from his fingertip. The taste wasn't exactly pleasant, but he enjoyed it. As they spent more time together, he had grown to love every part of Wu Xingzi's body, from his head to his toes. Despite Wu Xingzi's ability to frustrate him to the point of spitting up blood, Guan Shanjin still enjoyed every part of him.

Every time they fucked, Wu Xingzi's blush-pink hole would be teased to a fiery red. It only took a week of rest for it to revert to its original tightness and shyness.

Guan Shanjin licked his lips. Unable to restrain himself any longer, he spread apart the cheeks that had been marked by his handprints and pressed his lips right in the center.

"Ah!" Wu Xingzi cried out in alarm, shocked at what he was feeling. That nimble, agile tongue was...was... Guan Shanjin was devouring his asshole!

The general meticulously lapped at the tender pucker with the tip of his tongue. Exploring every inch of skin, he licked and licked until the hole softened under his tongue.

Wu Xingzi's taste spread through Guan Shanjin's mouth, somewhat astringent and slightly sweet. It fueled the flames of desire within him; Guan Shanjin desperately wanted to make Wu Xingzi orgasm using only his tongue. As soon as the thought crossed his mind, Guan Shanjin diligently applied himself to the task.

He forced the tip of his tongue inside. Wu Xingzi whimpered and whined, clenching up on Guan Shanjin's tongue, trapping it in place. But he didn't resist. As he writhed, his hole eagerly swallowed up the intruding tongue. His slickness dripped out even more, flowing down Guan Shanjin's tongue and into his mouth, as if there was a mountain spring deep within him.

Wu Xingzi whimpered. "Haiwang... Haiwang..." He trembled, his ass held up high. He tried his best to turn his blindfolded eyes toward Guan Shanjin. Tears stained the fabric, either the result of pleasure or fright.

Guan Shanjin jerked Wu Xingzi's little prick a couple of times, making the older man moan. Wu Xingzi's body had lost all its strength; his entrance relaxed, allowing Guan Shanjin's tongue to have its way with him.

Guan Shanjin placed great effort into tongue-fucking Wu Xingzi, mimicking a cock thrusting inside. He occasionally jabbed his tongue into the sensitive little spot within him. Wu Xingzi let out a quavering cry, his juices gushing out over and over. As Guan Shanjin pulled away, a thin, silvery thread connected his tongue to Wu Xingzi's hole.

Guan Shanjin's tongue left Wu Xingzi trembling. He was teased to the brink of orgasm, only for Guan Shanjin to step back at the last moment, leaving him teetering right on the edge. Wu Xingzi felt like he was being gnawed on by a million insects; the hair all over his body had become so sensitive that he could not bear to be touched.

Slick fluid dripped down his slender, fair thighs, soaking the bedsheets underneath. Every breath he took was tinged with the smell of sex.

Guan Shanjin leaned forward to kiss him. Tangling their tongues together, he shared some of Wu Xingzi's lewd juices with him. Mixing with their saliva, most of it escaped from the corner of Wu Xingzi's mouth, but a tiny bit was forced down his throat.

Wu Xingzi swallowed. It didn't taste like much to him, but it had come from his hole! Didn't Guan Shanjin think it was disgusting?

Wu Xingzi's face flushed a deep red as he twisted his hips restlessly. His empty hole clenched down on nothing, and inside was an ache that could not be relieved. He desperately wished for something thick and heavy to soothe the burning desire within.

"H-Haiwang," he cried softly. His tongue tingled from kissing, and it sounded like the inside of his mouth was coated with honey.

"Hmm?" Guan Shanjin reluctantly pulled his lips away, trailing kisses from Wu Xingzi's shoulder down to his waist. Frantic moans spilled from Wu Xingzi's lips.

"Inside me, please..."

Quivering, he groped behind him, wanting to touch Guan Shanjin's hefty cock. However, his current position left him barely able to move. After a few failed attempts, he grew even more impatient.

The thick, heated member sinfully brushed against his thighs and his hole like a dragonfly flitting across water. Before he could touch it, it moved away, leaving Wu Xingzi eagerly panting and close to tears. Even worse, he couldn't see; each time he tried to remove the strip of cloth around his eyes, Guan Shanjin patiently stopped him. Guan Shanjin's hands and lips took different routes, torturing Wu Xingzi with kisses and nips all over his body. Eventually, Wu Xingzi was pushed over the edge, teased to orgasm.

Wu Xingzi sprawled across the bed with his face pressed into the blanket, his fair skin flushed red. His mouth was agape, and his blindfold was soaked with tears. His feeble body twitched all over, almost broken from Guan Shanjin's ministrations.

Guan Shanjin studied the old fellow in his bed with great affection. Unfortunately, Wu Xingzi was unable to see the tenderness in his eyes.

"Come on, spread your cheeks apart a little." Guan Shanjin helped Wu Xingzi up. Reclining against the headboard, he guided Wu Xingzi's hands to grasp his buttocks.

"Uh..." Wu Xingzi was mortified, but he still obediently went along with Guan Shanjin's instructions. He timidly spread his cheeks apart, further exposing his twitching hole.

After being played with for so long, the pink hole was now a vibrant red. So tender and wet, it fanned the flames within Guan Shanjin even further.

The general hooked Wu Xingzi's thin, fair legs around his arms. When his heated cock glanced past Wu Xingzi's hole, the old quail shuddered violently, as if he'd been burned.

Guan Shanjin laughed quietly. He entered Wu Xingzi with a powerful thrust; there was no pause, no hesitation. His cock reached deep inside, fucking the old man into uncontrolled spasms. Wu Xingzi's head tilted back as his body trembled, moaning as if he was about to fall apart. He wanted to push Guan Shanjin away.

His hole was stretched to its limits, wrapped tightly around Guan Shanjin's thick cock. Wu Xingzi's tongue lolled from his open mouth, his gasps sounding almost like sobs. His moans were obscene, yet still tinged with a trace of bashfulness. Guan Shanjin was so aroused by the sounds he made that his gaze turned savage; gripping Wu Xingzi's waist, he started fiercely fucking into him.

At first, Guan Shanjin's thick cock couldn't fit all the way inside. After a few thrusts, his entire shaft was swallowed up by Wu Xingzi's tight, slick hole, the huge cockhead constantly jabbing him. His insides were sore and tingling; he wasn't sure if he felt pleasure or pain.

So many days had passed since they'd last fucked. His hole that had previously been conditioned to Guan Shanjin's cock now turned shy again, clenching tightly. However, with Guan Shanjin's tempestuous thrusts, its tightness would not last for long. As soon as his hole loosened a little, Guan Shanjin entered fully. The vague shape of his cock could be seen through Wu Xingzi's belly, bulging with every thrust.

Wu Xingzi was fucked so hard he felt his soul might shatter. Guan Shanjin's movements were brutal, his thrusts causing Wu Xingzi's body to sway with the force of them. The general's balls slapped against his perineum, and his buttocks rippled with each impact. Slick fluid escaped from where the two were joined, and it worked up into a froth from their vigorous motions before slowly dripping down Wu Xingzi's ass.

"D-don't... It's too deep," Wu Xingzi cried, hiccupping. Perhaps it was because he was blindfolded, but he was so sensitive that he could feel the pulse of every vein on Guan Shanjin's huge, heated cock as it spread him open. Wu Xingzi felt like Guan Shanjin might pierce his very soul.

"Be good," Guan Shanjin panted before lowering his head to kiss Wu Xingzi. At the same time, he grabbed Wu Xingzi's hand and placed it on his bulging belly.

Guan Shanjin dominated Wu Xingzi from both ends, filling up his mouth with his tongue and his ass with his cock. Wu Xingzi's tongue hurt from all the sucking and the nibbling. He could scarcely breathe, but he could not escape. The general's thrusts only grew stronger, as if he wanted to force everything, even his balls into Wu Xingzi. Again and again, Guan Shanjin impaled Wu Xingzi, torturing his red, swollen hole.

Every inch of Wu Xingzi's ass was brutally spread apart, and his entrance was fucked until it was swollen. The lightest touch was enough to make him thrash and scream. His entire body convulsed, having come two or three times in such a short period. Guan Shanjin seemed to think it was not enough; his hand went to stroke the little prick again, as if he wanted to wring out all the come Wu Xingzi had left inside him.

How could there be any left?! Wu Xingzi wailed and cried as his orgasms crashed over him. He had long surpassed his limits; his torso tensed up and he shuddered on the bed, nearly about to faint.

Guan Shanjin, too, was reaching his limit, gasping heavily. The slap of skin against skin echoed through the room as his thrusts became harder and heavier. Wu Xingzi was fucked into unconsciousness several times before being fucked awake again.

At last, Wu Xingzi's little cock gave a final quiver as he pissed the bed. Only then did Guan Shanjin groan and come inside of Wu Xingzi, the sensation so scorching that it made him convulse again. Wu Xingzi's head drooped down, his tongue hanging out of his open mouth as he passed out cold.

Guan Shanjin embraced the still-twitching Wu Xingzi and pressed kisses onto his skin before getting off the bed to clean both of them up.

Having been on the road for a number of days, Guan Shanjin was exhausted. All the same, he meticulously cleaned Wu Xingzi and changed the bedsheets before cuddling the older man to sleep.

When Wu Xingzi woke the next morning, the bed was empty next to him. Still in a sleepy haze, he timidly reached out to stroke the silk blanket. It felt cool to the touch, evidence that Guan Shanjin had left quite some time ago.

Unable to stop himself, he sighed. Flipping over, he buried himself in the blanket like a caterpillar inside its cocoon.

Although he'd been able to spend a great deal of time with his favorite pengornis last night, Wu Xingzi knew that things were far from good. He'd been feeling rather depressed recently. He kept on smelling the scent of peach blossoms, and at first he'd thought that was his problem— that the scent wafting from the neighbors' trees was reminding him of Yan Wenxin. However, after last night, he realized that those peach blossoms had nothing to do with his sorry mood.

Yan Wenxin did still have a place in his heart. However, what had really had him wallowing in his past heartbreak was not the scent of peach blossoms, but Guan Shanjin.

He might... Wu Xingzi might have developed feelings that he should not have toward this man he was not qualified to be with.

He pressed his palm against his chest as his heart wrenched painfully. He was unable to stop thinking about Guan Shanjin. His every move, his every frown, his every smile—how long had Wu Xingzi been storing them all inside his heart?

Before Guan Shanjin left, Wu Xingzi had been able to view their relationship casually. He knew from the start that Guan Shanjin was only fooling around with him—the two of them would eventually have to return to their separate lives. It took someone like Mr. Lu to be worthy of Guan Shanjin, and Wu Xingzi... He smiled diffidently to himself. He was only a little adviser from a poor county... Ah, no. He'd forgotten—he was not even an adviser anymore.

A bone-piercing chill spread through his body. Grabbing the blanket, Wu Xingzi shivered, quietly laughing at himself for being so foolish.

Wu Xingzi knew he was not a clever person, but he had never expected that he would actually be *this* idiotic. In his teens, it could have been said that he was naïve, but he was already forty years old. Foolishness at his age was not something that medication could cure—it was laughable.

How could he end up falling for Guan Shanjin?

The door to the room abruptly opened. Wu Xingzi curled up inside his blanket and shuddered. Only after he took a few deep breaths did he slowly peek his face out. He was met directly with Guan Shanjin's handsome, smiling face.

Rays from the spring sun shone in through the window, covering the beautiful man with a layer of golden gauze. His curving eyes entranced and dazzled Wu Xingzi.

"Hmm? Still sleepy?" Guan Shanjin asked, holding breakfast in his hands. He placed the dishes one by one on the table, then turned around, planning to pick Wu Xingzi up.

However, Wu Xingzi dodged him, scratching his nose and smiling awkwardly. "I'm awake, I'm awake."

After confirming that he was not naked under the blanket, Wu Xingzi slowly clambered off the bed. He walked barefoot to the table, salivating over the food.

Guan Shanjin's brows knitted together slightly. Staring at his empty hands for a moment, he then walked over to Wu Xingzi's side, and pushed him to sit. "Here, try the dumplings I made," he said with a smile.

"You shouldn't have gone to all this trouble," Wu Xingzi said, but his hand had already picked up a pair of chopsticks to dig in. Confusion was stirring within his heart right then, and he urgently needed to ground himself with a good meal.

After helping Wu Xingzi mix the dipping sauce, Guan Shanjin turned away to bring some flatbread and soymilk over. He sat down and accompanied Wu Xingzi as they ate breakfast.

The dumplings were juicy, filled with tender pork and firm, fresh shrimp. Paired with crisp chives, the flavors blended together harmoniously. The vinegar-based dipping sauce brought the tastiness of the filling out even further.

Knowing how much Wu Xingzi could eat, Guan Shanjin had prepared nearly a hundred dumplings. Afraid that it would not be enough to satisfy Wu Xingzi's appetite, he also made flatbread.

When faced with food, Wu Xingzi buried himself in it. His cheeks bulged out as he ate an entire dumpling in one bite, making him look like a little old chipmunk. Guan Shanjin couldn't stop himself from laughing.

"Don't eat too quickly," he said. "Be careful not to choke."

"Yes." Wu Xingzi lifted his head and smiled at the general before lowering his head again and gulping down more dumplings.

In less than half an hour, Wu Xingzi had cleared all the dishes on the table. He belched, then hurriedly covered his mouth as he glanced at Guan Shanjin in embarrassment.

"Did you enjoy the food?" Guan Shanjin asked, not minding the burp at all. Pulling Wu Xingzi's hands over, he wiped them with his handkerchief. He was about to help Wu Xingzi wipe his mouth, but Wu Xingzi dodged him again.

"It's fine, I'll do it myself. I'm not a toddler." His face tinged pink, Wu Xingzi took the handkerchief and wiped his mouth. Then he folded up the used piece of cloth over and over, as if he was trying to conceal the spots he'd dirtied. In the end, his shoulders collapsed in defeat. "I'll return it to you after I've washed it," he said, tucking the handkerchief away.

Guan Shanjin's brow creased. What was going on? He couldn't understand why Wu Xingzi was acting so differently.

Wu Xingzi's attitude was different now. In the past, he'd always been either subconsciously seeking intimacy or carelessly detached. Now, though, he awkwardly drew a line that distanced himself from Guan Shanjin—other than a glance and smile during their meal, Wu Xingzi had not looked directly at him since he got out of bed.

"Wu Xingzi," Guan Shanjin called out.

"Yes?" Wu Xingzi responded, tilting his head. His eyes fell to Guan Shanjin's chest, refusing to move his gaze upward.

Guan Shanjin wanted to question him, but he discovered that he had no words. What could he ask?

Wu Xingzi had never held Guan Shanjin in his heart in the first place, so for him to abruptly put distance between them was hardly unreasonable... But Guan Shanjin was extremely unsettled. He'd thought that after yesterday, the two of them had further solidified their feelings for each other, but today...

Wu Xingzi was the first to break the silence. "Haiwang."

"Hmm?" Guan Shanjin watched him in anticipation, but the old fellow still refused to look at him directly. A feeling of discomfort, as though he had swallowed a burning stone, spread through Guan Shanjin's entire body.

"If you still have feelings for Mr. Lu, shouldn't you go and bring him back?" Wu Xingzi asked. He himself was unclear about the intentions behind his words.

Guan Shanjin gritted his teeth, his knuckles cracking as he clenched his fists. The veins in his neck bulged out. "I have no such intention," he said.

The general was confused. After just one night, Wu Xingzi's attitude had completely changed. However, he knew that he had to control his temper, and he should not speak out of anger.

"Oh." Wu Xingzi nodded, sighing inwardly.

In recent days, it felt like Guan Shanjin was full of gunpowder, ready to explode with the slightest spark. Although he didn't take out his anger on anyone, the people close to him were still uncomfortable.

Mr. Lu was to be married in about two weeks, and no one could figure out what Guan Shanjin's thoughts were on the matter. After going to Yue Manor to see Mr. Lu, he announced that his estate was still in charge of managing the wedding. He then brought Mr. Lu back to his estate.

The Wang Shu Residence sprang back to life as though nothing had changed. The man Guan Shanjin longed for was still Mr. Lu, and Wu Xingzi was once again shoved to the back of his mind.

As expected, a substitute for his beloved could never compare to the original. Wu Xingzi had stolen a few days of doting away from Mr. Lu, but in the end, he had to give it all back.

It was Miss Yue who was left the most forlorn in this situation. However, she understood that no matter how much she liked Mr. Lu, he was essentially a fish eye disguised as a pearl without the general's support.

Not wanting to worry Mr. Lu, Miss Yue pushed her unhappiness away. She sent him away bitterly, now spending every day in anticipation of the wedding.

When Mint and Osmanthus told Wu Xingzi of Mr. Lu's return to the Wang Shu Residence, he simply smiled calmly. Even if his heart was filled with agony, there was nothing he could do. He was the one who'd told Guan Shanjin he should bring Mr. Lu back. It didn't matter whether he really meant it, or if it was only a test— Guan Shanjin had certainly given him an answer. With Mr. Lu back, a mere substitute was hardly necessary anymore.

Indeed, Guan Shanjin took all the attention he once lavished on Wu Xingzi with him, and he no longer visited every day. Although Wu Xingzi was not barred from cooking in his own little kitchen, he was given less vegetables, meat, rice, and flour than before. The intention was to make Wu Xingzi go and collect his food from the main kitchen itself.

This should have been the case from the start. In the general's estate, food was meant to be prepared solely in the main kitchen. Even Mr. Lu himself had never cooked in his own kitchen.

Hei-er hadn't made any more appearances either. Wu Xingzi did manage to catch sight of him following behind Man Yue at one point, though, rushing past him on horseback along the main road of the city.

As for how Wu Xingzi caught sight of him, the reason was simple: since Guan Shanjin no longer visited him, Wu Xingzi was free to do whatever he wanted. These days, he often dropped by the

Peng Society, seeking Rancui out for tea. After all, Rancui was the only other person he was acquainted with in Horse-Face City.

Today, Wu Xingzi once again visited the Peng Society. Rancui was dressed in an elegant robe, seated within the bamboo pavilion. It was simple, yet exquisite, like something out of a dream. Rancui plucked out a melody on a qin.

On a low table by the side sat an incense burner, its scent faint yet lovely. Wu Xingzi did not know what the scent was exactly, but he liked it very much. It was a perfect accompaniment to the sound of Rancui's playing.

Wu Xingzi dared not disturb Rancui, so he tiptoed over to a cushion placed slightly further away and sat down. Only when the melody faded did he wake up from his trance. Exhaling gently, he gave Rancui a small smile.

"Manager Rancui is so talented," Wu Xingzi said. "Even your qin playing is exquisite."

"You flatter me, Adviser Wu." Rancui cupped his hands toward Wu Xingzi. Nudging the qin away, he waved at one of his employees to bring over tea and snacks.

"No, no, I'm entirely sincere. You're too modest, Manager Rancui." Wu Xingzi looked at the qin with obvious desire and fondness in his eyes. Rancui did not mention it.

Rancui had investigated all eighteen generations of Wu Xingzi's family. He had a decent understanding of who Wu Xingzi's father was; naturally, he knew why Wu Xingzi loved the qin. However, sometimes it was enough to simply know; there was no need to say everything out loud. Smiling, Rancui accepted Wu Xingzi's compliment, and they began to make small talk.

A sigh escaped Wu Xingzi. He seemed rather absent-minded today.

After he'd sighed a few more times, Rancui couldn't hold back his curiosity. "Adviser Wu, is something troubling you?"

Rancui had a guess, but he hoped that he was wrong.

"Ahh... I'm sorry, I've been rude." Wu Xingzi now realized how distracted he was being today. Embarrassed, he covered his mouth and bowed his head in apology.

"You haven't. I'm just worried about you. After all, I consider us friends, Adviser Wu. You can tell me anything—there's no need to worry about offending me." Rancui refilled Wu Xingzi's teacup, his gentle smile so kind that it could lower anyone's defenses.

Wu Xingzi struggled for a moment before sighing heavily. With a rare deep crease on his forehead, he told Rancui, "In three days, Mr. Lu will be married."

"Yes. It's going to be quite a big event in this city. I heard that Old Master Yue has decided to hold a banquet in the square in front of the magistrate's office for three days and three nights. The general has approved this feast, and he will be temporarily suspending the city's curfew for those three days." Rancui laughed lightly. "Mr. Lu certainly has some powerful backing."

He covered his smile with a hand, his charming eyes fixed on Wu Xingzi, watching intently as Wu Xingzi's lips curled in distress. It seemed Wu Xingzi wanted to say something, the words at the tip of his tongue, only for him to swallow them down. Instead he picked up a pastry and shoved it into his mouth, not caring if he choked on it.

It seemed things wouldn't be resolved so easily this time. Rancui sighed.

The day after Mr. Lu was grandly escorted back to the general's estate, Wu Xingzi came by the Peng Society to look at *The Pengornisseur*.

Rancui had known at once that Wu Xingzi had realized his feelings for Guan Shanjin. He feared that Wu Xingzi's feelings were already too deep. A faint sadness permeated Wu Xingzi's expression; it was only Wu Xingzi himself who thought he was still concealing it.

Although Rancui was very adept at reading people, Wu Xingzi still eluded him. If he had feelings for Guan Shanjin, why did he want to deliberately distance himself from him? If Wu Xingzi was worried about his social status affecting the relationship, Rancui wanted to put his mind at ease. Guan Shanjin was a prideful man; he did whatever he liked. A person's status had nothing to do with the general's feelings.

However, Rancui felt that if he said that too directly—and Wu Xingzi changed his mind as a result—he would fall right into Guan Shanjin's hands. No matter what, Rancui did not want the general to have anything good in his life.

For Wu Xingzi, it was a choice between a long bout of suffering or a short one. If he chose to love Guan Shanjin, he would suffer for a long period of time. After all, who knew when the great general would find someone new to replace him? On the other hand, if he put distance between them now, the pain would only be temporary.

As a result, Rancui had spent quite some time in recent days accompanying Wu Xingzi in browsing *The Pengornisseur*. They even mailed out a few letters, receiving eight or nine drawings in return. Each was unique in its own way, and Wu Xingzi was delighted for a few days. However, this was merely a distraction, and it wouldn't resolve the root cause of his problem.

Rancui watched Wu Xingzi demolish the pastries and drink half a pot of tea before covering his mouth and releasing a burp. Apologetic, Wu Xingzi cupped his hands toward Rancui.

"Adviser, would you like more refreshments?" Rancui knew very well that Wu Xingzi relied on eating to steady his emotions. The Peng Society had no shortage of snacks, and Rancui waved at his employee to fetch some more.

This time the employee brought out freshly fried sesame balls, their aroma tantalizing. When the wind breezed by, Wu Xingzi could almost hear the crispiness of their coating. He'd wanted to speak, but he was inadvertently distracted by the devilish little sesame treats. Not caring if they were too hot for his mouth, he grabbed one and wolfed it down; the taste was so heavenly that it nearly made him cry.

After gorging himself on a third round of snacks, Wu Xingzi felt much more relaxed. Only when the smile curling his lips was genuine did Rancui calm down.

"I've been too rude," Wu Xingzi said. "I've just been eating and ignoring you." He wiped his hands and mouth clean, returning to his cautious and bashful demeanor.

"How is that so? It's a joy to watch you eat. The kitchen staff will be very happy as well." Rancui covered his mouth and laughed. "Do you plan on preparing a wedding present?"

"A present?" Wu Xingzi paused for a moment before he understood what Rancui meant. Complicated feelings swirled within him. "Yes. I've been living long enough at the general's estate that I've met Mr. Lu a few times. It seems proper to congratulate him with a present."

After all, they both lived on the same estate. To not express any congratulations would be rude of him.

"You're very considerate, Adviser Wu." Rancui tapped his fingers on the table, pondering for a moment. "However, in my opinion, it's better that you don't prepare a gift."

"Eh? Why is that?" In Qingcheng County, even the most ordinary family would prepare a gift once they knew of an impending marriage. Qingcheng County was, after all, a small place; people crossed each other's paths constantly. They would always display some courtesy toward each other and share in the joyous atmosphere of a wedding.

Did Horse-Face City not have such customs?

Rancui immediately understood Wu Xingzi's confusion, and he couldn't help but chuckle quietly. "No, it's polite for you to get him a present. It's a happy occasion, and it's good to take part in celebrating. However, I'm afraid that Mr. Lu might not be too happy receiving a gift from you specifically."

"What do you mean?" Wu Xingzi asked, confusion written all over his face. There was no conflict between him and Mr. Lu—Mr. Lu had even invited him to share a meal before.

They were now at the crux of the issue. Rancui deliberated over it, but decided to speak frankly. "Adviser Wu, in your opinion… Between Mr. Lu and General Guan, do you think it is an unrequited love or a shared affection?"

Wu Xingzi's face paled slightly at the question. Lowering his eyes, he answered, "It's probably mutual."

"I think that whether it's one-sided or not, Mr. Lu certainly likes the general." This sentence was cleverly constructed; Rancui only hoped Wu Xingzi could hear the meaning implied. He smiled. "Since Mr. Lu likes the general, and here you are, involved in a little dalliance with the general as well…your gift might seem like you're flaunting your relationship. I'm hardly bothered by how he might feel, but if you were to be the target of some petty revenge because of it, I'd be quite upset."

"Huh?" Wu Xingzi looked up, blinking foolishly. It clearly hadn't occurred to him that so many twists and turns could be contained within such a simple matter; his mind was about to explode. "But... it's not at all my intention to embarrass him. Isn't he the one in Haiwang's heart? Wh-what would I be flaunting, exactly?"

Even if he wanted to, Wu Xingzi did not have the confidence to pull it off! He understood now that Rancui had explained, but he still couldn't help but feel a little depressed.

"It's also yet to be determined if this wedding will actually take place," Rancui said. He opened the lid of the incense burner and stirred the ashes within, a scornful expression on his face.

The Peng Society had once been in the business of information exchange—even now, they had yet to fully give up on their old profession. Rancui was keenly aware of the undercurrent of turbulence in Horse-Face City, and he knew it was linked directly to the power struggle in the capital. The whole dog and pony show of Mr. Lu leaving and then returning to the general's estate had been shared loudly throughout Horse-Face City. If it turned out Guan Shanjin had no plans to stir up trouble, Rancui would eat all the past editions of *The Pengornisseur* stored in their warehouse!

It was no surprise that Guan Shanjin was distancing himself from Wu Xingzi. Although it was unclear if it was because he didn't want to involve Wu Xingzi in political matters, this was still an opportunity for Wu Xingzi to leave. Rancui could take advantage of this situation and urge Wu Xingzi to leave Horse-Face City and return to his quiet, peaceful life in Qingcheng County.

"Is there more to this marriage that I should be worried about?" Wu Xingzi was anxious. Although he'd taken the initiative in distancing himself from Guan Shanjin, he was still unable to let him go, and he was worried that an accident would befall the general.

"The general himself is probably the greatest worry," replied Rancui, feigning nonchalance. He gave a faint sigh. "Think about it.

Is he the type to share his beloved with anyone? He even got jealous over your pengornis drawings."

This reminder had Wu Xingzi convinced, and he nodded his head. Exactly! Guan Shanjin could not accept those drawings as competition, and Wu Xingzi was merely a substitute! Mr. Lu was Guan Shanjin's beloved, so how could he bear to share *him* with anyone else? Besides, in this marriage, Mr. Lu would be marrying into the Yue family, not the other way around. Was Guan Shanjin truly willing to let that happen?

Wu Xingzi rubbed his chest, which kept aching lately. When he thought about Guan Shanjin, the pain was especially fierce.

"Ah, it's really time for me to return to Qingcheng County..." Since those two men shared a mutual affection, why should he remain here and be an eyesore? Wu Xingzi looked up to the sky. Although it was the same sky, it looked so different from how it was at home!

Rancui heard Wu Xingzi's mumbling. He lifted his teacup, hiding a small smile behind it. A plan was forming rapidly in his head, but he revealed none of it on his face. Instead, he gently persuaded Wu Xingzi. "If you're starting to get homesick, why don't you mention it to the general? The general should have some free time after Mr. Lu's wedding. It's likely that he will be willing to take you back to Qingcheng County."

"Oh?" Wu Xingzi looked hesitant. He was reluctant to spend too much time with Guan Shanjin, afraid that his feelings would deepen. Unconsciously, he started to recall the day the two of them left his hometown after celebrating the new year, and how they had agreed to return together for the Qingming Festival to pay respects to his ancestors.

His gloomy feelings started to dredge up old memories. Wu Xingzi remembered how both his father and Guan Shanjin had said that he was passive by nature and never fought for anything, that he was someone who always reconciled himself to his circumstances. These words were too complimentary; he was only passive because he understood that he had no qualifications to fight for anything from anyone.

Wu Xingzi had no illusions about his talents. He was sixteen when he became the top scholar in his village. His father had already achieved this at the young age of twelve; in the entire dynasty of Great Xia, his father would be considered an exceptional genius. Wu Xingzi wasn't sure why his father had never attempted the higher examinations, but he had still been extremely talented as a teacher.

As for his looks, there wasn't much to say; he was plain at best. All of his features were present with nothing amiss, but that was all that could be said.

And finally, his family background... Because he was orphaned, everyone in the county said he was a cursed wretch who would live alone forever. In fact, they said it was because of his curse that his parents had died and he wasn't able to keep anyone by his side... He brought misfortune to everyone around him. If Yan Wenxin had not gone to the capital for the imperial examinations and instead chosen to spend his life with Wu Xingzi, who knew if he'd still be alive?

When he laid it all out like that, how could Wu Xingzi possibly have the confidence to fight for anything? Of course, if it was something he could feasibly fight for, he'd do it! You only had to look at his future gravesite—did he not fight for that special plot of land?

Recalling his grave, Wu Xingzi's mood greatly improved. He thought about the pengornis pictures he had tucked away, too. He did not dare to take home the eight new drawings he'd collected, instead asking Rancui to hold onto them for him. Among this new batch of illustrations was a Pan An among penises, straight and thick.

Wu Xingzi was not sure if Rancui had given the artist special instructions, but this drawing was in color—a pinkish hue shone through the fair flesh tones like a precious gem gleaming in the light. It was a truly magnificent member, second only to Guan Shanjin's!

Wu Xingzi never wallowed in self-pity for too long. Time marched forward, and there was no point in dwelling on the past. He might as well try to make his days pass in a happier mood. At least Guan Shanjin had not disappointed him; he'd even led him out of his well to take a peek at the big, wide world. Wu Xingzi should be satisfied with that.

Watching Wu Xingzi's brow gradually smooth out, Rancui was somewhat surprised. He'd never seen anyone with such a disposition before. It was as if no cloud could ever remain hanging over Wu Xingzi's head for long; he had the tenacity of a stubborn weed. Wu Xingzi looked quite shy and reserved, but his back was always straighter than anyone else's—nothing could make him bend.

"Manager Rancui, many thanks for the refreshments. I've bothered you for quite a while already, so I won't take up any more of your time." Wu Xingzi stood up and cupped his hands toward Rancui before sneaking another glance at the qin.

Rancui stood, too, and returned the polite gesture. "If you don't mind, I shall play again for you next time."

After some courteous small talk, Wu Xingzi bade Rancui farewell. However, just before he was about to turn and leave the pavilion, Rancui called out and stopped him.

"Adviser Wu, if you'd like to return to Qingcheng County, and the general is not able to accompany you... I'm willing to make the journey with you. I happen to need to return to Goose City four days from now, and if you like, why don't you...?"

Before Rancui finished his sentence, Wu Xingzi's eyes turned bright. He nodded his head, expressing his thanks.

"If Manager Rancui doesn't mind, let's make the journey together. We can help take care of each other along the way."

"That's great. You should ask the general for his opinion first, but my doors are always open for you." Rancui wanted to see what Guan Shanjin would do if Wu Xingzi announced his departure.

He walked Wu Xingzi out of the Peng Society as they conversed. It wasn't until he'd watched Wu Xingzi's thin, straight-backed figure draw a distance away that he turned back.

A towering, sturdy figure stood in front of him. Rancui's lips curled up in laughter. "Commander Hei, is it? Are you here to destroy the Peng Society again?"

"No." Hei-er's sharp, resolute face was tinged with anger. His brows knitted tightly together as he glared at the amused Rancui with fierce eyes. He clenched his hands into fists by his sides.

"Oh? Then why have you come to this little shop? Dare I ask if Commander Hei has any instructions?" Rancui remained standing by the door. He was dressed like a rich young man from a noble family and looked as placid and calm as a gently flowing river; however, his smile was gorgeous and his eyes were charming, giving his pure beauty a rather seductive edge. He cast a sidelong glance at Hei-er.

Hei-er took half a step forward. "Why did you goad Mr. Wu into leaving?" As he looked at the ravishing yet untouchable beauty in front of him, Hei-er felt his mouth go dry. But his loyalty was to Guan Shanjin, and he dared not delay the mission at hand.

Rancui snorted. "I knew it. How could it be possible for Guan Shanjin to allow Adviser Wu to roam alone in Horse-Face City? You're one loyal puppy, Commander. Why don't you let me hear you bark a few times?"

"This is a private matter between the general and Mr. Wu—you shouldn't interfere." Although Hei-er was not as clever as Man Yue, he could still tell that Rancui's actions had been deliberate—the manager clearly wanted to stir up trouble. Why did Rancui hate the general so much?

"I'm simply arranging a visit home with my fellow townsman. How is that interfering?" Rancui smiled sarcastically as he walked past Hei-er, not even bothering to look at him.

Hei-er faltered for a moment, but decided to follow Rancui. The salesman who'd accompanied Rancui from Goose City watched the two of them, and after some deliberation, decided to pretend he saw nothing. The manager had never been at a disadvantage before. Even if Commander Hei were to dismantle the place, it would still be difficult for him to gain the upper hand over Rancui.

Rancui knew that Hei-er was following him, but he didn't seem to be bothered. He led him all the way to the bamboo pavilion where he had just been chatting with Wu Xingzi. His qin had been packed away by his maidservant, and the seat cushion had been replaced with a new one. The tea and snacks had been replenished, too. With their seats on opposite ends of the table, Rancui felt they would be at a satisfying distance from one another.

"Take a seat." Rancui chose to sit down first on the side by the pond. Compared to the elegance and dignity he put on when meeting Wu Xingzi, in front of Hei-er, he was clearly more uninhibited. He sat with one knee bent and his leg folded up, a faint wickedness tainting his expression.

Hei-er sat. "Many thanks."

"Tell me, have you been secretly following Adviser Wu for the past few days?" Rancui lazily leaned against the railing of the pavilion, breaking apart the pastry in his hand piece by piece to feed the fish in the pond. He did not bother being polite with Hei-er.

Hei-er did not deny it. "I was following my general's command." He was transitioning from a visible position to one hidden behind the scenes, but he still had to appear in public alongside Man Yue on occasion, to better paint a picture of Wu Xingzi having lost favor with the general. He had never asked about the reason behind such actions—even if Rancui wanted to probe for information, Hei-er would have none to give him.

"What a tremendous game of chess," Rancui snorted coldly, glaring at him. "Don't you feel sorry for Adviser Wu? At the general's estate, you've been at Adviser Wu's side the longest. When you escorted him to Horse-Face City for the first time, did you never think about letting him go?"

Hei-er's head hung low. He was solemn and stiff as a stone; his breathing was so light that it could barely be heard.

Of course he had thought about it before. After all, at that time, the only person the general had in his heart was Mr. Lu; he barely paid any attention to Wu Xingzi. As one of Guan Shanjin's trusted guards, Hei-er knew all about Guan Shanjin's various dalliances. When Guan Shanjin liked someone, he would dote on him excessively, and once his feelings faded, he would toss him aside. Hei-er thought Wu Xingzi would be no different.

But to his surprise, Wu Xingzi ended up carving out a space in his master's heart. By extension, this meant that Wu Xingzi was his master as well. Naturally, he could not let Wu Xingzi be blinded by sweet words.

"Hmm? You don't have the courage to answer me?" Rancui dusted off the crumbs from his hands, then picked up a candy and placed it in his mouth. He seemed to have no intention of concealing the ridicule and annoyance in his eyes.

Wolfish men like Hei-er had always made Rancui uneasy; they were the sort of men he instinctively preferred to avoid. If not for his desire to obstruct Guan Shanjin, there was no chance in hell he'd be willing to be alone with Hei-er.

Hei-er could feel Rancui's distaste for him, and his eyes filled with resignation.

"It's been months already," Hei-er sighed, swiftly shooting Rancui a glance. "You're very keen, Manager Rancui, so you should know the sincerity of the general's feelings toward Mr. Wu. What is happening right now is a necessity. The general is not willing to see Mr. Wu get hurt."

"Hmph, what pretty words. Even I feel sorry for the general now." Rancui lifted his sleeve and made a show of wiping his eyes. The mockery cut Hei-er sharper than a knife.

"...Why are you speaking to me like this?" Did Rancui want to persuade him to conceal what had happened today from the general? Hei-er realized he was too unsophisticated for this. These quick-witted people were nothing but trouble, and every single word out of their mouths had a double meaning. Weren't they tired, living like this?

Rancui chuckled quietly; then his expression turned serious. "Commander Hei... You consider Adviser Wu to be your master as well, yes?"

"Of course." Hei-er straightened his back, responding with quiet solemnity.

"In that case," Rancui said, "what would you do if your master was met with injustice?"

"I would help him overcome that injustice, of course."

"Could you be a little more specific?"

Hei-er watched Rancui for a moment. Rancui leisurely consumed his tea and snacks, allowing Hei-er to size him up. He seemed to especially enjoy the candy. Rancui held a handful of them, tossing them piece by piece into his mouth. He crunched on them with his delicate white teeth. Some stray crumbs spilled onto his lips, and he swiped them away with his little pink tongue. Hei-er wasn't sure if it was deliberate or not, but the way Rancui licked his lips was tantalizing.

This image of Rancui was completely different from the one he'd seen before.

In the past, Hei-er only saw Rancui when he was accompanying Wu Xingzi, and the man was every bit the untouchable and elegant manager of the Peng Society. He had never been this bold, every action uninhibited. It sparked an indescribable desire in Hei-er's heart.

Hei-er's breathing sped up a little, but soon steadied. Without changing his expression, he stared straight at Rancui's bright, glistening eyes. "Manager Rancui, please clarify. I'm afraid I don't know how to answer your question."

"Hmph. Commander Hei, you're not as dull as you put on," Rancui said, his eyes curving as he smiled at Hei-er. The tip of his tongue peeked past his bright red lips, almost as if inviting him for a kiss.

Hei-er's eyes darkened. He lowered his head and averted his gaze, and his hands, resting on his knees, tightened into fists.

"What if someone has taken advantage of your master, and the person using him is not someone you can stand up against? What would you do?" Rancui's question could not be any more direct.

"The general is not taking advantage of Mr. Wu," Hei-er objected immediately.

"You know perfectly well whether he's taking advantage of him or not. First he doted on Adviser Wu, and now he's deliberately distancing himself from him. Yet he still assigns you to secretly protect him—you're telling me he's not using him?"

"He's not. If we are to follow your line of logic, Manager Rancui, the general is also using Mr. Lu." Hei-er had managed to avoid agreeing with Rancui, but he felt mysteriously uneasy, like he had somehow still fallen into a trap.

Rancui clapped his hands together, laughing. "That's right. With how things are currently progressing, the general *is* using Mr. Lu. That is the truth, and I'm happy to see it happen."

"Since that's the case, why do you..." Hei-er watched Rancui with uncertainty. The beauty in front of him had a certain reckless allure when he laughed. He was so bright, and his laughter alone was enough to dazzle one's soul; Hei-er was enchanted.

"But how will they make certain Mr. Lu thinks the general still has feelings for him?" Rancui's smile dropped abruptly. The change in his expression was swift and natural, momentarily stunning Hei-er into silence.

"You mean..."

"It seems like Guan Shanjin himself hasn't realized it. He's using Adviser Wu to set Lu Zezhi's mind at ease, letting him think Guan Shanjin has left his substitute and returned to him. In my eyes, that isn't noble at all."

Hei-er couldn't form the words to reply. Thinking over it carefully, he realized the general *did* seem to be exploiting Wu Xingzi, whether it was now or in the past. Things were different now, though.

"Manager Rancui, your logic doesn't follow."

"So what if it doesn't? What can you do about it?" Rancui crunched on a candy.

Hei-er was truly at the end of his rope. Sighing, he said, "Manager Rancui, will you get straight to the point? I'm a simple-minded soldier, and I can't compete with your quick wit."

"What a clever mouth," Rancui said, raising a brow. This time, his smile was more genial, but Hei-er dared not let his guard down.

"I'm not asking for much. There are two options," Rancui said. He held out his hand and raised one finger. "One, you look the other way and let me take Adviser Wu back to Qingcheng County for a few peaceful days. We'll wait and see if the general has any intention of retrieving him."

Rancui raised a second finger. "Alternatively...Adviser Wu is your master. Now that he has been met with such injustice, shouldn't you help him leave? The general will be heading back to the capital after Mr. Lu's wedding. What would it matter if Mr. Wu goes to the capital first and spends a few days enjoying himself?"

Hei-er frowned deeply. He had to squash the urge to storm out of the pavilion. "You want me to betray the general?"

"You're exaggerating, Commander Hei. Why don't you see it as a way to bring them closer together? If the general and Mr. Wu never face any setbacks, I'm afraid that the two of them won't last very long together. Besides, no matter which option you choose...if the general has the mind to do so, he'll find Mr. Wu, won't he? Where is the betrayal in that?"

Even if Hei-er were to grow another eight mouths, he would never be able to win an argument against Rancui.

Hei-er remained silent for a moment, carefully pondering every detail of Guan Shanjin and Wu Xingzi's relationship. He remembered Man Yue's orders, as well. Finally, he sighed and said, "All right. If you can promise not to deliberately try to separate General Guan and Mr. Wu, I can help."

"Now, why was that so hard? Let's shake on this oath! I definitely won't try to deliberately separate General Guan and Adviser Wu."

Rancui held his hand out toward Hei-er. His wide sleeve slipped down to his elbow, revealing a slender, smooth arm. Hei-er took in a deep breath at the sight. He just barely managed not to make a fool of himself by using his inner strength to suppress his reaction.

Hei-er held out his hand, clasping it with Rancui's and pumping it three times.

Thus, their oath was sealed. However, Hei-er did not notice the extra emphasis Rancui had given to the word "deliberately."

On one side of Horse-Face City, Rancui and Hei-er formed a secret alliance, planning to help Wu Xingzi leave the city as soon as possible.

On the other side, Wu Xingzi had just returned to Shuanghe Manor. Before he even had time to dust himself off, Mint and Osmanthus had to welcome an uninvited guest—there was no time to hide her away from Wu Xingzi's view.

Wu Xingzi did not know where this gentle and refined girl came from, but Mint and Osmanthus knew. She used to work as Guan Shanjin's maidservant, but when Mr. Lu returned to the general's estate a few days ago, she had been reassigned to serve Mr. Lu instead.

Now that their master had seen her, the two young maidservants had no choice but to welcome the visitor with a smile. "Han Xiao-jiejie."

"Mint-meimei, Osmanthus-meimei, is Mr. Wu around?"

Having worked for Guan Shanjin for a number of years, receiving his trust and favor in the process, Han Xiao was well aware of how she needed to behave. As the saying went, one should never hit someone who is smiling. If she was polite, there would be no reason for Mint and Osmanthus to get upset. Furthermore, the relationship between Han Xiao and the two young girls was quite cordial. The girls exchanged a look, then Osmanthus ran over to Wu Xingzi and dragged him into the house.

As for Mint, she remained where she stood. "Jiejie, you've seen it for yourself—our master is around," she said with a clever smile. "However, he's just returned from outside, and he's not prepared to meet anyone right now. Please wait for a moment."

"Please don't say that—it's me who has disturbed Mr. Wu."

Han Xiao, just like her name, was always smiling;[7] she wasn't bothered at all. She waited quietly in the courtyard, which made Mint feel rather sheepish. However, Han Xiao now worked for Mr. Lu, so it was prudent for Mint and Osmanthus to be a little more cautious. Who knew what the general was thinking? Mr. Lu was soon to be married, yet the general had still brought him back—ignoring and abandoning their master in the process. The general's deep affections and constant companionship from the days before felt like a fleeting dream.

Having seen Han Xiao, Wu Xingzi hurriedly wiped his face and hands. He was afraid to keep the girl waiting, so he quickly entered the courtyard; Osmanthus couldn't get him to slow down.

"Sir, this is Han Xiao-jiejie. She's currently Mr. Lu's attendant." Mint quickly stepped forward to offer a supporting arm to her master, placing an emphasis on Mr. Lu's name.

"M-Mr. Lu?" Wu Xingzi blinked, not knowing how to react. Rancui had mentioned Mr. Lu when he was at the Peng Society earlier. Now that Mr. Lu was back, his maidservant had come seeking Wu Xingzi. Did Mr. Lu want to invite him to another meal? How courteous of him...

---

7   Han Xiao (含笑) means to have a smile on one's face.

"Please excuse me, Mr. Wu. I've come at the wrong time and disturbed you." Han Xiao bowed. "Mr. Lu would like you to come over for a chat. Would you do him the honor?"

Especially compared to the unconcealed contempt from Hua Shu when he'd presented the same invitation in the past, Han Xiao was extremely courteous. It made Wu Xingzi feel rather awkward.

"You're much too polite. I'm more than happy to accept Mr. Lu's invitation." Wu Xingzi again thought about the whole wedding gift situation. Although Rancui had told him not to prepare one—and Wu Xingzi understood why—Mr. Lu did invite him to lunch that time, and it would be too rude of him to appear empty-handed. There was nothing wrong with preparing a small gift, right?

Having made his decision, Wu Xingzi instructed Mint to fill up a basket with the fresh eggplants, cucumbers, and other vegetables they'd harvested today, so he could give them to Mr. Lu for him to try. The cucumbers were fresh, sweet, and crisp; the eggplants were tender, and their skins were still thin. They could be eaten raw, but stir-frying them would make them even more delicious. With the skilled cooks in the general's kitchen, this gift would certainly not go to waste. After all, everyone had to eat.

Wu Xingzi had originally wanted to add a jar of pickled vegetables as well, but he remembered that for many years Mr. Lu had been such a strict vegetarian that he didn't even eat scallions, ginger, garlic, or peppers. Wu Xingzi hurriedly removed the jar of pickles from the basket to avoid any turmoil.

Han Xiao watched Wu Xingzi and his maidservants buzz about with no intention of hurrying them. She stood quietly to the side, waiting with lowered eyes.

Only when Wu Xingzi finally stood up, satisfied with his basket of carefully selected vegetables, did Han Xiao come closer and take the basket. "Thank you so much, Mr. Wu," she said in a gentle voice. "Please follow me."

"Uhh... It's fine, I can carry the basket myself." Wu Xingzi reached out to take the vegetables back. How could he allow this girl to lead the way with the basket while he followed behind empty-handed?

Han Xiao swiftly and nimbly pushed Wu Xingzi's hand away. She shot a look at Mint and Osmanthus, signaling them to attend to Wu Xingzi, before turning around and leading the way. Wu Xingzi had no choice but to follow. The entire time, he stared at the basket, periodically wringing his sleeves. He couldn't snatch the basket back, could he?

Wu Xingzi had been to the Wang Shu Residence once before. This time, the plum blossoms had withered, and the leaves rustled in the wind. It added a certain serenity to the atmosphere.

Han Xiao led Wu Xingzi and his two maidservants toward a courtyard behind the house. The spring sun was radiant, and a refreshing breeze was blowing. A shallow stream appeared in front of them with a bamboo pavilion situated nearby. A figure dressed in white was seated within, his clothes fluttering in the wind, as ethereal as a fallen deity. He looked untouchable, as though he didn't exist in the material world.

"Mr. Lu, I've brought Mr. Wu with me," Han Xiao said, leading Wu Xingzi and his maidservants to the pavilion and bowing obediently.

Naturally, the person in the pavilion dressed in white was Mr. Lu. He put down the book he was reading and stood up to welcome Wu Xingzi. "Mr. Wu, it's been a while."

"You're too polite, Mr. Lu." Wu Xingzi hurriedly cupped his hands toward him. Giving a few courteous greetings before he entered, Wu Xingzi sat down across from Mr. Lu.

"This is a gift Mr. Wu has prepared for you," Han Xiao said, lifting the basket in her hand. Mr. Lu glanced at it, and a small smile appeared on his lips. "Mr. Wu is much too kind. I don't deserve this gift at all."

"It's nothing, really. These are just some simple vegetables. I grew them myself, and they're quite delicious. You're a vegetarian, aren't you, Mr. Lu? Please try them." Afraid that Mr. Lu would refuse them, Wu Xingzi quickly called to his maidservants: "Mint, Osmanthus, help Han Xiao deliver these to the kitchen. They'll be ready in time for dinner later."

"Understood." Mint took the basket and asked her younger sister to stay with Wu Xingzi while she sped off to the kitchen alone.

"Many thanks, Mr. Wu." Mr. Lu sat down again, pouring out tea for them both.

The tea was excellent, but Wu Xingzi felt rather uneasy. He finished two cups, but Mr. Lu had yet to say a word. It was perplexing. *What is going on?*

Noticing Wu Xingzi's discomfort, Mr. Lu finally put his teacup down and smiled faintly at Wu Xingzi. Wu Xingzi responded with his own smile.

"What plans do you have for the future, Mr. Wu?" Mr. Lu asked, out of the blue.

Wu Xingzi froze, unable to provide an answer.

Looking at Wu Xingzi's bewildered expression, Mr. Lu lowered his eyes with a sigh. "I'm asking if you plan on remaining here in the general's estate, or if you are thinking of returning home."

Mr. Lu's words were too direct. Wu Xingzi shuddered violently, his face paling. He planned on returning home. After all, it looked like Guan Shanjin had returned to doting on Mr. Lu—and according to Rancui, there seemed to be some uncertainty regarding Mr. Lu's marriage to Miss Yue. Maybe Guan Shanjin had finally decided to snatch the groom away at the wedding. The entire matter really had nothing to do with Wu Xingzi anymore.

The only reason he had yet to go home was his reluctance to leave Guan Shanjin. In his heart was a faint hope he might see him again—after all, he should at least make his farewells, right? Perhaps Guan Shanjin might still...hold some affection toward him...

"Haiwang must have admitted this to you already. To him, you're merely a shadow of me." Mr. Lu had always dodged the issue; this time, he was so direct that the only thing missing was telling Wu Xingzi not to let the door hit him on the way out.

Wu Xingzi looked at him in silence. Was this man in front of him really Mr. Lu? Mr. Lu was typically so gentle and elegant, his words tactful and mild. Perhaps something was agitating him.

"Mr. Lu, you..." Wu Xingzi began to express his concern, but Mr. Lu interrupted him.

"In the past, my misgivings prevented Haiwang and myself from being honest with each other about our feelings," he said. "It caused some complications for us."

"Yes, yes..." Wu Xingzi knew what had happened between the two of them. From what he'd gathered, Guan Shanjin and Mr. Lu shared a mutual affection, but for some reason, they had been holding out when it came to each other for a long time; hence, they missed the opportunity to confess their feelings. Wu Xingzi rubbed his aching chest at the thought.

"So you already know," Mr. Lu sneered. "It seems you are a perceptive man, Mr. Wu."

"Huh?" Wu Xingzi blinked. After a stunned pause, he smiled wryly. "I don't have many strengths, but self-awareness is one of them."

His response was sincere, but Mr. Lu's fair face flushed violently in a bout of anger. Wu Xingzi felt rather lost. Had he said something wrong?

He watched as Mr. Lu opened his mouth, about to say something, but in the end, Mr. Lu bit his lip, picking up his teacup and taking a sip before opening his mouth again. "I fully understand my feelings now."

Wu Xingzi didn't know what to say. However, to not give a response seemed rude. "Ah, congratulations..."

Mr. Lu's brow creased slightly. A beautiful man, even when irate, had a certain flair. However, this anger seemed to come from nowhere, and it made Wu Xingzi apprehensive.

"Haiwang and I have known each other for many years. He's very gentle and considerate toward me. He has nothing but the utmost concern when it comes to me. However, in the past, I was worried that he was young and fickle—not someone who could settle down. I could only feign ignorance of his feelings."

Wu Xingzi scratched his nose, feeling even more confused. "What a pity..."

Shouldn't Mr. Lu be saying these words to Guan Shanjin? Why did Mr. Lu invite him over to say all of this?

"I finally understand this time. I shouldn't continue to disregard Haiwang's sincerity. To let him repeatedly seek out a shadow of me, to let him set his affections toward things so false... I've been hurting him deeply."

Keener men would register the ridicule and insult in those words. Unfortunately, Wu Xingzi was not one of them, and he nodded in agreement. "For you to have such a revelation... It's a blessing for you and Haiwang."

Talking to this man was like punching cotton! Mr. Lu frowned, unable to continue with the words he'd prepared. Wu Xingzi was truly so hateful!

Mr. Lu was worried that Guan Shanjin's feelings for him were not entirely the reason why the general was keeping his distance. He noticed that although he had once again been allowed to return to the Wang Shu Residence—and seemingly back to the days where he was carefully doted upon by Guan Shanjin—the general's care and concern lacked a certain affection from the past.

It all made Mr. Lu rather uneasy.

On the surface, Guan Shanjin had distanced himself from Wu Xingzi, but he had not sent him away. Wu Xingzi could still live and eat well in the general's estate—this was not how Guan Shanjin normally did things! Mr. Lu had thought he had a thorough understanding of Guan Shanjin's character. If Guan Shanjin really was tired of Wu Xingzi, the old adviser would have been sent away from Horse-Face City the day Mr. Lu returned to the general's estate.

Mr. Lu knew what was happening, but he was unwilling to believe that he had lost to someone so ugly, crude, and unrefined! Guan Shanjin surely still had feelings for him; it was just that he had some lingering sympathy for Wu Xingzi. He should help Guan Shanjin make a decision! The general wouldn't blame him for it; he'd loved Mr. Lu for many years. They'd let too many things slip through their fingers. There was no need to let anyone else create further complications.

"Haiwang has let you down, and I've let you down, too. We would be doing you further wrong if we were to keep you in Horse-Face City any longer." Mr. Lu schooled his expression and abruptly caught hold of Wu Xingzi's hand. "Mr. Wu, please don't blame Haiwang.

It's me who caused him to take such missteps. It's a shame you've been caught up in this."

"Your words are too serious, Mr. Lu..." Wu Xingzi was faced with a predicament. He wanted to pull his hand back, but it was caught too tightly. Mr. Lu exerted a decent amount of strength, leaving faint fingernail marks in his hand.

Osmanthus noticed this development. She stepped forward, wanting to help her master. Han Xiao held her back, shaking her head at the younger girl. Worried, yet unable to escape Han Xiao's grasp, Osmanthus felt tears form in her eyes.

"Ah, Mr. Wu. I'd like to apologize to you on Haiwang's behalf. We've wronged you greatly. However..." Mr. Lu's eyelids lowered, his brows tinged with sorrow. This expression always evoked others' sympathy, and Wu Xingzi was no exception. Feeling helpless, he allowed Mr. Lu to continue holding his hand, but it felt like there was a brand pressing onto his heart. The searing pain spread through his entire chest.

"Don't worry, Mr. Lu. I've never...blamed Haiwang..." It was the truth. Guan Shanjin had not let him down. Wu Xingzi only had himself to blame for falling for him, and there was no need to cry over it. "I've already made plans to leave."

Osmanthus's eyes widened at the words, and she nearly cried out. She quickly covered her mouth tightly with her hands, her eyes red.

"Is that so?" Mr. Lu's lips quirked up slightly, giving Wu Xingzi a pitying smile.

"Yes," Wu Xingzi sighed, barely managing to force a smile upon his face. "Please do not worry, Mr. Lu. I will not make things difficult for you and Haiwang."

Not having expected such grace, Mr. Lu was in disbelief. "You're... really willing to leave?"

"Of course. My relationship with Haiwang was only a tryst in the first place." Despite this, his feelings had deepened. But, now that he'd made up his mind, Wu Xingzi's smile only became more earnest. "It must have been difficult for you, to have missed so many years with Haiwang. I hope that the two of you stay together happily until a ripe old age."

"Thank you for your kind words." Mr. Lu had planned on cowing Wu Xingzi into submission. He hadn't expected things to go this way, and now he was at a loss, unable to discern Wu Xingzi's sincerity. How could someone so direct and honest exist in this world?

Wu Xingzi was still confused about the situation, considering Mr. Lu was engaged to someone else. In fact, Guan Shanjin was busy planning the wedding. Could Mr. Lu be afraid, having yet to clear up all the misunderstandings? Wu Xingzi was worried for him.

"Mr. Lu, you're to be married three days from now," he said. "Have you spoken to Miss Yue about all of this?"

This blow went straight to Mr. Lu's heart. His face paled, and he was struck speechless.

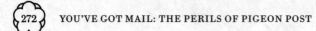

CHAPTER 7

THERE ARE PLENTY OF PENGORNISES EVERYWHERE

"Let me put it this way. The general is truly talented, but only in the court and on the battlefield. His mind has never been open to anything else. He lacks some of the emotions an ordinary person should have. I'm only helping him chisel open that brain of his a little."

Hei-er gasped. "We're killing him?"

Man Yue glared at Hei-er. "Don't be an idiot! I'm trying to open his eyes! He hasn't realized his feelings for Wu Xingzi. Do you want him to keep dragging Adviser Wu along like this?"

A SILENCE DESCENDED upon the Wang Shu Residence.

Wu Xingzi looked anxiously at Mr. Lu's ashen face, wondering if he should call the physician over to take a look.

Wu Xingzi understood that Mr. Lu probably had not thought about how to break off this engagement. After all, Miss Yue was very sincere about her relationship with him. Wu Xingzi had only met her once, but the young lady's love for Mr. Lu was clear.

He sighed, feeling a bit bad for Mr. Lu. His heart ached for Guan Shanjin, too... It seemed that these two men still had a long way to go.

"That is a matter between Haiwang and me," Mr. Lu said coldly, glaring at Wu Xingzi with fiery eyes. "It's none of your concern, Mr. Wu."

"Sorry, I've overstepped. Please forgive me, Mr. Lu." Wu Xingzi stood up and cupped his hands together in sincere apology. He wondered if he'd said too much. This was, after all, none of his business.

"I'm a little tired now, so I'm afraid my hospitality ends here, Mr. Wu. I hope that what you promised me today will not be easily forgotten." Mr. Lu did not bother standing up. With lowered eyes, he spoke in a weary tone; it seemed he was truly exhausted. "Han Xiao, send Mr. Wu back."

"Yes. Mr. Wu, please follow me."

"Sorry for disturbing you, Mr. Lu." Wu Xingzi glanced at him again with a sigh before stepping out of the bamboo pavilion and following Han Xiao.

On the way back to Shuanghe Manor, they happened across Mint, who was speeding back from the main kitchen. When Mint saw her elder twin, Osmanthus pursed her lips, grabbing onto Mint and chattering away. Mint diverted her attention to listen to her sister complain, frowning and sighing intermittently. Finally, Mint looked at her master in disbelief. Her mouth opened as though she wanted to say something, but when she caught sight of Han Xiao's quiet figure, she suppressed it.

Back in Shuanghe Manor, Han Xiao did not withdraw. Instead, she bowed and watched Wu Xingzi calmly, making him terribly nervous.

"What you said just now, Mr. Wu... Was it all from your heart?" she said at last.

"Huh? What exactly are you referring to?" Wu Xingzi was lost. He didn't know why Han Xiao would ask such a question.

Han Xiao decided to be direct. "Is it true that you're planning on leaving Horse-Face City?"

Hearing this, Mint and Osmanthus stared at their master, holding their breaths and waiting for his reply.

"Uh..." Wu Xingzi scratched the fleshy tip of his nose, hesitating slightly before continuing with a bitter chuckle. "There's no point in me staying here."

Guan Shanjin and Mr. Lu had finally confessed their feelings for each other. There was no need for a substitute anymore, right?

Han Xiao nodded. "Mr. Wu is bright and clever, just as Vice General Man described." She took a few steps forward and continued in a lowered voice: "Do you plan on returning to Qingcheng County, Mr. Wu?"

"Uh..." Of course Wu Xingzi had planned on returning home. However, at Han Xiao's abrupt question, he now hesitated. He did not believe that Guan Shanjin would go all the way there searching for him, but what if... Wu Xingzi suddenly registered the quiet anticipation within his heart, and his face paled involuntarily.

"I've been fortunate enough to be able to serve the general for many years. If you'd allow me to be so bold, I'd like to offer Mr. Wu some suggestions." Han Xiao drew even closer. Afraid that their master would be bullied, Mint and Osmanthus approached as well. Wu Xingzi could only take half a step back to avoid being the subject of estate-wide gossip.

Han Xiao shot a look at the two young girls, amused. Next, she continued in a respectful tone, "The general gets upset when things do not go his way. For you to leave like this... I'm afraid that it will greatly anger the general."

"Ah..." Wu Xingzi paused. "Maybe I should tell him, then? He should be able to understand."

He remembered when he'd wanted to go home for New Year... When he'd said that he wanted to leave, Guan Shanjin had been angered to the point of vomiting blood. But things should be different this time: Guan Shanjin had Mr. Lu now.

The general hadn't sought Wu Xingzi out in weeks, though. Finding the opportunity to inform him would be a rather difficult task.

Han Xiao observed Wu Xingzi for a moment, then nodded, her smile mysterious. "This is a good idea. Why don't I help you invite the general over?"

"Could you? I'd be very grateful." Wu Xingzi's eyes brightened as he smiled cheerfully. "Miss Han Xiao, it's so fortunate that you're here."

"No, no. This is part of my duties." Having completed her task, Han Xiao felt relieved. She gave Wu Xingzi a somewhat sympathetic look, then bowed and withdrew.

As Guan Shanjin's trusted maidservant, she was not someone Mr. Lu could order around, and she did not truly take Mr. Lu as her new master. However, Man Yue was different. That plump and honest-looking fellow was in fact the second most powerful man in all of Horse-Face City. He was an absolute mastermind, and no one would dare claim they were smarter than he. Han Xiao, Hei-er, and other close subordinates always listened to Man Yue. She didn't understand what he was planning, but Han Xiao followed his instructions to the letter.

After sending Han Xiao off, Mint and Osmanthus returned and, pouting, asked what Wu Xingzi's intentions were. When he confirmed that he really wanted to leave, the shoulders of the two young girls fell. They were close to tears, but managed not to cry.

Wu Xingzi's heart truly ached! He had doted on these two girls as though they were his own nieces, and he was just as upset at the prospect of parting with them so suddenly. However, Horse-Face City was not a place where he could stay forever; one always had to return home.

That day, all three of them were quite despondent. Wu Xingzi even ate two fewer bowls of rice during lunch—he did finish all the dishes, though. He leaned back sluggishly into the chair next to the cucumber trellis and dozed on and off, taking the opportunity to sort out his feelings.

Mint and Osmanthus each pulled up a stool to sit down near Wu Xingzi, working on some sewing. The spring sun was pleasant and not too hot; a breeze brought with it the comforting scents of nature. Somehow or other, Wu Xingzi ended up falling asleep.

Noticing that he was sleeping, Mint covered him with a cloak. However, in the next moment, the cloak was snatched away by a large, elegant hand. Mint quickly covered her mouth to keep herself from shrieking in shock. With widened eyes, she trailed her gaze up from the hand to see Guan Shanjin's flawless face.

"General!"

Osmanthus also noticed his presence, hurriedly tossing away the sewing in her hand and running over to greet him.

"You may stand down." Guan Shanjin casually waved at them, tossing the cloak to Mint. "How long has he been asleep?"

He gazed Wu Xingzi like a parched man finally finding water in a desert.

"Mr. Wu has only just fallen asleep, General."

"Mm." Guan Shanjin gave a brisk nod, bending over and carefully lifting Wu Xingzi in his arms, his motions steady and nimble. Wu Xingzi made a quiet sound, his head falling onto Guan Shanjin's shoulder. Nuzzling into it, he smiled and once again drifted into a deep slumber.

Guan Shanjin's heart softened at how trusting Wu Xingzi was. He desperately wished to tuck this man into his arms and never put him down, but he was worried that his actions would be too jarring and disturb the man's sweet dreams. He somewhat clumsily shifted about before he managed to seat the two of them together in a chair.

"The cloak," he said quietly, holding his hand out to Mint. The young girl seemed to be in a fog, and she only handed Guan Shanjin the cloak after he glanced at her.

"You may go now."

"...Yes, sir." Neither Mint nor Osmanthus was very willing, but Guan Shanjin's gaze was so frightening that they had no choice but to reluctantly leave.

After the two girls were a long distance away, Guan Shanjin chuckled. He carefully covered Wu Xingzi with the cloak, afraid he might get cold. Although it was warm in Horse-Face City, the wind of early spring still carried a slight chill. If he was not careful, Wu Xingzi could catch a cold—how could Guan Shanjin bear to let Wu Xingzi suffer?

However, Wu Xingzi was sleeping very comfortably. He exhaled warm breaths into the crook of Guan Shanjin's neck, and the heat sent tingles through Guan Shanjin's body. Pushing down his desires, Guan Shanjin managed not to take Wu Xingzi and have his way with him right there. Enduring the torture, he patted Wu Xingzi's lower back every once in a while.

Snuggled into each other as they were, Guan Shanjin was unable to see the old fellow's face. Unsatisfied with this arrangement, he pulled Wu Xingzi deeper into his arms and decided to simply close his eyes and rest.

When Wu Xingzi woke up, the sun was already setting. The air was tinged with the scent of sandalwood and orange blossoms. He huffed out a breath, thinking that he truly must have had a pleasant dream to be able to smell Guan Shanjin's scent.

"You're awake?" A familiar voice came from above Wu Xingzi. He stopped nuzzling into the surface he was leaning on and jerked his head up, narrowly avoiding Guan Shanjin's chin.

"You... You..." The arms around him were too tight. Even if he craned his neck, all Wu Xingzi could see was Guan Shanjin's elegant chin and neck. Guan Shanjin relaxed a little, and the two were finally able to look at each other directly.

The general greeted him with a faint, mischievous smile. "Did I shock you?"

"Uh-huh..." Wu Xingzi nodded slowly. He suddenly recalled that before Han Xiao left, she said that she would request for Guan Shanjin to come over. However, he hadn't expected that Guan Shanjin would come so quickly. Wasn't he busy preparing for Mr. Lu's wedding? It was barely three days from now!

Without thinking, Wu Xingzi asked, "Did Mr. Lu tell you already?" This was the only possibility—why else would Guan Shanjin take the time to come over?

"About what?" Guan Shanjin's smile faded away, leaving a certain iciness in his expression.

"Umm..." Just as he was about to answer, Wu Xingzi fortunately managed to cover his own mouth, preventing himself from revealing Mr. Lu's feelings.

Even though everyone knew that Mr. Lu had feelings for Guan Shanjin, there was still the matter of the wedding; Wu Xingzi should not be the one disclosing this to Guan Shanjin.

"Hmm?" Guan Shanjin pulled Wu Xingzi's hand down. Looking at Wu Xingzi's half-opened mouth, he couldn't stop himself from leaning down to kiss him, tangling their tongues together. When he finally, reluctantly pulled away, brushing Wu Xingzi's kiss-swollen lips with a finger, Wu Xingzi was left gasping for breath.

Wu Xingzi blushed red from the kiss, feeling both embarrassed and intoxicated. Everyone said Guan Shanjin had finally managed to win Mr. Lu over, so he should no longer be so enchanted by a mere substitute. Why was he still so passionate with Wu Xingzi?

"Why are you drifting off again?"

Guan Shanjin had never known that he could feel this satisfied just by looking at someone. He dearly wished that they could hold each other like this forever. Not even Mr. Lu had been able to make him feel this way. Exactly what was so special about Wu Xingzi? Guan Shanjin couldn't figure it out; he only knew that he could not bear to be separated from this little old quail.

For the past couple of weeks, he'd endured and suppressed his desires. To make Mr. Lu and the Yue family feel at ease, and to make sure the people behind the Yue family kept their focus on Mr. Lu, Guan Shanjin had had no choice but to distance himself from Wu Xingzi. He refused to even sneak a look at him, terrified that it would interfere with his plan.

However, when Han Xiao passed him a message saying that Wu Xingzi wanted to see him, Guan Shanjin could no longer stay away. Fortunately, he had worked hard enough these past two weeks to have half a day to slack off and spend time with the old fellow.

Squinting at Guan Shanjin, Wu Xingzi hesitantly opened his mouth. "Is Mr. Lu...really getting married in three days?"

"Yes." Guan Shanjin frowned at hearing another man's name on Wu Xingzi's lips. "Why are you asking this?"

Han Xiao had reported to Guan Shanjin that Mr. Lu invited Wu Xingzi for tea today, and that his words to Wu Xingzi had been rather grating. Guan Shanjin couldn't help but worry. Would Wu Xingzi air his grievances to him? Guan Shanjin was inexplicably delighted by the thought. His expression relaxed, and he rocked Wu Xingzi gently in his embrace.

"I'm thinking about..."

His decision to leave was at the tip of his tongue, but Wu Xingzi swallowed it back down. Bowing his head, he absentmindedly wrung the ties of the cloak. When Guan Shanjin saw this, he caught Wu Xingzi's hand in his. Their fingers entwined together, then separated and stroked along each other before interlocking again. It was as though flames burned inside Guan Shanjin's hand, so hot that Wu Xingzi's palm tingled. The warmth spread up to his face in a flush, and even the tips of his ears reddened. He obediently allowed Guan Shanjin to hold his hand, but he did not have the courage to look up at his handsome, bewitching face.

"What are you thinking about?"

"Ah, I'm wondering if I should prepare a gift." Once the words left his mouth, Wu Xingzi thought it was a rather terrible cover-up; the matter had long been decided. Mentioning the wedding now felt as though he was hurting Guan Shanjin's ego.

"A gift?" Guan Shanjin raised his brows and tapped the tip of Wu Xingzi's nose. "What gift? Are you close to Mr. Lu?"

How could they be? Han Xiao had told him some of what Mr. Lu had said to Wu Xingzi, and it had made him rather displeased. If those words had come from anyone other than Mr. Lu, Guan Shanjin would have properly punished that person.

"Uh... We've met three times..." Wu Xingzi sighed, his shoulders drooping slightly. He curled himself up into a ball in Guan Shanjin's arms.

"There's no need for a gift. Keep the allowance the estate has provided you; there's no need to waste it on other people." When he thought of Wu Xingzi's pitiful little stash of nine silver taels back in Qingcheng County, Guan Shanjin's heart ached. "Weren't you planning on treating me to a lamb feast?"

"Ah, yes. If you hadn't reminded me, I would have forgotten all about it." Wu Xingzi mentally counted the balance in his money pouch. Along with the monthly allowance he had received a few days ago, he estimated the amount to be nearly a hundred and twenty silver taels. The general's estate was truly too generous. Wu Xingzi knew he shouldn't bring the money with him to Qingcheng County, so he should take Guan Shanjin out for dinner.

"After Mr. Lu's wedding, you can treat me to a meal," Guan Shanjin said casually.

The expression on Wu Xingzi's face changed. "After the wedding?" he asked. He wouldn't be able to take Guan Shanjin out after the wedding. He would be well on his way to Qingcheng County with Rancui by then.

"What's wrong? Why do you look so glum?" Guan Shanjin asked. Wu Xingzi couldn't hide such a change in his expression from him; a chill permeated the general's heart. He pinched Wu Xingzi's cheek. "What did Mr. Lu say to you?"

"Nuthin', nuthin'..." Nervous, Wu Xingzi slipped into his local dialect. Although Guan Shanjin didn't hear him clearly, he could grasp that Wu Xingzi was denying things; it was clear that something had happened with Mr. Lu.

"Wu Xingzi, whatever Mr. Lu told you, don't take it to heart," Guan Shanjin said, lifting Wu Xingzi's chin and looking at him solemnly. "After Mr. Lu is married, let's go to the capital."

"The capital?" The capital might as well have been on the other side of the world. "What about visiting my ancestors' graves on Qingming?"

Guan Shanjin raised a brow and laughed. "All you do is worry about such trivial things! I'll wrap up everything in the capital before Qingming. We'll be back in Qingcheng County in time for the tomb-sweeping."

Without thinking, Wu Xingzi nodded, and, so doing, lost the opportunity to bid Guan Shanjin farewell.

This was the Great General of the Southern Garrison, after all, and he would need to return to the capital soon to make his reports. Add that to the wedding three days from now, and he was so busy that he barely had any time for a break. He couldn't even stay for dinner with Wu Xingzi. After hugging and kissing Wu Xingzi, Guan Shanjin had to leave.

Wu Xingzi sent him off, his mind in a trance. He pressed his fingers against his tingling, kiss-swollen lips. Even his tongue felt numb from the general's kisses; it felt almost clumsy in his mouth.

Should I still return to Qingcheng County? Hmm...

Under the setting sun, a tall, dark figure suddenly appeared in front of Wu Xingzi. Shocked, Wu Xingzi retreated a few steps, nearly shouting out in alarm with a hand pressed to his chest. Only after looking carefully did Wu Xingzi realize the mysterious man was Hei-er.

"Hei-er?"

"Adviser Wu." Hei-er cupped his hands at him, a certain resolute determination on his tanned face.

Wu Xingzi's heart missed a beat. Something about the man in front of him seemed a little different than usual. "Why are you here? Would you like a cup of tea?"

Hei-er took a couple of steps forward, his tone a little tense. "Would Adviser Wu like to return to Qingcheng County?"

Wu Xingzi was silent for a few moments before quietly replying, "Yes..."

Even though Guan Shanjin's offer had made him waver just now, he was still the same old Wu Xingzi: a little frog in the well.

"Then I'll take you there." Hei-er fell to one knee, his right hand on his heart. "You're my master. I'll keep you safe."

Hei-er's words left Wu Xingzi stunned. Was this fleeing, or were they...*eloping*? Hei-er's words spun around in his head, and he took a couple of uneasy steps backward, turning his head toward the direction Guan Shanjin had left. He only wanted to go home; he'd already agreed to go back with Rancui. Why did it sound so dangerous coming from Hei-er's mouth?

"I-I've already spoken to Rancui. I'll be going back with him..." Hei-er was, after all, one of Guan Shanjin's men. For him to continue accompanying Wu Xingzi—whether driven by his sense of duty or his personal feelings—was not quite appropriate.

"Where my master goes, I will follow. I will protect you." Hei-er was still kneeling, his swarthy face looking up at Wu Xingzi.

"Uh..." Wu Xingzi was bewildered. He tried to pull Hei-er up off the ground, but he didn't have the strength to move even a hair on Hei-er's head. Instead, he nearly fell down, and needed Hei-er's help to steady himself.

"I'm just going home."

"Mr. Wu, please pardon my directness, but... If there's a chance, would you be willing to spend the rest of your life with the general?" Hei-er looked up, his complexion almost blending into the sky. Although the lanterns had yet to be lit, the intense gaze in his eyes made them shine like stars.

"Uh..." Wu Xingzi could not give an answer. If it was in the realm of possibility, he'd want to be life partners with Guan Shanjin.

However, he was getting old; he had long since abandoned such unrealistic hopes. With Hei-er's sudden question, he could only give a self-effacing smile in reply.

Wu Xingzi was unaware of how much his expression had revealed. Hei-er watched him calmly for a few moments. "Mr. Wu, if the general finds out that you've left Horse-Face City, he'll immediately search Qingcheng County. I'm afraid that you wouldn't be able to withstand his wrath."

His wrath? Wu Xingzi shuddered. He had never seen Guan Shanjin quite that angry before, so he didn't know why he was afraid.

"Umm... But he..." Wu Xingzi sighed. "He and Mr. Lu can finally have a happy future together. There's no need for a substitute like me to stick around and be an eyesore."

Cleverly, Hei-er did not answer Adviser Wu directly. Instead, he asked another question in response. "Why not let me take you to the capital for a holiday? It can be a distraction from your melancholy, and it'll give the general time to calm down. Maybe this matter will be smoothed over in a couple of months."

The capital? No, that's not right! Wasn't Guan Shanjin returning to the capital to report on his work soon? *If we bump into each other...* Wasn't that the same as running headfirst into a spear?

Hei-er obviously understood Wu Xingzi's concern. "Everyone says that it's easier to hide in a big city," he said, his voice comforting. "The general won't know that we're right under his nose."

When he put it that way, it made sense. Wu Xingzi nodded his head.

He had never been to the capital in his life. He had heard from others that the roads in the capital were paved with stone slabs, and the city itself was extremely prosperous and bustling with activity. There were plenty of delicious foods to eat and fun things to do.

The most talented and good-looking people of Great Xia gathered in the capital. For example, there was that young man from *The Pengornisseur* who was talented with the qin. For all Wu Xingzi knew, he might have the opportunity to listen to that young man play—they could even become friends!

Would the young man's pengornis be as handsome, graceful, and bewitching?

Although Hei-er didn't know exactly what Wu Xingzi was thinking, he knew that the adviser had agreed to his proposal. He stood up and patted away the dust on his knee. Cupping his hands toward Wu Xingzi, he said, "Mr. Wu, I will personally assure your safety during this trip to the capital. To avoid the general's suspicions and his subsequent chase, let's depart on the day Mr. Lu gets married."

"Many thanks for your attentiveness." Wu Xingzi's head bobbed continuously, his mind rather distracted. The world was so big—were there not pengornises everywhere? *Maybe after a couple of years, I can meet another cock—err, man I can spend my life with!* Even if he didn't find a partner by then, he'd be able to reap quite a large harvest of drawings for his rattan case! Wu Xingzi was delighted at the possibilities.

"Then I shall take my leave first. Three days from now, we'll head off. Mr. Wu, if there's anything you need to bring along with you, please start packing—quietly." With that, Hei-er's shadow flashed past, and he vanished into the night.

Wu Xingzi stood in a stupor for a moment, pressing a palm against his heart. Then he returned to his bedroom and dug out the rattan case that stored his pengornis drawings. He took them out one by one to admire them, and even ended up skipping dinner.

After leaving Shuanghe Manor, Hei-er slipped into Man Yue's residence. Before he could even knock, Man Yue's voice drifted out. "Come in, Hei-er."

"Vice General Man," Hei-er said, pushing the door open.

Vice General Man and Commander Hei had known each other for many years. Other than addressing each other with their proper titles, they did not bother with formalities; a casual nod of the head was sufficient greeting. Hei-er took a seat on a chair to the side, pouring a cup of tea to drink.

"Is Mr. Wu willing to leave?" Man Yue asked with a smile, putting his brush down.

"Yes. Just as you said, Mr. Wu agreed without asking too many questions." Hei-er sighed, his face gloomy.

Looking at Hei-er's expression, Man Yue laughed out loud. "Do you feel that I'm helping Lu Zezhi bully Mr. Wu?"

"Uh..." Was that not the case?

"Let me ask you, when did you start feeling that Lu Zezhi had ulterior motives toward the general?" Man Yue asked, his face buried in scrolls of reports. He had to return with Guan Shanjin to the capital to deliver these reports, and in the past few days, he had been so busy that he'd had no time for any proper sleep. He'd had to make quite an effort to squeeze out the time for this conversation with Hei-er.

"I started having suspicions..." Hei-er frowned for a moment, then muttered to himself, "Probably the third year after Mr. Lu came to Horse-Face City. Was that only two years ago?" He counted on his fingers, a little surprised.

"Before that, didn't you think that Mr. Lu was noble and pure, and a perfect match for our general? Although none of us knew why they always referred to each other as teacher and student, did you not think that it was because our general loved him too deeply, and dared not desecrate the man?" Man Yue glanced at Hei-er, scorn curling around his smile.

"Yes, at the time, everyone in the estate thought that, too. The general only truly looked content when he saw Mr. Lu. Didn't you quite like Mr. Lu at the time as well?" Hei-er asked, skimming through his memories. Two years ago, everyone in the estate believed that Mr. Lu would eventually marry General Guan. After all, Mr. Lu's appearance was so outstanding, his aura so serene; standing next to each other, the two of them looked like a work of art.

"I never liked Lu Zezhi," Man Yue snorted. He used a little too much force on a downstroke, and the handle of his brush snapped in two. Vexed, he pursed his lips and picked up a new brush.

"But you've always been partial to him. These past two years alone, all your actions have aided him." Hei-er finally voiced his confusion. Most of the general's guards knew that Man Yue disliked Mr. Lu, since Man Yue had never concealed his disdain for the man. However, whenever Mr. Lu needed something, Man Yue always wanted one of them to attend to him immediately and settle any issues as soon as possible. This made all of them very confused about Man Yue's intentions.

Even this time, after Mr. Lu had returned to the manor, Man Yue had instructed Han Xiao to provoke Wu Xingzi as much as possible and erode his desire to remain in Horse-Face City. If this was not a plot conceived for Mr. Lu's benefit, then what else was it for? Just to make Wu Xingzi's life harder?

Man Yue laughed. "How did all of you manage to see through Mr. Lu?" he asked.

As for exactly how they finally saw through him... Well, it was more appropriate to say that they finally understood that Mr. Lu was only stringing Guan Shanjin along. Although they didn't understand why, people always tended to be biased; no one could stand Mr. Lu's behavior.

If he really had to say how... Hei-er suddenly came to a shocking realization. He looked at Man Yue. In the past, Man Yue did not interact with Mr. Lu. He wasn't interested in him at all and treated him indifferently, observing from the sidelines. At the time, none of the general's guards could understand why Man Yue always kept his distance from Mr. Lu, who seemed like such a good man. However, Man Yue's attitude changed eventually. He was vocal about his dislike for Mr. Lu, but he was very considerate of the man's needs. He even helped bring Guan Shanjin and Mr. Lu closer together.

It took no time for most of the people at the general's estate to understand the situation. They could see Mr. Lu had feelings for Guan Shanjin, but his attitude toward the general was rather passive. Rather than Guan Shanjin insisting on referring to Mr. Lu as "Teacher" out of love, it would be more accurate to say that Mr. Lu's haughty attitude forced Guan Shanjin to keep his distance.

Seeing this, everyone's opinion of Mr. Lu gradually changed.

Shocked, Hei-er looked at Man Yue with sudden enlightenment. "It was you, I see..." Hei-er nodded his head a few times, unsurprised. He didn't know how Man Yue had managed to pull it off so seamlessly. "So, that time Mr. Lu fell from his horse and broke his leg... You refused to let me suppress the information because you wanted me to make the general return as soon as possible."

"If you had suppressed the news, do you know what would have happened?"

What could have happened? Hei-er stared at Man Yue's seemingly innocent smile; he dared not answer right away.

"Here, let me explain. No matter how Mr. Lu fell from his horse, whether it was an accident or not—in the end, he still fell. Of course the general's heart would ache. Breaking a leg, after all, is no small matter." Man Yue crooked his finger at Hei-er, and Hei-er immediately handed him a cup of tea to wet his throat. After a few sips of tea, Man Yue continued. "If you had suppressed the news and informed the general a few days later, would his heart not have ached even *more* over Mr. Lu? He'd have punished all of you."

"You're right..." Hei-er nodded his head in understanding, but a frown appeared on his face the next moment. "Then why did you urge Mr. Wu to leave in such an indirect manner this time?"

"Well, firstly, it's something to do with the capital. Don't worry about that part now. Once Mr. Lu's wedding is over, I'll explain it to you fully. As for the second reason..." Man Yue's round, fleshy chin wobbled as he wearily spoke. "It's ultimately for the benefit of our general. Did Rancui mention that Guan Shanjin still does not hold any true affection for Mr. Wu?"

Rancui really had mentioned it. Hei-er could only nod. Exactly how did the brains of these smart people develop? Every one of them had such complicated, labyrinthine thoughts; they could stir up a storm over such a simple matter.

"I grew up with the general," said Man Yue. "I understand what sort of person he is very well. He's never taken the idea of love or true feelings to heart. He knows how to dote on someone, but there's a motive behind his pampering. Look at how he spoils Mr. Lu. What is he trying to do? If he really wanted to be with Mr. Lu, do you think that Mr. Lu could resist? He's just playing around!" Man Yue sighed. "Let me put it this way: when Wu Xingzi falls for the general and only has him in his heart, the general will quickly lose interest in him."

"If that's the case, then why don't we just separate them completely?" Hei-er asked. An image of the slight sorrow upon Wu Xingzi's face flashed in his head. How could he let this honest adviser's heart be broken?

"That's impossible." Man Yue waved his hand. "Guan Shanjin already likes him. Are you brave enough to snatch someone away from him? How many lives do you think you have?"

"But..."

"You think I want to do all of this? It's exhausting!" Man Yue massaged the center of his brows. Meddling with things behind Guan Shanjin's back was essentially offering his neck to the Chenyuan Sword.

"Then why?"

"Let me put it this way. The general is truly talented, but his talent exists only in the court and on the battlefield. His mind has never been open to anything else; it's always been tightly shut. He lacks some of the emotions an ordinary person should have. I'm only helping him chisel open that brain of his a little."

Hei-er gasped. "You want to kill him?"

Man Yue clucked his tongue, glaring at Hei-er. "Don't be an idiot!" he exclaimed. "I'm trying to open his eyes! If he doesn't experience a freezing winter, how will he be able to appreciate the scent of a plum blossom? He likes Wu Xingzi, but hasn't realized it himself. Are you willing to let him keep dragging Adviser Wu along like this?"

"You're right..." Hei-er sighed, recalling the words Rancui had spoken to him.

Was all of this just to bring the general and Wu Xingzi together?

Thinking of Rancui's exquisite smile, Hei-er shuddered violently.

Years back, Guan Shanjin had constructed the Wang Shu Residence especially for Mr. Lu. Brick by brick, room by room, even the large swath of plum trees—every single detail was a sign of Guan Shanjin's affection for Mr. Lu. Whatever Mr. Lu needed, Guan Shanjin would always have it ready, proving exactly how considerate and meticulous he was.

As for the name of the residence, it expressed Guan Shanjin's feelings: Wang Shu was another name for the bright moon. In Guan Shanjin's heart, Mr. Lu was like moonlight—noble, pure, and flawless, like a perfect piece of jade. If Guan Shanjin had no love and admiration for him, why would he see Mr. Lu in such a light?

Guan Shanjin stood in front of the Wang Shu Residence, staring at the signboard that he had written with his own hand. The characters were bold and forceful, the strokes strong and smooth; his handwriting seemed to give a tinge of violence to the moon. It was as though he had finally defiled the clear, shining moonlight, and he was reveling in it. Recalling his deep affections from the past, Guan Shanjin could not help but give a self-ridiculing smile.

It would soon be nine in the evening. Wispy clouds covered the starry night sky; it was dim and dark outside. This was a moonless night, and few lamps were lit in the Wang Shu Residence. There was only a small illuminated path that extended toward the plum grove.

The night breeze was slightly cool as it swirled through the plum trees and rippled the hem of Guan Shanjin's black robe. He was here at the request of Mr. Lu. Not too long after noon today, Han Xiao had sought out Guan Shanjin on Mr. Lu's behalf. She said Mr. Lu was missing the general, and that he hoped to invite him over for a chat tonight.

Guan Shanjin immediately agreed. For the past few days, he had been deliberately ignoring Mr. Lu. Surprisingly, Mr. Lu had been able to endure the cold shoulder; he'd only given in tonight, the night before the wedding. Guan Shanjin couldn't disappoint Mr. Lu now. Besides, he was curious—what exactly did Mr. Lu want to say to him?

At the end of the white pebbled path stood a pavilion with a thatched roof. That pavilion was one of Mr. Lu's favorite places to spend his time. It looked very plain, yet there were details hidden in every corner. Blending in with the plum trees, its simplicity emphasized the delightful serenity of seclusion. It was also the only part of the Wang Shu Residence that Guan Shanjin had not had a hand in—it was constructed by Mr. Lu himself.

Mr. Lu asking to meet in this specific location made Guan Shanjin laugh quietly.

Even now, Mr. Lu was still trying his best to maintain his image of innocence and virtue. He stood there proudly with his back upright as if he hadn't just snuck a glance at Guan Shanjin, pretending he wasn't frustrated or anxious in any way.

This was truly fascinating!

Guan Shanjin took an entire fifteen minutes to walk to the pavilion.

Lamplight flickered over the pale, orchid-like figure, bathing him in hazy gold. The image was ethereal, and the surrounding atmosphere felt serene. It seemed like if someone so much as breathed too loudly, the dreamlike scene would dissipate in an instant.

In the center of the pavilion was a seat cushion near a low bamboo table. Mr. Lu sat cross-legged there, upright and slender like bamboo, but also gentle and soft as willow. With his head raised, he looked up at the stars in the sky. His exposed skin was like pale nephrite; cool and smooth, it looked as though it glowed. His elegant face looked like it had been polished by running water. This man's appearance was unforgettable; it could easily be carved into one's heart.

Guan Shanjin watched him for a moment from a short distance away before greeting him. "Teacher."

Mr. Lu seemed shocked to hear his voice. His shoulders flinched slightly, and after a short period of silence, he slowly turned to look at Guan Shanjin. A smile concealed the sadness on his face. "Haiwang."

Guan Shanjin walked into the pavilion. Arranging his robes, he sat down on the seat cushion across from Mr. Lu. "Teacher, why isn't anyone attending to you?"

It was only them, alone among the plum trees. The night was soundless except for the rustling of the wind; not even the insects chirped. It was as if they were in another world, completely isolated from the rest of the universe.

"I asked all of them to withdraw," Mr. Lu answered with his gaze lowered.

"Oh?" Guan Shanjin was in no hurry. He turned his head and looked at the sky beyond the pavilion.

Silence fell upon them. Mr. Lu waited and waited, but Guan Shanjin still did not speak. Mr. Lu gritted his teeth, suppressing the panic rising within him. He did not realize Guan Shanjin could see his clenched fists, and because of his lowered eyes, he did not see the trace of mockery in Guan Shanjin's expression.

In the end, Mr. Lu gave in and spoke first. "Do you still blame me?" His words faltered at the end, his voice trembling. It was as though he had been greatly wronged and misunderstood, yet he still needed to restrain himself and maintain his dignity; he refused to bow. Such a bearing had once been extremely attractive to Guan Shanjin.

The general frowned slightly, feigning concern. "Teacher, why would you say something like that? I thought that it was you who still refused to forgive me."

"I refused to forgive you?" Mr. Lu snapped to attention, looking directly into the charming, alluring eyes that seemed to be filled with emotion. Even in the flickering light, those eyes still made Mr. Lu's heart pound. "For what?"

Guan Shanjin laughed wryly. "Because of Wu Xingzi." His long, elegant fingers dragged across the surface of the table, lightly brushing against Mr. Lu's. The heat of his touch was like that of a burning star, the flames encasing Mr. Lu's heart.

The name Wu Xingzi felt like a deluge of cold water on Mr. Lu's head, sending a shiver through his body. His face, which had been blushing just moments ago, turned ashen again.

"I know that you're doing it to agitate me." After a moment of silence, Mr. Lu sighed. "Do you still remember the Lantern Festival that year you returned from the northwest?"

"I do…" Guan Shanjin's heart was slightly moved, and he reached out to hold Mr. Lu's hand where it rested on the table. His skin felt slightly cool to the touch due to the evening chill, and Guan Shanjin could not stop himself from squeezing his hand more tightly.

Seeing Mr. Lu that day at the Lantern Festival had made Guan Shanjin finally feel at peace. It was also in that moment that he realized he no longer just held the feelings a student had for his teacher; it was a deeper affection that gradually intensified. After that, he invited Mr. Lu to live in his estate, granting him the status of a guest. Despite Mr. Lu's average intelligence—he was of no practical use at the estate—as long as he was by his side, Guan Shanjin could feel himself settle down.

Exactly when had they started walking down separate paths?

"I sought you out deliberately," Mr. Lu admitted, his voice slightly husky. Not waiting for a response from Guan Shanjin, he went on, "That day you returned, I saw you on the street. You had changed so much. Although you were still vibrant and magnificent, your eyes were empty."

Guan Shanjin raised a brow. "My eyes were empty?"

"Yes." Mr. Lu watched him, then smiled bitterly. "You don't believe me, right? You don't think I noticed. Haiwang, I've been by your side since you were ten. I know what sort of child you were. Days in the northwest were very difficult—you had to sacrifice so many lives to achieve these recent years of peace. How could I not know all of that? That day, you were riding Zhuxing, and you were parading the streets with your soldiers in victory. There you were, right behind the Great General Weiyuan, but it was as if you weren't really there at all. That roaring crowd felt like a joke to you, didn't it?"

Guan Shanjin's superficial smile faded away, his expression turning cold. He looked at Mr. Lu in silence.

He had truly never thought that Mr. Lu had managed to see into his head. Not even his parents or Man Yue had been able to see how difficult it was for him to remain in the capital. Everything in front of him was familiar, yet strange. The craving for violence still ran rampant in his veins, with no outlet to vent it.

Watching the foolish crowd, filled with people who had never suffered a day in their lives, made him feel like he was counting down the days in a dream, yet the day he was meant to wake never came. Guan Shanjin was not suited for those prosperous and peaceful days in the capital. He knew that he was a savage beast, and now that he had experienced the taste of freedom on the battlefield, how could he endure the shackles of such mundane days?

"I thought about it for days. During that time, there was always news of you stirring up trouble in the capital. There were some people who said that the protector general's family was heroic, yet their son was the devil incarnate—what a pity for such a valiant family."

These words made Guan Shanjin burst out laughing. His enchanting eyes curved up along with his laugh; they were like little hooks sinking into Mr. Lu's heart.

"The devil incarnate? These words really make me miss my young and reckless days." Guan Shanjin knew quite well how the citizens of the capital had spoken about him. Some of the names and words they used even came from him. "So you took that opportunity to meet me?"

"Yes. I wanted to meet you, to see how you were doing. I had always been thinking about you." Mr. Lu's expression was a little hesitant. His free hand that was resting on his knee twitched. Ultimately, he could not hold himself back; he cupped Guan Shanjin's face with that hand. "When I lured you over to meet me, I had no confidence at all. After all, so many years had passed, and I was no longer a young man. For all I knew, you might not even remember me anymore."

"I remembered you." The image of a reserved, graceful, beautiful man always dressed in white, like the reflection of moonlight on the water, had deeply etched itself into Guan Shanjin's heart, never to be forgotten again.

Mr. Lu's eyes brightened suddenly, seeming both shy and delighted. "Yes, you remembered... Under the revolving lanterns, you called out to me." Although Guan Shanjin was dressed entirely in black, looking proud and aloof, his image still stirred up feelings within Mr. Lu's heart.

They were sitting among the plum trees in Horse-Face City, but it felt like they were transported to that day of years past, when, under countless lamps, they only had eyes for each other.

Guan Shanjin sighed lightly. Laying a hand over Mr. Lu's hand as it caressed his face, he closed his eyes and leaned into Mr. Lu's touch. Mr. Lu's heart beat faster, his face turning red. Their hands interlocked, inseparable.

But the next moment, Guan Shanjin let go, and his tone abruptly turned cold. "Teacher, did you call for me today just to reminisce about the past?"

The joy and tenderness of the past only made them seem even more foolish now.

With the sudden dissipation of warmth, Mr. Lu looked at Guan Shanjin in stunned silence, as though he had not expected Guan Shanjin could change moods so quickly.

"Teacher, don't you have anything else you'd like to say to me?" His question sounded rather aggressive.

Mr. Lu pulled his hand back, rubbing at the heat that had yet to fade away. Momentarily, he seemed a little tearful. "I..." Mr. Lu gritted his teeth, and it seemed as though he had finally come to a decision. "Haiwang, I understand that the reason you were so good to Wu Xingzi was because you saw me in him. I'm the one who let you down. Because I was once your teacher, I was unwilling to let our relationship change. I've known all along that you had feelings for me, yet I didn't dare to return your affections."

"Oh?" Guan Shanjin's face darkened further. These words did not comfort him—in fact, they only added salt to the wound.

"Haiwang, in truth, all those years ago, I already...already..." Mr. Lu looked very conflicted. His eyes reddened, and he was unable to continue. Biting his lip, he gave up, bowing his head and refusing to speak further.

His hesitation only annoyed Guan Shanjin. The general kept his silence, staring at Mr. Lu with no intention to help him out.

The silence endured for more than a quarter of an hour, but General Guan still refused to speak first. Sighing internally, Mr. Lu felt resentful and uneasy; he was unable to surmise what Guan Shanjin was thinking. Anxiously, he tightened his fists, leaving marks in his palms with his fingernails.

"Haiwang, I do have feelings for you..."

Mr. Lu seemed to have gained courage from finally admitting it.

He looked up, meeting Guan Shanjin's eyes again. He saw Guan Shanjin freeze, then reveal an expression of disbelief. Finally, Guan Shanjin smiled lightly, like a flower blooming.

"Teacher, do you mean it?"

"Yes..." Mr. Lu quietly reached out and held onto Guan Shanjin's hand on the table, nodding his head vigorously. "I mean it completely and sincerely."

"Is that so?" Guan Shanjin said. He twined their fingers together, looking like he was cherishing something precious. "Then, let's cancel the wedding tomorrow! Since we've finally confessed our feelings for each other, there's no need for that Yue girl anymore."

"Hold on!" Mr. Lu had not expected Guan Shanjin to jump to that conclusion so quickly. He hadn't lost himself in the ecstasy of Mr. Lu's confession at all. Mr. Lu began to grow anxious.

"Hmm?" Guan Shanjin tilted his head at Mr. Lu, as though he didn't understand why he was being stopped.

"Haiwang, the wedding has to happen." This was the true reason Mr. Lu had wanted to speak with Guan Shanjin.

"Teacher, what do you mean?" Guan Shanjin's brows knitted. His displeasure was obvious.

"Haiwang, you know that I'm the only one left in the Lu family. Before my parents departed, their only wish was for me to continue the family line." Mr. Lu held onto Guan Shanjin's hand tightly, afraid that he would free himself and leave.

"This means..." Guan Shanjin's words tasted bitter. "Teacher, you still want to marry that Yue girl so you can have children? What exactly do you see me as?"

"Haiwang, the two of us belong to each other, but sometimes mere affection is not enough. I understand that I'm being selfish. If you're angry with me, then it's best that we part. From now on, we'll go our separate ways—just forget about me." Mr. Lu dropped Guan Shanjin's hand, turning his head away. Under the flickering light, a tear glimmered on his cheek.

"Teacher..." Guan Shanjin's voice was filled with pain. His warm fingers brushed that shining tear away, and he sighed. "Teacher, what would you have me do? Watch as the man who is supposed to belong to me marries someone else and has a child with her?"

"Haiwang, just wait for me. When Miss Yue gives birth to a child, I'll return to your side. Believe me, please." Mr. Lu threw himself into Guan Shanjin's arms and nuzzled into his chest, full of yearning. "You need to have a child yourself too. The protector general's family has had only one descendant for many generations; your family line cannot end with you. When you return to the capital, you should marry a woman and have a child as well—after that, we'll be able to spend the rest of our lives together."

Guan Shanjin hugged Mr. Lu tightly, burying his face in Mr. Lu's hair. His voice was muffled as he spoke. "Teacher... As long as it's what you want, I'll do everything you say."

Just like in the past, whatever Mr. Lu asked, Guan Shanjin would fulfill his desires. Sprawled in Guan Shanjin's arms, Mr. Lu exhaled heavily, finally at ease.

As for Guan Shanjin, he concealed his own feelings, his lips quirking up coldly.

They remained in each other's arms for a long time. It was nearing midnight, and Lu Zezhi finally showed signs of fatigue. After exchanging vows of love and loyalty with Guan Shanjin, he could finally relax and send the man away from the Wang Shu Residence.

Guan Shanjin put on a show, exuding gentleness and deep affection. He dragged out their farewell for as long as possible, acting as if he was unwilling to part. Only when Lu Zezhi could no longer control his expression did Guan Shanjin finally turn to leave.

Once he was out of Lu Zezhi's sight, Guan Shanjin immediately discarded his affectionate expression and snorted coldly. With no regard for decorum, he removed his outer robe. It was saturated with Mr. Lu's scent, refreshing and gentle. This was the scent of the incense that the general had searched for and bought specially to suit Mr. Lu all those years ago. The clean, crisp aroma had a gentle yet distant characteristic to it, like the silver moon in the sky—worlds apart from Guan Shanjin.

Everything felt like a cruel joke. The man whom he had cherished for so many years, whom he dared not toy with, and whom he had loved so deeply, had ended up being this selfish and unscrupulous. Mr. Lu had never been so foolish in the past. Was it Guan Shanjin's years of doting that had made him forget himself?

If Lu Zezhi's methods were a little more skillful, Guan Shanjin would have still been able to admire him. He might have even considered giving Mr. Lu a helping hand as compensation for his company these past eight or nine years. However, Guan Shanjin had not expected that the years of ease and comfort would make this seemingly bright person lose half of his previous capability—he had even become somewhat stupid.

Back when General Guan had lived in the capital, numerous daughters of noble families had sought his hand in marriage. Without giving them a modicum of respect, he rejected them all. Had Lu Zezhi forgotten? Didn't Mr. Lu see that the only reason the emperor turned a blind eye to Guan Shanjin acting like a dictator at the southern border was that he, the only child of the protector general, was a homosexual? Could Mr. Lu not grasp that the emperor allowed Guan Shanjin to do whatever he pleased specifically because he had declared he would never marry a woman or have any children, and that his family line would end with him?

Guan Shanjin pressed a palm to his forehead, laughing quietly. What a mockery this situation was. Just look at the idiot he had created as a result of his affections.

"Burn this," Guan Shanjin said, casually tossing his outer robe to the ground. A shadow flashed out from the dark, acknowledging Guan Shanjin respectfully. Just as the mysterious person picked up the robe, they were stopped by Guan Shanjin. "Tell Man Yue that there's no need to worry about anyone's dignity tomorrow. I can still afford to have such a small part of my honor trampled underfoot."

"Yes, sir." There was no sign of hesitation from the dark figure. In the blink of an eye, they had vanished without a trace.

Guan Shanjin stood in the dark for a long while. The stars were dim in the moonless sky. It was already late into the night, and the spring wind chilled the air. His clothes swirled in the breeze as he stood as motionless as a statue. It was not clear what he was looking at, nor what he was thinking about.

Finally, he exhaled a slow breath. As if possessed, he began to walk toward Shuanghe Manor.

He had not originally planned to seek out Wu Xingzi so soon after the matter with Mr. Lu concluded. Furthermore, Wu Xingzi was sure to be asleep at this late hour. Guan Shanjin didn't want to wake Wu Xingzi up, but there was a peculiar restlessness inside of him, and he could not stop himself from wanting to see that old quail.

It took him no time to reach Shuanghe Manor. In contrast to the tranquility of the Wang Shu Residence, chirping insects could be heard here, and the fresh scent of the earth, of the plants and trees, was everywhere. The atmosphere was more soothing than any expensive incense or perfume.

Guan Shanjin slowed his footsteps, heading to the garden first. As always, the vegetable patches were very neat and tidy. Vines twirled around their individual trellises, luxuriant and green. Every leaf was tender and fresh, the stems thick and strong. Some had blossomed, others had recently borne fruit, and some were covered by the lush leaves of various plants. They were all extremely pleasing to the eye—even cute.

Inadvertently, a small smile appeared on Guan Shanjin's face. He could see how joyfully and meticulously Wu Xingzi had taken care of these plants. Even when tending to the plot, the old fellow would still wear his Confucian robe, tucking the bottom hem up into his belt. When preparing the soil for planting, he would remove his shoes and socks and roll his pants up, revealing his slim and fair calves. He would step upon the soil with his bare, pale feet, all ten adorable toes occasionally curling up to try and get rid of the dirt between them.

When Guan Shanjin had witnessed this scene, it felt as though a butterfly was flapping its wings rapidly inside his chest; he could not decipher exactly what that feeling meant. He remembered that he was entranced by the sight of Wu Xingzi gardening. When Wu Xingzi bent over, his round, smooth buttocks would raise up, making his waist seem even more slender. Guan Shanjin knew how flexible that waist was, how he could bend the adviser in half without hurting him.

As he'd watched, a bead of sweat on Wu Xingzi's forehead slid down to the tip of his nose. Mint and Osmanthus wanted to help wipe his sweat away, but the old fellow wouldn't let them.

Smiling brightly, he refused their help, and wiped his forehead with his sleeve. In the process he left a few traces of mud on his face, making him look like a patterned cat. Even though he was an old cat, he was an adorable one.

When Wu Xingzi finished his work, Guan Shanjin had helped him wash his feet. He cleaned every toe carefully, causing a blush to bloom all over Wu Xingzi's entire body.

Guan Shanjin pushed all his troubles and dismay from tonight to the back of his mind as he walked around the garden. The fury and stifling pressure in his chest wasn't because Lu Zezhi was stupid; rather, he was angry at himself for not seeing it until now, after all these years.

Absentmindedly, Guan Shanjin made another round through the garden before heading toward Wu Xingzi's bedroom. When he pushed the door open, he could hear Wu Xingzi's steady breathing. Guan Shanjin perked his ears, listening to those slow breaths for some time. He deliberated over it again, but he still could not resist the yearning welling up inside of him, and he walked into the room with light steps, afraid to disturb Wu Xingzi's sleep.

Wu Xingzi lay on the bed, covered with a thin blanket. Sleeping sideways, he rested on a soft pillow, his cheek pushed a little out of shape and his lips slightly parted; the corner of his mouth was slightly damp. Occasionally, his mouth would move as if he was chewing on something; then he would reveal a silly smile. He looked entirely foolish, but this image only made Guan Shanjin's heart melt.

This old fellow clearly loved his food, but he never gained any weight. Even in his dreams, he thought of eating! Guan Shanjin had been too busy lately. When they returned to the capital, he would take Wu Xingzi out to try all sorts of famous restaurants and local snacks. Wu Xingzi would be absolutely delighted.

Guan Shanjin sat by the bed. Enchanted by Wu Xingzi's sleeping face, he reached out and played with his soft, silky hair. Wu Xingzi was thin and fair; when he had his hair down, he looked younger, nothing like a middle-aged man already past his prime. The contrast of black hair against white skin made him seem even more delicate—perhaps even pitiable.

The way Wu Xingzi looked only made Guan Shanjin adore him more. Guan Shanjin could not help himself from bending over and kissing his eyelids, his nose, and the corner of his mouth, before catching his slightly parted lips with his own.

The kiss was extremely gentle. Even so, it woke Wu Xingzi up from his dreams. He blearily opened his eyes. He felt he could not catch his breath, and an intoxicating scent filled his nose—a clinging, elegant aroma of sandalwood mingled with orange blossoms... Suddenly feeling suction on the tip of his tongue, Wu Xingzi responded eagerly. There was no way he could resist such a familiar scent.

"Did I wake you up?" Although reluctant, Guan Shanjin forced himself to stop. Removing his shoes, he climbed onto the bed, pulling Wu Xingzi tightly into his arms.

He was afraid that if he were to continue the kiss, he would not be able to keep himself from taking Wu Xingzi there and then. However, tomorrow was a big day, and he needed to be extremely alert. The only thing he could do now was to wait for the matter to be dealt with; he would return to settle this desire later.

"Haiwang?" Wu Xingzi was still groggy, but the kiss had lit a flame within him. Unconsciously, he ground himself against Guan Shanjin's thigh.

"Not tonight," Guan Shanjin said, hugging him tightly. He held Wu Xingzi's restless limbs and pressed a comforting kiss on his forehead. "Go back to sleep. I shouldn't have woken you."

"Oh..." Wu Xingzi struggled a little, but he could not free himself. He became a little more awake, huddling shyly into Guan Shanjin's chest and not trying to move again. The two of them remained in each other's embrace for some time.

Guan Shanjin looked at Wu Xingzi. "You're not going back to sleep?"

"I'm awake now; it's hard to get back to sleep..." Wu Xingzi sighed. This wasn't his choice! He was leaving for the capital tomorrow, and he'd even slept earlier to make sure he would be well rested! He hadn't expected to be kissed awake by Guan Shanjin. Now there was no way he would be able to fall back asleep.

"It's my fault," Guan Shanjin apologized sincerely, rocking the man in his arms. "Why don't I recite a book to help you sleep?"

"Recite a book?" Wu Xingzi blinked, then laughed out loud. He had never heard anyone use such a method to help another person fall asleep before.

"What? You don't believe I can get you to sleep?" Guan Shanjin raised a brow, staring at Wu Xingzi's smiling face.

At the very start, he had thought that when Wu Xingzi smiled, he looked like Mr. Lu. However, Wu Xingzi was reserved and didn't smile often. Instead, he would always fall into a daze when he looked at Guan Shanjin. Guan Shanjin didn't know what the adviser was thinking about; he looked rather foolish, yet also pure and innocent. It used to cause Guan Shanjin displeasure, as he felt that this fool was desecrating Mr. Lu's image.

The true fool was Guan Shanjin!

Looking at Wu Xingzi now, Guan Shanjin wondered how he could have ever seen a trace of Mr. Lu on this man's face. Guan Shanjin had never wanted to kiss Mr. Lu when he smiled.

"What book are you going to recite?" Wu Xingzi was curious.

He knew that Guan Shanjin excelled in both military and scholarly matters, and had read a hundred times more books than he. However, Wu Xingzi was a scholar! How could he listen to a book and fall asleep?

"*Qingcheng County Records*," Guan Shanjin said.

Wu Xingzi trembled, his eyes widening in shock. "Y-y-you... When did you read the records?"

Qingcheng County Records were like the records of most counties, the only difference being the people who compiled them. Coincidentally, Wu Xingzi happened to be the main compiler. After all, in such a small place as Qingcheng County, there were only so many people who could read and write. The person with the highest level of education was usually the magistrate, followed by the adviser.

The magistrate was busy with his official duties, so he didn't have time to prepare the records. Therefore, the responsibility fell to the adviser. Wu Xingzi knew that his writing skills were ordinary. He was hardly concerned if others read the records, but knowing that Guan Shanjin had read it made him feel very anxious. For his writing to be seen so plainly by Guan Shanjin... It was more embarrassing than being naked!

Guan Shanjin smiled. "Didn't you have a set of the records at your place? I was feeling bored at that time, so I read all of them."

"Oh, I forgot that I had a copy..." Wu Xingzi's shoulders sagged as he sank into Guan Shanjin's embrace. "You really memorized all of it? My writing is terrible—it's embarrassing."

"It's true that your words were not extravagant, but they were direct. You introduced Qingcheng County quite well." Guan Shanjin smiled and kissed Wu Xingzi's forehead. "How about it? If I recite the records, will you be able to fall asleep?"

"It probably won't work. Ah, let's just forget about it, all right?" How could he be able to sleep? He would die from mortification!

"Qingcheng County is a good place." Guan Shanjin did not push the subject. In any case, chatting casually with Wu Xingzi was enjoyable in and of itself.

"It is." Wu Xingzi nodded. Although Qingcheng County had barren soil and was prone to floods, it was still the place that had nurtured him. He would always hold an unyielding love for his hometown. Besides, many things contributed to his life; no place could compare to one's home.

"When Mr. Lu is married, shall we go back and stay for a few days?"

"A few days?" Wu Xingzi jerked violently. Guan Shanjin looked at him in puzzlement.

"Don't you have to return to the capital for work?" Wu Xingzi hurriedly came up with a response, but all he could think of was his journey tomorrow. He felt oddly guilty.

"A delay of a few days is nothing." Guan Shanjin thought that Wu Xingzi was refusing out of concern for him. Calmly, he smiled and tried to comfort Wu Xingzi. "The emperor is not rushing me to return. We have ample time—it doesn't matter if we delay our return to the capital for a few days. Besides, Qingcheng County is on the way."

"Oh..." Wu Xingzi forced a smile, nodding his head. He then immediately hid his face away, afraid he might reveal something in his expression.

"This time, Mr. Lu will return to the capital with us as well." Guan Shanjin spoke abruptly, a slight nervousness in his tone. However, Wu Xingzi did not register it; he nodded again, unbothered.

"It's good that the two of you have cleared things up." Wu Xingzi figured that Mr. Lu must have confessed his feelings to Guan Shanjin by now. After all, tomorrow was the wedding, and things could not drag out any further.

"You don't mind?" Guan Shanjin asked. Wu Xingzi's calm tone made Guan Shanjin unhappy. Did Wu Xingzi have no intention of asking why?

"Huh?" Why would Wu Xingzi mind? He was an outsider from the very beginning. Guan Shanjin and Mr. Lu would have a happy life together now, and Wu Xingzi no longer had any part in it. Could it be that Guan Shanjin was afraid that he would blame Mr. Lu? This thought flashed through Wu Xingzi's head, so he quickly reassured Guan Shanjin, "Don't overthink it. I understand that Mr. Lu had his reasons."

The expression on Guan Shanjin's face changed abruptly. Even the most casual of remarks could sound significant to a suspicious listener. He gritted his teeth. "Oh? So you also wish to marry and have a child?"

CHAPTER 8

A Journey of a Thousand Miles Together Still Must Come to an End

"You will definitely leave this world earlier than me. I can help take care of any unfinished business for a few more years."

Complicated emotions ran through Wu Xingzi. Never before in his life had someone made such a solemn promise to him.

Such sweet and sentimental promises might not hold forever. Even so, Wu Xingzi felt sweetness welling up within him.

The sweetness also made him feel alarmed.

He really had to leave.

MARRY AND HAVE A CHILD? Stunned, Wu Xingzi stared at Guan Shanjin's foreboding expression and shook his head stupidly.

Why would he have a child? Why would he marry a *woman*? He liked big dicks! Even if he wanted to find someone to spend the rest of his life with, that someone would have to have a perfect pengornis! He dared not even touch a woman's finger! The only women Wu Xingzi had ever had physical contact with in his life were his mother and Auntie Liu.

Seeing how confused Wu Xingzi was, Guan Shanjin realized that he had taken out his anger on an innocent man. Scrubbing his face, he sighed deeply. "That was wrong. Don't be angry with me," he said, his voice apologetic.

Wu Xingzi and Lu Zezhi were very different men. Right from their first meeting, it had been evident that Wu Xingzi cared about cocks, not the men attached to them. Could an old fellow like this marry a wife and have a child? He'd probably never even thought about it!

"What's wrong?" Wu Xingzi wasn't angry with Guan Shanjin, only curious. Logically speaking, Guan Shanjin and Mr. Lu had finally confirmed their affections for each other, so he should be happy! So why did he feel...a little weary?

Wu Xingzi's heart ached. Pulling at Guan Shanjin, he sat up. After a moment of reflection, he carefully pressed Guan Shanjin's head into his chest, gently patting his silken hair. "Tell me about it?"

Guan Shanjin's eyes fell half-lidded as he comfortably settled into Wu Xingzi's arms. The old fellow was thin, and his chest barely had any muscles on it. However, it still felt very warm, and his scent was mild and enchanting. As he took in a few breaths, the suffocating feeling in Guan Shanjin's chest evaporated. He reached out, wrapping his arms around Wu Xingzi's slender waist, enjoying the rare moment of warmth.

It was rather funny when he thought about it. When the two of them were together, they were always either eating or having sex. Among the desires of life, they neglected neither, but they did not confide much in each other. Guan Shanjin didn't even know the professions of Wu Xingzi's ancestors. He only had a vague idea that Wu Xingzi's father wasn't just a simple scholar. Putting aside how odd it was for a scholar from a tiny, rural area to expertly play the qin and write poetry, it was impossible that a talented man like him would willingly remain in his provincial hometown. Why would he become a teacher and raise his family on the bare minimum when he had so much potential?

Guan Shanjin had previously had no interest in knowing. Now, he had lost the opportunity to ask.

But he could handle it. In his life, he'd encountered countless dilemmas, and this was not a major issue in comparison. He could slowly make his plans, and once things in the capital were settled, he would have plenty of time to spend with Wu Xingzi.

Still, there was something that he had to find out right now.

"Are you the only descendant left in the Wu family? Do you have any other relatives?" It was rather amusing when he thought about it. Guan Shanjin, Lu Zezhi, and Wu Xingzi—all three of them were the last of their families. For them to come together in such a situation... It could only be the heavens making fools of them.

Wu Xingzi shook his head. "There's no one else left in my family," he said. He tilted his head and frowned. "My father's parents passed away before I was born, and my mother's parents died when I was young. After they were gone, my uncles left Qingcheng County, and I don't know where they went. When my parents drowned in the flood, my uncles didn't return to look for them. I'm the one who has been taking care of my mother's parents' graves. I'm afraid that my uncles, during that flood, also..."

Wu Xingzi sighed. He dared not continue.

No wonder there were some in the county who disliked him, saying behind his back that he was cursed to live a hard life. There had once been almost a dozen people in his family, but he might truly be the only one left alive.

"Oh?" Guan Shanjin noticed his melancholy and turned around to pull Wu Xingzi into his arms. Leaning against the headboard, he let Wu Xingzi sprawl across his chest and listen to his strong, steady heartbeat.

"Don't overthink it. Fate is out of our hands. Rather than dwelling on those who have died, why don't you allow yourself to live?"

"Oh..." Wu Xingzi closed his eyes.

Guan Shanjin's body was sturdy and full of inner strength. His heartbeats were steady and strong through his slender yet powerful chest; it felt as though his heart knocked directly against Wu Xingzi's ear. The feeling sent tingles through Wu Xingzi's body, making him blush a little. He tried to shift his position, only to have Guan Shanjin hold him tighter. Unable to move, he had no choice but to remain where he was.

"Then...have you ever thought about who will burn incense for you after your death?" These words came as a surprise to both of them. Guan Shanjin had never thought that he would ask such a question out loud, while Wu Xingzi had never thought anyone would ever ask him a question like that.

Wu Xingzi stayed silent for a moment. He was a little confused, unsure why Guan Shanjin would ask about something so private. The two of them had always been more like passersby in each other's lives than friends. Throughout the past few months, although they had paid respects to his ancestors and spent New Year together—and Wu Xingzi had found himself falling for Guan Shanjin in the process—the general had never asked him many personal questions.

Now, they were about to go their separate ways, so why would he choose a time like this to ask something so private?

"I..." Wu Xingzi murmured to himself and finally sighed. "I was originally planning to end my life on the day I turned forty."

He had never mentioned this to anyone before; he himself did not understand why he would speak of it now. Guan Shanjin stiffened abruptly, giving him a harsh pinch. The pain made Wu Xingzi cry out, and the general quickly gentled his strength. However, Guan Shanjin's breaths were burning hot. He was like a furious panther, exhaling hotly as it paced around its prey.

"Why?" Guan Shanjin asked. His normally gentle voice turned hard and cutting, as if it was a sharp blade gleaming in the cold light. Wu Xingzi shrank into himself, shuddering, and placatingly nuzzled his cheek into Guan Shanjin's chest. Timidly, he wrapped his arms around Guan Shanjin's well-defined waist.

"I..." He swallowed, his throat inexplicably dry. He struggled over whether he should tell the truth or not. Guan Shanjin looked angry, but Wu Xingzi did not understand why.

"Be honest. I can see through your lies." Lowering his head, Guan Shanjin could see Wu Xingzi's panicked expression. Everything that crossed Wu Xingzi's mind was written on his face, and Guan Shanjin was mildly amused at the sight. Still, he forced himself to harden his tone, and continued scaring the adviser.

Wu Xingzi trembled. He looked just like a real quail, huddling into a tiny ball. With great difficulty, he managed to reply, "I... At the time, I...was very lonely."

When he thought back to those days, the only thing Wu Xingzi could remember was being alone: all he knew was loneliness, infinite and endless. At the time, he was still Adviser Wu of Qingcheng County. The only two places he ever went were his home and the magistrate's office, and occasionally to the market to buy some vegetables and have a bowl of tofu. For holidays and celebrations, he would make the trip to Goose City to purchase some items, then return to his empty and lonely home, eating meals he made for himself.

Wu Xingzi had borrowed a sum of money from the magistrate's office to help Yan Wenxin, and then paid it off bit by bit. It had only been five years ago that he'd cleared the debt and interest. At first, he heaved a breath of relief; the burden in his heart was finally settled. However, it did not take him long to discover that without this burden, he didn't have anything to motivate him. Why exactly was he living like this—completely alone, with no one beside him?

He decided to buy a gravesite, and what a wonderful gravesite it was! Such a splendid location called for an excellent coffin. Thus, Wu Xingzi started to save up a stash of money. This fund was specifically to buy a coffin for when he breathed his last.

The coffins made in Liuzhou were the best in all of Great Xia. Wu Xingzi probably could not afford the most luxuriant ones, but a reasonably priced, high-quality coffin should not be out of his budget. He had already planned it all out. He would have a Liuzhou coffin made of pine, and his burial shroud would be made from the set of clothes his mother sewed him the year he took his examinations. Those clothes had not been washed away in the flood, and he had meticulously taken care of them over the years.

Before he realized it, Wu Xingzi spilled all of these matters to Guan Shanjin. His soft voice was very serious and earnest. To Guan Shanjin, it felt like a thousand needles piercing into his heart, hurting him terribly.

This was the first time Wu Xingzi had mentioned Yan Wenxin while sober. For him to be so open about it, it seemed that this painful part of his past was no longer quite so weighty.

"Do you hate Yan Wenxin for deceiving you?" Guan Shanjin asked.

"I..." Wu Xingzi blinked a few times, realizing he had accidentally talked about Yan Wenxin in front of Guan Shanjin. He glanced at Guan Shanjin carefully, his lips quirking up jokingly yet earnestly. "I don't know. But at least because of him, I've lived all the way until today."

If it wasn't for having to pay back his loan, Wu Xingzi felt that he would not have been able to endure the loneliness for as long as he did. However, he had never considered that the person to blame for his loneliness was Yan Wenxin himself. Guan Shanjin did not point this out; it was a rare opportunity for them to confide in each other, so there was no need for an extraneous person to be involved.

"When you pass away, what will happen to your ancestors' graves?" Guan Shanjin asked. Although the general was alarmed that Wu Xingzi had once thought of committing suicide, he was somewhat comforted by the existence of the Peng Society and those penis illustrations—this old fellow probably could not bear to die when he still had pengornises to collect.

Ah... This is a big issue... Wu Xingzi had thought about this before. There was a Guanyin Temple in Qingcheng County, and no matter how hard life was for the county's people, they would still spare some of their harvest and offer it to the monks there. They hoped that during Qingming, there would be someone to take care of the family graves of those like Wu Xingzi, who no longer had any living family. Their sincere prayers and offerings to the Guanyin Temple and the monks were enough for at least twenty years. Wu Xingzi had already planned to leave his ancestors to the care of the temple after his death. As for his own grave, it did not matter.

"I'm a lot younger than you," Guan Shanjin said. When Wu Xingzi didn't respond, he swayed the man in his arms, patting his back.

"Ah? That's true. You're not even thirty." Wu Xingzi laughed lightly. He had almost forgotten that Guan Shanjin was so young. Robbing the cradle was rather satisfying!

"Yeah, and my body is stronger than yours, too. For a skilled martial artist like me, as long as I don't die on the battlefield, I could easily live to be seventy." Guan Shanjin crooked a finger under Wu Xingzi's chin, smiling at him.

His smile was luminous, like Buddha holding a flower, or the sun coming out after the rain. Wu Xingzi's face flushed red, and he could not hide away despite wanting to. With no other choice, he could only stupidly watch that smile, his heart pounding so rapidly it might burst.

"How amazing to be able to live until seventy." People rarely made it to the age of seventy. For most rich families, it was already considered excellent to reach sixty. In Qingcheng County, a fifty-year-old person would be considered very old already. Old Liu and Auntie Liu were both over the age of fifty and still fit and healthy—they were truly a rare sight.

"So you will definitely leave this world earlier than me. When it comes to paying respects to your ancestors, I can help take care of it for a few more years." As Guan Shanjin spoke, he pressed a few kisses onto Wu Xingzi's lips. Like a dragonfly flitting across the water, the kisses left glowing sparks in their wake.

Wu Xingzi's attention had been entirely seized by these kisses. Unconsciously, he pursed his lips together and kissed Guan Shanjin back. At first he didn't register what the general had said. But Guan Shanjin had no intention of deepening the kisses—instead, he pulled Wu Xingzi back into his arms and patted him gently. If they'd kept kissing, Wu Xingzi would have had no time to ponder over the meaning of those words. Now that he was no longer distracted, he was shocked.

Guan Shanjin would help take care of any leftover matters? This meant that after he died, not only did Guan Shanjin want to arrange his funeral, he'd even help tidy up the family graves and make offerings every year? This, this...

Complicated emotions ran through Wu Xingzi. Never in his life had someone made such a solemn promise to him before. He'd lived a lonely life, and when he died, he figured no one would care. At most, Auntie Liu and her family would lay him in his coffin and deal with his funeral, and Wu Xingzi did not wish to trouble anyone with anything more than that.

What exactly were they? *Why...*

Joy, doubt, and confusion all mingled together inside of him. In the end, they converged to form a vision of Mr. Lu's face. A shiver ran through Wu Xingzi, and he immediately sobered.

Guan Shanjin and Mr. Lu were the ones meant to be together. Even in matters of life and death, Wu Xingzi had nothing to do with their future. Perhaps promises were just made when emotions reached certain heights. However, they would soon be going down their own paths. If someone were to ask Wu Xingzi what had left the greatest impression on him after being an adviser for so long, it would be that one could not depend entirely on anyone else.

There were even times when families turned on each other. A husband and wife might be together, but if disaster struck, they could still abandon each other. There was no friendship between himself and Guan Shanjin; they had yet to even know each other for a year. Such sweet and sentimental promises could not be relied upon. When people were caught up in tender feelings, their words would always seem touching.

Even so, Wu Xingzi felt sweetness welling up within him at Guan Shanjin's promise.

The sweetness also made him feel alarmed.

He really had to leave.

Even if Hei-er and Rancui had not urged him to do so, he couldn't stay here any longer. Guan Shanjin's every word and action felt like the spring rain: slowly dissolving the defenses around his heart. Without a sound, Guan Shanjin had stolen the heart that Wu Xingzi had closely guarded for twenty years. However, the general would soon be spending the rest of his life with another man.

Wu Xingzi lightly pressed his hand to his heart. He bowed his head, unwilling to expose himself and his thoughts to Guan Shanjin. The heartache he was feeling was something he had brought upon himself, and he could not blame anyone for it. Just like in the past, when he had loved Yan Wenxin, his feelings were willingly given.

However, why did they both refuse to properly bid him farewell? When it came to their separation, why did they always choose to leave him with such sweet words and promises? Wu Xingzi did not understand. He could not dwell on it any longer.

"What's wrong?" Guan Shanjin asked, frowning. He noticed that the man in his arms had suddenly distanced himself, but he didn't know why it had come about. He could only flex his arms fiercely, desperately wishing that he could absorb every part of Wu Xingzi into his bloodstream.

"I'm tired..." Wu Xingzi replied glumly. After struggling a little, he finally freed himself from Guan Shanjin's arms. He rolled deeper into the bed and pulled up his blanket. "Haiwang, you should get some sleep. It's going to be a busy day tomorrow."

Guan Shanjin frowned, a faint feeling of unease stirring in his heart. Wu Xingzi had always been very timid, and now was not a good time to explain matters regarding Mr. Lu.

After the wedding, he would take Wu Xingzi to the capital. There, he would prepare delicious food and fun things to do, and he would be able to appease the adviser. It would not be too late to explain everything to Wu Xingzi once tomorrow was dealt with.

Having made his decision, Guan Shanjin made no further attempt to mollify Wu Xingzi, but he did turn and hold him until he fell asleep.

Early the next morning, not long after Guan Shanjin left Shuanghe Manor, Wu Xingzi got out of bed. He sat for a long time, in a sleepy haze.

In the distance, he heard the joyful music of a marriage celebration and the sound of firecrackers going off. It must have been a bustling scene. He didn't know why Mr. Lu was still getting married... but it no longer had anything to do with him.

Checking his luggage one more time, Wu Xingzi changed into clothes that were more suitable for horseback riding. He paced nervously around the room, too anxious to eat breakfast. He shoved a few buns into his luggage, thinking he would be able to have them on the road later.

Wu Xingzi couldn't tell how much time passed. His palms turned sweaty, then they dried; then they became sweaty again. Suddenly, the half-open window creaked, scaring Wu Xingzi so severely that he jumped on the spot. His heart nearly leapt into his throat, but he calmed when he saw a familiar tall figure.

"Shall we go, Mr. Wu?" Hei-er asked. He was dressed quite simply and carried a small bag on his shoulder, looking ready to depart on an ordinary journey. He walked forward to grab the luggage in Wu Xingzi's hand.

"Don't worry, all the masters of the general's estate are heading to the Yue manor right now. No one will see you leave."

"Ah..." Wu Xingzi nodded continuously, swallowing thickly a couple of times. "Will Mint and Osmanthus get in trouble?" He was worried that if he left without giving any notice, the two young girls would be reprimanded.

"Don't worry—Mint and Osmanthus will be coming with us to the capital." Hei-er pointed outside. "They're both waiting for you in the courtyard."

Hearing that, Wu Xingzi quickly ran to the window. The two girls stood there with bags in hand, looking over in his direction. Wu Xingzi felt relieved, but at the same time, he felt rather apologetic. He hadn't dared to ask if the girls wanted to accompany him. After all, he was not sure when they would be able to return home. On the other hand, he was also worried about leaving them at the general's estate. He'd been worrying about this the entire morning.

However, the girls were much more decisive than he. It was a big world out there—there would always be somewhere for them! They were still young; they did not have as many attachments to their hometown as Wu Xingzi. Viewing the journey as a vacation and a learning experience, they were delighted. In any case, they could not bear the thought of their master having no one to take care of him! Fortunately, they would be there, and they could while away the time with him, could they not?

Thus, the final worry Wu Xingzi had in Horse-Face City vanished. With Hei-er's help, he tumbled out through the window. The master and his three servants secretly left the general's estate from the back gate, alerting no one.

Not long after, at the urging of a dark-skinned man, a simple carriage left Horse-Face City, flying down the road toward the capital.

The marriage alliance between Mr. Lu—the teacher of the Great General of the Southern Garrison—and the Yue family was one of the biggest events in Horse-Face City this year.

On the day of the wedding, the road from the general's estate to the Yue family manor was decorated festively, adorned with beautiful ornaments and lanterns. Many of the flowers used in these decorations had never been seen by the common folk before, and they feasted their eyes upon the splendid sight.

When the time arrived, a group of people left the general's estate to fetch the bride, making their way to the Yue family manor in a formidable arrangement.

At the front of this formation was an enormous horse, its entire body a perfect snowy white. Its coat gleamed under the spring sun, untainted by a single blemish. With a bright red saddle and bridle, it didn't just look festive, it was absolutely elegant.

Riding atop the horse, Lu Zezhi looked graceful yet stern, his back as straight as a board. He was like a meticulously carved jade statue, and his crimson-colored wedding attire made him seem like a deity of the high heavens.

Although his name was well-known in Horse-Face City, not many people had seen him in the flesh before. For many of the common folk joining in the revelry from the sidelines, this was their first time seeing the famous Mr. Lu. He certainly lived up to his reputation as the man fought over by General Guan and Miss Yue. He was truly gorgeous! They'd rarely seen such a beautiful man in all their lives.

This tremendous parade slowly made its way toward the Yue family manor.

The wedding goose had already been sent over, signifying the unity of the couple: unified and inseparable. The ceremony included gatecrash games, people knocking on the door and urging the bride to get onto the sedan chair, the groom entering the doors to greet his in-laws, and the bride bidding farewell to her parents. Finally, Miss Yue was led into the litter; accompanied by music and the boisterous crowd, they returned to the general's estate using another path.

After shooting three arrows at the bride to chase away any evil spirits, crossing the saddle, and stepping over a basin of fire for good luck, the procession arrived at the wedding hall. It was time for the part of the ceremony where the bride and groom paid their respects to their parents and to the heavens.

The scene was lively, bustling, and joyful. The seats in the main hall were reserved for the couple's parents, but Lu Zezhi's parents were no longer around. Although he was from another part of the country, though, his status allowed him to invite a local official to be a witness. The governor of Horse-Face City was a man of about forty. He was a warm and friendly-looking man who often had a smile on his face. Standing in for the elders of the Lu family, he was seated in the main hall, looking at the well-matched couple with a bright smile.

The master of ceremonies was about to speak, only for the governor to hold his hand up, putting a pause to everything. "Young man, would you like to reconsider this marriage?"

This abrupt question made the exuberant hall descend into silence. No one expected the official witness to ask the groom if he wanted to consider breaking his engagement!

Lu Zezhi was shocked as well. His brow creasing, he glanced up at the governor before turning to look at Guan Shanjin.

As a general, Guan Shanjin sat in the second most important seat. He happened to be holding his teacup, sipping lightly at it. He seemed completely unbothered by the official's actions, and looked as though he had no intention of rebuking him.

Old Master Yue could not restrain himself once he recovered from his stunned silence. "Governor Fang, what do you mean by this?" he asked, his eyes widening to the size of coins as he glared at Governor Fang.

"I don't mean anything by it. I just don't wish to see Mr. Lu take any missteps. After all...there are some stains that can never be washed off." Governor Fang was all smiles as he said this; however, the implication behind his words was rather profound.

Listening to him, Old Master Yue's face flushed in anger. Governor Fang was essentially insulting the Yue family! He sprang to his feet, but his wife hurriedly tugged at his sleeve. Governor Fang was a court official—and the general was present in the hall as well. The Yue family shouldn't poke the hornet's nest!

However, Yue Dade was a defiant man. Counting on the support of his relationship with the general's estate, he shook away his wife's grip angrily, pointing at Governor Fang and scolding him directly. "Fang Chongguang! You really think you're so damn special just because you're an official?! And doing this in front of the general— who gave you the gall to stir up such trouble?!"

"Ah, Old Master Yue, you've said it yourself: who gave me the nerve to try and start trouble in front of the general?" Fang Chongguang said, not the least bit angered. He looked at Yue Dade somewhat sympathetically.

Although Yue Dade was a little reckless, he was not a fool. He froze for a moment before the finger he pointed at Fang Chongguang started to tremble, and his voice grew hoarse. "What do you mean by that?"

The Great General of the Southern Garrison hadn't spoken up at all, so who else could be behind this? Trembling, Yue Dade looked toward Guan Shanjin. Although it was a joyous occasion, the graceful and charming man was still dressed in his typical black. Other than the gleaming jade pendant hanging from his belt, there was no color to be found on him; it looked like he'd dressed for a wake rather than a wedding.

Yue Dade shivered at the thought. He quickly controlled the rage on his face, exchanging it for an ingratiating smile. "General, you..."

"Hmm?" Guan Shanjin interrupted Old Master Yue. With a small smile, he looked at the bride and groom where they stood frozen in the hall. "Teacher, Governor Fang is asking you a question. Aren't you going to reply?"

Lu Zezhi seemed to have woken up from a trance. His face pale, he turned toward Guan Shanjin, clearly having suffered a great shock. His lips moved silently.

"Hmm? Teacher, I can't hear you." Guan Shanjin still sat imposingly, not moving an inch. With his cup in hand, he skimmed the film off the top of his tea. "Teacher, please think things through before you respond."

His tone was as soft as ever, yet Lu Zezhi trembled violently. Stumbling, he took a couple of steps backward, nearly tripping over himself.

"General, pardon my ignorance, but this is a wedding! Why, why..." Yue Dade wrung his hands, at a loss for what to do. This change had come too abruptly; although he'd weathered a variety of storms in his life, he did not know how to handle this situation.

Besides, the entire betrothal process had gone so smoothly until now! Why did this have to happen today, just when they were about to seal the deal?

"A wedding?" Guan Shanjin laughed quietly; he could not be bothered to even look in Yue Dade's direction. His alluring eyes were fixed solely on Mr. Lu. "Teacher, why aren't you saying anything? This is your wedding, after all."

"H-Haiwang..." With much difficulty, Lu Zezhi finally spoke. His voice was hoarse and scratchy, a far cry from his typically pleasant tone.

"I'm here." Guan Shanjin sounded practically joyful.

"What are you doing? I already explained everything to you last night. Miss Yue is a good match for me. You don't have to keep testing me like this." Lu Zezhi's voice was a little unsteady—he sounded almost like he was begging.

Lu Zezhi really was just a pretty face. On the outside, he looked enlightened and warm, able to make good judgments. In reality, he was too lazy to use his brain; he had never truly considered how to properly maintain his position and status.

In the beginning, he had merely wished to gain a position as an official, working alongside Guan Shanjin in order to support himself. He was not especially talented, and although he once had scholarly fame in his village, it was based almost entirely upon his looks. When it came time for him to rely on his actual talents to support himself, Lu Zezhi discovered that he would at most be a rank seven official[8] holding a mediocre position in some small town.

If he had never entered the protector general's residence, he might have been willing to contentedly walk down this path of mediocrity. However, having seen glory and opulence, he could no longer live without the luxury that had been provided to him.

When Guan Shanjin had returned to the capital, Lu Zezhi had been happy. In the crowd of the common folk, he was able to keenly detect that there was something wrong with Guan Shanjin. The heartache he spoke of that night was not a falsehood—he had meant it sincerely. After all, he had once seen Guan Shanjin running wild and in high spirits. But that heartache was overshadowed by the uncontrollable greed welling up in his heart. He knew exactly how he could get what he wanted.

---

8   Ancient China used the nine-rank system (九品制) to categorize court officials. There are nine ranks, with rank one being the highest, and there are sub-ranks such as standard class, secondary class, which can be further broken down into sub-sub-ranks.

Their reunion at the Lantern Festival had been the one thing he'd put the most effort into. Just like that, Guan Shanjin started feeling attached to him; as he expected, the general began to dote on him. Lu Zezhi understood the young man's thought processes. Guan Shanjin was as heartless and cold as a wolf cub. He was extremely guarded and highly intelligent, and everyone had a specific position in his heart. He had a clear method for how to treat everyone: his father, his mother, his friends, his confidants… Each had their own specific role in his head.

Lu Zezhi was no longer able to return to his position as a teacher, seeing as Guan Shanjin no longer needed one. As such, he took a risk. Relying on the twelve-year-old Guan Shanjin's disjointed feelings for him, he aimed for the position of "beloved."

This was a very special position, and he knew that he needed to exert every effort to maintain it. Only then would he be able to spend his days in carefree luxury under Guan Shanjin's wings.

Before long, he forgot that this youth was a wild beast hiding in the dark. Guan Shanjin was able to conceal his bloodthirsty nature and treat others very gently; yet he was also able to tear into the throat of his prey in the blink of an eye.

Guan Shanjin's cosseting of Lu Zezhi knew no limits; his devotion was intoxicating. Lu Zezhi lived in fear that someone would come along and replace him. Because of this, he kept some amount of distance between himself and the general, despite gradually developing feelings for him. A man might throw away love that was already in his grasp, but he would forever long for his pure first love, the one he desired but was never quite able to attain.

Lu Zezhi had thought he had managed to appease Guan Shanjin last night. He had truly believed that after he'd stayed by Guan Shanjin's side for so long and been his sole object of affection for so many years, the general would be willing to continue doting on him as long as he expressed his willingness to submit. He'd thought he'd done well, especially compared to that old man Wu Xingzi.

He may have guessed incorrectly.

"Yes, Teacher did explain it last night." Guan Shanjin quietly laughed at the way Lu Zezhi was panicking yet still trying to maintain his ethereal image. He sighed. "However, Teacher, you also have to understand that even the sun and the moon can bear witness to my affections for you."

Miss Yue could not tolerate such words. Before Lu Zezhi could attempt to pacify Guan Shanjin, Yue Mingzhu yanked off her bridal veil. Her beautiful features, further enhanced by makeup, twisted in rage.

She threw the veil to the ground. Her fingertips, dyed red, pointed unwaveringly at Guan Shanjin, and she began upbraiding him: "Guan Shanjin! I knew it! I *knew* you held filthy thoughts toward Zezhi-gege! Who in Horse-Face City doesn't know that you see Zezhi-gege as your property, keeping him confined in your estate? You've stifled his ambitions and made him the joke of the city! My Zezhi-gege cares for you, and he says that ever since you were a child, you've always been very arrogant and domineering. As your teacher, he said he wants you to change for the better, and that's why he has stayed by your side! *Hmph!* Now that I'm around, how can I let you continue bullying him?"

"Oh? I've bullied Mr. Lu?" Guan Shanjin burst out laughing. He looked at the frightened Lu Zezhi with feigned affection. "Teacher, have I bullied you?"

Lu Zezhi gritted his teeth at the question. After a moment of deliberation, he put on a stern expression and replied, "If you're not trying to bully me, why did you ask Governor Fang to disturb my wedding?"

He had many years of shared affection with Guan Shanjin, so he would be able to pacify the general after this. However, the Yue family was different. If he wanted to hold onto this family, he would need to preserve their dignity.

Having immediately discerned Lu Zezhi's thoughts, Man Yue, who stood behind Guan Shanjin, cackled. His laughter was not loud, but it stuck out like a sore thumb in the silent, tense hall.

Yue Mingzhu was a girl born and raised in Horse-Face City. She was outspoken and spoiled by her father. Ripping out her hair pin, she threw it at Man Yue. "Man Yue, the nerve you have!"

Man Yue was a skilled military official; a hair pin weakly thrown by a girl was no match for him. He easily caught hold of it, chuckling. The hair pin featured four large pearls the size of thumbs, dazzlingly radiant. How befitting of the third daughter of the Yue family.

"Many thanks for the gift. You needn't have gone to such trouble." Man Yue tucked the pin into his clothes, openly accepting it as if she'd intended to give it to him.

Yue Mingzhu had not expected Man Yue to be this brazen. Her eyes widened in anger. The finger she pointed at him shook nonstop, yet she could not say a word.

"Mingzhu, you're too rude! Quickly apologize to Vice General Man!" Yue Dade was more experienced, and he finally recovered from his shock to bitterly denounce his daughter's recklessness. Next, he smiled, adopting a subservient attitude and bowing to Guan Shanjin. "Great General, I've spoiled Mingzhu rotten. Although she's careless, her feelings for Mr. Lu are evident to us all! I'm very aware that Mr. Lu is your teacher, and the entire Yue family will not allow Mr. Lu to suffer in the slightest. Please, General, you don't have to worry."

Old Master Yue needed this wedding ceremony to be completed.

No matter what sort of relationship Lu Zezhi and Guan Shanjin shared, Yue Dade did not care! What he'd had his eye on from the start was the unlimited indulgence Guan Shanjin showed Lu Zezhi; it was the reason why he had worked so hard to make this marriage happen.

Guan Shanjin stirring up trouble in the wedding hall only further confirmed Yue Dade's suspicions. It seemed that the general truly held deep affection for this teacher of his. If the Yue family could hold on to Lu Zezhi, who in Horse-Face City would dare make any trouble for them?

"How amusing, Old Master Yue." Guan Shanjin turned his head, shooting Man Yue a look. The plump, smiling Vice General Man then unwrapped the package under his arm. He shook the contents out into the hall, and letters scattered through the air.

The attention of the crowd was drawn to the paper fluttering across the room. Other than Guan Shanjin and Man Yue, they all stared at the array of letters slowly floating to the ground.

It was impossible to tell whom these letters were from, but the name on the envelopes was large and obvious: the eldest son of the Yue family.

Whether veiled or direct, the gazes of the guests fell onto the eldest Young Master Yue. Some muttered to each other behind their hands as Young Master Yue's face paled. It was evident he knew where these letters came from, and that they were something that should not be shown to the public.

"Hua-er! What's going on?" Yue Dade demanded, his palms damp and his back soaked in sweat. His ears buzzed, and he could not conceal the trembling in his voice.

Old Master Yue could not entirely deny the fact that he knew what his son had done in private—and he'd even allowed it. After all, as a businessman, profit was more important to him than anything else. As long as he benefitted from it, why would he reject any backing or support? In the future, his business would belong to his son. Yue Dade was extremely gratified that his son knew how to seek profits for their family. However, he had never expected that this matter could be held against him.

Young Master Yue looked lost. He stared at the letters covering the floor in silence.

Yue Mingzhu, however, was the first person to pick up a letter and read it. She was a spoiled brat, and she had never shown any respect to Guan Shanjin. Furthermore, Lu Zezhi loved her, and he needed the Yue family. Guan Shanjin held Lu Zezhi in high regard, so she did not believe that the general could really do anything damaging to the Yue family.

After reading only a few lines, Yue Mingzhu's daintily painted face turned pale; even under her blush, the ashen tone of her skin could be seen. She looked at her elder brother in disbelief, her hand shaking as she held the letter. "D-Dage, th-this...this must be fake, right...?"

This letter was written by Young Master Yue, and from the name of the other party, it was very clear the recipient was from Nanman. The letter spoke of smuggling salt and saltpeter, and even mentioned mercury. From the way the letter was written, this was not their first time contacting each other; they had clearly been communicating for quite some time.

In Great Xia, saltpeter was rare, and it was mainly used in fireworks. However, during the rule of the previous emperor, the cannon had been invented; although it still could not officially be used on the battlefield, the country had kept a tight control over saltpeter as a precaution.

Nanman, however, managed to produce large quantities of saltpeter. Yue Mingzhu had heard her father and brother mention it before. At that time, her brother had a lot of complaints about Guan Shanjin. Because of Guan Shanjin's strict control, saltpeter could not enter Great Xia at all. Nanman had no clue what the substance could do, so there were piles and piles of potential money just sitting there going to waste. It made one's heart truly itch to do something about it.

As for salt, trading it could be very lucrative. However, the country had very strict control over it, and if one was caught smuggling salt, the punishment ranged from banishment to execution. People tended to pursue their own desires, and occasionally there was news of people selling smuggled salt, but since a specific department had been set up to control and regulate its trade ten years ago, salt smuggling had slowly started to die off. Yue Chonghua chose not to sell the smuggled salt to Great Xia, instead selling it to Nanman—it was clear how much he was willing to risk for the sake of profit.

The supplies of salt and saltpeter were tightly controlled by Guan Shanjin. Nanman produced little salt, and most of it was rock salt. By trading these two materials, the Yue family could earn an enormous fortune—but at what cost?

Seeing his daughter's awful expression, Yue Dade quickly picked up a letter himself. Before he could finish reading it, his eyes rolled to the back of his head, and he nearly fainted.

"You disgrace!" Yue Dade exclaimed. He could barely breathe. Recovering from his bout of dizziness, he threw the letter in his son's face. "Look what you've done! The Yue family... The Yue family doesn't have a son like you!" The letter had even mentioned cannons!

"Father, no! Listen to me! I didn't do this! I didn't!" Yue Chonghua crashed to his knees, desperately trying to explain himself to his father.

He crawled toward Guan Shanjin, kowtowing nonstop and pleading innocence. "Great General, please investigate this properly! Although I don't dare say that I haven't done anything against my conscience, I have absolute loyalty to Great Xia! With the heavens as my witness, I would never make such an exchange with those Nanman savages! I'd never jeopardize the safety of this country!"

His head smashed loudly into the ground with each kowtow until the skin on his forehead broke open. Blood slowly dripped down his ashen face; it was a frightful sight.

"Then who wrote these letters?" Guan Shanjin did not stop Yue Chonghua. He extended his foot to step on the open letters. One of them featured a discussion on how to smuggle seven horse carts of unrefined salt, eight horse carts of saltpeter, and ten jugs of mercury.

Written explicitly in the letter was how they should avoid the troops in Horse-Face City, where they should make the trade, what their secret phrases were, and how many people were involved altogether. Everything was listed clearly in the letter, proving just how daring and meticulous the person who wrote it was.

A fairly large number of troops were stationed in Horse-Face City; avoiding them was no easy task. The difficulty was compounded by the large number of goods they were transporting. However, if a man was willing to die for riches, he could become quite clever.

They'd decided to take a path through the river between Horse-Face City and Nanman. The river was located two miles away from the city. There was a large patch of dense forest located upstream, and very few people frequented the area. The army often detoured around the forest during battle, as it was not easy to traverse. The woods sat on top of a steep mountainside, and the trees grew in an intricate tangle. If one did not pay attention, all sense of direction could be lost.

This was where Horse-Face City's defense was the weakest.

Yue Chonghua was well aware of this. Hiring some hunters and woodcutters, he had slowly carved out a spot in the mountainside, building a few huts and docks for storing and transporting goods. By working secretively, he'd managed to earn quite a large sum right under Guan Shanjin's nose.

"I don't know anything! I didn't do anything! I was framed!" Yue Chonghua insisted, sobbing. It was as though he had suffered the greatest injustice, and he desperately wished he could slam his head into the ground and die to prove his innocence.

Guan Shanjin stared at him icily, making no move to stop him. When Yue Dade fell to his knees and tearfully begged for clemency for his son, Guan Shanjin sighed. "Stand up, all of you. It's a day of celebration—I don't wish to see blood." He then glanced over to Lu Zezhi.

Mr. Lu, having been lost in a daze until now, finally returned to his senses and opened his mouth. "H-Haiwang, there must be a misunderstanding somewhere," he said, his voice feeble. Of course he knew what was going on. Guan Shanjin wouldn't be flaunting all this evidence here and now if he wasn't completely certain of the man's guilt; he was merely taking the time to publicly humiliate these people.

A chill spread through Lu Zezhi. Harshly biting his bloodless lips, he did not even look at Yue Mingzhu, who was silently pleading with him with tearful eyes. Instead, his gaze was fixed beseechingly on Guan Shanjin.

This entreating look was not for the sake of the Yue family, but for himself.

"What was the misunderstanding, Teacher?" Guan Shanjin asked, looking at him with eyes full of softness, as though as long as Lu Zezhi provided an explanation, he would be willing to solve everything.

Lu Zezhi clenched his fists tightly, almost piercing his skin with his fingernails. His mouth fell open, but he hurriedly closed it again. Carefully watching Old Master Yue and his son kneeling on the ground, he finally lowered his lids. "No...I don't understand such matters. But Haiwang has always been meticulous in his work and has never maligned anyone before. I am well aware of this."

"Lu Zezhi, what did you say?!" Yue Mingzhu cried. Her eyes wide with shock, she started sobbing uncontrollably.

The meaning behind his words was obvious: he was drawing a clear line between himself and the Yue family, perhaps even recriminating them. He was announcing that he believed the Yue family had truly done something morally corrupt.

Yue Mingzhu shook her head continuously. Pressing her hand onto her chest, she stumbled two steps back, only to trip over the veil she had thrown on the floor. If not for the matchmaker's deftness, she would have taken an unsightly fall at her much-anticipated wedding. Even so, it seemed she had lost the strength to stand upright—with a pale face and trembling body, she collapsed, leaning into the matchmaker and her maid.

She stared straight at Lu Zezhi. With his otherworldly features and bright red wedding clothes, he looked just like the highest of all immortals. Miss Yue loved this man and had always believed every word he said. For him, she even stood up against General Guan and her own family.

But now, when the Yue family was in great danger, this man wouldn't even look at her.

"Lu Zezhi..." Yue Mingzhu would never forget the day they first met: how she had boldly abandoned all etiquette to meet this man, how her heart had pounded. Everything in her sight had seemed to beautify, as if bright flowers bloomed all around her.

Those bright colors were all fading now.

Her father and brother continued to proclaim their innocence to Guan Shanjin, declaring their loyalty to Great Xia. Guan Shanjin regarded them with half-lowered eyelids, a smile curling his lips, but he did not respond at all. Man Yue seemed to have lost interest entirely. Yawning, he picked at the plate of snacks next to Guan Shanjin and popped one into his mouth. Meanwhile Lu Zezhi... Lu Zezhi...

Yue Mingzhu shut her eyes. Two teardrops fell, staining her wedding dress. She took in a deep breath, pushed away the matchmaker and her maid, and yanked off her phoenix coronet. She ripped off her bright red wedding dress and threw it forcefully to the ground as the guests cried out in shock. Without blinking, she walked across to where Lu Zezhi stood.

Slap!

Silence blanketed the wedding hall once again. Yue Dade, Yue Chonghua, and Madam Yue all stopped speaking; Man Yue eagerly watched Miss Yue with gleaming eyes. Even Guan Shanjin looked over, though he remained motionless.

Miss Yue slapped Mr. Lu again. This time, she left Lu Zezhi bloody at the corner of his lips; red handprints soon began to show on both his cheeks. He seemed to be unable to recover his wits as he silently watched Yue Mingzhu attack him—he didn't even remember to dodge the third slap, which was so forceful that he stumbled a step backward.

"I, Yue Mingzhu, must have been blind to treat you like a treasure! From now on, we'll go down our own separate paths! I'd rather become a nun than marry an ingrate like you!" Yue Mingzhu

had slapped him so hard that she'd sprained her wrist. However, she could barely even feel it. Pushing Lu Zezhi aside, she walked over to Guan Shanjin and knelt behind her father and brother.

Regardless of whether her father and brother committed these crimes or not, as a daughter of the Yue, she could never embarrass her family. Honor one and you honor them all, hurt one and you hurt them all! She still had a spine!

Guan Shanjin watched Miss Yue for some time before chuckling quietly. "That's some backbone you have, Miss Yue. Mr. Lu has a good eye. Enough, all of you—stand up."

The Yue father and son exchanged a look, neither daring to kneel any longer. Yue Dade hurriedly helped his son off the ground. Yue Chonghua's face was dyed a distressing shade of red from his own blood. He did not dare to thank the general yet. He felt uneasy, like there was no way today could end well. Guan Shanjin would not let the Yue family off lightly, and he clearly had more evidence than just these letters.

"I'm a military man, not a local official, so I only know a little about criminal law. How your case will be judged is entirely up to Governor Fang." Guan Shanjin's smile and tone were kind, as though he was having a casual chat.

Governor Fang stood up, cupping his hands respectfully. "I promise a fair and just case."

The Yue men looked a little more at ease. Faced with Guan Shanjin's wrath, they felt nothing but fear. However, now that the case was in the hands of Governor Fang, they felt a little more relieved; perhaps they could even privately make some moves that were to their benefit...

"Ah, right. Man Yue, don't you have another big gift prepared for Young Master Yue?" Guan Shanjin refused to give them a moment to catch their breath. He was raised in an aristocratic family that teemed with political intrigue, and he'd come of age on the battle-field—he knew the importance of keeping up the momentum. He was simply toying with the Yue family, like a cat teasing a rat.

"Aiyah! Just look at the state of my memory, I nearly forgot all about it!" Man Yue smacked his own head, smiling brightly before he bowed to Young Master Yue. "Yue-gongzi, I do consider us friends. This present is from me to you, and there's no need to thank me for it." With a wave of his hand, two tall, sturdy soldiers dressed in the Guan family military uniform dragged a man into the hall.

Young Master Yue's pained expression had originally seemed quite natural. Although his misery and grief looked a little exagger-ated, he'd still managed to fool many people in the hall. However, when he laid eyes on this man, he could no longer maintain his facade. His entire body shuddered, nearly falling over; his eyes opened so wide that they looked as if they might fall out of their sockets.

"This person is named Liao Chunqiu, and he's from the capital. As for who his master is...hah! Yue-gongzi surely knows. He's been telling some rather fascinating stories, and the general has listened with much delight. He even forwent a few nights of sleep just to listen to these stories."

Man Yue signaled for his subordinates to lift up the man's face to the crowd. The man's expression was blank, and his eyes were bloodshot; he looked like he was one move away from crumbling completely. The moment he saw Guan Shanjin and Man Yue, fear immediately overcame him. With trembling lips, he mumbled hoarsely, "I-I've told you everything I know..."

General Guan did not look at him. It was Vice General Man who smiled and pulled out a letter of confession from within his robe, handing it over to Governor Fang. "Every profession has its experts, Governor Fang. I'm merely a military ruffian—I don't know anything about the law. However, I am somewhat skilled at garnering confessions. Don't worry, our general has never defamed anyone before, and neither has he forced anyone to say anything against their will. All the words in this letter have been expressed willingly by this man. Hopefully it'll save you some effort."

"Many thanks to the general. I'll accept it." Governor Fang accepted the letter from Vice General Man. He was already well aware of the truth; he was simply putting on a show with Man Yue in front of the crowd for accountability's sake.

Yue Dade and Yue Chonghua looked at the letter of confession being tucked into Governor Fang's robe and collapsed. In their hearts, they both knew there was no longer a way out of this. The Yue family was finished.

And all of this was thanks to... Yue Mingzhu glared hatefully at Lu Zezhi, desperately wishing she could peel off all his skin, tear into his flesh, and yank out his tendons.

The muttering crowd thought that the general was in a rage all because of a beautiful man. They didn't know that Guan Shanjin was studying their looks and covering his satisfied smile with his teacup. This was going exactly as he had planned.

What was supposed to be a jubilant wedding ended with members of the army and the magistrate's office surrounding the bride's family. They did not make things difficult for the women of the Yue family—Governor Fang only arrested the men. Bleak silence filled the wedding hall, and all the guests grew restless. They wanted to leave, but they dared not do so without permission. After all, the general was still seated in the hall, calmly drinking his tea.

Mr. Lu was still dressed in his bright red wedding attire, but he'd removed his headdress. Miss Yue stood next to her mother, quietly consoling the tearful, bewildered woman.

Unlike her daughter, Madam Yue was a woman so gentle that she was a little bit weak. Both her son and her husband were taken away—she lost both pillars of her family in the blink of an eye. She looked like she had aged many years in mere minutes, grasping onto her daughter with a trembling hand.

After a long pause that felt like eons, Guan Shanjin called to Mr. Lu: "Teacher."

His voice was soft, sweet, and affectionate. Lu Zezhi, standing frozen in the wedding hall, shuddered violently. The tips of his ears turned slightly red, but his face was full of anger. He looked over at Guan Shanjin with a frown.

"You don't blame me, right?" Guan Shanjin asked, his voice gentle and low. He feigned ignorance of Miss Yue's vicious glare, as if Lu Zezhi was the only one he could see.

"Now that it's come to this…" What was the point of asking? Lu Zezhi's head sagged, his pale, slender neck peeking out of his bright red clothes. His skin was uncommonly smooth, like a beautiful piece of nephrite jade.

Whether he felt resentment or pride, he did not know. In the end, he'd been unable to establish a connection with the Yue family… but it seemed clear that his position in Guan Shanjin's heart was unshakeable. At the end of the day, the Yue were only a merchant family. Compared to the Great General of the Southern Garrison, they were mere ants—Guan Shanjin could easily replace them with another noble family. Lu Zezhi had assumed that the Yue family could become his support, but it seemed he had overestimated Yue Dade's capabilities.

"Teacher, let's go home." Guan Shanjin stood up, dusting off his robes. Walking forward, he clasped Lu Zezhi's shoulder. "I need to return to the capital to submit my reports in a few days," he said, his voice sweet. "Teacher, you haven't been back in a while—you must miss your hometown."

"The capital?" Lu Zezhi blinked. After a light sigh, a small smile surfaced on his face. "All right, let's go back."

Miss Yue still stood in front of him in the hall of *their* wedding, but Mr. Lu didn't seem to care. The tenderness and affection he'd showed Yue Mingzhu turned out to be utterly false, and it disgusted her. She watched him with an icy glare, not even willing to spare an iota of her energy to curse him.

Guan Shanjin tenderly straightened Lu Zezhi's clothes for him before leading his men back to the estate.

When the hall was completely silent again, the guests all gasped in relief. They hurriedly bade each other farewell and fled the building. The Yue family was clearly on the brink of collapse, and Horse-Face City was on the verge of a massive shift in power. The wedding guests were all smart people, so they needed to quickly return home and start planning. If they were lucky, they might be able to seize this opportunity that the Great General of the Southern Garrison had given them to fill the void the Yue family had left!

Yue Mingzhu looked out at the now-empty wedding hall. Gritting her teeth, she refused to shed a single tear.

The wedding hall was not within the general's estate, but in a new residence two streets away that they had recently prepared for Mr. Lu. Leaving the hall, Guan Shanjin immediately stepped away from

Lu Zezhi. Swinging himself up his horse, he sprinted away without a word.

Man Yue grinned as he gestured for Mr. Lu to get into the carriage. "Don't mind him, Mr. Lu. The general's bad mood was inevitable—just let him cool down for a bit."

"Mm." Lu Zezhi looked at the black-cloaked figure quickly disappearing in the distance. He lowered his eyes to conceal the unease that was swiftly welling up within him. He could feel that there was something wrong with Guan Shanjin's attitude, but he could not put his finger on it.

The general had destroyed the Yue family for him in front of half of the noble families of Horse-Face City. This showed Mr. Lu's unique position in Guan Shanjin's heart.

However, the way he was acting was different from the deep affections he'd shown Lu Zezhi in the past... He seemed...a little too cold?

No, it can't be! Haiwang is just angry with me, that's all! Lu Zezhi comforted himself. However, he had a sneaking suspicion that his speculation was correct.

What he didn't know, though, was that while he was trying his best to reassure himself, Guan Shanjin bypassed the Wang Shu Residence and headed straight for Shuanghe Manor.

As usual, the fresh scent of earth surrounded Shuanghe Manor. The vegetables in the garden had nearly all been harvested; the only parts left were inedible stems and leaves. A few yellow flowers lay scattered across the dirt, most of them trampled.

Guan Shanjin's eyes darkened, and he inexplicably felt a sense of alarm. With great strides, he cut through the courtyard and burst through the carved wooden door, his uncontrolled strength almost splitting it in two.

There was no sign of anyone inside; the air was cool and still. With a grim face, he entered the house, walking step by step into Wu Xingzi's bedroom.

He found the blanket folded on the bed, so neat that it looked like a piece of dried tofu. Guan Shanjin could barely breathe. His footsteps lacked their typical steadiness; he walked to the bed with disjointed movements.

At this time of day, Wu Xingzi wouldn't normally be lazing in bed anyway. Guan Shanjin's slender fingers smoothed across the soft blanket, the coolness diffusing into his blood. An uncontrollable shiver ran through him.

The bedroom seemed no different from how it was in the past. Wu Xingzi had been living here for a few months, and he did not have many belongings. The ornamentations Guan Shanjin had asked others to deliver to him were all carefully kept in the storeroom, untouched, and the room looked as simple as the one he had in Qingcheng County.

Guan Shanjin finally recovered from his shock at the unusually cold bed and slowly surveyed the bedroom.

The qin he had given Wu Xingzi a few days ago was set neatly on its stand. If he hadn't paid close attention, he would have missed it, as it was placed in the corner of the room.

All the windows were closed. The rays of the sun peeked through the tiny gaps, scattering light and shadow on the round table in the center of the room.

Guan Shanjin saw something on the table. Moving closer, he discovered that it was a pile of silver taels, about a hundred and twenty in total. A note was tucked under the pile of coins, and the handwriting on it was intimately familiar to him—the clear yet somewhat fragile hand of Wu Xingzi.

Haiwang—

I'm leaving. This is the sum of my monthly allowance given to me by your estate, totaling a hundred and twenty taels. After accompanying each other for so long, we must say our farewells at last.

Don't look for me. Live happily with Mr. Lu.

—Wu Xingzi

Guan Shanjin clutched the note, shocked. He recognized every single word written on it, but could not understand what they meant put together. He read the note over and over again like a madman, desperately wishing he could peel apart every word and read them even more thoroughly.

The general could still remember the words he'd shared with Wu Xingzi last night as he held him. He had promised Wu Xingzi that he would bury him when he passed on and pay respects to his ancestors. One's fate was decreed by the heavens, and he would not fear it. Even if it was just one more day, Guan Shanjin would try his best to survive and take care of Wu Xingzi's grave.

He'd thought that once he exposed Lu Zezhi, he would be able to bring Wu Xingzi to the capital with him. He wanted to take him out to eat all the delicious food and explore all the fun sights the capital had to offer. Once he'd taken care of everything in the capital, they would be able to spend the rest of their lives together in peace.

However, Wu Xingzi had not waited for him.

This old fellow, who had thought about leaving him since the day they met, had run away for good this time!

A wave of dizziness crashed through Guan Shanjin. He staggered to a stool by the table, numbly staring at the hundred and twenty silver taels.

He should be furious at Wu Xingzi's departure—he hadn't even said goodbye! No one had ever stamped upon his affections like this before. Guan Shanjin regarded Wu Xingzi as the ultimate treasure, and because he was afraid that Wu Xingzi would be caught up in a political dispute, he had even pushed Lu Zezhi out into the foreground as a shield.

Were the promises he had given insufficient? Guan Shanjin was lost. With Wu Xingzi gone, he had no idea what to do.

Perhaps he should look for him. Wu Xingzi had Hei-er with him, that much was obvious—it was impossible for him to have left so silently without Hei-er's aid. There were only two serving girls taking care of Shuanghe Manor, and they were truly loyal to Wu Xingzi. There was no sign of them; it was likely that they had all left together.

This was not an impulsive decision. Clearly, they'd been planning this for a while.

When Guan Shanjin confessed his feelings to Wu Xingzi and promised him so many things...was that old fellow thinking about how to leave him?

Guan Shanjin burst out in a muffled laugh, cackling until his shoulders shook. His eyes turned bloodshot as he continued to laugh hysterically, unable to catch his breath.

Man Yue happened to enter Shuanghe Manor just in time to witness Guan Shanjin's chaotic laughing fit. Realizing something was very wrong, Man Yue shot forward. "General?"

When he placed his hand on Guan Shanjin's shoulder, he felt the general's qi pulsing out of control under his skin. The man was truly losing his sanity.

Alarm shot through Man Yue. "Haiwang-gege!" Before he could use his own inner energy to calm Guan Shanjin's, the laughter came to a stop. Guan Shanjin turned and glanced at him. His normally emotional eyes looked bathed in blood, the whites streaked deeply with red. His pupils looked like dull black crystals. The general's gaze was fixed tightly on Man Yue's face.

"Man...Yue..." Gurgles escaped Guan Shanjin's throat. His voice sounded hoarse and bizarre, as if he spent all his strength squeezing out the sounds from his chest.

"Haiwang..." Man Yue stared at Guan Shanjin in horror, watching as a trail of red spilled out of his lips. The vice general's mind went blank. Before he could reach out to help, blood sprayed from Guan Shanjin's open mouth, red droplets staining both their clothes.

Before the first spray of blood had time to cool down, Guan Shanjin spat out a second and a third mouthful. His fair complexion paled so quickly that it looked almost transparent; he exuded a vague aura of death.

Finally, after he expelled a fourth mouthful of blood, Man Yue jabbed at some of his pressure points, forcing his blood to circulate properly.

Guan Shanjin groaned, collapsing into Man Yue's arms. His robes slowly dripped blood onto the ground.

In distress, Man Yue yelled at the personal guards that had followed him to call for the physician. He pressed his palm into Guan Shanjin's back, sending his energy through him, barely managing to protect the general's vital organs. However, Guan Shanjin's inner force was much more powerful and advanced than his. This bout of madness had done damage to his heart, and Man Yue's aid wasn't enough.

Soon the physician arrived, and chaos unfolded. The doctor applied acupuncture needles and other medicines, and it took many hours for the ghastly look on Guan Shanjin's face to fade. He was still very pale, and his breathing was difficult, but those around him could finally breathe a sigh of relief.

Guan Shanjin had a strong physical foundation. Once he woke up and directed his qi back into its proper place, there would be no need to worry.

After seeing the physician off, Man Yue returned to Guan Shanjin's bedside, studying the general with a conflicted gaze. The man's blood-stained clothes had already been replaced. Guan Shanjin looked even paler than the snowy white inner robe he wore.

Although unconscious, Guan Shanjin still tightly held onto the note that Wu Xingzi had left him. Clutching the blood-spattered note, he painted a rather wretched picture.

Man Yue sighed deeply. He tried tugging at the note a few times, but to no avail. In the end, he had no choice but to give up.

"Did I...go too far?"

The Wedding Night, Part One

W U XINGZI HAD been locked in a secret room for around eight or nine days now. The only garment he had was a single outer robe; all he could do was wrap it around his bare body.

A few oil lamps were lit within the room. Every day, someone would come and change the wick, as well as top up the oil. These lamps were the only sources of light; there were no windows at all. With no way to tell whether it was day or night, Wu Xingzi would eat when he was hungry, and sleep when he was sleepy. After a few days, he was thoroughly dazed and lost, and he could no longer tell if he was dreaming, or if everything around him was real.

That man did not appear.

Wu Xingzi had always been a very adaptable person. He tried to recall how he'd ended up in this situation, but all he could remember was the face of a man so charming that seemed to have come from a painting. His eyes were emotive and alluring, and his smile held an iciness within. A single look was enough to make someone go crazy for him. Wu Xingzi wondered if he had met a human, or a demon. Why did that man lock him in this secret room?

Before long, his question was answered.

In his dreams, Wu Xingzi felt a heat burning through him. Moaning, he struggled to wake, but the fire inside him burned so hot that he fell into an even deeper trance.

"Who... who are you...?"

"You're awake?" The voice was very pleasant to his ears, like jade pieces striking together. Trembling, Wu Xingzi finally opened his eyes.

The face from his memories was now looking down between his legs. The fractured light from the lamps fell upon the man's long eyelashes, which fluttered along with his breaths.

"You... Mmm..." The moment Wu Xingzi's lips parted, cloying moans spilled from his throat. A blush burst across his face, and he quickly reached out to cover his mouth, yet he couldn't stop himself from releasing moans that were even sweeter.

"My dirty darling." The man's eyes curved with a smile. His hand that was pressed against Wu Xingzi's clit exerted a little more force, and the old man cried out, unable to catch his breath.

Wu Xingzi's legs were fair and slender, and although he was thin, he was smooth and soft to touch. Lying on the bed, his legs were already spread apart, both his knees held up by black silk ties. He was completely unable to free himself from this position, and his private areas were all exposed to the air.

A pink cock, a shy hole, and between them, a slit that shouldn't appear on a man's body. Where the testicles were supposed to be bloomed a beautiful flower.

The tender petals were tightly furled together, but as the man teased them, they were slowly starting to spread apart. Glimmering threads of slick clung to the skin, and above the petals was a hard little nub that had been forced out from the nonstop touching. Wu Xingzi didn't know how long the man had been playing with it, but it was swollen to the size of a red bean. Trapped between the man's elegant fingers, a gentle squeeze made Wu Xingzi release a soft cry, and he writhed continuously, trying to escape.

"Wh-what are you doing..." Wu Xingzi carried a lot of insecurity about his body. It was impossible for him to impregnate a woman, and although he was able to get hard despite his lack of testicles, he was unable to produce any sperm. Except while washing himself, he almost never touched the peculiar lower parts of his body.

The man revealed a look of satisfaction, bordering on intoxication. As he toyed with the soaking wet petals, he said, "I'm playing with you."

These words cut like a sharp blade, piercing straight into Wu Xingzi's chest. He struggled even harder, trying to get up, but the silk ties were too tight, and the man had already reached out to hold him down. As Wu Xingzi's thin, slender body twisted about, it looked more like an invitation than an attempt to free himself.

"You're already dripping wet down there," the man chuckled. He dragged his hand along the older man's entrance, holding it up on display for Wu Xingzi to see.

Under the dim yellow light, the younger man's palm was soaked. Smiling at the blushing, dazed Wu Xingzi, he held his palm to his mouth and licked every bit of the juice away.

"No... Don't do this..."

Wu Xingzi didn't know if the man appeared seductive as he licked at his fingers, or if it was he himself who was so innately lascivious that he was turned on by the sight. He could feel himself becoming even wetter below. Hot fluid gushed from his cunt, collecting around his asshole.

No, no, no! This can't be real! Wu Xingzi felt both mortified and confused. He had no idea that his body would be so sensitive to such manipulations.

"You're completely wet... How filthy." The man again flicked at his clit, which was now completely revealed to the air. The intense pleasure left Wu Xingzi gasping, and fragmented moans spilled from his lips.

"So sensitive? That won't do."

"Please... Please let me go..." Whimpering, Wu Xingzi started to cry. He'd been locked up for so many days; he'd barely caught his breath, and now the man was toying with him again. The way the man was touching him was one thing, but the pleasure he was feeling from it had him completely at a loss.

"You can start begging after I start fucking you." The man's tone was so gentle that it seemed as though he was teasing him, but Wu Xingzi shivered uncontrollably instead.

Shaking his head fiercely, Wu Xingzi tried his best to curl up, avoiding the warm hand that stroked him. However, his efforts were all in vain, and the man's finger dipped into Wu Xingzi's dripping wet entrance. A sharp jolt of pleasure and pain all at once made Wu Xingzi shriek, and he trembled all over.

"Hmm? I've heard that two-sexed people don't have a hymen. Seems like that's true..." The man's finger was now deep inside Wu Xingzi. He swiveled his finger around, making loud squelching sounds resound through the room. "Or has your virginity already been claimed?" This idea seemed to displease him intensely, and he shoved a second finger in without any warning, stretching out Wu Xingzi's tight cunt.

"N-no..." More whimpering came from Wu Xingzi. His face red from crying, he thrashed about to no avail. He didn't realize his movements only made the fingers inside him reach even deeper places. He clenched beguilingly onto them, as though trying to please the digits.

"No? But you're so slutty! Just look at your hole—it knows how to suck so prettily already." A smile appeared on the man's face, his fingers starting to thrust into the younger man, his other hand teasing Wu Xingzi's swollen clit. All the pleasure culminated in Wu Xingzi's nonstop wailing; drool trickled from his mouth, and his eyes became unfocused as they stared at the ceiling.

The man was too skilled, and when the two fingers turned into four, even thicker than the average man's cock, Wu Xingzi still didn't feel any pain. Instead, it felt so good that he couldn't stop twitching, and his juices gushed out of him in waves. There was an emptiness deep inside him that couldn't be filled. It gnawed at him so much so that he couldn't stop crying. Tears were smeared all over his face, and his buttocks clenched periodically, clearly seeking to be fucked.

"You managed to squirt from just my fingers?" exclaimed the man.

When he saw Wu Xingzi for the first time, he originally didn't pay much attention to him. This old man was thin and withered, and his appearance was ordinary. The only thing that stood out were his plump, delicious looking lips. It wasn't until later, when he discovered that he was a rare two-sexed man, that he gained an interest in him. It was said that two-sexed people were innately lewd, and they succumbed to the pleasures of the flesh more easily than ordinary people. They were born with bodies made for pleasure, and with how sensual and flexible they were, both their holes were weapons of sex. Just a taste would leave one begging for more, ascending to the peaks of ecstasy.

Knowing that he would be such a fun toy, how could the man let him go? Now that he'd had a taste, he saw exactly how lewd someone like this could be.

Under the dim yellow light, the lips of Wu Xingzi's pussy parted, and after all his handling they were now swollen. They looked very much like a delicate flower in bloom.

Mingled with the scent of Wu Xingzi's juices was a sultry sweetness, and with how much he squirted when he came, the scent permeated the entire room.

He seemed to be submerged in pleasure, his head falling back as his breaths came in stuttering pants. The muscles of his inner thighs twitched and jerked, and reflexive tears that had been forced out of his eyes rolled down onto the bedding. His face was scrunched up tightly, his expression one of agony and embarrassment, and all this made the younger man's sadism burn hotter, wanting nothing more than to break him.

The man's fingers ached from how tightly Wu Xingzi squeezed them. When he pulled them out, they brought along with them another gush of sweet, sultry fluid that ended up dripping onto the ground, forming a puddle.

With great difficulty, Wu Xingzi finally managed to catch his breath, and he started pleading, "Please... I beg you... Let me go..." Hiccupping with sobs, he felt a desire in his abdomen that was unfamiliar, yet intense. It was as though something was eating him up from within, like a fire burned inside him. The desire spread through his limbs to his brain, an overpowering emptiness that he was unable to resist. He desperately wanted the man to fondle his cock, but at the same time, his desire made him deeply ashamed.

"You really want me to let you go?" The man laughed softly. As Wu Xingzi watched with a teary gaze, the man removed his clothes, revealing a firmly muscled body and a thick, savage cock that was dark with blood.

Wh-why was it so big?! Wu Xingzi's eyes widened and he shivered. He dared not imagine how this weighty, veiny cock, almost a foot long and as thick as his forearm, could fit inside him. Its head was the size of an egg, and it looked so extraordinarily brutal.

Umm... umm... Without thinking, Wu Xingzi reached down toward his own stomach. As a two-sexed man, he knew the depth of his vagina was shorter than most females'. If such a thick, long cock were to thrust into him, wouldn't it tear right through him?

"Let me go... Please, let me go, I won't be able to endure it..." he pled pitifully. The man pretended not to hear him, instead climbing onto him and gripping his buttocks, dragging him down toward his body.

The rock hard cock jabbed right below Wu Xingzi's own swollen member, grinding across his slit that was shuddering with sensitivity. Occasionally, when the younger man's cock brushed past his entrance, it would mouth gently at the thick object. Tingling pleasure brought a flush to the man's beautiful face, and his charming eyes fell half lidded as he ground his cock even harder between Wu Xingzi's legs.

Wu Xingzi ached with need. A voice in his brain cried out, wanting him to do something. It would be best if there was something thick and hard to thrust inside and soothe him from within, but Wu Xingzi was far too shy to express this desire out loud. Unable to keep his hips from writhing, he reflexively angled himself toward the man's cock, desperate to swallow the burning-hot shaft.

"What do you want? Tell me." Sweat beaded on the man's forehead from the effort of holding himself back, but he knew that if he didn't tame the man underneath him now, he wouldn't be able to enjoy him as he pleased in the future. He endured, even as the sensitive head of his cock reveled in how well the hole sucked on it, even though he was eager to force himself inside and enjoy even more of this pleasure. With incredible determination, he forced himself to retreat a little, and with the attitude that something was better than nothing, he thrust against the cock that was about to be rubbed raw.

Wu Xingzi's attention had been shattered completely. "I-I don't know..." he whimpered. He continued thrusting his hips toward the man, welcoming him, only to keep missing. No matter what he did, he was unable to take the cock inside of him, and instead, his clit was getting the brunt of the pleasure, becoming sore from it. Fluid once again squirted out of him, and the younger man's cock was now dripping with it.

Wu Xingzi had always protected his virtue. Despite being near forty, he was still a virgin. He'd barely looked at any erotic drawings; he was completely new to matters of sex. He really had no idea what he should do, and the anxiousness left him twisting and jerking his hips wantonly, looking even more pitiful as he cried.

"Do you want my cock in your cunt? Do you want me to thrust inside and soothe it?" The general leaned down and nipped at the tip of Wu Xingzi's nose, his voice as sweet as honey.

"I want you..." Wu Xingzi stared at that beguiling face that could suck one's soul away and continued, his voice shy and soft, "to soothe me..."

"As you wish." The general smiled, his eyes narrowing. Grabbing his waist with one hand, he lifted Wu Xingzi's buttocks with the other, and with a loud *smack*, he forced his thick, long cock right into the soaking wet hole.

"*Ahh!*" screamed Wu Xingzi, his tears spilling immediately. The younger man was too big, and Wu Xingzi's vagina was too small. The pain left him trembling all over, and reflexively, he tightened around the intruder. Only a third of the way inside, the man found himself unable to go any deeper.

"Relax..." He frowned, massaging Wu Xingzi's buttocks in comfort.

Bending down, he pressed kisses to Wu Xingzi's lips and cheeks. "Come on, breathe. Relax a little. Otherwise I won't be able to reach all the way inside."

"It really hurts..." Having never experienced such gentle words, Wu Xingzi forgot that the pain he felt was caused by the man above him. Like a little kitten seeking comfort, he mewled, "Could you go a little more gently?"

"It always hurts at first. Be good, and don't clench so much."

As the general mouthed at Wu Xingzi's soft, red earlobe, he held Wu Xingzi's softened cock in his grasp, tugging at it. Soon, Wu Xingzi shifted his hips slightly as quiet moans slipped out. His cunt was no longer as tight, clearly more in the mood now, and slick fluid started to flow once again.

Naturally, the younger man would not let go of this opportunity. Grabbing hold of Wu Xingzi's waist, he yanked him down toward his groin, jabbing right into the sensitive spot inside.

A trembling shriek escaped Wu Xingzi. Tossing his head backward, his eyes rolled all the way back in pleasure. It was still very painful, but the pleasure of the man hitting his g-spot transformed this pain into a sort of ecstasy, leaving Wu Xingzi unable to do anything else. As for the younger man, he closely followed this victory with another attack, fucking vigorously into the man underneath him. The tightness did hurt him a little at first, since this was the first time this hole had ever been entered. However, two-sexed people had uniquely sensual bodies, and he didn't have to pound at it for long before the hole became so soft and pliable that it felt like countless mouths sucking on his cock. But this little cunt still behaved shyly, so much so that it was impossible to extricate himself from it.

Now that it had been fucked a little, the hole relaxed. Every entry brought out a gush of fluid, and the muscles within sweetly squeezed the man's long, thick cock. Wu Xingzi's extraordinarily sensitive hips writhed, and it felt so good that the man's thrusts became even deeper and more savage.

He suddenly came across something that felt different from the g-spot. It was a spongy nub of flesh deep within, and it was furled up tightly, as though it was protecting something.

Wu Xingzi's reaction was even greater. A few violent jolts shook through his body, and he burst into wails, reaching out to push the man away as he sobbed, "It's going to open... No, no..."

"Open?"

No matter how much Wu Xingzi shoved, the general remained where he was. The burning hot head of his cock again thrust up against that nub.

"I never imagined that you would have a womb."

"I don't, I don't..." Wu Xingzi shook his head nonstop. He didn't know if he was feeling fear or overwhelming pleasure, and his body flinched and shuddered. Every part of him burned with desire, and his cunt was dripping wet, as though a spring was hidden within him. "No one can go in there, please, don't..."

The general gave a bewitching smile, kissing him on the cheek. Gently, he said, "Be good. I'm going inside."

When he finished speaking, he pulled his cock out a little. Then, grabbing hold of Wu Xingzi's hips firmly, he forced himself through that little opening, fucking straight into the older man's womb.

Wu Xingzi's mouth fell open, his fragile, slender throat arching up. It was as though he had reached the peak of pleasure and pain, exceeding the limits he could tolerate, and his entire being went into a daze. The man fucking him, too, was swept away in ecstasy. The womb was even tighter than Wu Xingzi's cunt, and this was also because it belonged to a two-sexed man. Their wombs were smaller than most females', and thick, soft walls were hidden within. There was no resistance to them at all, and they would even mouth at the intruder in a honeyed fashion, just like a pliable cocksleeve.

Taking advantage of the fact that Wu Xingzi had yet to regain his senses, the man held onto Wu Xingzi's waist and thrust inward. The long, thick cock barged inside and brutally forced its way into Wu Xingzi's womb. Yet, when it retreated, the older man's entrance clung onto the head, as though he wanted it to stay. At other times, the man's cock would jab right at Wu Xingzi's g-spot, and a visible bulge appeared on Wu Xingzi's soft stomach.

This little hole was too slutty, the tight muscles quickly becoming pliant and sucking away at the man's cock. It felt so good that he was unable to pull himself away from the pleasure, and his actions became even more brutal.

"It's too deep, too deep... Please, be gentler..." Having finally managed to recover his senses, Wu Xingzi cried and begged. His pleas for mercy stood in complete contrast to how welcoming his pussy was, as well as how his hips writhed for more, wanting nothing but for the man to thrust even harder.

The feeling of having his womb fucked open was really too enjoyable. After the initial bout of pain, there was only endless pleasure. An aching fire burned through his veins, and Wu Xingzi had long forgotten who he even was. His lewd juices continued spurting out. His womb clenched up and released a wave of slick as Wu Xingzi wailed, reaching an intense orgasm.

The man nearly came from how tightly Wu Xingzi squeezed him in orgasm. He hurriedly stopped to calm himself down, leaning down and nibbling on Wu Xingzi's bright red tongue. "This is the only mouth of yours that isn't lewd," he said, giving the older man a fierce kiss. Wu Xingzi nearly fainted. He looked practically dead.

The long, thick cock invaded his womb, causing a huge bulge to form on Wu Xingzi's stomach. Having managed to hold back his orgasm, the younger man grabbed onto Wu Xingzi's hand and placed it on the bulge as a form of revenge for nearly making him come. The feeling of touching another man's cock through his own flesh left Wu Xingzi stunned, and without any instruction from the man, he reflexively caressed it.

"You're so obscene!" the general groaned. Ignoring that Wu Xingzi had yet to fully recover from his orgasm, his cunt still twitching away, he resumed fucking savagely into him.

"Ahhh!" The muscles of Wu Xingzi's womb was assaulted once more, and his convulsing vagina was again conquered by powerful thrusts. With a few jerks, it loosened up again. Wu Xingzi felt like a used hole, like he solely existed for this man's pleasure. He could feel every vein of the man's cock inside of him. Lewd juices gushed out of his swollen lips in waves, accompanied by the loud slapping of flesh. It was as though all the water in Wu Xingzi's body had been transformed into slick, drenching the man's savage cock, pushing him into another fucking frenzy.

"No... I can't... No more!" Wu Xingzi screamed. His entire body convulsed. Drenched in sweat, he squirmed about on the bed, reaching out to push the man away. But instead his hands were caught, pushed up and trapped beside his ears.

The man had gone in too deep, the tip of his hard cock all but pounding into the tender flesh in the deepest recesses of Wu Xingzi's womb. His coarse pubic hair rubbed against Wu Xingzi's clit that had now swelled even larger, and the intense pleasure made Wu Xingzi's entire body ache. He was both eager and afraid, his legs straight and tense in their ties as his ten adorable toes curled up tightly.

The sight of Wu Xingzi almost breaking down was very erotic, and the general lost control completely. His alluring eyes narrowed, brimming with madness. His fingers left marks all over Wu Xingzi's hips as he pounded even harder into the older man.

Despite having yet to recover from his previous orgasm, Wu Xingzi was coming again. He was lost in his desire, awash in the waves of pleasure, one after another, with no end in sight. As his hips tilted upward, his body spasmed, his entire face wet with tears. Even when Wu Xingzi's voice grew hoarse from crying, the man didn't relent. Before long, the friction on his clit brought him to yet another orgasm. Struggling in vain, he could only be held down by the man and endure the intense fucking.

Wu Xingzi's mouth was open yet soundless; he couldn't catch his breath. His vision was turning black as well, but he was unable to lose consciousness under the relentless pleasure, and he could only continue to hold on.

Enjoying how much the older man's womb trembled and clenched down on him, the younger man's cock grew even harder.

"No!" Wu Xingzi screamed amidst his sobs. He felt as though he was about to be torn apart, and he released another gush of fluids onto the man's cock. The man then thrust forcefully inside, reaching right into the deepest, most sensitive part of Wu Xingzi's womb... This sort of thrilling pleasure felt like hundreds of mouths sucking at him at once. He huffed out a heavy breath, and great, thick spurts of cum shot right into Wu Xingzi's oversensitive womb. The volume that spurted forth was so great that even through the thin layer of Wu Xingzi's stomach, they could both see the force of the man's ejaculation.

His body jerking and trembling from the younger man coming inside him, Wu Xingzi's head fell back and his eyes rolled up.

The muscles of his womb and cunt kept on wringing at the man's cock. This feeling of being filled up so completely left Wu Xingzi both terrified and satisfied all at once, and he felt as if he'd never be able to live without cock again...

By the time the man finished coming, Wu Xingzi was so full of semen that he looked as though he was three months pregnant. The man rubbed at Wu Xingzi's stomach in satisfaction, feeling his cock that had yet to soften still inside him. He undid the ties around Wu Xingzi's legs, pulling the entirely exhausted Wu Xingzi into his arms; this position only forced the man's cock in deeper.

Wu Xingzi moaned pitifully, experiencing another round of convulsions before finally managing to calm down.

"I'm the Great General of the Southern Garrison, Guan Shanjin." The man's petal-like lips sucked on Wu Xingzi's ear lobe. "From now on, you're mine."

"Yours?" Wu Xingzi repeated after him as if in a trance. The overly intense pleasure left him groggy.

"Yes." Guan Shanjin kissed his lips, then nibbled on his tender tongue. Chuckling, he said, "If you remain obedient and don't run away, I'll let you out of this room. In the future, you'll be my wife."

Wife? What? Wu Xingzi was wrenched back to his senses. His eyes widening, he looked at the impeccably attractive face in front of him in disbelief, as though it was a ghost.

Hold on, hold on. He had been locked in here for eight or nine days, and he had only met this general twice. They hadn't even shared a conversation before, so how could he become the general's *wife*? Was this how generals selected their wives these days?

"I...I don't know you," Wu Xingzi dazedly responded a beat later.

"It's fine. We can get to know each other later." Guan Shanjin was not worried in the slightest. He nuzzled noses with Wu Xingzi, his smile leaving a pleasant breeze in its wake. "We can slowly cultivate our relationship."

But... "Why do you like me?" Wu Xingzi was still conflicted. In his mind, getting married was not something done without careful consideration.

"I like to fuck you—is that not enough? In the future, I'll fuck only you, and having an official title will make things easier, won't it?"

Guan Shanjin had always done whatever he wanted. He liked this old man's body, and he had no interest in marriage. With a wife that was so good at being fucked, at least there would be no incompatibility in bed. Feelings were something that could come later.

Uhh... Wu Xingzi blinked. As though possessed, he found himself nodding, agreeing to the general's proposal.

The Wedding Night, Part Two

IT WAS SAID that there were four major celebrations in life—the first rain after a long drought, coming across an old friend in a distant land, succeeding in the imperial examinations, and having one's wedding night. Today should have been a joyous occasion for Wu Xingzi, as he would be experiencing the latter.

But this was a bitter tale.

He was dressed in a bright red bridal gown, with not a single item missing from the traditional outfit, including a phoenix coronet and an embroidered neckband. At the crack of dawn he was dragged out of bed, and under the deft hands of maidservants both young and old, his hair was combed and his cheeks were stained with rouge. He was forcefully transformed from an old man of forty into looking like a delicately pretty young man from a humble family. He was almost unable to recognize the reflection looking back at him.

Next was a flurry of activities that could barely fit into a single day's schedule, including fetching the bride and performing the wedding rites. Covered by a red bridal veil, Wu Xingzi was dizzy from being spun around. When he was escorted to the bridal chamber, he almost collapsed from exhaustion. The main issue was that the phoenix coronet was too heavy on his head—the weight made his neck and shoulders ache.

Guan Shanjin was thoughtful. The moment the doors to the bridal chamber were shut, a young maidservant came forward to help him remove the coronet, saying that she had been instructed to do so by the general—he didn't want his wife to be too tired. Later on, for the unveiling of the bride, they would just go through the motions. For now, Wu Xingzi could eat, drink, and rest.

It had to be said that Guan Shanjin—now his husband—was very good at doting on someone. A burst of sweetness bloomed within Wu Xingzi, but he was also secretly a little uneasy. He was, after all, a two-sexed man, and an old and ugly one at that. He couldn't understand why such a handsome and promising young general would like him. When the young man became tired of his body and discovered he could not bear any children, would he not want him anymore?

It was a stifling train of thought, and it made him a little weary.

Of course, this inexplicable gloominess didn't last for long. Guan Shanjin entered the room and removed his veil, and they exchanged their nuptial wine. After the younger man deftly stripped him of his clothes, there was only bashfulness left in Wu Xingzi's heart.

"What are you thinking about?" A smile curled around the corners of Guan Shanjin's lips. He seemed to be a little drunk already, with a haziness clouding his charming eyes. Just one look from him was enough to leave Wu Xingzi enamored, unable to resist the general at all. Dizzily, he shook his head, not even noticing that his legs had been pushed apart, and the embarrassing part of his lower body was completely exposed to the man's gaze.

It truly was a pretty sight. Wu Xingzi's cock was smaller than average and light in color. In its current soft stage, it was only slightly longer than his thumb, looking delicate and adorable. Under his cock was not a pair of testicles, but a vulva. Right at the top of the slit was a small clitoris. Not too long ago, Guan Shanjin had touched it for the first time, forcing it to emerge.

Under the general's burning gaze, Wu Xingzi's clit swelled up a little, looking just like a little red bean. Slick fluid started to seep from his opening, leaving a sheen across the lips.

"My dirty darling." With his long, slender fingers, Guan Shanjin played with the bud, and the sweet juices flowed even faster.

"G-gentler..." Wu Xingzi grabbed the blanket and covered his face. He was easily embarrassed, and despite how intimately familiar his body was by now with the man's touch, he was still as bashful as a blushing virgin.

The man gave a low chuckle, pinching Wu Xingzi's vulva and kneading the lips. More blood flowed to them and they swelled up like a blooming flower. Juices continued gushing out, soaking Guan Shanjin to the wrist. His eyes darkened, and he thrust two fingers straight into Wu Xingzi's cunt.

Just as the general expected, it was already wet and soft inside, and the moment his fingers entered, the muscles clamped down on him, refusing to let go. Wu Xingzi's pussy sucked and mouthed at the intrusion, urgently wanting the general's fingers deeper inside. Guan Shanjin's fingers twisted and thrust into the warm, wet heat. His neatly trimmed fingernails occasionally scraped across the inner walls, sometimes pressing into Wu Xingzi's sensitive spots, leaving the older man writhing nonstop as moans and wails spilled from his lips.

Still unsatisfied, he started rubbing at Wu Xingzi's clit with his free hand. The intense pleasure made Wu Xingzi yelp, and not too long later, lewd juices squirted from him.

"You're coming already?" Laughing softly, Guan Shanjin removed his fingers. His dirty darling's body was very sensitive. Just toying with him a little was enough to make him squirt. "Your stamina is always so terrible! What are we going to do later, hmm?" His words ended with a charming lilt, like a little hook catching Wu Xingzi's heart.

Wu Xingzi panted, yearning for the general and buzzing with anticipation. He sneakily pulled down the blanket, revealing his eyes and glancing at Guan Shanjin. Ah, this man was truly handsome...

"You... you..." Wu Xingzi stammered, unable to speak. Tonight was their wedding night, and it didn't make sense to ask Guan Shanjin to stop. It was likely that he would fuck him to his limits. Nervous, Wu Xingzi twisted his hips, and he must not have completely recovered from his first orgasm yet, because he squirted again.

With such a beautiful scene in front of him, how could Guan Shanjin endure it? He leaned down to kiss his newly wedded wife's ear, gently murmuring, "Your husband will make you squirt so much that half our wedding bed will be soaked. Don't disappoint me."

The general didn't wait for a response but went on to wrap his mouth around Wu Xingzi's small, soft cock. He gave a hard suck, making Wu Xingzi shriek and kick his legs out, shuddering. He didn't know if he should push Guan Shanjin away or pull him close; his fingers tangled in the younger man's shiny black hair.

Wu Xingzi really could not endure it. Guan Shanjin's tongue was nimble, and the little cock in his mouth was soft and malleable. Its taste was somewhat obscene, and its head was still tucked within its foreskin. He slipped his tongue inside the foreskin with the tip of his tongue. The flavor was a little acrid, but he didn't dislike it; bit by bit, he teased the head of Wu Xingzi's cock out.

This teasing left Wu Xingzi feeling both pleasure and pain. Having hidden within its foreskin for a long time, the head of his cock was pink, round, and unbelievably sensitive. It was possibly even less able to endure Guan Shanjin's touches than his clit. Normally,

Guan Shanjin didn't pay much attention to his little cock; this was the first time he'd teased the head.

Feelings of anticipation and fear made Wu Xingzi start to cry. Clutching at the blanket, he writhed about, his hips continuously thrusting upward. Even more fluids dripped out of him in an unstoppable stream.

"*Ahh–!*" The head of his cock had finally been teased out fully by Guan Shanjin. As the general gave another hard suck, Wu Xingzi kicked again, yelping. He trembled, pleasure shooting straight to his head. His eyes were unfocused and his entire body went limp, but Guan Shanjin didn't stop sucking on his cock. He nibbled and licked away at the tender, leaking head. The tip of his tongue continuously slid against the slit of his cock, probing at it as he attempted to dig his tongue further inside.

"No... You can't..." Crying, Wu Xingzi pushed at his head fruitlessly. Both rapture and fear rushed through him. He felt as though he was about to be eaten alive.

Guan Shanjin didn't listen, taking Wu Xingzi's cock entirely inside his mouth and swallowing half of Wu Xingzi's exquisite vulva as well. Sucking hard, his tongue licked at Wu Xingzi's cock, then teased his swollen clit. Simultaneously, his fingers kneaded at the exposed part of his lips, thrusting into his slick, wet cunt. Wu Xingzi convulsed, squirting so much that a huge wet patch spread on the blanket. He was even squirting from his cock, and Guan Shanjin swallowed everything down before shooting an amorous look at Wu Xingzi. It seemed as though he hadn't had enough.

Having experienced two consecutive orgasms, Wu Xingzi's body twitched and jerked. When Guan Shanjin moved his mouth away, a surprising emptiness took over him.

Without realizing it, Wu Xingzi twisted his hips, murmuring, "I want... I want... Mmm..."

Wu Xingzi's sluttiness made the general inhale sharply. His eyes darkening, the general looked like a leopard about to lunge at its prey. He pulled the whimpering man onto his thigh, his diamond-hard cock fitting seamlessly right against the trembling lips of the older man's dripping wet pussy as he drove his hips up.

"Ahh—!" The thick, savage cock pierced right inside him.

The action made more lewd juices squirt out, as though Wu Xingzi's cunt was a ripe, juicy fruit. Guan Shanjin's cock, which had yet to fully enter the older man, was drenched, and so was his entire pelvis. Mingling with the younger man's incense-like scent, the wedding chamber filled with an obscene aroma.

Guan Shanjin leaned down and kissed Wu Xingzi, his tongue forcing its way into the other man's mouth and blocking all his moans. He tangled their tongues together before sweeping across the sensitive spots inside. It felt almost as though his tongue reached his throat; Wu Xingzi was left gasping, his eyes rolling to the back of his head as he drooled.

But Guan Shanjin's hips didn't stop moving. Gripping Wu Xingzi's waist, he fucked into him, every thrust brushing against Wu Xingzi's g-spot and ramming right into the entrance of his womb. Each thrust was harder than the last, and in no time, the entrance widened, mouthing shyly at the head of his cock.

The brutal thrusts left Wu Xingzi whimpering and moaning. His soul had pretty much left his body; his mind was blank. Despite having no strength left in his entire body, his fair, slender legs still unconsciously wrapped around Guan Shanjin's waist. Without realizing it, he lifted his buttocks, welcoming the cock that was about to fuck right into his womb.

"Be good..." Guan Shanjin moved his mouth away, his crimson tongue flittering across Wu Xingzi's kiss-swollen lips before licking his own. He smiled with his eyes half lidded. The general's appearance was unparalleled, and the long-dazed Wu Xingzi was completely smitten.

With his tongue foolishly hanging out, Wu Xingzi murmured, "Husband... Fuck me, my husband... Quick, fuck me..."

"Am I not fucking you right now? You greedy old thing." The man's amorous eyes turned red with lust, his cock tingling from how hard the insatiable hole clenched around it. Wu Xingzi's cunt seemed to be stretched to its very limits already, yet it still continued tightening continuously around the general's huge shaft.

Wrapping an arm around the older man's waist, Guan Shanjin thrust even deeper inside. His large, full balls slapped against slick flesh, and the thick, coarse hair at his groin rubbed against that swollen nub as he fucked right into Wu Xingzi's womb. Trembling and unable to take any more, Wu Xingzi screamed, a visible cock-shaped bulge appearing on his stomach.

"So deep... So deep... My husband has reached all the way into my belly..."

Guan Shanjin felt heat around the head of his cock, and a gout of slick spurted from Wu Xingzi; it was as though he had found the source of a spring. However, as the entrance to Wu Xingzi's womb was been completely obstructed by Guan Shanjin's cock, none of the fluids could escape. The warm liquid stayed trapped in Wu Xingzi's womb, and the wet, slippery texture felt incredible.

Drained of his energy, Wu Xingzi collapsed onto his wedding bed, trembling. He had once again been fucked into an orgasm, and the pleasure flowed through his veins to all parts of his body. It was more than he could endure. Every single inch of his skin was flushed pink, and even the slightest touch was too much. As soon as the general touched him again, a towering ecstasy would rise up within him; very quickly, he reached his peak again.

His lips parted, to plead with Guan Shanjin for mercy, but when his mouth opened, his tongue drooped out and he couldn't speak a single word. All that came out were short, stuttering moans.

At the sight of Wu Xingzi like this, completely fucked out, the flames of desire within Guan Shanjin once again blazed fiercely. He leaned down and carefully nibbled at his tongue. Full of gentleness and passion, he said, "My wife has yet to leave half the wedding bed soaked."

The general really was about to fuck him to death! Fear and anticipation tangled in his heart, and Wu Xingzi's lips puckered up to return the man's kiss. The next moment, the general held his legs apart and entered him. The huge cock forced its way into his womb with every thrust, every movement evident from the bulge of his stomach.

Each time Guan Shanjin pulled out, he would leave the head of his cock inside, and Wu Xingzi's lewd juices gushed outward, leaving a large wet spot on the blanket beneath them. Then, Guan Shanjin would once again impale Wu Xingzi with the full length of his cock, piercing through the entrance of the womb before it could get a chance to tighten back up. The general's thrusts would sweep past the sensitive spot at the bottom of his uterus, causing even more fluids to well up within and flow outward. Wu Xingzi shrieked and cried, convulsing as he orgasmed once again.

Guan Shanjin did not give him any time to recover. With a look of intense, animalistic lust on his face, he frowned and gritted his teeth as he panted. Wu Xingzi's quivering cunt and his greedy womb sucked at his cock like hungry mouths. The series of powerful orgasms in such quick succession left all of Wu Xingzi's muscles tense and rigid, clamping down on Guan Shanjin's shaft so fiercely that he could barely move, yet it still brought about a pleasure so great that thrills ran through his body.

Guan Shanjin gradually lost control, fucking Wu Xingzi until he forgot who he was. His stunned and stupefied eyes were exactly what Guan Shanjin wanted to see. He was a proud, arrogant man; a scoundrel born into a blessed life, with a good family and education. Despite his background, brutality and savagery thrived within him, and this was evident in how he fucked.

Exhaling roughly, he grabbed hold of Wu Xingzi's legs and placed them on his shoulders, lifting up the thin man's lower half so that Wu Xingzi's shoulder blades were the only part of him still on the bed. Before he could catch his breath, Guan Shanjin resumed driving into the man under him.

Wu Xingzi's tight hole was fucked wide open; although it twitched constantly, it could no longer tighten around the intruder. Wu Xingzi gasped and wept, beginning to break down. His hazy eyes were still directed at his stomach, watching the visible bulging of his abdomen. The general's cock was too deep inside him, and it felt as though it was about to tear through his womb. Lewd juices erupted with every thrust, spraying across his own face and body, as well as the bed beneath him. Guan Shanjin smeared the fluids with his fingers, then pushed them into Wu Xingzi's mouth. The sultry flavor mingled with the older man's scent.

"Taste it. Isn't it sweet?"

"Please... have mercy, husband..." All he could taste was himself. As the general teased his tongue, he didn't stop fucking him, his pace even more frenzied. Wu Xingzi's mewling pleas continued, but he didn't even know what he was begging for; dizzily, he watched the bulge of his stomach appear and vanish over and over again. Tensing up, he shuddered, reaching yet another orgasm.

This time, not only was his orgasm accompanied by fluids spewing from his pussy, which drenched the bedclothes, pillows, and everything else, but also from the head of his cock, which had been teased out into the open. The little prick spurted a thin fluid that was almost colorless. The cum landed in Wu Xingzi's own half-open mouth, and, reflexively, he swallowed.

Some people were simply born to fuck. Their sluttiness was practically engraved in their bones. And if they didn't realize just how lewd they were, it only made them sexier. This was Wu Xingzi's nature. He whimpered pleas for mercy, yet his crimson tongue licked away the cum on his lips, curling every bead of moisture into his mouth and savoring it before he swallowed. Watching this scene unfold, the general's eyes turned bloodshot, and he wanted nothing more than to fuck this man to his ultimate end. He reached out and pressed his hand against Wu Xingzi's bulging stomach. Through the thin skin, he kneaded at Wu Xingzi's fucked-swollen womb, attacking it from outside and within.

"*Ahhh*—!" Wu Xingzi let out a tragic wail, his entire body jerking violently. He grabbed the Guan Shanjin's hand, wanting to push it away, but his effort was futile. Instead, the man grabbed his hand and pressed it against the bulge, making Wu Xingzi feel just how deep Guan Shanjin was inside of him.

The general's actions slowed down considerably, and it seemed he was catching his breath. However, every thrust was still deep and powerful, and his balls slapped loudly against Wu Xingzi's skin. His tender, tight womb was merely a sleeve for the general's cock. Every inch of flesh inside him was swollen and ripe from fucking, mouthing and wringing the general's shaft. The general kept driving into him until Wu Xingzi's muscles relaxed around his cock, allowing Guan Shanjin to have his way with him.

Wu Xingzi was unable to recover from the nonstop orgasms. His thin chest heaved with every shaking breath. His dazed, unfocused eyes stared blankly into the air. His face was wet with tears, and he looked incredibly foolish.

Guan Shanjin freed a hand to tweak the small, pitiful, soft little cock that had only just come, wanting to squeeze out every last drop of cum from it.

"Has my wife pissed from his vagina before?" This question, spoken gently, did not register in Wu Xingzi's head at all.

Right now, his mind was mush, the continuous orgasms having pushed him to the edge. He kept thinking that he was going to reach the ultimate peak, but never did he imagine that an even more intense pleasure awaited him. He wanted to die, yet he was also reluctant to stop.

"My wife?" Unlike the general's soft, gentle voice, his hand around Wu Xingzi's cock tightened harshly, forcing Wu Xingzi to return to his senses. The pain caused his face to crumple, and he whimpered softly. He looked up pitifully at his husband, who looked completely at ease.

"H-husband," he responded shyly, his little prick still twitching in pain. He didn't realize it, but there was a fawning expression on his face.

"Good boy." The man leaned down to kiss him, his cock nudging deeper inside his womb. Wu Xingzi gasped, quivering instinctively as his muscles wrung tightly around the thick, hard member. The general expelled a breath of satisfaction, almost unable to stop himself from fucking into the man again. However, the bed was not as soaked as he wanted it to be, so he had no intention of letting his wife rest just yet.

Guan Shanjin patted Wu Xingzi's fair and tender buttocks, then used his calloused palm to play with Wu Xingzi's shriveled cock, smiling as he repeated his question. "My wife, have you ever pissed from your vagina?"

"My vagina...?" Wu Xingzi froze for a moment, needing a moment before understanding the man's question. His cheeks immediately burned, and he shook his head in a panic.

Before meeting this man, his vagina had been basically ornamental; it was a shameful secret, and it wasn't of any use. Not only had the man brought it to ripeness with his fucking, he even wanted him to... to... *No, no, no!*

He stared at the man pleadingly, fear taking over his embarrassment. He was well aware of the man's skills. Normally, the general would pamper him, go along with him, and behave very considerately. However, once they were in bed, he turned into a savage beast; no matter how much Wu Xingzi begged and cried, it was useless. No matter how embarrassing or how ridiculous the position was, as long as the general wanted to do it, he wouldn't stop until he was satisfied. Wu Xingzi's female sex organs had been ornamental for the past forty years, and he was starting to wonder if it even had a urethra... *Perhaps not! Then...*

Reading his thoughts with one glance, the general smirked, undoing the ribbon from his hair and tying it around Wu Xingzi's small cock. The silky raven hair cascaded down, its ends tickling Wu Xingzi's sensitive, reddened skin and making him tremble and moan weakly.

"Today, I want my wife to piss from her vagina so that I can witness it. Grant me this wedding gift." The rough pad of the man's finger started massaging the area where a woman's urethra would be located.

That area was extremely secretive, hidden within the folds, and it normally couldn't be seen. Wu Xingzi barely even touched his vagina, at most cleaning it during his daily bath, and he didn't even know where this little unused hole was located.

But one touch from this man ignited the fire within him. That spot was terrifyingly sensitive, but the feeling it brought about was less intense compared to his clit and his cunt. The tingles were small and ineffective at bringing him to his climax. Without realizing it, Wu Xingzi tilted his hips up, wanting his more sensitive spots touched. However, Guan Shanjin only exerted a little pressure, pushing him back onto the bed as he stubbornly rubbed his urethra.

Wu Xingzi felt as though thousands of ants were biting him right where Guan Shanjin touched; a feeling that was difficult to describe swelled up and hardened, spreading through all four of his limbs. He struggled, legs flailing, sobs spilling constantly from his lips. He quickly understood that the mysterious feeling was the desire to urinate, and his face paled before reddening in embarrassment; he couldn't help but plead for mercy.

It wasn't the first time he had been fucked into pissing. Every time they had sex, the general wouldn't stop fucking him until he peed himself, but peeing from his male urethra was completely different from his female one! Wu Xingzi was frightened of this peculiar body of his, and he didn't want this very last boundary to be broken. He reached out a few times in an attempt to untie the ribbon around his cock, only for his hand to be waved away. Whenever this happened, the general would use even more strength to tease his urethra; soon, he would reach his limit in holding back his need to urinate.

Wu Xingzi was unable to free himself from the other man holding him down. Then, Guan Shanjin wickedly pressed down harder on Wu Xingzi's stomach, and lewd juices again gushed out from Wu Xingzi's vagina, some of the fluid splashing onto his urethra. Guan Shanjin slowly smeared the fluids all over Wu Xingzi's intimate parts; with how wet it was getting, Wu Xingzi felt as though he had pissed himself already.

"Husband, my husband... Have mercy... Please, have mercy," Wu Xingzi hiccupped, desperately trying to free himself from the man's hold.

The general's finger crooked against the entrance of Wu Xingzi's swollen urethra. Wu Xingzi froze, then released an anguished wail as pee came flooding out.

It was only a trickle at first, flowing across his vagina and soaking into the bedspread. But more soon gushed out, mingling with the juices from Wu Xingzi's orgasm and squirting everywhere. Very quickly, the fluids were all over the bed.

As for Wu Xingzi, he seemed to have completely lost his mind. His eyes were fixed on the canopy above, his body periodically shuddering. Drowning in insane amounts of pleasure, this seemed to have broken him. He couldn't stop twitching, his limbs jerking uncontrollably. His cunt tightened around the general's cock, almost forcing the younger man into orgasm.

The general groaned in pleasure, intensely satisfied at the debauched look of the man beneath him. There was no trace of the old fellow's usual shyness now. His entire body and heart had been conquered by Guan Shanjin, and whether it was pleasure or pain, it all belonged to him! The general had completely marked Wu Xingzi as his own.

An overwhelming excitement came over Guan Shanjin. He was unable to put to words what this feeling was—perhaps it was the ecstasy of Wu Xingzi's cunt clamping down on him, or how their wedding bed was completely drenched with their fluids.

Supporting the older man's lean waist, Guan Shanjin bent down and pressed his lips onto Wu Xingzi's. His cock thrust even deeper inside, slamming all the way into Wu Xingzi's womb. The barely conscious man gasped roughly as he again twitched violently. Instinctively, he wanted to escape, but the arm around his waist forced him down further, and the intense pounding only continued.

Guan Shanjin seemed to not know what exhaustion was. Holding his newly wedded wife tightly, he pounded away. His thick, hard cock only became harder, the huge head of his cock brutally yet skillfully attacking the sensitive spot within Wu Xingzi. His shaft tortured Wu Xingzi's walls like an iron rod, as if he had forced Wu Xingzi's channel to fit around his cock. Wu Xingzi's entrance was red and raw, his juices foaming up from the extreme friction as they flowed down toward his still-untouched asshole.

Wu Xingzi squirted continuously, the juices drenching the head of Guan Shanjin's cock over and over. The heat made the younger man growl, his savagery piqued even further. His thrusts now left Wu Xingzi's inner muscles completely limp, unable to tighten anymore, and Guan Shanjin now faced no resistance as he pounded into Wu Xingzi.

Wu Xingzi was now in a state of constant orgasm, and the intense pleasure brought him back to his senses only for him to lose his wits again. As the cycle repeated over and over, his eyes fell half-lidded, and his fingers clutched fruitlessly at the iron grip around his waist, silently pleading.

The loss of bodily fluids left Wu Xingzi dehydrated, not to mention how he even peed himself. He wasn't even able to produce any more tears as he cried. He howled like a wild animal, but he didn't know why exactly he was wailing. The only thing he knew was that he was about to be fucked to death by his husband. This wedding night was going to kill him!

Guan Shanjin, having already lost all reason, gave a low groan. He jerked his hips violently into the man under him, jabbing right into the deepest spot within as large amounts of come erupted from his cock. The heat sent Wu Xingzi into another bout of convulsions, and he fainted dead away.

The general came for a long time, filling Wu Xingzi up so full that his belly swelled before he carefully pulled himself out. Then, he shoved a dildo into the gaping hole, plugging Wu Xingzi up with his semen still inside him.

Embracing the unconscious man, Guan Shanjin panted for a bit before he got out of bed to wrap Wu Xingzi up in clean clothes. Only then did he summon his servants to clean up the room, as well as commanding them to heat up some water.

The servants were quick and silent. They didn't dare to even sneak a glance at the general, who was currently holding his wife as though he had the world's greatest treasure in his arms. Despite not looking at him, they were still able to sense that the general was in a great mood, and there was no sign of his usual deathly cold aura.

The man was undeniably in good spirits as he massaged Wu Xingzi's slightly swollen belly. The older man was full of his cum, and each time the general kneaded, Wu Xingzi would shiver and whimper, his brows wrinkling. These little actions tugged on Guan Shanjin's heartstrings, and he couldn't resist pressing a few more kisses on the older man.

It was said that two-sexed men only rarely got pregnant. The general had originally been unbothered by this information, but having spent so much time with Wu Xingzi recently, he couldn't help but anticipate having a baby. He hoped that their child would inherit his intelligence and wits, along with his wife's gentleness and bashfulness. If their child was a girl, there was nothing more that he could ever want.

"Don't worry. Before you get pregnant, your husband will fill you up every day," he murmured into his wife's ear with a doting chuckle.

THE STORY CONTINUES IN
You've Got Mail: The Perils of Pigeon Post
VOLUME 3

CHARACTER & NAME GUIDE

Characters

WU XINGZI 吴幸子: A lonely, gay middle-aged man who recently gained a new lease on life when he discovered the Peng Society.

GUAN SHANJIN 关山尽: The renowned and formidable young general of the Southern Garrison; a playboy who only has space in his heart for Mr. Lu.

PEOPLE IN QINGCHENG COUNTY

ANSHENG 安生: Wu Xingzi's crush, who introduced him to the Peng Society.

OLD LIU 柳老头: Wu Xingzi's neighbor, who provides transport to Goose City.

AUNTIE LIU 柳大娘: Old Liu's wife, a gossip who is fiercely protective of Wu Xingzi.

CONSTABLE ZHANG 张捕头: Wu Xingzi's colleague in the magistrate's office, and Ansheng's life partner.

AUNTIE LI 李大婶: A gossipy woman who doesn't think much of Wu Xingzi.

PEOPLE IN HORSE-FACE CITY

MAN YUE 满月: Guan Shanjin's vice general and childhood friend.

HEI-ER 黑儿: One of Guan Shanjin's bodyguards.

FANG HE 方何: Another of Guan Shanjin's bodyguards.

MINT 薄荷 AND OSMANTHUS 桂花: Sisters who work as maids for Wu Xingzi at Guan Shanjin's compound.

MR. LU 鲁先生: Guan Shanjin's teacher and his unrequited first love. Full name is Lu Zezhi, 鲁泽之.

YUE MINGZHU: A headstrong young woman from an important local family. Engaged to Mr. Lu.

OTHERS

RANCUI 染翠: Manager of the Goose City branch of the Peng Society.

YAN WENXIN: Wu Xingzi's first love, who took advantage of him and abandoned him.

Name Guide

Diminutives, Nicknames, and Name Tags:

A-: Friendly diminutive. Always a prefix. Usually for monosyllabic names, or one syllable out of a two-syllable name.

DOUBLING: Doubling a syllable of a person's name can be a nickname, e.g., "Mangmang"; it has childish or cutesy connotations.

DA-: A prefix meaning big/older

XIAO-: A diminutive meaning "little." Always a prefix.

-ER: An affectionate diminutive added to names, literally "son" or "child." Always a suffix. Can sometimes be a fixed part of a person's name, rather than just an affectionate suffix.

Family:

DI/DIDI: Younger brother or a younger male friend.

GE/GEGE/DAGE: Older brother or an older male friend.

JIE/JIEJIE: Older sister or an older female friend.

Other:

GONGZI: Young man from an affluent/scholarly household.